My Personal Fables
Book: 2

The Legends of the Mystical Horses

Written and created by
Sadie Chapman

Copyright 2023 by Sadie Chapman

All rights reserved. This book or any portion thereof may not be reproduced or used in any manner whatsoever without the express written permission of the publisher except for the use of brief quotation in a book review.

ISBN 978-1-957956-98-5 (Paperback)
ISBN 978-1-957956-99-2 (Hardcover)
ISBN 978-1-961017-00-9 (Ebook)

Sadie's Logo was created by Aiste chapman since 2021

Inquiries and Book Orders should be addressed to:

Leavitt Peak Press
17901 Pioneer Blvd Ste L #298, Artesia, California 90701
Phone #: 2092191548

The Legends of the Mystical Horses

Reviewed by K.C. Finn for Readers' Favorite

My Personal Fables is a work of fiction in the animals, fantasy, and adventure subgenres, and it forms the second book in The Legends of the Mystical Horses series. It is suitable for readers of all ages from young to the young at heart and was penned by author Sadie Chapman. In this enchanting continuation, we find ourselves reunited with the Unicorn King, Seequest, as he enjoys his time with his close friend Princess Helena. But the mystical horses of Earth, Day, and Night will soon find a new challenge in their midst as more fabled equines of the past begin to make their mark on the world.

Author Sadie Chapman weaves a truly charming story that will keep readers engaged for a long and lovely time. I was most impressed by the immersive quality of the descriptions, which detail so many vibrant and exciting magical realms, as well as bringing the many horses of the storyline into cinematic life. This makes for scenes filled with atmosphere and action, driven forward by some really excellent dialogue that is enticing and easy for younger readers to access, but also suitably enjoyable for older readers to explore in greater depth. This is a work that I can see being read across generations of the same family together, especially those who have a special place in their hearts for horses already. Overall, I would not hesitate to recommend My Personal Fables to fans of epic fantasy novels, and to readers who want a highly immersive tale that they can turn to every night for wonderful adventures.

Is about how there were once Mermaids; Hippocampus; Seahorses, and Kelpies.

This is my story of how they may have become today's legends of the present day.

Contents

In the loving memory of my dear friend Fran

I would like to dedicate my second book to Helena Frances Clohessy (Sheehy), who was a remarkable friend and my amazing boss in the past.

She did not just believe in me but also changed my life forever and made me the person I am today.

We sadly lost her to cancer on 19 August 2017.

May she live forever in my book as the legend that she is to everyone who knew her for her wonderful talents, amazing heart, and tremendous kindness.

I just want to say thank you for everything, and that you will be always in my heart. Love Sa x

The Explanation to previous Book One

This is the continued story from *The Legend of the Horse.*

This time, it is about Seequest's life once he decided to give up his horn and gave it to Neptune to help him create mysterious creatures & water horses in the future!

Seequest's energy was lying inside his amazing horn where there was great incredible magic and in return was allowed to live out his life as a hippocampus.

Until Neptune's eldest daughter, Helena wanted to go onto land for twenty-four hours for her sixteenth birthday.

This is their story: about two close friends and their destinies which changed both of their lives forever.

Chapter One

Seequest life now in the sea

Seequest felt that he did not belong with the other species of horses anymore.

As he remembered how much fun he had swimming with his friends the dolphins where he feels free, so he spoke to Neptune about living in the sea permanently and the sea god said yes of course dear friend.

"You can become the protector of my Princess Helena and the rest is history!"

One gorgeous morning, just after sunset, the sun glowed amazing orange and red tones sitting in the sky and the ocean, where the sun always looked like it was actually disappearing into the sea itself (like magic) the aqua blue hippocampus was playing with his friends Mini and Tuck, the dolphins, when he wanted to go back to Neptune's palace.

They dived deep into the bottom of the ocean, where there were beautiful green seaweed and colorful corals with pretty jellyfish and a school of all different types of fish swimming by them.

How Seequest loved his new life of peace.

They swam through this large dark cave that felt like it went on for hours.

But once they were through, it was the most astonishing sight that you could ever see, as there were magnificent buildings made of pure gold and silver with loads of incredible statues of Neptune and dolphins beside the palace gates.

Seequest said goodbye to the dolphins and galloped onwards using his front legs and his stunning fish tail and fins which swooshed quickly with great speed to the main gates, where two mer-knights were guarding the gates of the great sea god.

Seequest changed his color from aqua blue all over to white and blue so the knights could recognize him, as he is all blue only in the ocean to camouflage himself from any danger.

Even though he still had some powers, he promised to do no harm to Neptune's creatures unless he had permission from the king of the sea himself.

As when Neptune created all his creatures, they all always had a purpose of protecting the sea or keeping it safe and clean for all to live there.

The mer-knights had opened the gates.

There to greet them was Neptune.

"Well dear friend welcome back from patrolling the sea with the dolphins this evening's sunset".

When Neptune says "as you know, my home is now yours too Seequest."

Even though Seequest loved his new life he felt sometimes alone and afraid of missing his old life and his mother Moonbeam from time to time.

As he wondered how his forest friends and his own horse family are doing because Seequest had been away from the land for fifty years.

"Thank you, my dear King."

They both swam gracefully to the palace to catch up with the rest of the family before bed.

A month had passed when she was feeling lonely has been brought up with Seequest by her side as a protector.

Who taught her how to ride a hippocampus and been the gentlest and most patient of them all.

Sea Spray and Tidal Wave together were just the most powerful seahorses of the sea which now create high waves and control them when needed to be rough or smooth.

The mer-folk had great respect for him.

Helena was the eldest of six other brothers and sisters and they all had their jobs in the palace.

Some became protectors of the sea creatures and the others become protectors of the palace.

Neptune had a soft spot for Helena because she seemed to be the only one that could communicate and hear the sea animals and the mer-folk with her mind as well as her voice.

That was classed as a special gift that only she; her mother and her father had, it's called telepathic.

Helena heard that her mother Queen Sera (Neptune's wife and high priestess) had bred Sea spray to Tidal Wave to see if they would produce more like them-selves or something completely different.

Knowing that they were first created in the sea by Moonbeam's actual horn many years before.

From what she heard by her friends and the guards on the palace grounds.

That it was a complete success and now she wanted a hippocampus of her own!

She was becoming a mature mermaid now going to be turning sixteen very soon.

Helena was so interested in the king of unicorns' previous life on land that she would sit for hours while he is telling her many tales, which she enjoyed a great deal.

One morning on their swim in the ocean she mentioned to Seequest that she wanted to visit this great land and she wondered if her parents would grant her this wish.

But that was not all she wanted.

She wanted to actually walk; breathe and sleep on the land for twenty-four hours as well.

Living has a temporary Piscean, part fish and part human type of form.

Still been a great swimmer and could breathe in the sea and yet was close to a human type on land as well.

Seequest did not like this idea as there are many dangers on land.

But he agreed as he thought he could see his friends once more and his own horse family.

But he still felt like it was too dangerous.

If Princess Helena's parents agreed, then he would be the best one to take her and protect her from danger there.

The sun was shining down in the ocean, as the sun god also had a soft spot for the princess.

Next, the mermen were all beautifully dressed up in gold, blowing their trumpets and celebrating the princess's sixteenth birthday in the town close to the city.

Suddenly they stopped playing and announced by saying, "Happy Sixteenth Birthday Princess Helena" and blew them again afterwards.

This time saying "everyone, please wish Neptune's eldest daughter a happy birthday and may she always be happy and at peace."

This time everyone was wishing the princess a great day from all the kingdoms of Vissen.

The mermaid princess had beautiful dark hair and blue eyes, with a gorgeous pretty green swallow tail that matched her fins beautifully.

She wore some large elegant pretty silver pearl shells across her top line and a silver delicate crown sitting on her head.

She had flung open the door from her quarters and swam as fast as she could to her father's palace which was a mile away from their actual home to protect them from dangers.

She saw Seequest who neighed at her wishing her a nice day.

He bowed down before her as she jumped on his back to the palace.

"Quickly, dear friend, let's see father" acting excitedly.

Seequest galloped and swam as quickly as he could by using his tail to and fro to the palace gates, where the guards let them straight through.

"Your highness," they said and bowed before her.

Helena said to Seequest "I wonder if my parents will grant my actual wish?"

Seequest replied "your Highness all you could do is hope?"

"Seequest, you're right, as always."

"I shall just do that!"

They both reached the great doors of Neptune's throne room when Helena barged straight through them without waiting to be told to come in due to her excitement of it been her birthday today that she forgot all the rules.

"I am sorry, father but it's my birthday."

The sea king laughed.

"It's OK, dear daughter".

"I shall allow it only for today," he swam towards her and gave her a big hug.

"Oh, I do love you"!

"Now hurry on your mother and I have a special surprise for you".

"Now go to the stables?"

"But father, I know that I said I wanted a hippocampus of my own!"

"But I want something more precious than that now."

The king looked confused.

"I thought you would be pleased."

"Oh, I am very."

"But my wish is to go onto land and see and feel what it is like to live on it for twenty-four hours please?"

"Oh," Neptune replied, "well, that is a completely different gift from what I was hoping you would ask for Helena."

"Does that mean you won't let me?"

"Daughter, you do not understand the dangers there."

'Fine' and started to cry where she storms off fluttering her tail quickly back home unhappy.

"Seequest, what am I to do?"

"She is my daughter and I know that her mother will say no!"

"But I also know this will help her become a great queen in the future?"

"Because I believe it is good for us all to know about how magical the land is as well as my seas"

Seequest agreed with the king and turned around to catch up with the princess when the king called out to him and said "wait"!

Has he swum to him holding on to Seequest's neck saying, "Leave it with me and I will get back to you after speaking to Sera?"

Later that day Seequest was called back in to be given the news that he did not expect to hear as he approached the sea king's throne.

Neptune smiled at the hippocampus in his eyes and said "Yes she can go to Scotland, as long as you Seequest go with her and protect her with your life!"

"Or don't come back here!"

Seequest was shocked that Neptune granted the princess's wish.

"I promise, my king I understand."

"Now, go and let her know the good news."

"Queen Sera is waiting to surprise her at the stables, so take her there now."

Seequest replied, "Yes of course your highness right away."

The hippocampus sped off catching up with Helena while she's attending to the dolphins and calls her "Princess, I have some good news for you."

"You can go to Scotland with me".

"But you are going to have to listen to my rules and obey them."

"Otherwise, I will bring you straight back to the sea in a flash!"

The mermaid princess turned around, moving her arms and hands in the sea to keep steady when she smiled back at him like a Cheshire cat.

She was happy that she did a somersault backward in the water.

She replied "Seequest, I promise with all my heart."

She was smiling with happy tears in her eyes and hugged his neck.

Which he loved as he now felt that his life was worth living again.

"Great, now get on my back as I need to take you to your mother, the queen."

"Yes, dear friend let's go."

Seequest swam three miles into the east part of the ocean to the stables where queen Sera waiting for them to arrive.

The mermaid princess reached the stables and saw her mother talking to Tidal Wave.

She said, "Well done boy."

While now Seequest swims up to the hippocampus and their mother with her baby seahorses as the father give birth to them like Seequest did to his daughters, yet slightly in a different way.

As then the mother takes over and feeds them on her milk and they both bring them all up together as one.

As Sea horses mate for life and are loyal for a life time by treating each other has equals.

The queen said, hello my darling, happy sixteenth birthday, as Helena is staring at these beautiful creatures where she jumps off of Seequest and swims quickly up to her mother and hugs her with pure delight!

"You can have one when they are older."

"Helena, I will let you pick it yourself too."

She looked at her mother and said "thank you, mother with great joy in her tone of voice expressing complete happiness in her heart.

Helena could not believe what her mother had just said, as this was her wish.

Helena decided that she would stay with all the hippocampus for the rest of the day, where she had a great birthday after all,has she spent the rest of the day been taught by her mother how to look after a hippocampus properly while she was patiently waiting for them to be old enough for her to pick one for herself.

Queen Sera spoke about her other birthday gift too.

Looking nervous at this time and yet said "Helena, promise me that you will be careful up there and you do as Seequest tells you!"

"As remember he was once the Unicorn King of the lands, please promise me?"

«I do not like it but I know that we must trust you.»

"As I know one day you will have a kingdom of your own to rule, I believe."

The mermaid replied, "I understand mother."

"I promise," looking at her straight into her eyes of happiness and yet Sera felt also fear at the same time for her daughter.

Chapter Two

Helena's wish becomes reality

The next day, Neptune and Helena were riding Seequest to the surface of the sea.

When they reached the top and poked their heads out to see if it was safe to carry on towards the beach.

It was dawn so most of the animals and birds were resting in their cozy beds.

Hades had heard from his shape-shifting creatures that turn themselves into sharks who spy on the kingdom for him.

That Helena and Seequest were coming on land soon.

Because at times he would change into one to cause some trouble in the waters for his dear brother too.

Because he would put a spell on Neptune›s guardians to see what was going on down there feeling jealous and lonely.

The sharks had mentioned to him that Helena wanted to see what it was like to live on land for twenty-four hours and that it was her special time of showing her independence on her sixteenth birthday from her parents.

He smiled and thought this news had made his day and now he decided he will turn himself into a large handsome fox as they would never of guess it's actually him.

Seequest knew some foxes in the woods and yet not all of them.

Hades' saber-toothed tigers were all killed by Zeus with his lightning bolt, as they tried to kill too many deer in the past.

But he was lucky to save his favorite Pain again and kept him hidden until he was needed.

Hades thought that he would like to see and meet the princess face to face.

When he said a Greek verse next his body started to form into a stunning dark fox with a beautiful bushy tail.

"Now what can my name be", he thought

"Oh, yes Jinx!"

He liked it so much he started to laugh, as he ran through his cave till he reached Mysterious Woods.

There he found a burrow and a mate to play along with his game and plan.

Back in the sea, Neptune told his daughter that she had only twenty-four hours on land and then she needed to return with Seequest without fail!

She agreed with great excitement on her face and just wanted to go and explore this new land of mystery and beauty.

The mermaid princess blew her father a kiss as she grabs hold of Seequest's scaly mane and tells him to go, which he then neighs with excitement towards the beach cove.

There they both were swimming against the waves and eventually became closer to the shore where they both could see the beach in sight.

Neptune could see that they reached their safety and his daughter was so happy.

He said a magic verse and stirred his trident into the sea.

There was a bright light that appeared and glowed brightly when it began to travel through the sea where Eldest Daughter was.

The light touched her beautiful swallow tail.

First, she saw Seequest changing into his original form of a real horse with a beautiful glossy white coat with a touch of soft blue chasing through his mane and tail and his eyes were dark blue too.

Within seconds his tail had changed now two solid back legs.

That made him gallop even faster than ever before.

He neighed with happiness and yet nervousness.

Thinking he had been away for fifty years from land.

Where he hoped that everything was still the same?

While they were approaching a few horses were running on the beach having fun.

They heard loud splashing noises in the sea.

They stopped and looked where in the distance they could see this strange image approaching the shore.

They neighed loudly where the stallion heard them and passed on the message to their leader of the herd, a beautiful large mare.

The mare was told that an unusual creature was approaching the beach at a fast speed.

Seequest was galloping and jumping the waves like he did when he was the Unicorn King, he jumped in and out of the water so fast that Helena was so fascinated with his transformation that she did not even realize that she had a nice pair of long legs and feet now.

Until she lost her balance and fell off when looking down instead of holding on as he was going faster than normal.

Has they had to reach the shore before the tide was going to go back out?

Otherwise, they would be pulled back again making the hippocampus become tired and where Helena could possibly drown as not a mermaid no more at the moment.

Because she has never had legs and feet before as she will have to adapt to them, which will take a least an hour to get acquainted to them probably.

The mare was told again that they are coming to the shore rapidly where she plans to go and see them for herself.

She tells her stallion to follow her as she gallops down the hill to meet the incredible creatures.

But she was hoping it was her great grandfather as the mare was Spirit's daughter Honour.

The two horses get closer.

There appeared a water horse with a female rider on its back of a form the horses have never seen before.

The mare approached them carefully and studied them closely as she did.

Then Seequest spoke and said, "We come in peace".

The Honor recognized his voice and knew that it was Seequest somehow.

She neighed back as he looked up to see his family had been running towards them.

Even though he was very happy he also told Helena to stay close until he explained who she was.

"Helena, keep near me," so she crawled to him as she was still getting used to her legs, as at that moment they felt like jelly.

Because for Seequest it was easier for him to adjust as he had done it many times before in the past.

Eventually, Helena started to get her balance where she was leaning against him for support until she felt confident and could feel her feet properly without falling over again.

Seequest looked around to see this beautiful skew-bald mare with blue eyes running towards them with great force wondering if this horse was related to him or just through the creation of his horse's history.

There were loads of different types and colors of horses in the herd as well.

It was an amazing thing to see.

Princess Helena said to her dear friend "are these horses which you have told me about?"

He replied, "Yes I believe this is my bloodline and family from my daughter Spirit, who was born a unicorn like me once."

"But later in her life, I took away her horn and powers so that she could live with her family forever without feeling different from them."

That is when I left the land and decided to become a hippocampus for good.

Where years to come I then became your personal teacher and protector too

Then Honor came over and said, "Seequest if that is you then we come as friends."

"If it's not, then please beware."

The dear old sea horse said, "Yes it's me and I believe you are my great granddaughter through Spirit whom we lost a few years ago, am I correct?"

"Yes, that is correct."

"As I was told that Queen Celestial appeared in the beautiful night sky and flew down to collect her where she takes her to Heaven to rest and meet her old family again as well.

Because she left her body behind where it was washed out to sea as now only her shell because her spirit and soul went back to the place they came from.

"How did you know this?" with a quizzical expression on her face, knowing that he has been away from land for a long time now.

"Oh, Queen Sera told me" the high priestess of the seas and mother to Helena who is the Eldest Daughter who is with me now.

The princess could not believe after all these years they still remembered him and all the great things that he had done for them and the land.

Well, without him they would not exist now.

Honour was delighted to meet her great grandfather who used to be the Unicorn King.

With great powers of magic, he sacrificed to live the rest of his life in the sea.

He died on land when he became a full hippocampus by giving up his horn and the rest of his powers to Neptune to help him create his amazing sea creatures instead and protect the oceans from Hades too.

Plus Neptune then became the god of horses instead of Seequest.

He neighed and told Helena to gradually slide down his body until she reached the floor safely when he gradually walks away from her and begins to run up to Honour.

As with the rules of horses, they were meant to both meet halfway.

Both horses decide to greet each other, while the Princess was sitting on the beach quite happily now.

Putting the sand in her hand and feeling its unusual texture on her skin.

While the horses continued to gallop towards each other.

Seequest was just a little bigger and taller than her whereas in the past he was twice their size which was quite daunting for them all.

At least now he felt more like them.

For this moment he felt happy and at home again on land thanks to Neptune changing him into a horse as there was no more magic on earth at this time.

Apart from in the ground, thanks to the earth unicorns' ashes that are scattered across the lands through their deaths in the past.

While he was running towards her still, he could see a pretty elegant mare with great potential for full leadership.

Where he could see why his actual full bloodline was chosen to be a Leader again like his daughter Spirit in the past.

They stopped in front of each other and reared on their hind legs showing their strength, leadership and protection of their fellow friends as well.

Next, the mare calmed down and walked slowly towards Seequest as they were both looking closely at each other.

Once smelt each other gently blowing their nostrils as they did meaning been cautious of each other for the time being.

Eventually they felt happy that they nuzzled against each other's necks and put their noses together as a family would, which made the other horses relax as then they were recognized as an acceptance to the herd.

Honour was pleased to see and meet him at last, as she had heard so many great stories about him from her grandmother.

The princess then called out to him, knowing that she felt good about her legs and said, "look I can walk, not realizing then she was actually walking with great balance and straight at last."

The two grand horses turned around at the same time and looked at Helena and could see her walking up towards one of the bay colts she took a fancy to.

Honour felt unsure but Seequest reassured her that she would do no harm to him probably good as Helena had the magic touch with all animals everywhere in the sea and hopefully now on land?

While she was touching the young colt, she collapsed once more, as she kept having pins and needles, which made her lose her balance and feeling in her legs properly because her feet had gone numb.

But the bay colt could see that she needed his help and began to bend down as she leaned against his muscled body to pull herself back up again creating a powerful bond with him, that she named Fortunate.

Meaning lucky and blessed that he was around to help her, the colt seemed to love his name and neighed with joy and pushed Helena saying he liked her too.

A few hours later she started to get the feeling back in her feet and walked slowly one foot after the other to readjust for a while of having legs and feet instead of her beautiful swallow tail.

Once she got the hang of it, she started to dance like she was a true natural, as if she'd lived on the land for a long time.

'" Bravo", they all said, and then she curtsied to them.

All the horses reared with delight as she did have the gift of communicating with animals and the horses loved her for it as well.

As all the horses could feel all her emotions and that's how they react back towards her showing courage and love for her too.

Seequest felt so pleased about this.

Helena jumped with the excitement too, later they all rested on the beach after having some food.

They all lay together watching the sun go down which was a stunning sight to see.

Seequest had agreed to take her to the woods to meet the rest of his friends.

They met back with the horses as they had to move because it was not safe for them to be on the beach anymore as the salt in the sea was good for swimming and healing and yet only doses at a time, otherwise it would make them sick.

As they are not allowed to drink it like Seequest and Princess Helena can as they live in the sea always.

As these horses cannot drink the salt water like Seequest and his mother Moonbeam or the sea horses could, thanks to Neptune giving them that power to in the past.

They decided they will show the Helena how the land can change so quickly and differently regarding the sea and rivers alike.

The mermaid princess was more excited than before as she had never seen woodlands and she loved any-thing to do with the mystery of the unknown.

The horses galloped on in front of them with Honour leading them where Seequest bent his right leg and his left under himself so Helena could jump onto his back easily for the ride of her life on land.

They traveled at great speeds where she saw so many different birds and heard all these beautiful songs from above in the trees and red and grey squirrels jumping from tree to tree looking for hazelnuts to eat as they go.

The birds were beautiful colors and sizes that she felt like she was in a new heaven as she loved the sea.

But the land was becoming more interesting, as it had loads of textures for her to see and touch as well.

They arrived in Mysterious Woods at night.

The princess wanted to stay up and watch the stars but Seequest knew that she needed her beauty to sleep more.

Eventually, they saw a beautiful cave on Moonbeam ridge where Seequest used to live with his mum when he was younger.

As after she died and became a mystical horse being and left him there on earth by himself he named it this, expressing all the great memories they shared together there, as watching from the distant the dolphins jumping in and out of the sea at night too.

He told Helena to get off his back and go for a rest and stay there until he came back to sleep by her side later as knew it was overwhelming even for her what she's seen and experienced in one day!

She was actually tired from the excitement of coming to stay on land for a while.

So she agreed by lying on the soft green grass which they pulled between them into the cave to sleep on.

She felt like she was a child again and yet needed her rest and fell fast asleep in the back of the cave.

At this time Seequest was enjoying the time with his family, as he thought that they would have forgotten him once he left in the past.

Has Moonbeam been the first Night unicorn and Seequest's mother, where she is now known as the Celestial, Queen of the Heavens who look after the horses in their afterlife!

Who comes and collects the horses and animals when they die and takes their spirits before they leave.

But their souls go back to Pegasus' home as they were from the winged horse's bloodlines originally.

Before this happens, they stand and mention the great Seequest as he was their superior at the time of their lives.

Where there will be no one ever like him again on Earth.

When Seequest hears this, he is chuffed to bits and that tears start to fall down his face because of happiness and sadness as he was proud and yet missed his mother.

Because now living in the sea was the only place she was never with him.

He felt that he could accept this easier.

Knowing it was a new life and a new beginning for him without her.

Chapter Three

Helena is comforted
by the black fox

While enjoying waking up to these different surroundings she thinks about exploring with Seequest or maybe
without him soon as he is still fast asleep beside her.

Because she was going to break all the rules he and her
parents told her possibly due to curiosity.

But she was thinking that she was now sixteen and
was old enough and wise enough to go and adventure
on her own.

There in the cave, Helena has properly woken up lying
beside Seequest's body for warmth and protection.

She stood up gradually, as she was still getting used to
her legs where they were cramped.

She stretched them to help the stiffness that she was feeling at the time when standing outside the cave she heard beautiful tweeting noises from up above her.

Where above it were some great trees were loads of pretty birds of Blue Tits singing along to the beginning of the day.

She said, "good morning my little ones", as they tweeted back and then flew off.

"Oh, come back, dear sweet ones."

She then decides that she's going to follow them and so slowly she walks back into the cave to get dressed properly as when her tail changed earlier in the day, Neptune put a beautiful bright green dress and tights for her to put on instead on the beach to wear.

She now crept past Seequest quietly trying not to disturb him as he looks so peaceful still sleeping after a long night with his family and friends.

She walks out of the cave carefully walking further into the woods and followed the birds wherever they went.

"I am not going to hurt you" and she decided to follow them further into the forest to explore some more.

She walks through some high dark green grass which felt like silk to her feet and brushed it against her hands too while she smelled the pretty flowers as she went on her way quite happily.

She enjoyed smelling the Roses and Sunflowers best.

Because back home there were no smells like this in the sea and so she wanted to enjoy it as much as she could.

She seemed quite confident now that she started to dance and spin around in circles.

The princess thought that she belonged more on the land than she did in the water because she always knew that she was different from her siblings back home and yet never knew why?

There a young fawn (female deer) with red and white spots on her back crossed her path bravely when she said, "Hello."

"What are you?" putting her hands out to touch it.

The young fawn did not reply and ran away feeling really scared, as it had never seen a pretty creature like her before.

Because the princess was stunning with a pale complexion with bright blue eyes and now gorgeous blonde hair as her hair had changed when she produced her legs.

As her hair is normally a dark color.

It changed due to protecting her identity from Hades hopefully.

She had ripped her beautiful green silk dress running through the bushes so now she finds some leaves and made another outfit to wear instead.

She was wearing a bright green top and loose flared skirt that she had made from all the leaves that fell on the ground as she was quite creative in that way.

She was about five feet six inches with a slim-like body with perfect curves.

I believe that's because all her life in the sea she developed the strength and shape of her body due to the movement in the water with her tail.

The mermaid princess was singing with an unusual sound that the forest animals loved as to them it sounded soothing to their ears and encouraged them to all come towards her even some of the horses from the herd too.

Suddenly after the big black fox had been watching in the shadows from a distance it decided to come out and introduced itself to the princess.

As it had been watching her having fun with the animals for ages.

Hades now been an image of a large black fox came slowly out of the burrow acting all nervous and scared which caught her eye and pulled her away from the others.

The fox looked at the other animals and snarled and glowed red eyes at them.

They knew then that it was not a true friend, and they all ran off.

"Please don't go," said Helena who seemed a little upset but the fox drew closer to her so she forgot about the others due to she was fascinated with this unusual creature as well.

She sat still on the ground where she was sitting earlier stroking all kinds of forest animals.

She seemed scared and yet anxious to see if the fox would run away or will it come up to her.

She froze has she could see this big black fox walking closer towards her.

Feeling adventurous, she looked right at it and saw these amazing orange-yellow-amber eyes stirring big with inquisitive expressions in the sunlight's background.

The fox's eyes seemed to put her into a trance of her falling in love with this creature that she never ever had seen before and yet she felt like she loved it a long time somehow.

Because of been in this trance it made her feel different than ever before has it made her feel good has he wanted to be her friend and so she forgot all about Seequest and did not go back to where he was still sleeping again.

Eventually in the cave he was now steering and woke up wondering where Helena had gone as not there anymore.

He then thought she'll be back soon and so waited for her to come back knowing what she is like disobeying the rules has being so adventurous all the time.

But time was getting on and Seequest was becoming worried more each second had past.

Hoping that he was dreaming about her breaking the rules and yet she was not in sight still?

He decides to go and see his forest friends to see if they have seen her at all that early morning?

Back in the woods near the darker parts of the forest Helena was still fascinated with this fox that she was now listening to what he was telling her, which was the wrong thing to do at this time.

As really it was a Bad god in disguise who wanted Helena, so he could claim the Seequest's horn for himself from her father Neptune god of the sea that now processes it in his kingdom.

Instead, she started to listen and obey the fox's voice like she was hypnotized and vanished with the fox out of sight.

In her heart and mind she's been trying to call Seequest for help for ages?

He then thought it may have been her calling to him somehow earlier in his sleep.

So got to his feet and shook his body to relax his muscles again before trotting out the cave and starting to gallop as fast he could to the Woods where his friends now lived.

He arrived when the animals appeared thinking that they don't recognise him as he isn't as large as he was all those years ago and looked like an ordinary white horse.

So they appear to be not sure of him until he tells them who he really is, which then they are revealed and pleased to see him where they tell him that they missed him and yet they were pleased that he was happy and ok.

He asked his friends the squirrels; bears and rabbits the same question over and over again about Princess Helena from the great seas and yet no will tell him the truth.

But an adult rabbit starts thumping its foot and there appears a young rabbit that hops over and approaches him where it told the white horse that a large black fox whom they had never seen before had taken her to his den further away on the other side of the woods.

Seequest started to panic inwardly as he knew that he must get her back home and into the sea before the next sunset or she will die.

Because living in the sea all the time.

Neptune had given them oxygen to breathe the fresh air there for this short period of time only twenty-four hours.

He runs back to mysterious woods where Honour and her herd were still resting and tells them that it was lovely to meet them all at last and yet he had to go find her as she has disappeared with a creature no one had seen before.

But he knew that he must go and find his friend before sunset.

They understood and he gallops off further to where he remembers as a colt where his mother loved to go.

It was the main part of the Mysterious Woods.

He knew he would possibly find some help, as he had an idea that it could be Hades in disguise as there were never any black foxes before, only gorgeous burnt-orange ones.

Back in the forest Helena had fallen into a trap of fascination for this creature.

Hades was still in disguise as the fox was studying her beauty and thought that he wanted her to be his queen of the underworld.

The fox was very cunning and crafty that he gave her some water to drink and inside it was a potion to let her breathe longer on land, as he now wanted her to stay with him forever.

The fox said, "Come my lovely jump on my back and I will show you my home."

She agreed and the fox bent down for her to climb onto his back she grabbed hold of his black thick and yet soft fur and ran as quickly as he can further deep into the Forest of Dreams.

She seemed so relaxed and happy at the time.

Hades had her exactly where he wanted her and he thought that it was easier to get her back to his lair than he thought it would be.

Where he started to make howling noises through the excitement he had her.

Eventually, they reached a massive cave where the fox picked up stuff in his mouth and opened a gateway.

He started running even faster into the cave that seemed to go on forever.

They eventually reached his lair and he dropped off the princess onto a beautiful soft blanket made of silkworms where she fell asleep.

"Rest", the fox said and started to change once more into the form of Hades, King of the Underworld.

He says "Sleep my queen sleep with a smile on his face."

The princess did not know this was her father's nemesis and brother of hell.

Eventually, she woke up not hearing the beautiful birds in the trees or she could not see the sun shining above her anymore but only a dark, cold old lair full of complete darkness apart from some candles here and there.

She begins to panic and falls onto the ground shocked thinking now that maybe her parents were right as she should have stayed in the water after all.

She wished she paid attention to what they and Seequest said to her about why there were rules for her to obey, she now realized they were there for her safety.

All now she could think of was that Seequest will hopefully find her in time and hear her call earlier in the woods in his mind?

As Helena then realized that she had been tricked only by the king of tricks himself, her uncle Hades.

"Don't worry my love you are safe here with me and that is where you will stay from now on."

The mermaid princess replied, "No I am going home and you cannot stop me!"

"Oh, Princess that's not true as what you have forgotten is that everything you have seen around you recently can all disappear with a blow of my breath to the land".

"Now if you want all your friends to perish and die, then please go ahead and leave me".

"Otherwise, I suggest that you stay here with me and rule my kingdom as my queen."

Poor Helena was terrified that she was trapped forever now with Hades.

She wondered now if Seequest would heard her cry and will find her here in this underworld kingdom?

Poor Seequest was wondering, what if he did not get any help in Mysterious Woods and would he find his old friends of his mother's to help him?

Because if not, he would then have to go back to the sea empty-handed and see King Neptune and say that his daughter has been kidnapped while he was enjoying being with his horse family and old friends of the forest once again as she was sleeping in a cave unattended as he was sleeping too instead of watching her every move.

He also knew that it will not go down well for him where he will possibly be deserted or even killed for it.

He did not like the thought of that and so galloped faster off into the woods as quickly as his legs could carry him.

Eventually, he approached the famous silver birch tree of his dear uncle Truth, the Old Earth Unicorn.

There above him in a chestnut tree was the great wise owl that was looking down at him and said "are you the great Unicorn King?"

And he said, "yes, once, and yet no, as magic does not exist anymore."

"That's why I look like a normal white horse now."

"Oh", the owl said, only in your eyes, and then said, "Are you looking for Max the wolf?"

Seequest replied "Yes I am where is he?"

The owl said, "Go to the stream where it connects to the field where Pegasus once touched."

"There, you will find the cave of the great wolves themselves."

"Thank you," he said.

The owl said, "You are welcome old friend," as it spread its wings and flew in the direction where Seequest had to go.

Once he found the path the owl flew in another direction and said, "Until you rein again great king."

The white stallion did not understand what the owl meant.

But he did it in another way and replies "thanks!"

Where he gallops closer to the stream until he reached the golden field where Pegasus left some special supplies all those years ago.

Because on this side of the woods it grew everything you needed.

The stream was beautifully clear light blue, that when he approached it for a drink he could see some Mallard ducks with elegant green heads and brown bodies with their brown hens swimming happily on the stream just relaxing in the sun.

"Oh, excuse me," he said.

But the ducks did not realize it was him and felt threatened and so they quacked and then flew off into the sky.

Poor Seequest was disheartened as he felt that no one wanted to know him anymore.

He felt in his heart that some animals sensed that they thought he had abandoned them when really he was protecting them all from Hades.

He walked out of the stream and lay down as he knew that the wolves do not hunt until the evening.

So even though he did not want to rest and waste his time he also knew he needed to keep up his strength to get the princess back in time before sunset tonight hopefully.

Poor Seequest at this moment felt like he was defeated and dreamt of the times with his mother as a young colt until the wolves arrived.

There on top of the hillside was the alpha a beautiful grey wolf twice the size of a regular wolf.

The wolf saw this strange white stallion lying near the waters and ran down to see why it was there.

He approached Seequest without disturbing him and grabs him by his neck and said "you are not welcome here, horse growling as he speaks."

Seequest woke up and dropped the wolf to the floor as he stood and said "I may look like a horse but I am not!"

"I was once the Unicorn King of the lands," and said, "I knew Max and Ash now back off before I kill you wolf."

"They were close friends to my parents who were the night unicorns."

"They were the herd leaders who were known as Moonbeam and the great Jecco himself".

"Max was a great friend to my mother as he helped save her and my life when she was excepting me, where is he now?"

"My apologies great one I did not know it was you!"

"It's OK, dear friend."

"No one is meant to!"

"How can I help you," said the young wolf.

"I need to see Max, where will I find him?"

The wolf was holding his head downwards and said, "I am sorry."

"My father died a year ago"

"His mate Ash is resting further in the woods with the females, as it destroyed her when he passed and retired her position of Omega."

"Oh, I am so sorry to hear that."

Seequest then knew that he had no choice but to go back to the sea alone and face Neptune and queen Sera!

He felt confident and yet scared as well as he had lost their pride and joy.

He started to wonder again if they will listen to what he needed to tell them and forgive or kill him.

When he realized he had no choice and had to take the chance.

As he says thank you to the grey wolf and looks up in the sky and says rip old friend as he neighs loudly with respect of losing like a family member of another kind.

Paying his represents that Max died and went on to heaven.

He gently brought down his head again.

When he thought in is mind, I must face my fate and galloped all the way back to the beach.

As he reached the beach and began to gallop into it he turned back into a hippocampus again.

There in the sea were his dear old friends the dolphins Mini and Tuck waiting for them to come home again.

But what they did not know was he was coming alone.

Chapter Four

Seequests Fate or Not

As he approached the water, his body was starting to change once more into the handsome light blue hippocampus with an aquamarine scaled mane with gills to breathe under water and beautiful scales on his body that are beautiful deep sapphire blue to protect him like a shield from been hurt or bitten hard as loads of smalls shields put together which created a coat.

His eyes changed to aquamarine which shone brightly if you had a chance to see them.

He swam towards his friends the dolphins when they were starting to jump and do somersaults into the sea and splash their tails in the water by squirting it from their mouths through the excitement of knowing that Seequest and the princess were coming home to stay.

They also started to make squeaky noises of happiness knowing that their friends were safe once more back in the sea.

But as he was getting closer they stopped and looked angry as they noticed that Princess Helena was not with him.

They were ready to bump him with their noses to make him go back and get her.

As they were telling him off as he left her there in danger because they too are guardians of the royal highness as well.

'Seequest, where is the princess?' the dolphins were talking to him angrily.

He replied, "sadly, the large black fox taken her called Jinx who is new to the forest, has taken our princess back to its lair somewhere in the woods."

"It happened while I was sleeping."

She must have woken up and felt safe in the woods with my friends that she wanted to explore more and let me rest, bless her.

I was told by one of the rabbits and a fawn deer that they did not like the fox.

"Helena was singing and dancing around with the other forest animals happy and safe when he approached her and frightened everyone away because of his scary stare of red eyes."

"The rabbit said the fox's voice seemed to put Helena under a love spell or something so she went peacefully with him to his den which I still cannot find?"

Seequest's face was looking upset and felt that he failed everyone with tears in his eyes and held his head down towards the water.

Daring not to look into the eyes of this friends as feeling embarrassed.

"The worst of all I have wondered if it is Hades up to his old tricks again?"

The dolphins' faces seemed to change and felt sorry for Seequest and said "then let's not delay and get back to the Palace straightaway and tell Neptune what has happened and get her home quickly and safely as possible."

They nuzzled their friend and he neigh as water came out of his gills at the same time as he was swimming where he replied, "yes, you're right."

The dolphins and the hippocampus turned around and put their faces towards the waves and pushed with all their might and dived deep into the ocean where they saw the darker shades of the water which is the portal to Neptune's hidden kingdom of Vissen.

They continued to swim deep until they reached a golden light that takes them through to the great golden gates of Neptune himself.

The guards recognized Seequest and let him in with the dolphins following behind him until they reached the second gate where his friends said "good luck" and swam away from the palace.

Seequest said to himself in his thoughts, "Thanks, I am going to need it", and approached the stunning golden gate that had the emblem of dolphins on it.

The hippocampus gulped and approached the open gates, where the guards said, "Seequest, where is the princess?" He just ignored them and swam further toward the palace doors.

Seequest knew that Neptune will be very upset and angry and also disappointed in him so he felt scared.

But he knew that he had to do this and face up to his mistakes by telling the truth of what had happened as he wanted his dear friend home safely once more where she belongs when he starts swimming with his head held high.

The guard opened the door and there sitting on his throne was Neptune looking quite happy himself until he saw that his dear friend was not carrying his daughter on his back.

The sea king panicked and swooshed his large swallow tail two and fro as he was standing up and said angrily and yet concerned in his voice,

"Seequest, what has happened to my daughter?"

"Why is she not with you?"

The great sea king was worried now and started to cry and said "I must tell the queen now"

"Wait, I can explain."

"She is safe and well I can promise you that."

"But I must ask one thing of you."

"You must give me back my horn so I can get her back from the black fox in the woods please."

"Why does a fox have my daughter? Seequest, what happened there?"

"Your Highness I am sorry to have let you down!"

"I promise that I will never return here again unless I have Helena with me."

Neptune said, "Why do you say that, dear friend?"

"Because I have failed you both and Helena who is my dear friend and I am her protector."

The king could see that he was very upset and quietened his tone towards the stressed hippocampus at this time.

Neptune asked the white and blue hippocampus to tell him what had happened to his daughter and then he will decide on Seequest's fate to live or die.

An hour had passed and even though he seemed to still been angry he understood that his daughter was also adventurous and would go and explore on her own if she felt it was safe to do so.

"Wait", the King said, "do you think that my daughter is in danger?"

The hippocampus said, "If I am correct, yes and no."

Neptune did not like Seequests answer and said "explain yourself!"

Seequest mentioned to Neptune the times that Hades would play tricks in the past and he told him that he possibly thinks that he is doing it again to get his horn and use his powerful magic to rule the land as he has tried before when Seequest was then the Unicorn King of all the lands.

The sea King sat back on his throne with a quizzical expression and his hand on his chin thinking is this possible that his brother could be up to his tricks again?

Neptune then said, "Seequest, I think he wants your horn!"

"But if he gets my daughter to marry him he then will become more powerful than me, so that means he would be able to defeat me and become the King of the underworld and the sea and of the land as well."

"We cannot let this happen at any account."

"Agreed," Seequest said, and they both swam up to the temple where the queen was doing her work, and there inside was Seequest's beautiful silver horn energizing the four crystal skulls of his Kingdom.

They were four actual skulls in this crystal temple where the queen would charge them up for the protection of her people, the sea, and its lands.

First, there was the aquamarine skull, which represents the power of creativity and spiritualism, which are the connection to the other planets above.

Then there is the emerald crystal skull that represents healing and peace.

The rose quartz represents love, hope, and family, and the last one is the sapphire crystal skull, which represents protection and courage to its people that believe in them.

But there was a myth that there was one more, it was the purple crystal skull which has been said it was more powerful of them all put together.

Neptune then called his queen, who has great wisdom and knowledge of everything. The queen turned around and looked at them both.

She appeared to be beautiful wearing a stunning silver-and-white dress with a cloak around her with the emblem of the moon on it.

And for her swallowtail, is aquamarine and light blue running through it.

She has a pretty pale complexion with long, wavy blonde hair and rosy lips with pearly blue eyes that could make you melt just by looking at them.

"You called Your Highness, always respecting her husband's role as the god of the sea. "How can I be of service to you today?"

Neptune replied, "My dear queen of great wisdom, please share with us your knowledge."

She replied, "Yes, of course, what is it that I can help you with?"

Neptune said, "Seequest feels that our daughter Helena had been captured by my cruel brother Hades.

As he knows that I would give in to him and that he also knows as well that I will give him Seequest's horn in replace of our lovely daughter back home safely with us again in a heartbeat."

Queen Sera seemed puzzled and angry at the same time and yet she kept calm, so she could use her powers to see if this was true.

"Let me look into my clear crystal ball called "the eye of wisdom."

The queen took out one of her beautiful silver hairclips and with magic, she clapped her hands and it began to shine and change into a stunning crystal ball.

It eventually stopped glowing and floated in front of her.

She then put her hands onto the ball and said "hear me now my eye of wisdom."

"Show me the fate of Seequest and my daughter"

"Will they both come home safe and together again?"

It replied to her "yes your highness but they will with a price to be paid in the future."

It now begins to dull down when she clapped her hands again and then it changed back as she puts the silver hairclip back into her hair.

The queen also saw something else that involved Seequest.

But she knew that she had to keep this to herself for now as it represented good and bad, which is a balance with Gaia (Mother Nature).

She had to keep the secret from everyone for now.

Neptune was happy with the answer that was received and said, "That will be all."

"Sera was good at what she preached, where for now she kept her feelings in control to prevent any more worry for Seequest or the king at this time."

Again her husband repeated "that will be all my high priestess yes, my king," and bowed her head softly, looking at him as she did, "thank you" and then swam off gracefully towards the great tall doors of the temple which opened up on her presence near them and swam further towards the stables crying as she went.

Neptune was still wondering what the right thing to do was for everyone's sake.

Mainly for the safety of getting his daughter back in one piece, without her getting hurt by Hades' wreath.

He thought long and hard and then decides and replies "my dear old friend Seequest do you really think that you can defeat my brother Hades with your powerful magical horn?"

"Please Neptune at least let me try as Helena is family to me."

"Let me go back to the surface and talk to my friends and bring back your daughter to you."

The sea king said, "OK, I agree to give you back your horn for now temporarily."

"But once we have defeated him you will have to kindly return it back to the temple of the crystal skulls where it helps my people and your fellow sea friends."

"Yes, Neptune, I agree to this and I totally respect why as well as you have taken me under your wing as one of your own for many great years now."

"This how I pay you back for your love and understanding."

"Good well that's settled" and they swam to the doors of the crystal temple where he reaches for the large silver horn that shone its rays toward all the crystal skulls every day.

Neptune asked Seequest to bend down a little so he can put his horn back in the middle of his forehead without any pain.

He also put extra protection on from it getting broken or being taken off him as the agreement was if this happened Seequest's powers will fade and he will then die and be no more!

Poor Seequest did not like the idea and yet knew that it was the only way that he could possibly defeat Hades at his own game.

Then Neptune puts his trident towards Seequest's head and says a verse in Greek, where the trident begins to glow, there as magic was once more.

You could see his horn growing beautifully back on his forehead where Seequest felt a slight tingly sensation as it grew to its full size once again.

Neptune looked at Seequest and said, "Rise, my unicorn hippocampus and Unicorn King."

Seequest had grown bigger too and he shone like a horse angel from the heavens once more!

Seequest was magnificent; strong and bold and felt that he could defeat anything.

"Before you go I have also given you all the powers you had before so if you need to you can take someone else's energy like you did in the past with the Earth unicorn"

He bowed to Neptune, and he said, "I expect you to be coming back with my daughter next time you come home, my boy. Otherwise, our friendship will end and you will die alone on Earth."

"Yes, my King I promise you this as I agree by giving up my own life to save hers!"

"Thank you, Seequest, my true hero and friend" and he then swam back up to the Unicorn King and hugged him around his neck with his arms as the Uni-hippocampus closed his eyes and put his muzzle into the hands of the sea king showing affection back.

Seequest responds "She will be home soon safely my King, I promise you."

Neptune knew that this was true, but he felt sad about what Seequest had said as if he felt like The great Uni-hippocampus knew he will never be back anymore to live with them again.

Neptune sensed that it was him saying his goodbyes in a different way not to alarm him and the king respected him greatly for that.

Neptune said, "Wait, remember this if you need my help or advance."

"All you need to do is put your horn into the sea and I will be there for you. Now go!"

The powerful Uni-hippocampus turned around and swam away with tears in his eyes knowing what he had to do.

Seequest knew that the sea king was only protecting himself and his kingdom, so he respected Neptune's wishes.

While the Uni hippocampus had already swum away the king slammed his trident hard onto the floor and said "May all the strength and wisdom of the seas be with you now my dear friend."

The great Uni-hippocampus swam back to the golden gates where this time there were the mer-knights of pale complexion and dark hair and blue eyes.

The guards were waiting for him wearing their golden armor and holding powerful golden spears.

Seequest then knew that these were Neptune's most loyal and strong mer-knights of the kingdom.

No one will dare to enter the palace while they are on guard, knowing that Neptune was possibly getting ready for war against his own brother Hades again.

At the second gate he sees his dolphin friends who are guardians to Helena to before Seequest come along.

They we're aware of the plan already as Neptune had already briefed them by talking to them through their minds earlier before they met back up with their loyal friend for one last time possibly?

They looked at their friend and saw not a hippocampus anymore but a bold; strong handsome Uni-hippocampus and he looked stunning with his beautiful long flowing fins that looked like small angel wings.

They first bowed at him as he approached them as he bowed his head back.

He said with bolder tone to his voice "Come my friends and the guardians of the princess, let's go to the surface and get her back."

The dolphins nodded their heads up and down and smiled at him.

They all swam very fast to the entrance where they would have to climb the surface as they swam through lots of beautiful colors of greens and reds, seeing crabs walking sideways at the bottom of the ocean and golden starfish sticking to the rocks to feed.

Seequest remembered why he loved living in the ocean as they swam passed clownfish; rainbow mackerel; cod and plaice.

Plus the massive string rays, which they had to be careful of so that they did not get squashed by them as these beautiful creatures would bury themselves in the sand to catch the prey that they would eat on a regular basis.

They swam close to each other as the sting rays could easily knock the dolphins or even Seequest flying as they were massive.

These creatures were enormous to him, so they would have to wait until they were ready to move on.

Eventually the stingrays are gone and so they swim on happily again towards the shallow part of the sea where the passage to rise to the surface was.

The guardians eventually stopped and looked up to the top of the ocean which was much colder in the British isle waters as they originally came from Greece.

It was pretty and clear even though it was turquoise blue that they could see.

The whales and fish swam passed them as they were swimming to this long passage to the top.

When they reached the surface, it is now sunrise as this is the only time it shows up in the ocean and also Neptune's way of keeping his people and the sea creatures safe from Hades' preying eyes and his shape-shifting creatures.

Seequest had to say a verse and said 'Pisces.' The double doors would appear like a magic as if they were there all the time, but they could not see them until now.

The doors appeared as heavy metal of bronze for strength and security as well with elegant blue markings of mer-folk on it.

The door opened and they swam through them quickly.

As they did the sea changed into a darker shade of blue and the entrance vanished.

As they continue to swim closer to the beach they could see that the sea color was changing on and off to light and dark between certain areas, which meant the sea was still deeper because of the shading and it was a warning for them to be careful.

They swam through the deeper waters they approached sharks of all kinds that respected them as they too then were guardians of the ocean to Neptune and would never touch them unless ordered to by the sea king.

They nodded their heads as they swam away the sharks seemed more scared of Seequest than usual.

Then just before they reached a lighter part, they came across the whales happily swimming in between them and the sharks as there had to be good and bad in the waters to keep a true balance on things.

They seemed happy at this time.

But Seequest also was sad as he knew that as soon as he reached the beach he would never be able to go into the sea ever again home properly.

It was just a gut instinct he felt and hoped he was wrong.

He decided that he would enjoy every minute with his friends and so he took his time having one last play before going alone on his next adventure.

Later Seequest could feel his gut telling him it was time to now go to the beach.

When he heard a faint sound or something which could have been a cry for help from Helena perhaps?

So he stopped playing straight away and got ready to carry on swimming on his own back to the pretty shore-line of bonnie Scotland.

Before he did that he swam up to the dolphins and touched them individually with his horn glowing an white light which lit up the sea and sparked like Luna the moon herself as if she was shining above them at this time.

The dolphins squeaked back as they felt the warmth of love and goodbye from Seequest through his mind as he then swam closer on his own toward the beach.

The dolphins were beautiful shades of blue and grey jumping out of the waters sadly knowing too that they were saying goodbye to their dear friend the Uni hippocampus.

Seequest swims as fast as he could now which made the sea very rough and aggressive where it starts to produce large waves that he started to ride with.

Eventually, he was jumping with them as he gets closer to the beach where Seequest's gills were opening very quickly even though he can swallow the seawater too.

It just made it easier for him to then have the energy to jump and gallop the waves at the same time.

As the sea was lit up with the gorgeous white light of the moon more than before as in the night sky Luna was watching from afar.

He now, at last, reached the beach.

When he touched the golden sand underneath him his tail begins to change into two powerful back legs and his gills closed around his head as his whole body becomes solid too, not now a water effect like earlier.

He now trots out of the sea in his true form of a great pure white Unicorn king that he was once before with a difference as he had a platinum horn instead of the silver one as he also processes the power of the crystal skulls too.

He galloped further and further towards the beach which hurt his feet as his not been on land for a while.

The sun lit up the Scottish lands as it was beginning to creep back in again for the next day to start.

When walked further in his hooves touched the sand which then became more solid, he then shakes all the salt water off his body.

With a beautiful coat of white tones with long wavy soft streaks of black in his mane and tail and part of his coat here and there making him feel the strength of his original self and presence of his father with him too (the night unicorn power)

That now his appearance was of a dapple grey affect, which was outstanding as a mixture of all his true form and his fathers too.

He looked like he had gained full wisdom now.

He made sure he was dry before resting for a while and he feels exhausted by the worry of his dear friend, the princess.

He looked to his left and remembered the rock where he was born and went to lie down there and falls fast asleep thinking of Helena and also his mum.

There Seequest was all curled up as he was when he was younger.

He felt great to be back on land for a while but his gut instinct made him also feel it was not going to be for too long.

Seequest the Unicorn King once more dreamt of all the good times as if they were coming closer to an end.

Chapter Five

Back in Neptune's Kingdom of Vissen

Back in Neptune's kingdom of Vissen, Helena best friend noticed that the princess did not meet her like usual and went and spoke to her mother and asked why.

Helena's friend is called Emerald, as she had beautiful bright shades of green all over her fins and tail.

She also wore a pretty Basque top with her green hair which also matched her bright green emerald eyes as this is where she got her name from.

Her parents were close friends with the king and queen of the sea.

Emerald swam further into Neptune's kingdom until she reached these round buildings made of the strongest sand there was.

She approached the second one, which had the initial S engraved on it stood for being friends to the queen.

All the other- buildings had the letter N on the doors as it was where the Guards and Knights lived.

But further on there were more homes with the initial S that belonged to the mer-helpers and mer-carers to the queen.

It's just that Emerald's parents were very important to both sea royals and the home of Vissen, that's why it's the only one connected to knights' homes too.

She opened the door, and there inside was her mother cooking some fish looking quite glam as well for one that is cooking.

Emerald's mother looks like her form with bright orange hair, glowing orange eyes, and a tail to match. Her name is Citrus.

She approached her mother quietly not to disturb her and she cried, "Mother, the princess is not around here anywhere.

"I think something terrible has happened to her."

Her mother replied, "Hush, child, I am sure she is fine and at the palace grounds."

"I bet she is not," interrupting her mother's conversation.

Citrus knew that her daughter had special powers of knowing things sometimes, so she decided to listen to her this time.

She said, "OK, my darling, if that is how you feel then I believe you.

We must go and see the queen and tell her what you feel and know now."

She takes off her apron, which floated onto the table.

Emerald's mother grabbed hold of her nicely and went to the front door and said, "Come, my child, let's go and get the dolphins in and get the chariot ready."

They swam the pool both blowing through these large conch shells.

Where there appeared two handsome male dolphins bigger than Seequest's friends.

The dolphin's came swimming towards them, squeaking as they went excited to see them both.

They approached the mermaids gently, and Citrus said, "Hello, my beauties."

"We need your help as they swam back to the chariot, where Emerald and her mother put on the soft shimmering gold bridles on their faces and the thick soft golden harnesses to the bodies which they connected to the chariot so they can pull it freely."

The chariot was stunning, as it's big and yet elegant with oranges and greens with an S on the middle of it too.

They both swam onto it, where Citrus calls to the dolphins and said, "Go, my boys, take us to Queen Sera at once."

In a flash, the dolphins dipped their noses downwards then they started shaking their tails up and down quickly so they could feel the big mammals pulling the chariot with all their might and yet quick and very calm at the same time.

The dolphins reached the south of the sea where Neptune's kingdom lay secretly.

They swam and swam until an hour later they saw Neptune's actual home, which was the prettiest sand building you had ever seen covered also with silver as that was the queen's line and power as she received her power from Luna, the moon.

Luna is the goddess of the moon and is the mother to Queen Sera.

Neptune and Sera met centuries ago in the skies before the Earth was even created.

There they fell deeply in love with each other.

Neptune is also the name of the beautiful bright blue planet where he originally lived as it was renamed by Zeus then.

After beating the Titans in the heavens he wanted to come down to Earth as at the time Zeus decided that he wanted to live closer to his creations and loved Earth himself.

At a later date, Zeus agreed with his brother that he would give him a gift for all his hard work in helping Zeus kill their father, the horrible Titan of them all.

Zeus named him the god of the sea, as the planet Neptune was full of water so Zeus knew that his brother would be perfect for this task.

So as Sera and Neptune got closer and wanted to be together forever, he was given the sea and the oceans to protect.

Princess Sera agreed to be his queen and was then named Queen Sera, the high priestess of Vissen and of the Crystal Temple.

As a gift from her mother she was given the power to breathe underwater and on land and the knowledge and wisdom of the universe, which she knew one day will come in handy from celestial friends from afar by each of the crystal skulls they gave her in the past.

Once Citrus and Emerald reached the silver building, two mermen guards were wearing silver armor and holding silver spears with the moon logo on their shields.

Citrus told the dolphins to slow down, so they started to move their tails and bodies at a slower pace.

When the chariot stopped, they swam off it and Citrus said, "Away with you," and the dolphins swam miles away not to be seen.

Emerald and her mother approached the large silver gates with the moon logo on them, where the strong mer-knights crossed their spears in front of them, which were their job to protect the queen, which shocked the daughter.

The queen's friend said, "We come in peace and will not cause any harm to our queen," and then said, "We must see her urgently about her daughter's safety."

The knights then laughed and then refused her, so she said, "Cancer."

As it's the queen's code to her mer- friends and workers in her realm, as the name of her guardian the Crab.

As these merfolk would only ever know this or see it for that matter unless there was any danger or a war coming!

It was her true guardian from the Cancer star that Luna kindly gave her daughter to protect her and the seas.

The large red crab still had the same name as its star sign and was a close friend to the queen, as it was never far away from her when she needed it, as it protected her at all times now that she lives in the skies no more.

The crab was also a symbol of love, peace, and creativity to the mer-folk as well.

Within that the knights shut up and pulled back their spears and smiled as they opened the doors for them to enter freely.

There inside was the prettiest palace you had ever seen.

There were statues made of silver of the queen's favorite dolphins and actual herself and her husband, King Neptune.

The sand floors even sparkled with silver and gold too, as this was Neptune and the queen's actual home, as he and his family not only love their people very much but also need their privacy from everyone.

The palace is where he is during the day to see his people and have meetings with others from all parts of the ocean, making sure that the sea and the creatures were safe.

This also is where the stables of the great legendary Sea spray and Tidal Wave, live happily together as one.

Because they were the first hippocampus created which made them very special, so the queen would hide them in secret stables that no one knew were there, as the queen did a spell that cloaked them from others.

As these were the first seahorses of their kind who are very powerful and dangerous if they got into the wrong hands, they were born thanks to Seequest's mother giving her horn up to save herself and her unborn son fifty- years before.

The queen's knights called her through a clam shell.

She heard the call at the stables straightaway and quickly finished what she was doing, said a verse and made the hippocampus invisible to the mind's eye,

The hippocampus is the precious and sacred creature to Neptune and herself as Tidal Wave also is the sea's Aquatic supreme champion, which has never been beaten yet.

She then swam from the stables back to the quarters where her guests were waiting to see her.

She rushed as quickly as she could to the throne room of pink, blues, and silver with diamonds blended into the floor and above on the rooftop was a copy of the stars and the moon above in the ceiling representing her mother and her home to prevent ever becoming home sick living in the sea now.

She quickly got her breath and sat on her throne wearing her beautiful white dress and her silver-and-blue cloak.

On top of her head was an elegant crown of the hippocampus and the moon and stars around them with aquamarine and Topaz on it too.

It was stunning.

The knights escorted the mermaids to the throne room and opened the doors. There in front of them was Queen Sera, who was pretty and glowing with her beautiful, long wavy, blonde hair.

She said, "How can I be of assistance to you, my dear friend?"

Citrus replied, "My gracious queen," with a bow, "sorry to disturb you but my daughter has some important news that you must hear.

It's regarding your eldest daughter, Princess Helena."

At this moment Sera was panicking wondering what this child had seen or known as she too could feel her powers.

The queen thought that she already knew and played along to not upset her friend's daughter.

"Come forward, dear child.

What do you know about Helena?"

Emerald approached the queen with fear and tears rolling off her face as she spoke, she bowed and then said, "My sweet queen I am best friends with your daughter and I feel in my gut that she is in great danger."

The queen reassured her and then expressed that she knew already and yet was prepared to listen to this young gifted child to see if her powers were true.

"It is OK, dear one."

"Please don't forget that I know you care for my Eldest Daughter, a lot and that you both grew up together."

"My daughter is safe, as Seequest, our dear old friend from the land who was once the king of the unicorns and now known as Seequest the Great Hippocampus has gone back to get her from whoever has taken her into their care," with great confidence in her voice at the time.

"Please let me help you, oh, Queen, while she is away."

Emerald's mother straightaway rejected and said, "No, I will not allow this."

The queen replied, "Yes, you can by looking after my dolphins while Helena is away."

Emerald smiled and agreed Even though she meant about helping out on the land above.

But knowing that Citrus refused, the high priestess thought it was one way of pleasing them both.

"Now I must go back to the stables.

Thank you for coming today and be safe."

"Love and light to you both my darlings"

Straight after they have gone Queen Sera was planning on going to actually see Neptune himself and tell him what she saw before as it was time!

"Thank you Your Highness, for your time today."

"No, please the pleasure was all mine!"

Citrus, do not be too hard on your daughter, as one day in the future she will save many lives to come.

"I shall come and visit you soon and see what great dolphins you have for our knights' chariots and mine but for now, good day."

Emerald and her mother bowed to the queen and then were escorted back to the gates, where they called on their dolphin chariot and there it appeared in a flash.

They swam onto it and went back home happily.

In the meantime, Queen Sera, or the sea queen, swam back to the stables and said, "Cancer" and there it appeared right before her eyes, as this stable was protected.

She said, "My legs" and within a glow of light they were there.

She was walking through the great sands of the bottom of the sea breathing perfectly fine as she went.

Queen Sera quickly changed into her stunning blue-and-white mermaid dress with silver armor with dolphins and moons on it, with her helmet of her favorite dolphin friend Spirit's tail.

She rushed to the stables and went into Tidal Wave's stall, there he was floating gracefully.

She put on his golden bridle and shell saddle and jumped on him and said, "Tidal Wave, take me to see your master and then the surface."

Within that, he neighed and said, "My queen, hold tight," and swam as fast as he could through the sea like a cloud of smoke.

He reached Neptune's palace within seconds, which was further east than their home.

She knew that she had to tell him before her friend did, so he would do an announcement about Helena's disappearance before this happened.

"She reached the palace doors and said Open up, I say."

The great doors to his throne room opened widely, as she swam in and said, "oh dear husband, we must make it known today that Helena has been kidnapped and that Seequest is going to rescue her."

He agreed, and then she said that she had to go and see her mother, the moon, for some advice on what to do next, as she is all the eyes and ears in the sky.

Neptune hugged his wife and he agreed and gave him her blessing to go and visit Luna, the moon, that night.

Tidal Wave and the queen reached the surface, where he galloped across the waves, making more as he galloped out of the sea.

He was more than a hippocampus.

He was a beautiful white seahorse with aquamarine eyes, mane and tail, with blue hooves as well glowing as see through.

He was magnificent to see.

They reached the beach, where he bowed to let the queen jump off his back gracefully.

Automatically her tail changed into legs, while Tidal Wave changed into a proper form of a horse.

"Thank you", she said and he got up and turned, ran back into the waters once more as he quickly changed into his true form again in a flash.

At this time, it was late and dark out.

The queen was looking up at the moon. She called, "Goddess Luna, I seek your guidance. Show yourself to me, please."

Within a few hours later, she appeared in an image of the great beauty of a fine goddess with grey-silver hair and a white-and-silver garment with a moon crest on her dress.

She was elegantly standing gleaming there the great moon right in front of her.

"You called my daughter? How can I help you?"

"Mother, I need your help?"

"Our eldest daughter, Helena, has been kidnapped by Hades."

"Is there any way of finding her?"

"Yes, my child".

"I know he has her in his underworld."

"What does he want with her?"

"At this moment maybe, nothing but he does know that she is very powerful in the future and knows that even though she is his brother's daughter that he would do anything to get her back."

"Oh, now what shall I do?"

"Well, I am going to contact Jecco and Celestial, the Guardians of the Sixth Dimension of Heaven, as they are Seequest's parents before and they would know how to defeat Hades as they did once before."

"Oh, Mother, yes, please can you do that?"

"I will go back to the crystal temple and see if I can use the crystal skulls for advice as well."

They both agreed with the plan and disappeared before the beautiful sunrise was pulled by Apollo (the sun god) and his amazing sun horses which one of them was once a day unicorn herself who kindly sacrificed herself to save Moonbeam and her foal in the past.

Has they bring the great sun to shine its light and share its heat with earth for another day?

Chapter Six

Seequest Is Trapped?

When the sun had risen, Seequest decided it was time to go after he drank some fresh spring water and ate some apples.

He would investigate this strange yet mysterious black fox.

He galloped further into the beautiful woods and the forest where he came across wolves and foxes.

He asked them if they had seen or heard of this fox before and everyone said no.

Seequest was getting really scared and worried for the princess, as he now believed it was Hades in disguise that had taken her for himself or possibly using her to get to him for his horn once more so he can rule Earth, which is Hades' dream and Seequest's and the Gods' nightmare's.

A day had passed when he was approached by a great grey wolf.

It reminded him of some friends he knew in the past.

"Fear not, the great one.

I am Storm, son of Max and Peacemaker, who is the second generation from Max's and Ashes' original pack, your late friends of the Peace clan."

"I hear you met my brother recently?"

The wolf ensured that he was a friend who could help him find the princess and where Hades' den is hidden.

They talked for a few hours and then galloped and ran to the forest called the Unknown where there is darkness lurking.

At the bottom of it near a silver birch tree, there was the secret entrance to the den where Hades had taken the mermaid princess to.

Much had changed since Seequest's reign.

There was more disease and decay to the plants and trees, thanks to Hades' magic around which was agreed with Gaia (Mother Nature) herself.

As she too needs to obey him, as the rules of Earth had to be obeyed.

So, every six months of the year everything is to die sadly and the following few months, it is meant to grow even stronger than before.

But this time, Seequest put his horn down on the ground where it started to light up and within half an hour the forest was alive and well again.

Storm said "this is a permanent thing now and that's how the season Gaia named their spring, summer, autumn, and winter after the strengths of the sun and moon."

Of course, Hades' favorite was the darkest and dullest of them all, winter.

Storm smiled of reassurance that there still was a chance for health and peace once more on Earth, thanks to the Unicorn King appearing in the nick of time.

They reached the forest of the Unknown.

Everything that still grew there had no color anymore, just one color of green and dirt where the badgers and snakes live.

Seequest did not like it here.

He could feel the sadness and pain of the forest.

He tried to do the same as he did earlier, but it stayed the same.

He knew then he had to find Hades' home, as no color was anywhere because of death around it.

The grey wolf told that Hades had cursed the land and there will be nothing or no one that can heal it so he said kindly, "Seequest, please save your magic"

When he gave up and walked further into the darker parts of the forest until Storm was sniffing and came across a strange smell of seashells, which he thought was strange.

Then the Unicorn King said, "Helena, she must be here", as he began to trot through the cave of darkness into Hades' home.

Helena did not know where she was and who to trust anymore, as Hades seemed to be nice to her.

He didn't react the way that she thought he would and wondered if her father Neptune, had ever told her the truth about him; as it seemed that he didn't at the time?

Because he acted as if he wanted to protect her and yet seemed not to want to tell her that he was actually a truly powerful god related to Zeus.

Because of this, he treated her well with color and gemstones around her like home and was kind and considerate.

Helena was not aware that she had been fooled once more by this great god of death.

Days had passed.

Hades seemed to make Helena feel that he was caring and loving to her, thinking if he could keep this up and make her his true queen.

"He asked her to put on this beautiful red and black velvet dress to keep her warm in his lair."

She agreed because this was only as she did feel that it was cold down there.

Once she put on the dress she felt warmer and yet Hades felt that she now was his too as wearing this to please him!

Hades had a plan.

Back in the cave, the Unicorn King remembered that his horn was a beacon and lit it up as they went and walked through a slushy and muddy pathway.

They heard growling from a distance.

Seequest touched his horn at Storm's side where he jumped when Seequest said "sorry I had to."

Within seconds, Storm started to grow four times his normal size.

"Oh, I see", and he said "thanks."

"It's only temporary until we're away from here."

The unicorn knew that the growling was only Cerberus the faithful guardian hound who looks like a three-headed black Great Dane with red eyes with the strength of a dragon who sometimes could change its image to parts of a dragon too.

On this day, that is exactly what they walked into.

There was Cerberus guarding the grounds with his large Dane heads and a dragon one too for extra protection and his feet and his tail were dragon-like as well.

There were very dangerous as at this moment in time he could also blow out fire from his mouth.

He also was covered in dragon scales to prevent him from being hurt or bitten.

With green powerful eyes, he could see in the dark caves and night skies easily and clearer with them.

Seequest mentions to Storm about the evil guardian dog before he approached them to be extra careful as he could still kill him with one blow if it wanted to.

Seequest also says that his name at this time was no longer Cerberus but Soul Taker as he would shock you and grab you and take your soul from your body.

"When he is his true self the guardian of soul's acts nasty and will bite and crawl on its victims".

"So please be careful, as he is highly dangerous and approaching quickly."

Even though they were both brave warriors, they were also scared of this creature, as it has never lost a fight before but they were hoping it would this time.

They heard its cries as they walk slower.

The cave became a dark deep tunnel to nowhere they were hoping it will take them to Helena at least.

As they knew it was worth doing this.

They approached the end of the tunnel there standing in front of them was their worst nightmare.

It was Soul Taker in the flesh.

The monster's body was glowing with fire and there at that minute, Seequest was lighting up the cave like a beacon with his amazing horn.

He told Storm to run away quickly into another small path on the left of them.

He stood there in complete silence away from harm quietly.

Seequest approached the creature with great caution.

Even though his powers were at his greatest level and he was glowing all over his body, his eyes lit up a beautiful blue like the sea.

He was walking with his head bent down so his horn was protecting him.

Soul Taker saw Seequest and said, "that won't protect you".

"I am stronger than you put together."

The unicorn replied "we'll see about that."

He charged towards the creature and stabbed him in the chest with his horn just missing his heart and said "I missed."

The creature said "yes you did and now it is my turn" and its mouth opened.

Its dragon head blew out the fire and burnt Seequest where he reared up in pain.

But he was not defeated yet and carried on the battle until they were both exhausted and both fell to the ground.

While the creature was asleep, Seequest woke up and jumped right over it and thought he had gotten the better of it this time as he galloped away through the dark tunnel.

Soul Taker accepted that Seequest was his equal and changed back to Cerberus as he cowardly walked away finding Storm at the same time.

So he took him instead to Hades as another problem for Seequest.

In the meantime, the Unicorn King felt he was lucky to get away alive and that Storm would be safe too.

He reached another pathway to a colorful cave of amazing colors and nature.

He knew this was not right as it was a very strange thing to see in Hades' lair, knowing that he is the king of the darkness.

He began to trot forward freely cautious when Helena walked over to him and said, "You found me."

"I now want to go home, please."

Within this, a large black fox appeared once more and says "that is not possible, my dear".

"You are staying with me now".

The plan has changed a little and he laughed.

Helena said, "why not?"

Then the fox started to change into an image of a large man covered in jet-black warrior clothing and appeared as Hades himself.

The poor Princess seemed scared and yet confused as if she was meant to know him, but she doesn't.

"My child I am your uncle Hades and you are the daughter of my brother, the sea god Neptune."

Helena said "and what of it?"

"Well, my dear one, I want something in return."

She then replied "name it and you shall have it."

Seequest said, "No, do not say anything but it was too late the agreement was already placed."

Poor Helena did not know about the rules of the Gods.

Because if they ask for something that they cannot have, they will take anything that they want, even if it is not normally possible.

That's exactly what he did.

Helena had now landed herself and the others into a complete trap by accident of not knowing this rule.

Hades was very clever and witty and said, "Very well, I will do just that.

I want Seequest's horn so I can create my own horses of darkness and have the power to rule Earth with Mother Nature as my guide and be part ruler to humans in the future."

Helena realized now what she said and tried to change the agreement.

She replied in shock "No, no, no, this you cannot have, as it is not mine to give you."

Feeling very upset and wondered what she could do to change it.

Hades replied if I ask I get!

"But, my lovely, if I cannot have his magnificent horn, then I shall tell Neptune myself that Seequest found you and killed you with it!" in a blunt voice.

"No, no," Seequest and Helena both said.

"Never will that happen!"

"Oh, dear friends, you forget."

"I can make you do anything if I want you to, as you're in my home now of death and destruction."

Seequest knew what he had to do.

When he answered "Promise me you will let the princess go unharmed and I will stay and you can do what you want of me in return for her safety."

"No!" she screamed and was very upset.

"You will die, dear friend."

"Yes, but you will be alive and well" and he smiled at the princess.

Hades agreed with a big smile on his face and said, "Cerberus, take the wolf and the princess out of this cave before I change my mind."

She cried and hugged Seequest throwing both of her arms around his neck as he bent down his head to her hands comfortably, showing their love for each other as great friends they were.

Helena then pleaded again to Seequest saying "please my unicorn king you cannot do this he will kill you!"

"Seequest, please do not, there must be another way," she said.

"It's OK, Helena. This is my fate and I promised your father that you will be home soon safely no matter what the cost was.

Now you go back to him and have a good life to the fullest in the sea and don't come back for me."

"I love you" and he nuzzled her arm when she was walking away from him.

Her eyes were flooding with tears but she knew that she had no choice but to go and leave him here to possibly die.

"Enough of that" and Hades pulled her away, when Seequest was now under his control as he bowed to his princess for the last time to say goodbye.

The mermaid princess said, "oh my goodness, what have I done?"

She began thinking hard about how she was going to fix it.

In her mind, she spoke to Seequest and said "I will do my best to free you, dear friend".

Seequest said, "No please Helena, it is not your thought Hades has been waiting for these moment for many years now!"

"Please do not beat yourself up over this"

"I knew one day this would come".

"So please do not blame yourself as I said before this is my fate!"

Hades' powers sensed something was going on due to their body language.

As he commanded Cerberus to take Helena back to the beach he takes hold of the princess's arm by his jaw gently and looks at her as if he is warning her to do as she is told for her safety and that the wolfs too.

She agrees to nod her head when looking very upset.

She then gets on his back for him to take her to the beach where she can swim safely back home again.

Before they left Cerberus said, "Seequest I beat you twice in one day,"

The poor unicorn put his head down to the floor in shame of defeat.

Cerberus is getting ready to start running through the dark tunnel once more.

Helena looked back seeing that the Unicorn King was now trapped helplessly with fear in his eyes not because he was afraid of Hades.

But for what he will do and use his horn for, as it will give the evil god power to use on her best friend and everyone else in the world?

Thanks to her trusting a complete stranger who pretended to be nice to her to get what he wanted.

Where really was an evil god undercover to gain the power of her best friend and everyone else in the world at last?

Seequest wanted to show his strength in front of the princess one last time when called her as she turned around quickly and he said, "Helena please go with Cerberus and be safe."

Everything will be OK or that's what he was hoping for.

Quickly she jumped of Cerberus and ran back to listen to old friend for one last time.

Next, she nodded at the Unicorn one last time as she again climbed onto the dragon dog has he ran out of the cave with the wolf following behind him.

Storm howled as he too did not like leaving Seequest there either and the howl was a call to say he will try and get some help to save him somehow and quickly followed after the dragon dog as he was faster them him.

The hell dog was knocking the princess up and down through the bumpy cave as he did not care for her comfort so she grabbed hold of his fur carefully and held on for dear life.

They reached the end of the tunnel where there was pure sunshine in the pretty forest.

Halfway through the journey to the beach, Cerberus frightened off Storm to another direction and warned him not to follow otherwise he will be killed.

The wolf nodded and looked at Helena as he closed his eyes in respect for who she truly is and ran off with great sadness with tail between his legs.

Hoping to find some help along the way or at least try?

Cerberus ran as fast as he could through the lands until it was dark and arrived at the shore at around midnight with a beautiful moonlight shining above them.

The poor mermaid princess could not wait to get off this massive beast and fell asleep on the journey.

As he arrived on the beach and knelt down to jump off.

When he said, "you better hurry as Hades' magic is going to wear off in a minute unless you want me to drag you in as a fish, which you will be."

"Otherwise you will die here."

"No thanks I can manage" has she falls to the sand where she was already starting to change.

She felt the sand for the last time on her toes and in an instant her toes became her beautiful swallowtail and fins once more.

She crept into the sea with her hands wriggling as she went until she could swim further into the ocean.

Luckily enough she had jumped into the deepest part of the sea before she fully changed back to her actual full mermaid self.

Where she heard and saw her Seequest's and her friends the dolphins waiting for her to return.

But it still was not right as they were happy to have the princess back but now lost Seequest.

They were all pining for their dear friend as he said that he wasn't coming back and they hoped that was not true.

She told them that Seequest was in great danger and that she must get back and see her parents urgently to see if they can save him somehow.

The dolphins squeaked and agreed, and they dived back into the deep once more with Helena grabbed hold of their dorsal fins as they are faster swimmers than her.

Making sure she gets home once again with a full guarantee.

Chapter Seven

Is Seequest Doomed?

Back in Hades' cave, Seequest was still standing there helpless.

"What can I do with you?"

"I cannot take your horn otherwise it will kill you and I may need you for something else and you need to be alive."

"Um how can I get your powers, without killing you?" he wondered.

Next he remembered his beautiful yet mysterious Friesian type demon black mare called Knightmare.

He thought that she was a good age to birth a foal

"Yes, I know what I am going to do with you, old friend!"

Knightmare was not like any other horse.

She had red eyes red flowing mane and tail with bat wings.

She was an underworld fire Pegasus.

She was named Knightmare by him because of her nasty temper and that is what Hades liked about her that she had a nasty spirit due to what happened in her past.

He took her in as his own and trained her to obey him.

She excepted this offer as at last she wasn't ever alone and she had a friend she could trust from there on, or that's what she thought?

Seequest replied "Hades I will not mate with your mare".

"I will choose my own mates and you cannot make me."

"Oh, dear boy that's where you are wrong!

"Well, if you won't mate with her then I shall have to kill you"

"Wait, I have another way that I can give her a foal without mating with her."

"Yes, I am listening."

Seequest replied, "bring your mare to me and I will show you"

"Good" Hades replied with great happiness.

Hades called for her by making a whistling sound where they was a noise of heavy neighing and breathe coming from a distance and seemed to becoming closer as this incredible jet black winged creature flew in flapping her bat wings until she landed beautifully in the door-way and walked to the Unicorn King.

He looked at her, which overwhelmed him because of her death but he recognized the soul's body of one of his late family of the horses that had passed many years before.

Has her herd called her "Velvet?"

She answered it even though she is dead and said "so you are going to mate with me, Great King?"

Seequest answered "No you are one of my granddaugh-ter's foals so I cannot and I shall not!"

"But I will grant you this".

"It will hurt you so beware".

"This is not what I want to do but your master wants this."

"Good then get on with it as where I am living with pain as it's normal here."

When she said that he felt sad for her and yet had a duty to try and save his life and escape somehow.

"OK, I shall do this Hades but just remember you may be the god of the underworld but you have feelings too!"

"If I hurt her, it is your fault!"

"Seequest I command you to mate or impregnate her another way, I do not care which"

"Or I shall kill you by cutting off your horn while you are in a deep sleep."

The stallion nodded his head sadly agreeing.

He asked the mare to lie down and he lay beside her.

"Close your eyes" and then he did too as his horn began to glow a stunning pink light.

In his mind, he was thinking of his children for their highest good.

Knightmare was wondering what was happening as she was still lying there comfortably.

He then put the pink bright horn onto her belly.

She began to scream and she said, "It stings."

But he told her that she must stay still for this to work.

He moved his horn further to where her womb is and pierced her stomach gently where through this he had now impregnated her by his magic of will and mentioned that he will never do it again.

As when he closed his eyes in his mind he versioned a healthy foal appearing in her womb and growing quickly so he could escape possibly sooner than later.

An hour had passed when he was exhausted and felt weak and light-headed and fell to his side with a massive noise to the ground as if there was thunder.

The mare had not yet awoken herself from the deep sleep the magic had put her eventually in.

She did not feel too much of the burning pain that was involved to achieve this miracle once again.

While Seequest was asleep, Hades created a spell of an invisible cage around the tired unicorn.

Later on, the mare woke up and went straight to her feet.

Another hour had passed when her stomach began to grow and become heavier with foal.

"Excellent," Hades said "you are pregnant dear friend with Seequest's foal."

"Now I will have the power to rule Earth once more."

Knightmare neighed and reared with joy and then said "I am going to be a mother to a foal of the great Unicorn King" and galloped off into her stables further in the cave grounds to rest.

Chapter Eight

Eldest Daughter's Plans to Rescue Seequest

Helena was swimming back with the dolphins in the beautiful ocean she saw colorful schools of fish going past them as they reached the golden gates.

The mermaid princess decided that she could save him and escape the palace grounds at night.

She stayed in her hide out telling that she was going back to the palace.

But she decided that she would go to the library instead to see if she could help Seequest instead.

She found what she was looking for and slept here for the night, hoping that she would not be seen.

She arrived back on the beach at sunrise the next morning after finding a spell from her mother's book in the temple that night before.

Where tells her how to change into a Pisces once more or that was her plan?

But she reached the shoreline when she remembered what Seequest had done for her all because she did not listen to him the first time.

She thought about it and then thankfully came to her senses that this time she will do what Seequest told her to do.

As she believed she owed him that much!

She knew then that she needed to talk to her parents first knowing that it was the most sensible thing to do in this case.

She had learned her lesson through her experience by being caught by Hades, who disguised himself as a cute fox who was kind to her.

So, knowing this she decides to not carry on and turns back and runs towards the sea and jumps straight in as she once again quickly changes to her mermaid form and swims straight home.

Being home in Vissen she felt safe and happy again where she belonged.

And yet she felt awful for what had happened to Seequest putting him now in great danger like that which will also cause a great war on her people and Earth.

If Hades worked out how to claim Seequest's powers without killing him or what if he did just kill him, she thought?

Before she reached the gates this time the dolphins knew that she had not been home yet and wanted to make sure this time she will!

The dolphins stopped at the gates and she swam up to their faces and kissed their noses gently and they swam away into the distance.

There, Helena was excited and frightened to tell her parents what she had done to their dear old friend, where this possibly may jeopardize their lives completely as well by accident.

Eventually, she swam up to the mer-guards has they bowed their heads straight away and opened the great gates where she swam into the city, seeing the mer-folk happily doing their jobs and being with their families.

She reached Neptune's golden palace where she bumped into her mother and she stopped and stared at her with pure love and sadness at the same time.

Queen Sera could not believe her eyes.

She thought it was just her imagination playing tricks on her as said "Helena you are home, is that really you?"

Helena said "yes mother I am home."

The queen swims right up to her and hugged her tight and said "my dear daughter we were worried about you and Seequest kept to his word, bless him."

Helena pulled away and said "what?"

In a shocking and upsetting tone in her voice, "you knew that Seequest gave up his life to save mine?"

Looking so confused and yet in her mother's eyes she replies, "yes my darling it was the only way to save you my dear child!"

"I am sorry" with great grief in her voice and heart has she said out loud to Helena while still cuddling her tightly.

"No, this cannot be true".

"You let him come back to save me knowing that he was going to sacrifice or die for me instead?"

"Yes Helena Seequest, your father and I know this is to be his destiny and it had to be done this way to save you!"

The mermaid princess was horrified to hear what she just heard from her mother and swam away from her and rushed through the throne doors and fell in front of her father's tail and said, "Father how could you let my best friend and protector give his life to save mine?" with tears in her eyes from a broken heart.

Neptune said, "my child you are still too young to understand what it means to be a protector and a friend at the same time."

"But one day you will completely understand why he had to do this for us all."

"Now know this" in a strict tone in his voice "I forbid you to try and help save Seequest from Hades' wrath."

Helena looked the other way as her father was saying this to her face.

"My darling, I am not just the sea god for nothing."

"Have faith in me and great Zeus himself."

"I cannot promise you my darling but we will do anything to save him somehow?"

"But we may have to kill him ourselves."

Hating what he was saying and dreading that might be the case.

"As if his powers get into the wrong hands then all the life that we know and enjoy will be gone forever."

"Otherwise if we don't."

Helena shouts in a pleading voice "please Father save Seequest I beg you."

Neptune at this moment in time felt helpless and knew there was possibly one way it may work but it will take time as he will have to go to Olympus and see Zeus himself.

He insisted that the princess was not allowed out of their sight and could not go anywhere out of the kingdom.

She was sent to her quarters where the mer-guards guarded her doors.

Until one night she realized that the mer-guards changed for the night and in that split second she slipped out of her round sand window and swam towards the dolphins that pulled the great chariots for her parents.

Thinking she should listen to her parent's rules often as they were for her good.

And yet she could not get it out of her head that Seequest is now under Hades' control accidentally because of them.

Wanting to get Seequest home again with her even though he said it wasn't his destiny in the end!

She opened up the coral fence and the whole pod of dolphins swam around her until she reached the pair that stayed always together called Coral and Reef.

Everyone came out of their homes quietly and tried to get them back in their pen before the king find out while they were doing this.

Helena was holding on to these two dolphins' dorsal fins as they wanted to now play with the other free dolphins around them, as they never went out of the kingdom unless on a chariot run for her parents.

The dolphins felt completely free now that they just wanted to escape into the large ocean, as the gates were accidentally left open so they and the princess could escape through it.

But first, she had to get hold of chariot wear that she swims as fast as she could where she had tied them up to the other side of the fence with strong seaweed twine.

She swam straight back when the dolphins are calling their friends when she grabs them and puts on their golden bridles and harness's quicker than she had ever done for her mother and then takes them to their chariot where she connects them and jumps and on it and calls their names softly and off they go towards the open gates from the city.

Quickly they disappeared like dust.

Once out of the gates Coral and Reef needed to go up for air so they rose to the top where Helena thanked them and set them free they started to swim away from her and began to jump in and out of the ocean enjoying their freedom once again.

The mermaid princess must remember a verse that she saw in her mother's Book of Wisdom and hopefully prayed that she had the power to say it and make it work for her again.

She did just that when she had legs once again and swam to the beach where she rested for a while thinking about how she was going to save Seequest from this great evil danger on her own.

The next morning, she woke up after feeling exhausted from her swam by using her legs.

Once she had changed properly the power from the magic this time also formed a beautiful blue and silver gown and her hair of golden locks was put up in a bun out of the way.

It was a sunny morning.

There she was lying on the dried golden sand feeling warm as back in Scotland.

The birds are singing in the blue sky above her.

She noticed that the sand was getting hot to stand on she quickly gets to her feet and runs into the sea where she drank to energize herself where she remembered that she had some seaweed in her hair and remembered that too will strengthen her quickly.

She seemed to have a plan and quickly started to heal her feet with salt water.

Helena felt better and begins to run towards the forest where Cerberus had brought her recently.

Has she was running, she started to remember the route back into the forest of Dreams.

There she noticed the den that the black fox took her through and wanted to run again fast as she could and go into it to save her friend from the bad god Hades.

Helena forgot that her legs could only do so much in so little time as different from her tail now.

When she started to feel some tightness in them and thought of what her father said that legs are as not strong as her tail and they will fail her quicker whereas with her tail she could swim for hours in the sea.

The difference was that the legs are made of bone and her tail was made of the cartilage more powerful because of survival like the shark which gave her great speed too.

She did not like this pain or discomfort she had never felt before and so she agreed to herself to rest and heals them before entering into possibly another trap.

Luckily before she collapsed she had reached a smaller part of the woods where it had beautiful rainbows roamed around freely like magic.

Because Seequest had covered it with a powerful spell to protect them while enjoying themselves in the past.

She believed it was there so they could rest from the danger of the unknown that lurked at night or day while staying there for a while on land.

Helena was astonished by this that she decided to walk further where she saw a lake where Seequest and his friends and his horse family must have been recently while she was sleeping safely in the cave.

When looking in the lake for fish she saw her father's image reminding her to not over do it for the first time and she started to understand why.

While she was resting under the willow tree in the gaps of the branches crept a glistening light from the sun shining through so gracefully.

Helena was still in great pain and blacked out on the green grass luckily in a safe place where no one would ever find her, thanks to Seequest.

Two hours had passed when a pack of wolves started to sniff her body and scent who were curious as they had not seen a creature like her before on land.

To make sure that she was not dead, they smelt her gently without waking her up or frightening her.

As the male smelt her the wolf recognized another smell that they have smelt before and it reminded him of the great unicorn that lived here in this forest in the past.

But that was quite some time ago and they wondered how his smell was on her dress and knew then she must be a friend of his?

Because of this the male was encouraged to go up to the princess and licked her face to wake her up.

She started to feel a type of wetness on her cheek, which startled the young Piscean girl.

She opened her eyes and saw this large black wolf looking right at her with his incredible amber eyes staring into hers looking at her soul.

She was frightened and yet she knew that she had to keep still.

Where she was taught by her mother in the library about other creatures on land through the Book of Wisdom back home regarding how to protect herself from certain animals she may come across and how to defend herself if approached.

Where back home she was taught that if it a shark was near, she would have to keep still until it passed by as it could eat her whole.

So, the technique she was using was similar.

The wolf did not feel scared of the princess.

It seemed it was fascinated by the beauty and kindness in her eyes.

The princess didn't feel any fear either they were complete opposites and yet felt part of each other's spirits at the same time.

As she looked the wolf right in the eyes too she could see that they were communicating together.

The wolf's head kept tilting back and forth as if he understood what she was saying to him and eventually backed away as a friend.

Helena gave a sweet smile and the wolf sat down and lifted his paw showing peace.

He also opened up his mouth where the mermaid freaked out thinking she had upset it by getting up and quickly sat back down again as the wolf came up to her and brushed his tongue gently against her face once more.

She laughed as it tickled her and now felt confident around him that she then stood up brushing off the dirt from her dress.

She then decides to be brave and walks over to the wolf, where he and his mate are playing with her and run off into the forest.

Helena felt confused and yet relieved that they did go.

She got her breath back where her legs were tired out.

So, she crawled into the pond to drink and keep from drying out, as otherwise, she would die.

She was leaning on the grass when she saw a reflection in the water and thought of home with her family once more in the sea.

Oh, how much she felt like jumping into it.

But you knew that it was not possible because of her living in salt water all her life as the lake was completely different due to its origin of fish that lived in it.

But thanks to Seequest he knew that they would need somewhere to go to gain their strength once again.

As he blessed it and purified it so they could use it to do just that.

"Thanks, Seequest"

She thought about him when she dipped her feet into the fresh blue pond to relax her legs for a while.

When she was just chilling in the water she realized that the unicorn must have mixed with her mind somehow as she could see through his eyes and that is why she find this hiding place, she thought.

It must have been a gift that he gave her earlier when he nuzzled her arm.

"Wow", she said and realized what had happened to him and thought she must get home and tell her father straightaway.

She was sad for him but pleased that he was still alive.

She thought she would try something that she had never done before and dived deep into the bottom of the pond and could see her family back in the actual sea in Vissen.

She cried and then a fish jumped in front of her and ruined the connection.

She was upset and angry with herself for ever wanting to come on land as Hades would not have not had the opportunity to capture Seequest after all these years of hiding in the sea away from him.

And for his peace of mind, he wouldn't have known about her either or that's what she thought.

The mermaid princess was thinking about how she could make this right again and save her dear friend from this underworld god.

She enjoyed the rest in the sunshine sitting in the pond.

As she started to feel better, so she climbed out of it carefully and dried her legs with her dress while wiping her hands over her cheeks making her feel nice and fresh again where she then decides to lay back down near the willow tree to dry off slowly.

Looking at the beautiful view she could see the birds tweeting and flying happily above her.

She fell asleep because of all the thinking she did on how she could help Seequest somehow.

The wolves had been watching from afar and agreed to protect her from now on seeing that she was in great pain with her heart been broken and her tiredness in her legs which made them sore as she did not have enough time to heal properly because of the freshwater fish swimming in it too.

Both of the wolves crept up while she was sleeping and thought they could help in some way as if she's friends with their late mighty king of the lands then their happy to protect her now.

Both wolves were starting to lick her legs gently as their tongues produce a savor that heals them.

As they too get hurt at times while fighting and hunting for food.

This is how their wounds heal quickly and help them to survive.

Once the brace had finished licking all her legs,Helena felt a wet sensation of healing energy on her them which made her smile and turn over in comfort once more.

She slept for many hours dreaming of back home.

The male wolf seemed to like the princess and lay right beside her body while the female was not quite sure of her yet and kept her distance a little longer.

The evening had come and Helena woke up stretching her arms out she could feel a large warm body of fur besides her keeping her warm.

She panicked inwardly but she stayed calm due to her legs were all magically healed, so she was laying there with the wolf comfortably enjoying some company too.

Later, she feels that she had to get up because her back was unusually starting to ache.

So she crept past the male wolf trying not to disturb him in his slumber.

But it was too late.

Her foot tripped over the wolf's tail where he lifts his head and looks at her thinking what had happened?

She looked the wolf in the eyes and said out loud, "I am sorry.

"I didn't want to wake you, so I tried to climb over you my mistake is your tail ok?"

The large male wolf looked at his tail and wagged it fast as if saying yes.

Helena then was shocked as he said "yes, Princess it is fine and I understand every part of your body language and your voice, as you must have the gift that your voice changes into the language of which animal you are talking with?"

"Well, that's a first" she says back to him.

Helena thought as she normally only read minds (telepathy) and she did not know that she could do this too!

The princess seemed excited about her gift and it made her more powerful than ever before.

"My name is Troy and my female is Crystal."

"She's OK."

"She's just unsure of new things around her at times that's all."

"She will warm up to you in time but for now give her space to breathe."

Helena then realized that she can communicate with all the animals as she does with the dolphins and hippocampus at home. "Wow", she said "That's cool."

Because there is now trust and friendship she put out her arms to Troy and he walks over to her.

Where she hugged him tightly, showing that she had no fear anymore.

They both enjoyed the hug as Troy pushed his body closer to Helena's face.

But because he was much bigger than her she had to get up and walk away as he was starting to accidentally suffocate her with his thick soft fur.

"Are you ok, where is the Unicorn King?"

The princess started to cry again as she mentioned what had happened to Seequest and that it was all her and her parent's fault.

The Piscean girl tells the wolf that she is a mermaid princess really and that she must go back to the sea again as she knows that her friend is alive and will be used to produce Hades powerful horses of darkness and that it may be too late for him now as Knightmare is pregnant with Seequest's foal!

As Helena's mother told her that if they ever meet up again there will be a death trying to save him!

That's it is why the mermaid princess was determined to help her friend before it was too late.

After thinking long and hard she was prepared to put her life on the line for a change hoping that it will not come to that though she hoped.

She was thinking to herself that she must go home to find out how her father is going to get Seequest back without being harmed himself or his kingdom and people.

The wolf looked upset and concerned so he asked her 'what can I do to help you get back home?'

Princess replied "well if you could kindly give me a ride on your back to the beach as you can run faster than I because I only have a few more hours before the spell runs out and I become a mermaid again."

"I need to get into the sea before the moon rises as otherwise, I will die."

Troy agreed to help her.

He then walked away proudly and knelt and bent his neck so she could climb on his back by climbing up his left shoulder and putting her left foot over until she was sitting comfortably.

Now he tells her to hold on to the scruff of his neck and hold on tight as it's going to be a bumpy and fast ride to the beach if they want to get there on time.

The beach was five miles away from the forest and the woods.

They were going to set off when Crystal approached and growled thinking that Helena was trying to dominate her mate.

"It' is OK, my love, I am helping the princess."

"You wait here and I will be back soon."

The female cowered and put her head down looking at the ground obeying his command.

She walked backwards as she howled and disappears, the princess felt tense and the wolf felt it.

"Don't worry Princess she will be fine"

"I' will meet her back home after dropping you at the beach."

After him saying that to her she relaxed were they set off to the woods towards the beach?

"Hurry", she said.

"I do not have much time left."

The large black wolf runs as fast as his legs would take them.

Halfway into the journey Crystal came running from another angle of the woods and howled at Troy and followed behind him.

Troy just carried her onto the beach as the sun had just set and the moon will rise very soon now.

Helena was starting to panic thinking that she will not make it home in time and could die.

She was scared and yet believed that her new friend would not let her down.

The wolf ran so fast that poor Helena started to feel dizzy as she was not used to the speed on bumpy grounds and sitting low as she was now.

Yet she held on tightly as she drifted back into a deep sleep.

Even though she had blacked out she seemed to hold on for dear life.

She was lucky.

An hour had passed when they reached the beach with the sea crashing its waves roughly against the shore.

He took the chance of walking on the wet soft golden sand and trotted into the sea being careful as he went.

He took a deep breath and shut his mouth to prevent himself from swallowing any of the water as he walked further into the sea.

It was rough that it could pull him in and he could easily drown.

So, with his strength, he digs his paws deep into the sand for extra grip on the land and then gradually he started paddling, and now he feels that it's time to get the princess back into the water.

Troy shouted "Helena it's time to wake up!" but she didn't so he thought that if he swum out towards the ocean she will hopefully wake up by energized again.

The sea was getting too rough for him to stand and also to cope with as now he is out of his depth.

He rolled to his side where Helena then fell off his back.

He licked her face and she woke up in perfect time before he gets pulled under because of the current.

Luna the moon goddess saw the wolf trying to stay afloat in the heavy waves crashing and shines on him to give him some extra strength to survive this.

So that he will not get pulled under as they went on he started to taste the salt sea water in his mouth.

Helena turned around to see that he was struggling and swam up to him and said, "Troy hang on I got you" and grabbed hold of him as though she was bigger than him now as she pulled him back to the shoreline.

Where his mate come running down and dragged him by his neck to the sand where he collapsed through exhaustion.

Helena managed to get him closer to the shore where Troy slowly pulled himself out of the sea in time.

She wanted him respond to her and so she kissed his nose and said thank you, hoping he feels and hears her voice that he comes too soon.

Helena still saw Troy laying there on the beach soaking wet and hoped that he will be OK?

She calls Crystal and says "give him some of the seaweed."

"It will be safe for him to eat for now just to get him up and about".

So, Helena told her to go near these rocks and collect some which she did and she encouraged him to eat it.

Eventually, she howled as he started waking up looking weak and tired and started to eat a little of it.

The mermaid princess is watching from afar in the great distance hoping that Troy be fine in time.

Helena was not aware that Troy was in a bad way at all.

She thought that he was just resting and so she left him there thinking it was the best thing to do for him as on land again and he'll be safe now?

Then the moon rose when Luna knew that the wolf was not fine at all.

Back on the beach there Troy is struggling for his life, hoping that Helena was OK too?

Luna decides to help the brave wolf.

Helena feels that her friends are OK and it was safe and so begins to go back to the sea where she changes back into her original self again.

The beautiful mermaid now with true black hair and her gorgeous green tail jumped up with excitement that she made it back in time thanks to her new friends.

Another hour had passed when Troy did not realize that the princess was safe and was herself again, thanks to him.

She still was watching him from a great distance and yet hopping that he will be OK in time, she heard a voice in her head say that he will be and this made her feel reassured.

The mermaid princess also heard a voice say its time go home Princess and speak to your father about what has happened to Seequest.

She paid attention to the voice as if it's her intuition telling her that she needed her parent's help after all.

Before she went she said by shouting across the waves 'thank you for everything!

"I won't forget you."

Storm lifted his head gently off the wet sand and repeated 'nor will I now go with a low tone as his heart was slowing down.

But poor Helena could not see or hear him say this as she's now a far distance.

So, she's swimming deeper with a smile on her face and turned towards the deeper part of the ocean where she swims further out to the darker parts of the sea where they could not go.

In the distance, Crystal can just see her and howls in great joy that she's ok and yet sad that her mate is not.

Heading back towards a spot where there is a special place that will take her to depths that will eventually get her home to Vissen, Neptune's kingdom.

The mermaid started to repeat to herself many times before diving deep "I am going home and dived where she disappeared into the rocky waves."

While this was all going on the moon was shining brightly more than normal on the ocean like a pearl in the night sky.

Helena did not know that her actual grandmother was watching over her all the time when she can, of course.

Back on the sand, the wolf was panting heavily and still struggling to get his breath where possibly dying because of fighting the waves and protecting Helena making sure she got into the sea before she changed back to her original self as she would of drowned and by doing this he was drowning instead which exhausted his body through and through.

Crystal, his mate, knew that he was weak to walk and could not stay there much longer, as the tide was coming in and would take them both back out to sea.

She howled to give herself the strength and then again grabbed with her mouth gently biting his neck of thick fur she began to drag him as far away from the beach as much as she could.

She continued to drag him further away from the beach with all her strength she had left.

The female wolf would not give up on him no matter what as it was her true mate for life.

Crystal has found an open space between the beach and the woods where she felt safe for them now and feels exhausted too.

Lying beside her mate until they both recover by building their strengths back up once again and keeping him warm too.

Crystal licks his face as pure comfort where she's showing him that she loves him, which will make him feel better and that they were safe now.

She snuggled up to him keeping them both warm for the night as it's chillier in the night-time in Scotland.

Luna, the moon could see that the poor wolf was still suffering badly so she came down to see him in person.

The wolves are cautious but Troy has no strength to protect his mate Crystal who feels like it's her turn for a change, has her shackles come up on her back showing her body language to Luna saying please beware that she is guarding and protecting them from harm so when Crystal saw her she feels nervous about what she wants from them both?

She started to growl warning Luna that she would bite her if she came closer to them.

Luna says "It's OK, girl".

"I promise not to hurt you or him."

"All I want to do is help him."

"Please let me try?"

She looked closely into the female wolf's eyes gaining trust as she did.

As she walked slowly over to them, where now Crystal felt calm safe and trusted her.

Luna came over she gently stroking her head and Crystal licked her hand as she accepted her.

She then continued and approached Troy carefully knowing it was safe too and began to stroke both of them around their ears which they both enjoyed very much as it was comforting.

Crystal got up and made way for Luna to get even closer to her mate and as she did Troy was just trying to open his eyes to see this beautiful magical figure leaning beside him again gently touching his body with love and great care not to hurt him anymore than he already is feeling.

Luna had an amazing healing touch, which he needed to get better.

He saw briefly a stunning young lady of white and silver glistening like a star in front of him.

"Please do not be alarmed."

I am Luna, Goddess of the moon I am here to help you like you just did earlier for my granddaughter Helena of Vissen.

"Please let me try?"

Troy was weak at this point and possibly dying so he blinked with his sweet amber eyes and agreed as fell back into another deep sleep feeling stone cold.

His mate sensed this and she came back and lay closer to him once more to try and get him warm again.

Poor Crystal was looking very worried.

"Don't worry girl he is going to be just fine you'll see, Luna put her hands onto his body and they began to glow."

He starts to become dry and his fur is now feeling some heat more healthily again.

His mate started to see that he was changing from a black wolf into a beautiful pure white one instead.

Where she- the wolf becomes frightened that she gets up and ran's off for a while and watches from the trees nearer to the woods for safety.

Troy was starting to feel better now and more himself when Luna said "wake up".

It's time to go back home to where you belong.'

He heard her voice and looked at her now with extra special vision as his eyes were now stunning solid sapphire blue and he now can see for miles at night.

He saw his mate in the woods hiding behind the trees when she come out with a quizzical expression and looked at him differently.

First, she reacts towards him by giving a vicious growl at him as if he were not her mate anymore.

This upset Troy as he didn't want that.

"Relax dear one give her time."

"She will warm up to you and your new look and realize you are still you inwardly just not on the outside anymore, that's all."

Troy did not understand what Luna meant about him being different from before as he had not seen his reflection to notice that he now had become this mighty powerful white wolf.

It was nearly halfway through the night when Crystal decided to come and see her new version of her mate.

She crept up to him and started to sniff him to make sure that he still smelt the same but just didn't look it anymore.

She made whimpering noises because of confusion but she wanted to be with Troy still so she started to brush her face to his face and rubbed her body on him and wag her tail showing a submissive state.

Troy responded to her actions and then they were playing together again.

Luna seemed pleased to see he was well safe and with his mate again.

The wolf said "what have you done to me to make my mate act like that towards me?"

The moon Goddess said "dear one I have helped you recover from death with my powerful caring healing powers, I process."

"I can only use my white and silver in my magic because my powers have been powered by the moon itself and that is where I have come from tonight"

"Oh", replied Troy "thank you for saving my life."

"Thank you for saving Helena's too", replied Luna.

Both wolves were feeling strong enough to go back home so they both got up and ran as fast as they could together back into the woods to their pack.

Luna smiled and clapped her hands and she flew back to the moon in a silver ball of light.

"Farewell", she said, and the wolves howled to her passing them as she went.

Months later Troy started to realize that he could see better at night-time as much as he could in the day as he was more powerful than any other alpha around the lands.

So, he changed his name to Moon Cloud.

That gorgeous night the moon was full of all her glory.

He decided to howl to her while he was standing on the cliff top as close to it as possible looking at the beautiful scenery as he did.

Hoping that he also would see the princess swimming around the sea hopefully?

But no luck this time where he wondered if he would ever see her again.

He did not mind standing up there as his white coat shone brightly in the moonlight due been thicker now and warmer as he was now fully grown and the true alpha to his kind of his family before him.

He looked at the moon once more before leaving thanking Luna for saving his life when she appeared inside it.

While this was happening, the moon was shining fully onto this great wolf.

"Hello, dear friend".

"I see that you are looking for her again, where she and I are very grateful to you for getting her back home safe and sound risking your own life to do it."

"I would do it again as she is a very special Goddess."

"Moon cloud said I don't think anyone realizes that she can change the world as we know it today."

"No, I think you are right but for now you, Seequest and I are aware of this and it must be our secret for a little longer to protect her from harm."

"Agreed my great one" and he looked up at Luna on the moon and howled deeply with sincerity from his heart that he was showing his love and respect for her and Helena.

"I must go now back to my pack as Crystal has had puppies."

"Congratulations my dear, yes go home to them at once."

The warrior wolf turned and ran down the cliff top to his home.

As he did the moon disappeared and the sun rose in the most beautiful shades of gold and orange.

As the sun did this it looked like it was raising out of the sea such an amazing sight, Moon Cloud thought.

Therefore, this is why all the wolves in our time howl to the full moon, as they are respecting the Legend of the Goddess Luna, when she comes and says hello to them.

Also, it's the time they see their ancestor the great white wolf warrior around as well who was named Moon Cloud for his greatness and wisdom that he has passed down to the present wolves of today.

Chapter Nine

Helena Reaches Vissen Again

Helena had dived into the darker part of the sea where it is a portal to her home.

She was getting closer to the main gates seeing all types of fish of all colors and sizes swimming beside her, below and above her.

What an interesting view, she thought.

How glad she was been back in the sea with all her water creature friends.

She knew now that she had to swim closer to the floor surface.

Helena saw many crabs walking sideways on the seabed below her and starfish sticking themselves to the rocks.

She laughed as she also saw a clever place hiding in the sand to catch its prey.

She replies "your clever fish" and swims on.

Helena then smiled as she saw an old friend of hers the great blue whale where she grabs hold of his large dorsal fin as he passes by her and catches a ride because he will get her home quicker.

As tired Helena had to get used to using her tail again.

The whale was a large yet the fastest mammal of the sea and a guardian to Neptune himself as well.

He requested that they would be protectors and healers of the sea too.

Helena noticed that they were nearly there so she said "thank you and let's go of the whale's fin."

There in front of her were the golden gates once again to Neptune's kingdom.

She flapped her tail up and down as quickly, as she could.

She reaches the gates where she calls out to one of the mer-guards, who then approached the gate for a closer look and there floating in front of him was Helena.

He recognized her and said "Princess what are you doing out here on your own now?"

She refused to answer and said "just let me in, please?"

"Yes, your Highness straight away."

Helena ordered the other mer-guard to open up the gates for her to enter.

She swam through the huge golden gates and asked "where is my father?"

The mer-guard replied "he is out on business on the other side of the ocean."

"Oh, no" she sighs.

"OK, where is my mother?"

"She is up at the Temple of Knowledge."

"Good, then I shall go and see her first she said to them."

Helena swam to the palace where it begins to turn right towards the temple.

She reached this stunning gold and silver crystal temple and whacked on the door hard with her tail full blast.

"Mother, mother", she cries out acting all anxious through her movements.

The queen recognized that voice and said, "It couldn't be as she was told to stay in her room by the order of the sea god himself.

Hoping that her daughter would listen to her king?

Or would she be like her disobeying an order because there was something more important to deal with?

Which was still concerning to the queen and so she begin to question herself "what could be so important now?" as the high priestess did not retrieve this information from the crystal skulls yet.

Because she was still charging them up with the sun and moon's powers

She said a Greek verse and the enormous doors started to open out and there in a stance was her daughter out of breath.

She said, "Helena, my darling it's you" and swam right to her and hugged her tightly thinking that she should be at home resting because of what had happened to her recently.

"Mother, that's enough."

"I must see Father now as Seequest is trapped and it is our fault!"

"Calm down my child and catch your breath."

Helena explains what she did and her mother is not impressed and yet proud of her at the same time as that is also what she would have done it herself when she was younger.

The queen smiles at her dearly knowing that Helena is becoming the age of greatness and she is so happy yet she keeps it to herself for now.

Because there are more important things to talk about and sort out first!

Queen Sera spoke and said "first you must go back to the palace to see the rest of our family so they know you are all right".

"As you have been in her quarters and resting quite well now"

Then go back to your quarters and get cleaned up as you smell like animals and whales".

"I will see if your father is back from his business and then I shall come and get you, so you can tell him your-self what has happened."

She said "yes mother".

"Please go now as Seequest is running out of time".

"I shall go with you, though".

"No, my child not this time you won't".

"I do not want to lose you again knowing that your father will be cross that you risked going back on your own accord and luckily she did not get caught or killed this time round either".

She nodded and turned around with her head looking down feeling disappointed.

she fluttered her tail hard and whooshed back out of the door back to the palace and to her room to tidy herself up before hopefully going later to see her father when he is back home.

Forgetting that her mother sees what goes on no matter if it is done behind her back as after all she is the high priestess.

And yet this time Helena was shocked that she did not know and was glad that she went and spoke to her straight away instead of waiting.

Back at the temple, Sera was wondering if she should just help or go and see her husband first.

By telling him the full truth that Helena disobeyed them or should she just mention that she had seen this already in the crystal bowl, knowing that she thought Helena had done wrong but she understood why she did it and forgave her quickly knowing she went by her true instincts and kind heart!

Sera decided to go and see Neptune and swim faster than her daughter could as she has a large swallowtail.

The high priestess swam elegantly in her special gown to the throne room hoping that the king of the sea will be there to talk to.

While the princess was waiting patiently for her mother to come and collect her from her quarters she thinks that she could hear Seequest's voice in her mind.

Saying "dear Helena I hope you're home safe and well, that you have spoken to your father about rescuing me as you need to hurry as Hades is getting ready to get rid of me for good."

She replies telepathy "don't worry dear friend I am waiting to speak to father, I know that he will help me and that he will be on his way to you soon!"

Back in Hades' liar Seequest heard Helena's reply and felt relieved that they had not forgotten about him.

Chapter Ten

Seequest and Knightmare

Seequest felt that the only way he may survive and escape was to play along with Hades' plan for a little longer.

Knowing has been left in an invisible cage which also has been draining all his powers while he has been asleep at night.

He decided he liked Hades' demon horse Knightmare and offered to be her mate forever.

When Hades comes back the Unicorn King mentioned this offer to Hades and he agreed with delight.'

"Splendid as she always wanted a stallion and I have all your magic anyway"

"So, you will not be able to escape me."

"You are trapped here" he started to laugh horribly.

Poor Seequest was at least happy to know that Helena got away and was safe at home again as that was his promise to Neptune many months before.

Because Seequest told Hades he would stay with Knightmare now!

As now he lets him out of the force field for a while and when he did he warned the Unicorn stallion any funny business of trying to escape he will go back in it again!

Seequest agreed as he was beginning to like the mare as she seemed to be quite nice company for a change than him being alone all the time.

He started to feel something for her and yet he could not explain it himself yet either.

But he knew it was completely different from what he has felt for any other mares in his herd before.

A week later the mare was snuggled up with the unicorn when he felt two heavy kicks from her stomach and she also neighed in pain.

She got up and walked over to the soft straw and blanket that Hades put down for her to lie on for comfort.

Seequest said "is it coming soon?"

She neighed back with discomfort in her sad red eyes.

He started to feel sorry for her and knew that once she was one of his progenies.

He gets up and comforts her as they both wait for the foal to arrive.

The days carried on the same as Knightmare was still there lying in pain while the stallion started to feel her pain and felt bad for her so he said, "Let me help you."

She looked at him as if for the first time she felt some kind of love and comfort and seemed to like it.

She nodded her head gracefully and said "ok."

Seequest then put his horn on her side and it began to glow green.

He told her to close her eyes as the light will become too bright for her to bear.

She lay there trusting him.

As he did this she seemed to think about her foal and of giving birth soon.

Once she become calmer he placed a little touch of magic to her mind which healed the pain but not the discomfort due to the mare will have to feel something so in time she will know when to push.

He was touching her forehead gently when he saw that there were two foals (twins) and kept it a secret till they are born.

Knightmare woke back up feeling better and said 'thank you with a soft glare in her ruby red eyes.

"You're most welcome" when he thought the mare isn't bad-natured it was just because of her master that makes her act this way.

As time went on Seequest became closer to the mare as a friend and eventually, he enjoyed her company as having someone other than himself to talk to.

How he missed his kind; his mother; dear Helena and his sea life too.

Seequest thought that he had another twenty years to go.

But he knew that he won't be seeing her for a long while as autumn was approaching.

One autumn evening in September the mare could not keep still in her bed.

Seequest asked "what is wrong?"

"The baby!" she cried and stood up and moved around a little because of the discomfort as the foal was growing bigger now.

But she was too weak and fell back to the floor again instantly.

The mare tried to stand up again this time feeling very stiff in her legs but managed to stand eventually.

Again, the unicorn stallion touched his horn on her legs and eased the pain.

Then the mare fell and collapsed safely to the floor with a thump.

"Knightmare" Seequest said many times but she did not answer him.

He seemed to be worried even though he should have been worried about himself, as Hades has nearly drained him of all his magic.

But he went and rested beside the mare to protect her while she slept on.

The twenty-seventh of September came and it was quite a warm day.

The comfort of his love had woken her up when he explained to her what had happened and mentioned that she needed some fresh air away from this dark and dry cave.

Hades had turned up and saw the two of them together.

"Arr, my girl got a mate."

How cute in a cheeky kind of way knowing that Seequest was trapped, where he had to keep to his word to prevent the earth and everything on it from being destroyed.

Seequest did care for this mare strangely and was prepared to stay with her forever if he actually could somehow.

But Hades was not aware of this.

Even though Seequest's powers were draining he still seem to care for Knightmare and he showed his love for her which would help him to reboot his magic due to love been a positive energy.

And can then strengthen us all.

The mare noticed that she was helping him regain his powers back.

But because he showed kindness to her she did not tell her master.

Seequest asked Hades if he could take Knightmare out for some fresh air and see the sun once more.

He said that the sun and fresh air will help her and the foal grow even stronger.

"If you care for her in any way you will do this for her."

Hades agreed and says "as long as you don't try to escape me?"

The old unicorn said, "I won't."

"Fine, old king, take her to see the forest and sunshine."

The unicorn stallion slowly walked over to the mare and said, "Get up and follow me."

So she did just that with a struggle and yet slowly started to follow Seequest through the dark cave until they could see some actual bright light.

Knightmare closed her eyes as she was not used to the bright light as it was her first time out because of being underground.

She closed her eyes when he told her to bite his tail and said "I will lead you out to the beautiful safe place of mine."

"Do you trust me?"

She said "yes, not knowing that she started to have a soft spot and feelings that she has never had before for him too."

They reached the forest Seequest quickly put a spell on her regarding her eyes as they were not used to bright light anymore.

So he continued the second part of the spell without her knowing any difference her eyes changed to the original color they were before when she was alive, which was a pretty light blue.

Velvet was an unusual mare that's why the stallion of the herd wanted her at the time.

She then winked and then she bit his tail and he directed her through the entrance to the forest.

She trotted out, as she could feel was pure heat on her body that she hadn't felt for a long time.

Suddenly, the pregnant mare felt some soft green grass touch the hooves that made her remember her previous life.

Knightmare was starting to feel alive and well and yet not alone anymore due to Seequests magic inside her that has given these sad feelings also back to her.

Seequest told her to relax and lie down and look at the view to take her mind off it.

She did with her bat wings tucked close to her body, when she felt she was lucky and started to feel some powerful warmth come over in her heart.

She opened her eyes to see this handsome unicorn stallion proudly looking at her while approaching the great silver birch tree where he and his mother used to sit.

While he was standing there, he told her to be quiet and looked behind him.

He gradually moved out of the way as they both saw the pretty blue lake with the elegant male pure white swan and a female black swan swimming together as a life time pair.

He thought it could be a good omen about them.

Knightmare looked up above her as she heard the birds of many colors tweeting and flying around as well.

She first felt happy and then became sad as she again remembered how she died alone as different from her kind.

He bent down to her and nuzzled her gently and said, "It is ok you're safe."

"That was your past life and this is now your present life, as I am here now with you now."

Seequest could see that there was a tear in her eye and asked why.

Crying in a neighing type of way she explained how she was different and sensitive as no one wanted to be with her in the past so eventually, she died sadly alone.

He then explained that being a king he too was sad at times, where he was alone most of his life until he had the opportunity from Neptune to change it by becoming a full-time water horse or a hippocampus forever.

"Don't worry my love, you will never be alone again as we have each other in the present and that's what counts."

After lying down with her being careful because of her rough bat wings he put his head over her neck feeling the bones on her wings.

She seemed to smile and enjoy being outside and seeing the beauty in the place once again.

He boldly got up and said "wait here while I go and get some fresh food and water for you."

The pregnant mare agreed to stay as she was feeling happy to have her dreams come true at last.

He nuzzled her once more and galloped off into the deeper part of the forest where he saw the squirrels and the badgers and the birds that came and greeted him.

He stopped and asked them permission if could take back to his friend their juicy fresh berries and flowers.

They agreed while he was getting some berries and flowers.

The animals kindly made him a basket of leaves to secure the food into and he said thank you and headed back as quickly as he could go.

He was pleased that the forest animals had not forgotten about him has explained why he left them in the past.

He says his goodbyes as he galloped back to Knightmare, he thought that it was so nice to see his friends and their families again and knew that this would never happen anymore as for the moment he was trapped by Hades.

Plus, his real home is in the sea with the dolphins and Neptune now for a long time.

But he felt sad as he wondered how Knightmare would feel knowing that he could not stay with her or his children.

But he then thought of a way he could make that possible.

He thought when he eventually gets home maybe he could speak to Zeus and ask him if he could help him.

But he shook his head and neighed and galloped onto the great birch tree where he left his love for a short while and hoped that she was ok with being left so long alone back in a world that she does not know about anymore.

He had the plan to save her and maybe take them with him when the foals are older.

Seequest was galloping through the forest having flashbacks of the time with his mother and friends here when all of a sudden, he stopped so quickly.

He had to dig his two back hooves into the ground for stability to stop instantly as there was a large white wolf in front of his pathway.

Straightaway he went into protection mode and started scuffing the ground with his left front leg showing that he was ready for a fight if needed.

As he bent his head showing that he was ready to charge his horn into the wolf as he felt threatened because the wolf was standing in his path.

"Wait, are you Seequest?"

The unicorn stallion's ears perked up to alert position as he heard his name being called.

He pulled his head back up to look at the wolf face-to-face.

He answered him "yes I am Seequest."

"Who are you and how do you know my name?"

The wolf replied, "thank goodness I found you". I am now Moon Cloud, the alpha of the peacemaker clan.

I was Troy before you knew my great-grandfather Max many years ago and meet Storm my brother earlier.

Plus, I am a friend of Princess Helena.'

Seequest started to panic thinking if this was one of Hades' tricks so he quizzed the wolf to see if he knew the truth about where she is now.

'Right what have you done with her?' with a panicked voice.

"Slow down their old-timer".

"I said I was her friend."

"She is safe as I took her back to the beach and risked my life to doing it."

"That is why I am like this now as a gift from Luna for saving Helena's life."

Seequest was still not sure so he asked the wolf a question that is a secret that he Neptune, Queen Sera and the Goddess Luna knew.

"Tell me, is the moon Goddess related to the mermaid princess?"

"Yes, she is" Moon cloud says.

"Luna told me herself that she is her grandmother from Queen Sera being her actual daughter."

The unicorn was so relieved to know that the wolf was telling the truth and he explained why he was being so cautious previously with him.

The alpha wolf understood and they eventually calmed down and started to walk together.

"As I mentioned before I am related to Max."

The white wolf told Seequest many great stories that his family had both experienced in the past and how the Unicorn King had helped save them from saber-toothed tigers and the pack as well "Thank you he says."

Seequest said "yes that's history now."

He mentioned "I must get back as I have Hades' pregnant mare waiting for me near the lake and she will be worried if I don't get back there soon."

The body language of the white wolf changed within seconds with his shackles showing on his back growling showing now his teeth to him.

"How can you be with her after she killed your kind and mine?"

"Look, she had no choice."

"She was under Hades' orders and she was put under the god of death's nasty spells, which made her do it."

Seequest then mentioned that she was once a descendant of his bloodline.

"So please no harm will come to her."

The wolf was not happy.

He agreed for now seeing that Seequest was quite sensitive when talking about her.

"OK, I have an idea."

"I am going to go back to Knightmare and take her back to Hades' cave."

"I will need your help to possibly escape from him."

"Can you howl loudly and call our friend Luna the moon queen as there will be a full moon a month from now?

Which gives me time for the foals to be born and become strong enough to run away from there?"

Moon Cloud could see that Seequest was serious about what he said regarding trying to escape with Knightmare and his children.

"Will you help me?"

"Yes, great one, of course."

"As I said earlier I am going back to Hades' cave in the deeper part of the forest."

"As I go back I will mark the trees carefully brushing my hooves against them as my powers are gradually coming back from time to time."

"I will be able to speak to you through your mind for caution in case any of Hades' creatures are spying on me when I am underground."

"Then can you let Luna know when we are ready?"

"Now, I must go otherwise the mare will get suspicious about why I am away from her for so long as she is just starting to trust me."

"Thank you by the way for getting the princess back home and trusting me."

"I will see you around."

The wolf agreed and bowed to the unicorn.

Seequest bowed his head back too and then galloped away back to the lake as fast as he could, thinking about his plan to escape in the future with his new family.

Moon Cloud was puzzled about why Seequest was with Knightmare and how he is the father to her foal.

But straightaway he realized that in the talk Seequest gave him the answer to his question without actually saying it in case Hades was spying on him somehow.

The white wolf ran back home and remembered that he must call Luna, especially in a month's time explaining that Seequest had a plan to escape.

Back at the lake Knightmare was hoping that her mate will be back soon as she was hungry and started to feel that Seequest was leaving her there as his way to escape her and Hades.

But thankfully she heard a sound of thunder coming through the woods and in front of her stood Seequest carrying in his mouth leaves full of juicy red berries and sweet flowers especially for her to eat.

She could not look too much as her eyes were not used to the sunshine yet so Seequest said, 'Close your eyes for a minute and with that, he said 'keep still and I will help you see better".

His horn glow a green color on the tree when he began to shade her more.

Knightmare couldn't believe that she could look at him clearer and sharper as the Unicorn King had made it for her eyes to see even clearer and sharper than before so she could see everything properly.

"Oh, wow", she said.

Seequest then mentioned to Knightmare that in her life before as Velvet she took him up here to this forest to show him how the herd's doing and how it was been protected from Hades' creatures.

As then she was the Leader at this time.

"Do you remember?"

The mare started to have flashbacks of her past until she became upset as she remembered that she was abandoned by her herd and that no one wanted to mate with her again as her mate died of an unknown death and she was blamed for it.

So, she left the herd and lived on her own until she died of a broken heart and was abandoned by her own even though while she was thinking about it she kept saying "It wasn't my fault.

Please don't leave here."

She freaked out and jumped up bucking around and flapping her wings as she got angry and upset.

Seequest could see that these memories were cruel and hard to bear, so he quickly tapped his horn to the berries and put a healing spell on them and told Knightmare to calm down has its was past which is now gone and this is her future.

She calmed down listening to his voice and she bent down to eat the berries.

As she forgot about her past and thought that they were delicious and wondered if she may have this opportunity to do this again with him someday after her foal was born.

When she ate the berries, it took her upsetting memories away as if they never existed.

At least Seequest could make her life a little easier even though she was now living with Hades underground.

The Unicorn King said "the evening is drawing near and we better get back to the cave soon before Hades gets upset and never lets us do this again."

They both ate the sweet flowers and drank from the lake and had a quick cuddle together and then decided it was time to go back.

As they did Knightmare started to feel the kicks of the foal in her stomach and said "It's ready."

"It's coming soon."

Seequest agreed and licked her face and said "Ok at nightfall we shall go back home for now rest while you can and I will explain to Hades when we get back there."

The mare nodded her head and pushed herself closer to his body.

"Thank you for everything and for giving me this opportunity to live once more the way I always dreamed I would, even though it is temporary."

"I could never repay you for your kindness."

He replied "there is no need my love as you're carrying my baby in you and I wouldn't want it any other way."

They nuzzled their faces as if they kissed and Knightmare's heart lit up inside and she believed that he would never leave her again.

The pregnant mare knew she would never live out here again because Hades' home is in the dark and dead and was very hot to bear sometimes she thought.

Seequest put his large thick elegant neck on her shoulders and looked out into the beautiful forest and how he missed it,

Where he knew it was his past life as he lives in the sea as a hippocampus with Neptune and Helena for at least the last fifty-five years.

They were there still chatting away for hours when it started to get dark.

They got up and started to walk back into the cave to Hades' lair.

As they did Seequest quickly changed her eyes back to red again to adjust to the darkness once more.

Chapter Eleven

The Secret is out that Tidal Wave & Sea Spray's babies are born

Back in the sea, Queen Sera had sent home Helena earlier and quickly saw the sea king and told him what she knew about Seequest's fate.

As she did not tell him before and now needed to as it was happening the way she saw in her crystal in the past.

Later, Queen Sera was riding Sea Spray back to the stables where she went and checked on Tidal Wave as he was pregnant with his and Sea Spray's babies.

When she arrived, there were two tiny seahorses that had just been born.

But as the day went by they were actually seven born altogether that looked like the seahorses of today but much bigger.

Sera was pleased with them all when she noticed that one was completely different and unique from the rest regarding its body shape and fins and yet was pretty with her mother's shaped head.

Months had gone by as they grew very quickly to look like their parents.

Hippocampus is part horse, part fish.

Apart from this one, they all were colorful and different from the next.

One was blue and another pink, pure white, and green and also a beautiful jet black one too.

But the main two that Queen Sera had her eyes on were the one with four flippers and the black one that had the soft white star like Moonbeam had.

She felt that this large boy was special somehow.

As his sister was much bigger than them all put together and had four flippers instead of horse legs and a massive fish tail with a gorgeous long neck possibly like a water dragon?

She thought to herself that these two will be her gift to her husband, the god of the sea.

Queen Sera was worried about Seequest and how he was doing.

But was relieved to know her daughter was home safe and sound again, thanks to him giving himself up to Hades.

She remembered what her mother told her about her magic and how to use it once more without Neptune ever knowing about it.

One night, she rode through the sea on her sea mare, galloping fast and swishing her tail as well for more speed through the port hole up in the ocean and towards the beach where Helena had been recently.

The seahorse galloped so fast that she could not even see that her tail had now changed to legs and she was jumping and galloping very fast through the rough waves as quickly as she could as the queen wanted to get to the cliff top where Seequest and Celestial said their goodbyes as mother and son for the last time previously.

There Sea Spray now is a beautiful aqua blue water horse with a see-through solid body that you had ever seen so she could walk on land.

"Come on, girl, we do not have a lot of time left."

So, she galloped faster than she did before.

Even the poor hippocampus mare was tired, that she ran until she could not run anymore up the hill.

The queen said that she could rest later, so they continued up the hill like lightning until they reached the top where the moon was at its brightest.

Queen Sera jumped off and patted her and said, "Good girl thank you now you can go and rest somewhere until I call you for our return.'

Sea Spray bowed and then trotted down the hill carefully so that she did not slip or fall.

She got to the bottom and walked near the rocks to eat the seaweed and rest for a while.

Queen Sera was tidying up her beautiful blue and silver dress when she took off her cloak and then her stunning silver and aquamarine and diamond crown and shook her hand.

As she did, a gorgeous moonstone and silver staff appeared before her.

"My moon staff of magic, I ask for your assistance."

"Please send a message to Celestial; Legend; Pegasus and Zeus that we need their help most urgently to save our friend Seequest from danger to save his life and others."

He had his magic taken away from him by Hades himself to use it to create his own horses of darkness and to rule Earth!'

She slammed her staff down and called "I call on the old magic of the unicorns and Luna, the moon Goddess Help me now."

Her staff started to shine brightly and she pointed it at Legend's star which then went flashed as she looked away.

The light was too bright even for her eyes.

The queen's power was generated through her body and her eyes lit up like Moonstones.

She then could see far into the distance of the stars and universe from where she was standing.

She could also see Celestial and Legend in the sixth dimension protecting the world called the heaven where the horses and animals go when they die on earth.

She then can see Legend galloping across the universe shining brighter than normal as his true image appeared he was told by her voice that he must go and see the high priestess of the moon and find out what happened.

He appeared as a true black Pegasus that he was with sapphire blue running through his coat and stardust sparkling on it as well.

He opened his wings and then flapped magnificently toward the earth.

Has Legend been flying downwards toward the planet as if he was in another dimension?

It did not take him too long to reach her as Sera had opened a portal for him to come through quicker at this time.

Eventually, he reached the third dimension and landed on his star once again.

Now she can see his image in the sky clearly.

This is the closest he can get to where she was because he has no reason to go back there anymore 'my dear queen of the great seas and old friend why do you call me here today?'

She answered "because it is about your son Seequest."

"He is in great danger and so is earth as we know it."

"Ok where is my son?" he said.

She replied back "he is locked up in Hades' underground lair."

"Then I must contact Zeus and let him know as I cannot come down there without his constant."

"Yes, I am aware of this."

That's why I have told you first so you can give him a message that his brother is up to his old tricks again.

"Of course, thank you, Sera.

I am sure that I will see you soon."

"Thank you old friend, it is lovely to see you in the flesh again too."

Legend liked what Sera said to him and in his reply, he stood up on his hind legs and neighed loudly flapping his wings beautifully as he went, which also caused a slight breeze to blow into her face below.

In a flash, he disappeared and the star dimmed.

Legend jumped off the star and started flying to the ninth dimension where Zeus and Pegasus themselves live.

Queen Sera called her mother next, and there you could see a faint light flying upwards in the night sky once again.

The queen is called Luna.

As she did, her face appeared on the moon this time.

"Yes, my dear child, I was listening, and I know you have called me.

The only way I can help you is with this last special gift.

But use it wisely.

This crystal can change things completely from what you already have or want.

I call it the New Beginnings Crystal."

Queen Sera put out her hand, and then appeared this amazing clear Lemurian crystal shaped like a unicorn horn.

"Thank you Mother, I will."

The moon was starting to fade as the morning is on its way.

The queen clapped her hands once again and her staff vanished into thin air.

She stood there just looking at the beautiful view of the sea from afar and called Sea- Spray in a flash she appeared near her.

She climbed onto this pretty now white seahorse with a light blue mane and tail with blue hooves has been on land for quite a while and so changes it colour to survive the sun and heat longer because where the sea mare had stayed a long while on land her complete form changed similar to an original horse.

As she gets on her she can see that the mare was now fully energized again as her eyes were glowing bright blue like the sea itself.

Where has she got her name from?

She's glowing at the moment powerfully.

Sera decided to go back into the sea while waiting as the Hippocampus cannot stay out of the water for too much longer, the water horse neighed loudly.

"Come on let's go home she reached out for the silver bridle and held on tightly."

The seahorse trotted to the end of the green where trees started to take them back into the woods.

She then turned around and quickly galloped towards the cliff top and jumped perfectly facing her whole body downwards towards the sea again.

The mare was facing her head into a straight diving position with her front legs thrown out in front of her.

As she did the queen tucked her own head inwards towards her neck and took a deep breath as the mare was diving straight back into the sea head first.

The queen was still holding on tightly to the reins so that she would not fall off as they both changed back into their natural forms again.

When they touched the sea water they made a massive splash into it which creates a big wave in the sea as well.

They had both landed safely and caught their breaths as Sera's actual gills appeared on the side of her head.

Because she was not a true mer-person from the begnining!

Sea Spray starts to swim as quickly as she could back home to Vissen to see their families again.

Once they had gone back through the portal in the dark blue part of the sea they reached both gates which the guards opened and quickly swam calmly back to the stables.

She put Sea Spray back in her stall and said, "thank you girl for your service today you have done well".

"Now rest with your family," as she patted her neck and kissed her muzzle before she made sure that everyone was fed and watered and that the babies were all right before she headed back home.

She called her brace of dolphins Coral and Reef through a conch shell as they started to swim towards her.

When they were close enough to her she hooked them up to her chariot and she then headed back to the palace for the night.

As she was arriving back she was thinking how much she hates that no one else knows that she is the princess of the moon and wondered if maybe in the future she could tell her people where she actually comes from?

Because her people do wonder sometimes where she gets her powers from as hers are completely different from theirs.

No one else has anything like it in her kingdom they stop sometimes and make inquiries to Neptune as they say that is why she's special.

Everyone just sees her as the Queen of the sea or the High priestess as her main duties are to make sure that all the children are brought up properly and trained for battle.

Plus, she and the princess mermaids would look after the dolphins and now seahorses.

While Neptune makes their sons look after the sea; land; and the larger sea creatures like the sharks and whales, as they protect them from pollution and death.

There were also mer-knights who were mer-men but bigger and broader kind.

Living in the ocean was magical, she thought.

She would see all the kinds of fish swimming around all with different colors who protected the sea from germs as they ate it all and discarded it where these germs could not harm anyone or anything anymore.

The ocean was magical too as it has different shades of blues and greens every day as it was the color through the actual reflection of the sky above her.

Yet deeper under the sea there were strong colors of deep purples and reds of seaweed and coral and sea Anemones they too had their own purpose.

Finally, the queen reached home and took off the harnesses to her dolphins and put them in a peaceful place for the night, and fed them their favorite fish pink salmon.

She fed them and thanked them by kissing their bottle noses one at a time which the dolphins loved and they squeaked and swam away doing acrobats in the water which also made the queen smile.

"Good night my darlings I shall see you tomorrow."

She turned around and opened a golden round door and arrived in her daughter's room.

She approached Helena carefully as she was still looking quite sad and said "what is wrong my child?"

"You know what is the wrong mother" Helena feeling so upset with them and herself.

"We have left Seequest my best friend and protector in the hands of Hades" speaking with a broken heart.

She says "how could I have been so eager to want to go on land so badly and not obey the rules and go off with that sweet fox, knowing that what Seequest said to me about being careful with animals, who I did not know about at all?"

She continues talking and then says also "mother you were right!"

"I should have not gone".

"At least Seequest would be with us now safe happy and swimming around with his friends outside near us instead of me here sobbing my heart out."

Her mother hugged her and said "there there, my child".

"He will be fine Seequest isn't just a hippocampus".

"He is a powerful unicorn as he was once the king of that land before coming here to live in the sea with us".

"Don't fret he will be ok because he has his horn back which your father gave him before you came back to us".

The Secret is out that Tidal Wave & Sea Spray's babies are born

"You know that he gave himself up to Hades recently" his horn will protect him from any harm coming to him' her mother replied.

"How?" the princess replied.

"Hades has now captured him and is draining him of his magic as he is trapped underground and his magic is getting weaker as he impregnated Hades' mare."

"Knightmare is having a foal which will be even more powerful than he put together as it will have Hades' powers as well as Zeus."

"That's what I am afraid of, as he may then discard Seequest and have his foal instead which he can train and control!"

"My dear Helena, listen"

"What you do not know is that Zeus is the superior brother and he is stronger and more powerful than Hades so Seequest's powers will be too."

"Do you really think so mother?"

Queen Sera wiped her daughter's tears and said 'I know so' thinking to herself I hope?

Because Hades has produced magic that no one has ever seen until now so she is worried for her friend and her people.

After their little talk Princess Helena felt a lot more reassured that her mother would not lie to her and they headed to the library.

Queen Sera was not just a queen she was psychic.

She could see what has happened so far to Seequest and what will happen if she does not save him soon.

So, she knows that when Neptune is back from this business they will have to talk seriously and what they will do next?

For now, she enjoyed some time with her daughter and taught her about her magic as Helena was now coming of age that she was changing into mer- woman, and her mother felt that one day she too will be more powerful than herself.

They looked up in their archives of magic and crystal spells of the crystal skulls.

They spent quite a while there when Sera said, "It's time for you to go to bed, my darling."

Then Helena yawned and said "ok, then."

Helena swam to her room slowly as she was feeling tired and overwhelmed from what had happened recently.

The queen then rushed back to the king's palace thinking as she went at least practicing the magic with Helena and reading up about the knowledge of the crystal skulls would have helped her take her mind off her guilty conscience and this will helped her to use magic as well in time.

One day she will use it to protect their land if needed.

The Secret is out that Tidal Wave & Sea Spray's babies are born

But most of all Helena seemed to have more peace of mind so she can rest well as tomorrow will be a day that she will never forget ever again.

Chapter Twelve

Seequest's Love

Seequest walked back into the dark cave and shook his head and his horn lit up the cave.

"Do not tell Hades" and he winked at Knightmare.

She was actually starting to feel that warm feeling in her heart and earlier that evening, Seequest told her that the fuzzy warmth of security and happiness is called Love.

The pregnant mare felt this and she knows it was because the unicorn stallion who is the true heir of the earth itself was her mate and father to her foal.

Knightmare could not believe that she was chosen to actually have his children the normal way and seemed scared.

Knightmare was falling in love with Seequest and he was starting to feel the same way about her and he had not told her this yet.

He thought she was not the prettiest of mares you had ever seen but she was beautiful in her own way with her feminine Friesian build her amazing large bat wings with claws sitting on them and red traits running through her feathered legs mane, and tail.

Plus of course, her ruby red eyes that he could stare at her for hours as she could put him or anyone into a trance with them.

Seequest thought that he had fallen in love with her sweet and stubborn personality which he seemed to like a lot as it reminded him of himself.

Of how he became a true leader as he had to do things sometimes even though he did like doing them sometimes too.

He thought that she was unique as he noticed even his daughter of Truth in the past did have this too.

He was thinking maybe these foals will be the best thing yet to happen for the earth when he eventually he dies and leaves it to them one day or will they be the worst thing and destroy all that his unicorn bloodlines have recreated again?

Poor Seequest's mind was ripped in two of the unknown.

He also wondered while trotting back into the cave the way he feels about her if there is any possibility that she could be changed back to good once more.

He could take her home with him to the sea with help from Neptune his great friend.

They were trotting back when he heard a massive neigh of a cry that shook the cave.

It was Knightmare, she had blacked out.

Seequest turned and galloped as quickly as he could go.

When he did not realize that she was so far behind him.

When he eventually he reached her, she was looking helpless and unconscious.

Now he was thinking the worst that he was going to lose her and his children.

"Knightmare, please wake up."

Seequest was bending down his head nudging her to wake up.

But she would not budge or respond to his voice.

Seequest started to feel that he could not do any-thing as he was weak to even help himself so he knew then that he had to find Hades and get him to help them home.

Even though he hated the idea he had no choice at this moment but to save her and the foals.

Before he left her he bent his head down again and licked her face and said "don't worry my love I will get help."

Then Seequest galloped off to find Hades.

He ran, as fast as his legs would go, and arrived in the lair calling for Hades to come quickly.

As he called the whole cave was reacting as if there was a volcano blowing.

The underworld god felt and heard Seequest's voice and wondered what had happened.

Hades appeared like a cloud of smoke and said "what is wrong?"

"Where is my mare? What have you done with her?"

"I knew I shouldn't have let you take her outside."

At this time Seequest was trying to tell him that Knightmare had collapsed half back in the cave entrance and that she needed help.

The unicorn stallion for a second could see that Hades was concerned for this mare and that he had caring feelings for her after all.

It looked like if anything happened to her it would break his heart at this time.

He remembered that Neptune told him in the past that there was a battle between Zeus and Hades to rule Olympus and that Zeus won.

For his challenge in the first place, he was chosen to rule the second-best thing which was the underworld.

As Zeus created all things Hades will deal with the bad souls and death a complete balance of life on earth.

When there is birth there must be death otherwise the earth would be overpopulated by all creatures and would be destroyed in the future if this did not happen.

Seequest thought he was wrong about him and they went back to the cave to see Knightmare.

She now looked even more drained than before.

The demon mare woke up and she was neighing in great pain.

Seequest was thinking in his mind that Hades should have never made him use his magic and should never use it on his own horse.

He believed this was against the rules of the gods.

But it was well too late as the job is done and he forgot about that feeling completely.

Seequest said "let's get her back home and we can discuss what I shouldn't do when she is ok again."

Hades said "agreed" and drew a circle all around them.

In a flash of smoke, they were in with a click of fingers they both appeared in the stables in their stall.

There was Knightmare still looking helpless.

Seequest requested Hades to give him back his full magic so he could help her properly and save her.

Hades loved his horse so much that he actually agreed.

Hades put his hands on Seequest's forehead where blue sparks started to fly and his horn had turned bright gold as he now has his full power back and then could have escaped.

But he knew it was the wrong thing to do as the foals were too young and may die due to the change as will be too much for them at a young age of being inside her at the moment.

He agreed to himself that he will help her.

The Unicorn King then knelt and put his horn, touching the mare's stomach once more.

It lit up in green for healing this time.

Minutes later she awoke looking stronger and got up as if nothing ever happened to her.

Then Hades took his full magic straight back from Seequest.

Knightmare asked what had happened to her and Seequest explained that the foals were getting powerful and stronger and that they were taking her energy away from her at times to help them grow strong as well.

All for the love of this mare and his children he knew now that he was trapped forever and a day as even their magic foals did not grow that quickly.

He just hoped that they will remember and never forget about him in the future when he plans to escape hopefully with them all.

But maybe without them too he thought also might have to happen if Hades catches them.

He thought about this a lot and it broke his heart as he remembered that he is the Unicorn King first and that his powers were more important than his actual feelings and his life itself.

Chapter Thirteen

Helena's Plan to Help Seequest

Back in Vissen, Helena was starting too really panic and worry about her dear sweet friend Seequest and how they were going to free him from Hades' grip.

Later that day she met up with her friends from the sea and told them what had happened they asked her where he was because he was always by her side or she was riding him around at times.

One of her friends slipped up and also spoke about what had happened and that she had told her father about it.

He told her that Neptune has the plan to get him home.

The mermaid princess was pleased to hear this.

But her friend did not tell her everything because her father made her promise not to worry the princess anymore, as really what she held back was the actual plan that could get everyone killed in the process.

Helena was excited and yet upset as she was meant to speak to her father herself about it as she now knows that her mother did it without her now.

She was angry with her so she said "guys I must go back and help the queen at the stables now have a nice day,"

When she swam off towards the back of the palace see her mother.

As she went the mer-people were waving and bowing to her as she swam past them and she smiled and waved back as she went being polite.

She reached the stables where she caught up with her mother who was attending to the baby sea horses that had grown big and magnificent as they looked like their father Tidal Wave who is also related to Seequest too.

The high priestess was delighted to see that her amazing idea had worked beautifully knowing that the sea horses or hippocampus were created by magic in the first place by Moonbeam's horn.

Even if Neptune told Sera not to try and breed them in case there were problems or deformities involved.

The queen used her own magic to prevent this from happening and went ahead with it anyway trusting that her powers would never fail her as she believed in them highly.

Maybe that's the reason why there is one that is completely different from the others but still has a sweet temperament all the same.

Because after all there is great magic in being used that was given by Pegasus himself and remember he is the God of all winged horses and others of his kind in the future too as well.

The queen was feeding the sea colts and sea fillies when Helena came up to see them and approached her mother with a smile and says, "Hello, Mother", thinking that her mother will explain why she went and saw her father on her own.

The queen knew straight away that Helena was angry through the expression on her face.

The queen said, "Helena, look you are only sixteen now and still a young mermaid princess."

"These sorts of things should not concern you yet my darling I am sorry but I thought it was in your best interest".

"There are some things that have to happen that I don't want you to worry about as you're too young yet!"

"Mother, you should have told me the truth I am a young mer-woman now."

"I know and I see that now".

"Can you forgive me?"

The queen looked deep into Helena's eyes and seemed to put her in a trance to forgive and forget the question and it worked!

"Yes, Mother."

"Good, now help me with these young ones."

The stables were a stunning part of the deep blue ocean which was peaceful and colorful.

The dolphins and the sharks swam together protecting and guarding the area, plus loads of different fish swimming around in schools, Helena thought it was a pretty sight to see.

She also forgot about the question she asked and went over to the young hippocampus where she looked at them very carefully.

There were two that caught her eye.

He was a beautiful black sea colt hippocampus with dark blue tones in his scales and when he swims the lighter blue shades show up on the front of his body as the sun shone into the ocean depths in the daytime which made him stand out from the rest of his siblings.

He also had a stunning Arabian-shaped head with a soft white star on his forehead a pointy type of mane with an elegant arched neck; tail where his fins looked wing-like and yet soft going down his back on both sides.

His eyes were like a sapphire blue.

Sera could see that Helena had a good eye for sea horses and was happy to see that she had a gift like her.

"Aww, you have chosen well my daughter".

"I do believe he will become a fine hippocampus stallion in the future and that he will be strong and fast like his parents".

"Oh, Mother, he is gorgeous."

"Yes, I know."

The Colt seemed to like Helena and her mother noticed that the black sea horse colt liked her too and she said, "I think he has chosen his owner."

"Sorry, what do you mean?"

"Well, I had picked him to give to your father as an anniversary gift and for his races which he loves doing once a year across the ocean with the other kingdoms."

"But I think that this colt has chosen you instead."

The princess was shocked by what her mother had just said and forgets about the worries for the moment about Seequest.

"Would you like him if I gave him to you for your sixteenth birthday present?"

"And if I do, you would have no more time worrying about anything as he will need your love; time, and patience always".

"You cannot forget him any day".

"He will be a true commitment as you will have to train him with me".

"So, we can keep a close eye on him because of his growth, as his cartilage (skeleton) is not an actual one like Seequest has because he is more fish than a sea horse this time."

"But he is still very strong!"

"I can see he will be a great hippocampus in time."

"Mother, really, yes, yes".

"You know I have always said when I was a little, that I would love to own a hippocampus in the future and if only dad had the power to create them himself."

"Yes, my dear sweet girl, I remember well."

Helena swam closer to the stable door and the colt heard what they had been saying.

And she too talked to the sea creatures and animals telepathically.

Because they understand her being the daughter of the moon goddess Luna, who has these powers too that is also why Helena has the gift as well.

The colt turned around and neighed at Helena as they both looked each other in the eyes deeply and felt a telepathic connection together.

He reared up in his stall and she smiled when he did a somersault too.

They both just stayed staring at each other as if she was a dream coming true.

Princess Helena knew then she had the gift of talking to the hippocampus and the sea creatures plus land animals as well now.

She thought from that moment then she was dearly blessed with this amazing gift.

She wondered if that means she could live in both worlds in her future.

Dreaming up an idea that she plans to possibly have and do when she's much older if her parents allow it?

For now, she was happy to own her own hippocampus at last.

Mother he spoke to me

"He did my child that is great".

"Well, that means you are telepathic and understand all kinds of living things like me and your father."

The queen explained.

"It means that you are one with them all."

"Oh, wow, that's incredible."

"I have it too as my mother Luna is the sister of Gaia (Mother Nature) herself".

Now my darling you have this amazing gift too.

"I am so happy for you."

"Oh, wow, thank you, Mother."

"Please don't thank me my lovely you have earned this gift by being caring; loving, and kind to all kinds of creatures great and small here and on land".

"This is their gift back to you my wonderful Helena", it is classed as abundance.

Helena was swimming around in circles through excitement and then slowly swims back to the stall where the colt was waiting for her to come back and see him again.

Eventually, she returned with a beautiful gift seeing if he would accept it from her as this also meant the hippocampus had chosen her for life.

She quietly approaches the young sea colt.

She first put her hand out to him and gave him a sea flower to eat and said, "It is ok, boy".

"I am Helena your new friend and owner"

"I promise to love and look after you forever."

The colt took the sea flower from her hand gently not to bite it.

She then gently stoked his forehead.

He felt her warmth and she thought how gentle-natured and silky soft he was.

He also seemed to like her touching his ears which made his eyes seem to glow brighter when he closed them occasionally as he felt her love for him and she felt his too.

Within that, they bonded and became one.

Her whole body felt like she was shining from the inside out.

She asked if that was normal and her mother said,"yes".

"That's called bonding my child that means he has accepted you as his lifetime rider and friend".

The queen was a little upset that she had to distract her daughter this way and yet knew well that it was the best thing for her.

Helena was always good with his parents and the other hippocampus.

Sera saw a true strong friendship within them as they bonded as if they became one instantly.

Her mother is thinking and talking in her own mind saying to herself

Maybe it was what Seequest had wanted from the beginning as she did not know that he will be with them for only a certain time in the sea either.

Her mother says "now feed him and as you do watch him carefully".

"Make sure you choose a great name for him as I have called him Onyx for now".

"I do have another special surprise that I know you would really like."

After he had eaten he came up to Helena again and nuzzled her from his stall.

She thought of a name that means "great friend forever and protector".

She said "mother I am going to call him Louis."

The queen smiled and replied back "yes, that's a great name."

Louis neighed too that he liked it which made the mermaid princess and her mother laugh and smile.

The princess did exactly what her mother told her to do and kissed Louis on his muzzle, which made him neigh loudly, making bubbles everywhere.

She told him to calm down and that she will be back to see him later but for now she had to go with her mum.

Louis understood and swam away from her and went into the stall to eat the rest of his seaweed which is on the floor below him.

The queen had already left.

"Wait for me mother I am coming."

Sera turned around and stopped to see her daughter swimming as fast as she could to her and saw her gills making bubbles as she rushed and puffed herself out.

"Now slow down and catch your breath."

They waited a few minutes for Helena to recover and then swim on together to another part of the stables a bit further in.

Sera was so excited to show someone else her beautiful unusual creation and wondered how her daughter would react to this special creature that she was preparing to show Helena.

See, she loved her other children but they did not have the extra special touch she had around these creatures.

Like their horses which feed on emotions.

They were nearly there to the bigger stables when Helena heard a sound slightly different from what she had heard before and was excited and scared of what and who was making it.

They approached the enormous stable doors and swam through and all Helena is thinking about is that she felt a soft cozy feeling in her heart as if this creature was very special indeed to the future.

Her mother called the beast through and there floating beside them is the biggest creature that Helena had ever come across with gentle eyes.

"Mother, what is?"

"Well my dear this too is a child from Tidal Wave and See Spray's spawn".

"How is this possible?"

"I guess magic and been designed by the gods."

"Oh, she is beautiful in her own way, I guess," Helena said.

The creature looked at Helena and licked her face as the wolf did on land.

"Hey," she said.

The queen started laughing.

"Ha, ha, she likes you, daughter".

"I haven't named her yet."

"Can we call her Kessy?"

"After all she is a mess in a pretty kind of way."

"After all, it does mean she is pure like a delicate butterfly that flies in our skies above us in the day and kind with a gentle nature as well?"

Her mother replied, "yes, that's a perfect name for her, Helena."

"Wow, Kessy you are a pretty creature indeed."

Kessy is five times the size of a blue whale with four elegant flippers as feet and a beautiful long tail.

Her neck is very long with a beautiful sea horse head.

She somehow looked like she had similar traits to the other sea horses but was still different too.

Queen Sera mentioned to her daughter that she must not let anyone else know about her, as she feels that she may have crossed the lines of a new creation which will be called the sea dragon!

As she had been told through the crystal skulls to be prepared as even the gods have never heard of or created one before so she is yet another miracle.

It is similar to the rein of the unicorns in the past.

"Yes, mother, I promise."

"Good, then you can come and bring Louis down here as they get along very well together."

"At least you can help me look after her when I must attend my day in the Crystal Temple, and I will help you train Louis as well.

"If you are wondering she is the family of the Hippocampus."

"Her mother continued by saying this Helena, is a four-legged sister to the others but she seems special indeed."

They stayed with her for a few hours to feed her and give her water.

Her mother said"the next couple of months you will be busy helping me train her and your boy too."

At this time Helena had completely forgotten about how she was going to help Seequest escape from Hades' lair.

Chapter Fourteen

The Foals Are Due

Back in Hades' cave, Knightmare had to rest up as the foal was taking a lot out of her where she was blacking out a lot these days.

Seequest had to come clean and mention to her it's because of his magic!

Because she is carrying two foals, not one and but two as they are draining her every day due growing quickly and getting ready to be born soon.

On the afternoon up above on June 11th, when the sun was at its hottest and there were clear skies, the forest animals were teaching their young ones the ropes of life and the birds were tweeting away happily above the gorgeous trees.

Seequest was keeping an eye on Knightmare closely when he also was thinking that he missed his family

Very much even though he loved being with this mare, which he knew was not normal and yet right for him.

He wondered if he had the chance again to be above and visit his uncle/friend Truth the Earth unicorns Presence which lays inside the silver birch tree further in the forest.

He thought that he would like to pay his respects to him while he was living temporally on land.

Yet he thought would he recognize the tree if he got the chance to find it again?

Does he then consider if his plan works he may become possibly free soon to find it again?

He said to himself of course I will find it due to the scent and Truth's image of his head is still poking out of it as he lived in it for so long it created an outline in wood as the tree grew around him for years.

It was Zeus' kind idea of leaving his image there as a remembrance to him for his greatness in helping the animals and the earth itself so he was never forgotten.

Later Seequest dreamt about being able to fly again like he used to with his mother when he was younger.

Due to Moonbeam's mother being an original bloodline of Pegasus's winged horses her magic was then transformed from her wings into her third eye.

Where it grew a beautiful powerful horn instead on her forehead when they were picked to stay on earth and heal it.

The Day and Night Unicorns were the only ones that still had this power to fly through producing a special pretty dust from their horns to create this magic for them to fly safely as their duties were to protect the day and night skies.

It also helps bring the sun and moon closer to the earth as well.

Knightmare woke up from her restless sleep and slowly stood up looking very heavy as if she was ready to pop that she felt uncomfortable at times as the foals had hooves and kicked her hard that she was badly bruised from the inside.

She told Seequest about her aches and pains which he tried to keep at bay for her in secret.

As she was stretching her body she ate her meat as much as she could to keep her strength going remember after all she is a horse of the underworld now.

This put Seequest off her at times and hoped that one day he could stop this.

But he knew that she would not survive without it.

So, he said nothing and respected that she had no choice in the matter even though he really did not like seeing her this way.

He did hope that one day he could possibly change her feeding habits again?

But this did concern him because she had to do this so he did wonder would their children do the same.

Will it make them more like her in a bad way?

This did frighten him a little and hoped that his power would be stronger than Hades to keep it at bay he thought.

She eventually came back over after Hades had visited her and rested down next to Seequest again.

Hades disappeared at this time.

It's not that he didn't feel these emotions it's just that it reminded him of his good memories back home.

When he was a young man in Olympus with his brothers when they decided to kill their father the last of the Titans and then Zeus was chosen to become the king of the heavens of birth and creation he was chosen to be the king of death and lost souls and destruction.

Knightmare neighed and within seconds there poking out her was the first to be born.

Seequest's eyes lit up and his horn began to glow as there appeared a sweet pink foal with a little horn on her head and pretty feather wings which were wet and stuck to her body making her look cerise pink at the moment.

Knightmare was strong enough to help open the bag for the foal to breathe properly and the foal was free resting there all dark pink and wet.

At this time Seequest wondered if she would stay this colour?

Another hour had passed Knightmare was going to rest again when she neighed loudly out in great pain and said "the other one's coming."

She pushed and pushed but it seemed to take longer as it was bigger and she said "this one really hurts."

Seequest said, "let me help me you and put his horn on her stomach."

At this time Hades came and said "I knew you still had your powers" with anger in his voice.

Seequest was annoyed now that he knew his secret was out.

But at this time his mate was more important.

The male foal was born of his true self.

The reason why he caused Knightmare so much pain was he like was like her with small bat wings with crawls on them.

They were scratching her as he was been born Poor Knightmare was exhausted and slightly sore inwardly too.

Yet it was all over now and there they were resting beside their mother (magical he thought!)

Seequest was amazed that he created these tiny creatures of two different species and then wondered if there was more good than bad in them both?

But hoped and prayed that his magic and guidance will make sure that the good would prevail in them in time through love and patience.

Just by loving them for who they truly are his children.

There the male is laying in the straw resting with his sister between them.

They both licked and cleaned them all up.

Later they were fed on their mother's milk.

Seequest was startled by what he had just seen has he never was around before to see the actual births of any of the other mares in his past.

Or be involved with it before either, so for him it was a magnificent and magical thing.

Moonbeam at the time was the leader of the herd of night unicorns in the past, Seequest's mother!

Poor Knightmare was over-exhausted still from the births.

It took a few days for her to recover before she became herself once more.

Two days had passed when Knightmare stood up and saw her foals properly for the very first time since they had been born recently.

There they were trying to stand by leaning against Seequest body for support where she could see that both of their children had a horn like their father.

She had something to drink as she then walks over and stood close to Seequest while watching their foals practicing to stand up on their own.

The foals stood eventually and looked at each other Seequest stood up all boldly and nuzzled them saying "well-done children."

The two foals understood him clearly and walked over to their father and they nuzzled each other.

The Unicorn King said to the foals "that lovely mare over there is your mother."

"Now let her rest, you can say hello when she's stronger but come and lie with me until she is ready to feed you later.'

The foals nodded and went and laid with their father once again until dawn came for their feed.

Hades was watching from afar by the crystal ball he got from one of the witches.

He was pleased that Knightmare gave birth to an actual black male foal as he will possibly have the power that he wanted, like his grandfather before him (Jecco), again Seequest's father who was known in the all realms of the been the strongest and greatest unicorn that had lived for his strength and bravery a crossed the lands.

So now Hades thought that he will not need Seequest anymore?

Although Hades was hoping that his son will be more powerful than he put together because of having Seequest's powers and the power of his mother's blood too which was Hades' power as well!

The underworld god was so pleased with the foal that he kept it a secret from them all until the time was right for them to know his true interest in him.

Months had gone by when the foals were starting to show their true colours.

Seequest was looking at them and was thinking about eventually taking them out to the woods to train and teach them about the rules of life and explain to them who they really are and what their purpose is in this life time for the greater good of living things.

He was going to show them a way of escaping for good hopefully as well while doing this.

When Knightmare woke up all she could think of was that she now had the family of her dreams and she couldn't believe it was real.

The foals were awake and so she walked over to them and fed them.

She spoke to Seequest.

"Well, what do you think of our children my love?"

Seequest's answer was vague as he noticed that his son looked like her and was worried that he will become one of Hades' evil horses in time if he gets his hands on him lone?

So, he tried not to think that way.

Where looks are deceiving as he knew his son was a good foal on the inside.

Which made him change his mind to a positive one that he was his actual son and nothing else mattered.

Only because he may look like a demon horse it does not mean that he would act like one unless pushed Seequest believed.

The unicorn king wanted to get away from Hades as quickly as he could, so he can train his children before he could get hold of them himself.

Knightmare walked away from Seequest as she called her foals that walked freely to her nicely.

Seequest was just watching happily in the distance.

She nuzzled them lovingly and was proud of her achievements and how the Unicorn King loved her too.

When Hades was not there they were wondering if they could escape together as a family.

Seequest knew better that it may not be possible but agreed that they all for now keep Knightmare from worrying.

After all, she had enough to deal with regarding looking after the two foals.

Seequest really wants to escape quickly.

But the foals were not strong enough to run that far yet or their wings were not ready to fly either too.

Where the unicorn king had to be patient so he decided to just enjoy his time that he had with his family while they could...

Chapter Fifteen

Training Louis and Kessy

Back in the ocean, Helena as really getting the hang of looking after her sea colt and Queen Sera was astonished at how Kessy had grown twice the size of her brothers and sisters.

"Oh, my goodness Kessy," she said "what will I do with you?"

Then she had an idea that there was a beautiful place far away that does need guarding for the future and was big enough for her to live on her own, now.

As Kessy was completely different because she had four flippers instead of two legs and fins which also meant that she could walk on land at any time possibly in the future.

Kessy had a long neck that she could see also underwater and above without being seen.

She was also a pretty creature.

Her colour was bright green with blue shades running through her body with emerald-green eyes.

So, from the point of view of being a member of the hippocampus bloodlines, she looked closer to a dragon type of creature.

Sera called her not a hippocampus with four legs but a new species that she named a sea dragon.

The queen knew that somehow in the future Kessy would be able to live on land and there was a possibility that her skin will become tougher and protect her from the sun and others in time.

She thought to herself that she was very special and will be important in time.

But the queen discovered while observing her that Kessy well being in the water seemed to enjoy it so much that it made her shine.

That night after visiting Kessy in the day the queen was wondering while she and everyone were in bed if she would take her through to this other place as she was getting too big even for their sea stables.

As the salt water did not actually suit her anymore as she was changing quickly into something else that no one had seen before in this lifetime.

Personally, she thought that she would feel more comfortable in freshwater as she seemed to struggle for long periods of time with her breathing.

As she preferred to keep her head out of the water and breathe the fresh air from the sky above.

The queen thought of using her magic crystal skulls tomorrow to create an invisible shield over her face until Sera could get her to the freshwater possibly in a place that was sacred she thought.

Sera was in her shell bed and was still thinking about it, that she then realized as she could not sleep that maybe the best time to do it was now! while looking at the colourful fish swimming passed her window happily.

She got out of bed and gently swam to get her dress with her cloak and put her hairpins in her hair and then opened the royal doors to her chambers and swam quietly out of there.

Closing the door carefully not waking up her husband who needed his sleep has been on a long journey the day before about the kingdom been in danger now.

Then she called for one of the dolphins telepathically which came and took her to the royal stables where Kessy; her parents and siblings were living.

That night in the gorgeous moonlight above Sera shone onto the stables where she was resting with Moonstone her hippocampus sister and spoke to her.

As she told her what she was going to do to help Kessy.

Kessy so young felt delighted and let the high priestess put on her harness and collected Sea Spray too.

"Come on, my beautiful."

I have a job for you to do for me' she said.

But Kessy would not leave the stables and pulled the queen off her hippocampus where she landed on her face.

The queen then realized that Kessy had feelings and she knew that she was not coming back here so she wanted to go and see her brothers and sisters for the last time first.

While in the stables the queen let all her siblings out of their sea stalls so they could play.

And then they pushed their faces to each other's bodies and said their goodbyes.

Next, she swam quickly up to her father's stall where his head was leaning out of it as she was very close to Tidal Wave because he actually gave birth to her in the past not her mother as normal horses do.

Once she had done all her goodbyes her siblings held their heads low being sad and yet respecting that she needed to go so that she could enjoy life to the full herself.

The queen once again was riding her mother and escorting Kessy through the kingdom and into the main part of the sea where it came lighter where there is a porthole to get to other places and lands on earth if needed.

They eventually swam through the porthole.

As they both arrived on a beautiful loch of green and blue shades with a load of fresh water and space which was in Scotland!

This gorgeous place was known as the Loch because it's the largest part of fresh water in the British Isles.

Kessy poked out her head first while her mother followed behind her with the queen.

Sera named her a sea dragon as it was possibly its own proper species.

Kessy looked excited yet so scared with mixed emotions of happiness; sadness too.

The queen saw her expression and was concerned that she did the right thing and asked 'what do you think girl it's gorgeous here, isn't it?'

Kessy could see that there were loads of green trees and grass on the land where there were loads of open waters for her to explore when she feels comfortable too as well.

She decided to swim and jump up and splash back into the freshwater as she was so happy as the queen had taken off her harness and mask by saying a magic verse.

She felt for the very first time that she could breathe on her own again and be truly free to be her!

Queen Sera told her that this would be her new home only.

She said, "See you soon."

But Kessy was not ready to be left on her own, as she followed Sea Spray back through the portal.

The mermaid queen realized then it will take time for Kessy to be ready to live on her own.

So, she said, "you can stay with us until you do not fit in the stables anymore."

Is that agreed?

"It doesn't mean we have abandoned you as you will be always part of me and all of us."

"It's just that you are different from your siblings and I feel you have another calling my girl"

"Do you understand, girl?"

Kessy nodded and totally understood what the queen had said and agreed with her.

They swam back altogether to the stables to rest once more.

As Queen Sera decided to leave her alone until she was ready to leave on her own accord Sera thought?

As she then realised that Kessy would adapt easier to her new surroundings and home as well, if she did it this way.

So another year had passed already when Kessy was walking up to the paddock of shells and saw her sibling sisters practicing their skills of riding and pulling the sea carriages too.

They stopped after their session seeing her watching them quietly as they neighed at her and they swam towards her, as they were as big as the size of a blue whale but she towered still over them many times more.

They did not mean to but even though she was big she also felt that her siblings suffocated her as too many swam around her in one go and made her feel overwhelmed again, after all she is their big sister too.

Now she was in her prime.

She swam gently back away from them like a dragon would have swam and they knew then it was time to say their goodbyes properly for good this time.

They all swam up to her individually showing that they would miss her dearly when she is gone.

When they approached her, she had to be careful that she did not hurt them because of her size now.

She made neighing noises back and they danced in sync with each other.

The queen and Helena thought it was amazing to see because of all their lovely colours moving around all together making beautiful shapes as they did.

Sera could see that it was time for Kessy to move to her new home and she believed it was too after training that day in the Mediterranean Sea.

Sera and Helena went on to get things ready for their beautiful friend to take with her and to help her readjust from her true home as well.

From what she had just witnessed she thought that the seahorses could also be a little entertainment as well and thought of doing a dance sequence with them all.

But Kessy looked like she had fear in her eyes because of her knowing that she will not see her family anymore for a while at least and picked up her flipper and cuddled her sisters and then the mer-trainer called them all back and they neighed and went away again.

Further back in the other stables were her brothers the stallions which were handsome beasts.

They looked like they were ready to carry the ocean knights now as fully trained and ready for the new jobs in the royal palace.

She made this dragon noise which echoed through the sea and shook the mer-folk around a little.

The queen said "Kessy calm down girl please."

"With her making this noise the stallions were swimming around and came straight to her showing the dominant side to her and yet friendly and loving."

They had to look again as they knew her voice and yet did not recognize her so even though they swam up to her nicely they were prepared to attack her if needed.

Eventually the male Hippocampius's quieted down not throwing their front legs and hooves around as they noticed her smell was like theirs, as they then calmed down completely.

They swam beautifully with her for an hour then real-ized that it was time for them to say goodbye to her as well.

The stallions saw the queen approaching them so they started to swim away.

The queen was thinking that they were her babies that have grown into very strong and handsome Hippocampius's who were also swimming quite grace-fully now.

She then wondered about how time had flown by for all of them.

Helena's mother was glad that she went ahead with the mating after all.

As the babies now ready to go their separate ways as time flew by too fast she thought.

Sera knew that it was time for all the Hippocampius's to do their duties and for Kessy as well.

Queen Sera knew it was time for her to take her back to the Loch where she will stay for the rest of her life.

The difference with the Hippocampius's is that they must be ready to meet their rider telepathically con-nect and become one with body and mind.

With Kessy, she knew that it was not at all possible as she was too large for anyone to handle her apart from herself.

"Kessy, it is time."

The sea dragon looked sad as she nodded and swam up towards the queen where she cuddled her by putting her head on her back.

"OK, girl I think it is time for you and me to go back to the Loch tomorrow morning for your new start as an adolescent."

Kessy felt that she was not quite ready to let go of her siblings, yet but knew in her heart it would be the best thing for her to do.

So she thought hard and long that night back at the stables further in as she was too large to be with her siblings now.

She thought should she let her heart rule her and struggle with breathing all the time or rule with her head and face the fear knowing it was the right thing for her to do in the end even though she was scared of coming out of her comfort zone?

She knew that she had to do this for herself at last and yet felt terribly sad.

But thinking about it carefully that there was no one else like her in the world and felt lonely.

The high priestess could sense and feel her sadness and said "it's okay girl to be scared, I was too when I moved from living on the moon to here in the sea."

"But it was the best thing I have ever done".

"You don't know how you are going to react until you try?"

The queen told her she was a new creation and her kind will come again because of her having both male and female genes inside her body, like a worm.

So, it meant that she could have babies as she has both hormones in her body to produce them herself in time when she is ready.

Kessy liked this information that she swam to the top of the sea and jumped up in the air and bounced back deep again accidentally upsetting the merfolk once more.

Kessy then cried with a smile and frown at the same time.

They went back there that day and Kessy then real-ized where she belonged now as they swam back to Vissen together one final time.

She looked at Sera and said "It's time my friend"

But Kessy wanted to see Helena before leaving the sea for the freshwater life so the next day she will start a new adventure of her own.

Chapter Sixteen

A New Species of Winged Unicorns Are Born

In the sea, time is slightly different from living on land.

As in the ocean sea creatures mature quicker due to survival of living in the sea as predators are swimming around them always and cannot actually get away from them like on land, so they need to grow strong to defend themselves at an early age as well.

Back in Hades Liar

Knightmare awoke after a loving kiss from Seequest.

The foals had grown into two elegant creatures not seen or heard of before like Kessy and a new species to earth.

Knightmare woke her beautiful children from their deep sleep and asked them to get up and come and have their milk they did this quite happily and she smiled at the Unicorn King while they did.

She knew that these foals were very special and she was proud to be a part of them.

They fed on her every day that which created a great bond with her.

And through that she believed that even her dreams had come true at last even in death she as now lives a new life with Hades and for that, she had to thank him.

Hades arrived with Cerberus beside him for his protection as even a mare who loves their owner can change when they're with their young, so he did this as a precaution for all.

While Hades was there Seequest could see that he had a loving side and smiled when he saw that his mare was happy and with two foals of great brilliance.

Seequest thought is it at all possible that Hades could change his ways and let them all be free as a family?

But what the unicorn stallion did not know was that Hades was putting on an act to fool even him to let him get close to the foals and stroke them.

By doing this with his hand on their foreheads where their little horns were growing quickly he put a spell on them for when he needs them they will come to his side.

"What beautiful children you two have created and these two will be a magnificent pair in time."

He smiled and walked away back to his lair with his faithful friend.

"Mother who was that they said?" she replied "he is your owner, my darlings."

"Don't fret there is nothing to be scared of"

"He won't hurt you."

Both Knightmare and Seequest were fooled by his kindness which they had never seen until they were together and the foals had been born.

But then Seequest thought really hard to himself thinking, is this his way of getting to his foals and using them for something terrible in the future?

Hades couldn't have Seequest's horn of great power?

But he has more than that now as the Unicorn King's children have the powers of greatness and darkness as well from their mother!

Seequest quickly said to Knightmare that they must escape when the foals are older as he had a horrible feeling that they will never be together again.

They both hated this feeling but they made the best of it now.

It was now a year ago when the foals were becoming their own character and winged unicorn.

The filly (Firefly) was pretty.

She had the build of her father very elegant and yet strong looking.

Her coat was pink velvet representing her parents' colours combined together pink and white mane and tail with an elegant horn on her forehead of rose pink and silver with a beautiful rose-quartz-colored eye of pure love and kindness.

She had a stunning pair of small angel-like wings of the same colour as her mane which were now a foot long when opened to their full glory.

Seequest called her Firefly as she had the feisty side of her mother's strength and she will fly as well one day.

Because he believed she will be as outstanding as the great Pegasus himself and the winged horses in time too, that for the moment she followed her great grandfather's genes which Seequest was delighted with as he represented the greatest good of them all put together.

But his son was the complete opposite!

He was a handsome colt with a strong build with feather legs like his mother and his mane and tail were flowing like his father's with Seequest's elegant swan-arched neck.

His coat was jet black like his grandfather Legends of course and his mother's too

He also had a deep red fire running through his coat red bloodstone eyes like his mother with a small deep red horn where he had a small pair of bat wings with

Claws on the tips which had red veins pulsing through them too.

His mother called him Knight after her because he was her Knight in shining armour, which has come to her rescue at last by changing her life forever.

Seequest was worried about is that he also had Jecco and Legend's strength and charm and he was worried that he could possibly hurt or cause great problems if he was trained by Hades!

Seequest was so concerned about the way his son looked and yet remembered not to judge him based on his looks but through his true loving personality, as Knight had a sweet disposition to him as well.

And that's what Seequest hoped would always stay with him?

Seequest was proud of his family and yet was scared of what Hades had planned for them when they are older.

As with them both, he could possibly get what he wants as he always wanted to rule Earth and somehow Seequest always seemed to make sure that never happened.

One good thing was that Firefly seemed to have telepathic abilities like him which he told her to keep a secret from her mother and brother until one day they were all free once more.

The great stallion told his children why they were born and to be prepared to fight this man Hades if ever they needed to, as everyone's life depended on it.

When Hades went and did his errands of collecting the souls of the dead.

Seequest taught his children and his partner some home truths about their owner and his plan is to possibly use them to destroy earth or Zeus himself.

They all promised to prevent this from happening, that they will fight to the end to prevent it.

For now, they all lay together enjoying each other's company until that day comes.

In the meantime, Seequest was planning a way to escape and see Helena and his friends again whom he missed so much.

Yet he wondered would his foals now be able to change into hippocampus (water horse) like him in time and will Neptune kindly accept Knightmare as a friend instead of a foe?

Seequest was hoping that he would give her the blessing to live with him in the sea as well as give her the gift he gave to him in the past.

The Poor white unicorn now was so confused and sad but he did not show this to his family as he was happy to be with them too.

The poor old unicorn king was split between two worlds once more which he thought had now ended.

He thought of new beginnings for us all and fell asleep next to Knightmare hoping this to be true in time?

Chapter Seventeen

Pegasus Visits Olympus

Since receiving the message from the Queen of the sea a year ago

Pegasus had been watching from above on the clouds closely regarding Seequest knowing that he was the last of great magic alive on Earth and had noticed that it was true that he had been captured by Hades himself and knew that he must report it to Zeus straightaway.

At dusk, he leaped off his silver cloud and dived into the sky, and flapped his amazing huge angel wings with all his might towards Greece where Olympus was high up in the mountains in disguise from anyone.

He thought that he will fly in the night, as Hades' spies will not see him.

He arrived at Olympus before the sun was about to rise.

He landed elegantly onto heaven's path and walked into Zeus's kingdom of gold.

He bowed in front of Zeus and Hera as they were sitting in their mighty thrones with the sun gleaming on them throwing great light into the room of the peace reign.

Pegasus told Zeus what had happened, and Zeus became upset at once.

He was close with his brother when they were children, and he did not choose his brother to rule the underworld.

But their father the Titan before them did as the Titan could see weakness in his youngest son.

That he felt that he had not the strength to rule any other kingdom apart from the underworld as this job was easy as all he had to do was keep the dead at bay and keep the bad punished if needed in the future.

The Titan King could see that Hades was loving and caring and would not kill anything.

But Zeus would, to show that he could rule if wanted to be a leader in time and yet too loving and kind as well.

Yet he did not show it as Hades did.

So, the Titan King gave him a test and told Zeus to kill his brother and get rid of him forever.

Zeus loved his brother very much but also wanted to rule Olympus in time so they went out one day and had a great time together.

Zeus poisoned him secretly with an orange that carried some snake venom in it.

Zeus did not have the heart to tell Hades that his father wanted him dead and said that it must have been an accident in the fruit as Hades died and he told their father he was gone.

The Titan king seemed happy about this while Zeus was pleased it was a lie.

Zeus said, "Brother I love you so much."

"I cannot bring you back to life the way you were once."

But I can bring you back in death but he never knew that it would change his brother's ways forever.

This was the only way that his father accepted that Hades was gone for good.

Hades had to live down in the underworld which Zeus personally created for him to be free and happy.

The only difference is that he could not stay out in the sun or attend Olympus often only twice a year without their father there.

Many years went on and the brothers still had a close relationship until Zeus came of age to rule Earth and all his brothers came together to destroy their father once and for all because of his bad spirit and wanting to destroy the lands.

They did this before he died by all their powers put together as one.

As their horrible titan father was dying he saw that Hades was still alive somehow and so cried out in spite "Hades, Zeus killed you for Olympus!"

From that day Hades' heart broke and became bitter and changed to the Hades we now know and hate as he decided that what was the point of loving and caring if you were stabbed in the back by your own family?

But it was not Zeus' thought it was their father's.

Yet Hades would not ever listen to the truth anymore.

Zeus tried to ask for forgiveness and help Hades as much as he could.

But it was too late.

Hades had gone mad and now wanted revenge but instead of just wanting to rule Olympus.

He wanted Earth as well to destroy it as he felt why should Zeus see the beauty of life in everything when he only now sees death?

So again when Zeus heard this was horrifying news by Pegasus that Hades had Seequest thinking that it was his way of getting back at him for all the years of torture he went through.

Zeus called for all his brothers and sisters across the lands and kingdoms where his children would all together help destroy Hades' plan and rescue the Unicorn King.

The great god felt threatened that Hades now has the upper hand as Seequest is even more powerful than Zeus himself as he has the powers of Pegasus the horse god and his powers too.

In Zeus' thoughts he did not like what he was hearing and planned to stop it straight away.

Later Zeus asked Aphrodite to send out one of her beautiful owls to spy on Hades' lair.

Days had passed when the owl returned and told her that what he had seen were two foals with wings of a difference and that they were both children of the mighty Seequest and Hades' mare.

Zeus was very worried as now Hades had all the powers of good and evil at his fingertips and what was his plan to do with it?

That was the true mystery.

In the afternoon some great warriors of Olympus turned up: Ares; Diana; Hermes, Athena, and some others too came to discuss how they were going to conquer Hades again.

The only god who was missing was Zeus's middle brother Neptune as he was still on his way there.

Zeus had his last conversation with Pegasus before they came together for his great meeting still waiting for Neptune to arrive knowing that Seequest is now his friend and his ocean protector too.

He said to Pegasus "thank you friend."

"You must go to the sixth dimension of the heavens in the divine and see Celestial and Legend as they were once Seequest's parents".

"I believe we will need all the help we can get as this battle is going to be the greatest one yet"!

Pegasus agreed and bowed to Zeus as he galloped quickly up into the sky towards the sixth-dimension portal and flew into the light and disappeared.

Chapter Eighteen

Helena and Louis Have a Secret

Helena and Louis were becoming great friends and it seemed like Helena had forgotten about her old dear friend Seequest completely.

Her mother said that she was becoming so good at riding that she wanted to put her and Louis in for a special event in which Neptune her father also competes with Tidal wave for ten years running and they have never lost it so far.

The queen was interested to see if Helena could beat her father at his own game.

Within that Helena's eyes shone and she smiled like a Cheshire cat as she sat on Louis and whispered into his ear a word that Seequest taught her in the past.

In a flash Louis had changed from a stunning black hippocampus to a strange slim and narrow-faced horse looking like creature.

He swam like the wind showing her mother that Louis could slip through small holes in the rocks and reefs that no other hippocampus so far could do.

"Wow, my darling I never knew that he could do that."

"Nor did I until recently as I heard Seequest say it when he changes into an actual horse/ unicorn on land."

"I wondered what would have happened if I said it to Louis so to my surprise this was the result as after all the Hippocampius are all related to Seequest from his mother's horn right."

"Yes, you're right but I never knew that they could do this."

"It's amazing and out of this world", her mother said.

Helena said "please mother doesn't say anything to Father as it's our secret!"

"I want it to be a surprise when I am competing with him in the future, agreed?"

"Yes, Helena agreed" and the queen laughed as she liked a little bet and cheekiness at times as well.

Sera asked "Helena show me again this incredible magic that Louis has".

Helena agreed and within seconds the queen saw Louis's whole body begin to light up in a blue shade and change in a flash to this very unusual creature of brilliance as he looked fast.

He had a slim body and his tail curled underneath him with a large fin on his back away from where Helena sat.

His neck had also grown longer and more curled too.

His head was stuck under it and his head was narrow with a short snout with beautiful aqua-blue eyes.

His coat had changed as now he looked scalier and had a thicker coat for hard wearing in the sea and it protected him from getting hurt as his skin was like bodied armour.

The queen realized then why Kessy was like she is.

And now wondered if she would change as well one day and what into?

But this will be another story to be told in time!

Helena's mother thought hard knowing that she could see the future and yet could not say anything about it in case it changed things for the worst.

After finishing her practice for the sea aquatic event soon Louis was exhausted as this change takes a lot out of him.

Helena told her mother that she was taking him home to rest as now Louis had changed back to his handsome black and blue Hippocampus form once again as she escorted him back to the stables to be freshened and fed and watered as well.

The queen said she will meet her back at the stables later.

Queen Sera thought as Helena did this that she was very proud of them both and that she loved Tidal Wave.

But knowing that his son Louis is got more of a handsome head and seemed to be powerful than his father.

Because he had beautiful velvet skin and yet soft scales with a stunning swallow tail elegant fins and pointed ears small fins on his head with two slim-shaped front legs that give him extra speed

What caught her eye was how his mane is flowing like seaweed in the ocean gracefully.

She was hoping one day maybe Helena would let her breed him to another.

She also had a sensed that he was meant for a special purpose as well and yet did not know what that was yet.

It was now summer when it was getting closer to Helena trusting him to behave outside.

She would practice all the time and then decided that Louis was ready to go out of the grounds and explore the ocean properly and see the life that she knew and loved so much.

One morning she did all her jobs and then went to the shell stables and saw that Louis been restless.

She put on his colourful bright blue and silver saddle and harness on him gently that her mother had specially made for him.

Where she also had another smaller one for when he changed into a slimmer type that Helena called sea horse or sea dragon.

She gave him his breakfast and attended to his brothers and sisters and later she swam up to him and said, "my dear Louis would you like to see the world today?"

As Helena could talk to sea animals he neighed gently and said "my princess I would love that".

"Yes, please but I am scared."

She came up to him and he appeared over his stall and she hugged his neck and face and said "no harm will come to you dear one I promise.'

"Then what are you waiting on your Highness Let's go."

She opened his stall door of shells and put on his gear and jumped on him gracefully with his front hooves like fins they swam off towards the gates out of Vissen with great speed.

They reached the last large golden gate when Helena said "Are you ready Louis to explore my world?"

He replied, "Yes I am."

"Then off we go" and they swam as fast they could out of the gates by a massive pod of killer whales which were black and white and very elegant to look at.

Even though Louis was big now these sea mammals were enormous to them both and they enjoyed swimming beside them further into the deeper parts of the sea.

As the killer whales were guarding the other sea creatures and protecting Vissen too from harm.

It was clear she decided to say the word again and made him change once more into a true sea horse.

He could swim faster through any slim hole of any kind and miss being caught or being eaten many times thankfully.

Helena enjoyed herself so much that she could not wait to tell her mother their adventures that day as they swam through the coral reefs and sea grass where they also saw plaice lying on the seabed.

Louis seemed to feel more confident now as he swam more freely.

Because of this, he changed back to his proper form again.

The princess tapped her friend on the neck and said "well-done boy."

"That's impressive".

"Come we better get back home and tell mother what you now can do."

She wondered if the others could do this too.

She also mentioned to him "I could see you been a Champion in time and a great specimen of your kind."

Louis liked the sound of that as they swam back the kingdom through the gates and to the stables once more.

They reached the stables quite late and missed her mother due to she had already left for the day.

Helena was disappointed but she was not surprised as her mother was the queen and had other things to do as well.

The mermaid princess slipped off his back and escorted him back to his stall where she took off his shell saddle and bridle and gave him a nice rub down with seaweed to get rid of the sweat on his skin and brushed his mane with an old crab's claw for comfort to his mind to rest.

Later she swam out and locked his stall.

He turned around to say goodnight to her and she kissed him on the nose before she left to go to the library to do some research on his kind.

If there was any then it would be in the Archives of Wisdom, she thought.

The princess swam happily and was excited about her new life.

She then remembered before him she rode the great Seequest her dear old friend.

She then started to feel awful as she did forget about him for a long while and wondered if he is ok from being trapped there in the underworld with Hades under his commands to save her and the Earth's life as they know it.

She knew then that she must try and do something to help him somehow but what.

That she did not know yet?

Chapter Nineteen

The Yearlings

Back in Hades' stables, the foals had come of age to see what they can do.

Knightmare asked Hades if she could kindly take them out and see the outside world for a while as she felt like her strong self and wondered what powers they both had of their own.

Seequest felt the same way.

Because of what happened before they were banned from going out again.

But Hades changed his mind and thought this could be his advantage as he then could let Seequest teach the yearlings the ropes and duties.

Where all he had to do is change their way of thinking in the future when he was ready.

"Yes, Knightmare you can but do not be out too long please as we do not want to drain them as they have a lot to learn my gal."

She agreed.

The two foals followed their mother through the dark caves.

Seequest was walking right behind them and lit his horn once more.

They saw the sunshine and adapted to its light quickly whereas Seequest had to change Knightmare's eyes again to enjoy it.

Knightmare said "welcome my darlings to the upper world as you live in the underworld where nothing grows."

But this time they had to stay near the woods of Dreams.

"But here everything grows with magic connected to it thanks to your father the unicorn king and his family of unicorns and the horses too."

"But until now the magic only lied in the earth and the trees and your father's horn."

The foals loved the look of the grass where they started to gallop and jump on it as it felt soft and smelt good to eat afterward being weaned now completely from their mother for quite some time.

Seequest said "I am going to introduce our children to my old friends of the forest."

"Is that ok with you?"

"Yes, of course."

He said "great as they trotted away from the birch tree where their mother rested and enjoyed the change of scenery."

Seequest asked the foals to follow him to the Mysterious Woods to introduce them to his friends the forest animals.

To let his animal friends, see his children and also to show everyone that he's still alive and well at the moment.

Has Hades not used him and his powers so far for creating this new species of unicorn which in the future he may try and use to his advantage to conquer them at last and the world as well?

He also told them the animals where they were just in case he cannot escape.

Hopefully, they will come and rescue him and maybe his family too he hoped and thought that they had not forgotten him yet?

They met loads of different animals like foxes bears; badgers and of course the pack of wolves his best friends.

Seequest had a plan that if everyone knew about them everyone then could help or call in any way.

Knightmare loved the forest and felt warm and safe and it was colourful that she really did not want to go back and yet had no choice in the matter.

She knew that their father felt the same way and said that he would do his best to achieve this.'

Back in Mysterious woods, Seequest said to his children "we must get back to your mother before she starts to worry."

They said their goodbyes and galloped back to the great birch tree.

They got reached back where their mother was grazing happily.

Later that day they all walked up to the mountain where Seequest was trained when he was younger, where he would practice walking into the sky with his mother those many years before.

Now it was his turn to teach his own and yet slightly different because they did not have to produce dust.

They just had to use their beautiful wings instead.

First to try was Firefly as Seequest's horn lit up in bright silver across the sky.

As he walked off the mountain he was walking in the air (magic!) he said "Firefly it is your turn."

The filly seemed quite keen to please her parents and believed she would be a great flyer because of her pretty powerful looking wings.

So, she turned around and then came back galloping as fast as she could flapping her incredible pink and white angel wings which still looked a little fluffy as she was still young.

She jumped off the mountain with great fear in her mind that she would fall as not aware of how her wings worked properly yet.

But trusted her father's judgment, and she was now ready to try.

As she is moving her wings up and down as quickly as she could and yet had also had to get aquatinted to the weight of them as well at the same time, which was fun and yet tiresome too.

Eventually she accepted them being part of her and so her wings were now one with her, has she now could control them through her mind which helped her to flap them freely as they held her up in the air and the wind helped her glide across the sky quite freely.

"Wow, brother come on."

"You're next", as she was flapping her wings beside their father.

"Come on Knight your turn son", said his mother and he too was determined to achieve this and did the same.

But because he does not have feathers but skin for wings when he flapped them, which made a gust of wind whereas his sister's wings are feathers and slid through it.

Because his wings are made of pure skin this also makes them heavier in flight.

Now their mother came up into the sky as well.

They all were having fun together in the air away from danger when Seequest told them how to land without hurting themselves.

He would go first and jump back onto the mountain elegantly and Firefly followed.

She seemed very scared of doing this.

Seequest said to them both "calm down enjoy and believe in yourself you both were blessed with these beautiful gifts."

Seequest was amazed as his great grandfather or god of horses Pegasus's gene had gone through five generations of horses and now these two as well.

He then thought it happened because Knightmare must have originally been born from one of the first mares of his beautiful daughters long ago as he guessed in the past when they first met.

When he left them to get on with their own lives has ordinary horses.

He thought somehow, they must have had a little magic left that stayed in them.

As he changed them so that they all could be accepted in their herds as leaders before he decided to go and live out the rest of his life in the sea.

Seequest wondered what other great gifts his children would both have and had to wait until they were much older to find out.

So that day was one to remember as they were growing up quickly in the underworld all together as a family.

But Seequest felt like that was going to change soon as the foals were becoming of age now.

More years had passed when they became two years old and were coming to the woods for quite some time.

The colt was the stronger of the two as he had more of his mother's traits of Hades' powers than his own which made Seequest worry for him.

He knew that if Hades found this out then they would lose their son forever.

So, when Hades asked how they were doing he tried to change the subject and Hades becomes annoyed as he did not trust Seequest anymore and spied on him from above himself.

A large black vulture came up in another oak tree nearby.

Hades let Knight's parents continue the training until he felt it was time to take over.

Luckily too Pegasus now knew what was going on and was in sync with Seequest's mind and could also see through his eyes what was going on for himself without anyone else knowing.

He did this in the past as well to keep an eye on the herds when Seequest was the king of the unicorns and horses on earth.

As it was his job to make sure they did their duties all properly to create beauty again and also protect Earth and not damage his reputation for their purpose.

Now that Seequest's children were much older and wiser he felt that he could quickly leave them in the care of their mother for a short period and decided to find his late uncle Truth tree again.

So one day when they had done their training he told them to rest with their mother and that he would be back soon, saying his looking for some special berries as award for their hard work!

He gallops off alone and he finds birch tree quite easily as he thought that next time they are there in the woods he would like to take them to see where he is and tell them his story as it is important to them for him to explain where they came from originally and who they are today.

He eventually comes back with the black berries which they loved and later went to Hades cave to rest properly for the day.

Seequest was waiting for them to be stronger in every form before taking them to Truth's tree as they too had to understand what he was telling them and take it seriously as well.

Were one afternoon month's later back in the woods of Dreams after the children's training session they rested beside their mother as usual?

While Seequest he said to himself this is the day!

Has he told his family they were going on an adventure before going home back to Hades' lair this time!

They all discussed that they would find the tree again and he will take them all there for a history lesson of their kind.

Seequest first leads them until they are close by and felt that they were been watched.

So then lets Knightmare lead instead.

Seequest was galloping towards the old birch tree which did not feel right and began to slow down as he walked behind his children happily.

Still felt there was something wrong all the same and kept it to himself for a while.

They came closer to the woods of the great birch trees Knightmare took her children as they came across the image of a unicorn head embedded in the tree.

She stopped and looked and said to Seequest "is that it by any chance?"

Seequest replied sadly, 'yes he was one of the greats and knew my mother very well because they can see an image in the bark of their great uncle Truth, the leader of the past Earth unicorns.

The yearlings noticed great colour and beauty all around them as well.

It was an amazing sight to see as they all felt a magic presence all around and below them too.

As they came closer they saw that there was no horn sticking out the tree where Seequest told them that the horn fell off as some of his ashes went back into the tree in the past after the reign of his generation.

"As the horn turned to dust on the ground and now brings magic into the woods everywhere you tread."

"That's would feel now," he said

The dark mare asked "so was he an earth unicorn that looked after the land; trees and waters that made it as beautiful as it is today?"

The unicorn stallion replied, "Yes, my love he was the ruler of the Earth unicorns and uncle to me."

"His name will always be remembered here as Truth."

"He was one of the greats that had to fight many battles with Hades himself and his sabre-toothed tigers once too.

"He also helped me so I could create today's horses as well"

"Fifty-three years ago, he helped me produce the first horse and my unicorn daughters by emerging our magic together."

Seequest mentioned to them to touch the wooden image of him as they did they saw what happened in their minds of the past in a flash.

Afterward, their children both knew they were born for a special purpose and were proud to be who they were, a new species of mystical horses now!

"Wow", the children said "will we be as powerful as you both?"

"No, my dears as I am the true king of the unicorns and horses and also I am hippocampus which means I too now can live in the deep blue sea and drink all kinds of waters which horses and unicorns could not, you might not be able to either but we will see?"

But to his surprise, his children shocked him at a later date regarding this.

Seequest told them when they are older that he will tell them more.

But at least they know of their family's past.

They now could understand what the Unicorns before them did which was to help the planet grow its beauty again and protect it from Hades' grasp.

Now that his mare had rested and had a little of his magic in her he could see that she had a kind soul and that she too was a great mother while she was waiting for them to be ready to go home.

But before that Seequest wanted to take them somewhere else first.

They reached a gorgeous green meadow where Seequest used to play games with his own mother Moonbeam which brought back some great memories and sad ones too.

In memory of her, he thought it would be nice to visit the mountain they used to climb together and share this memory with his new family.

A few hours later they had reached the top where they decided to separate and let their children wander for a while.

Seequest thought it was time that they knew why they were born and what their purpose would be.

Knight got upset and angry at his father as he told them about the true horrible Hades but Knight Thought this guy was nice and kind to him and ignored the warnings that Seequest tried his best to get through to them both.

But Knight decided not to listen to his father's lies again.

Poor Knight does not see that all Hades wants is his powers and control over him.

Knightmare said nothing now and changed the subject quickly.

The day was becoming night so they all galloped as quickly as they could back to the liar.

From that day Seequest felt that he was losing his son through Hades' powers were getting stronger in him and he was worried that Hades would see this and take him away for his doing.

Another month passed when Seequest felt that Knight would not listen to him as he did before since he mentioned bad things about their owner.

But Seequest hoped that one day he would see the truth before it is too late and prayed that it would be very soon now.

Because of this Seequest seemed to be more involved with his daughter and said to them all "come let's gallop in the fresh air while we can."

They all agreed and followed as he watched his daughter who was the prettiest filly as she too was a Friesian/ Arabian type with strength and stamina of true speed.

She had a stunning light pink coat when she was happy.

She had rose pink running through it showing that she was happy most of the time.

She had a heavy flowing pink and white mane and tail that held quite high when she was proud her eyes were rose quartz and glowed like rubies when she was angry like her mother.

Her wings were now powerful with pink shades running through the white angel feathers that matched her body perfectly.

Now that yearlings had great trust in their wings their parents decided to take them to Moonbeam's Mountain where Seequest was once trained and this is where he believed that his children will show their true powers and strength.

"Why is it called Moonbeam's Mountain, Father?"

"I named it after my mother your grandmother who died here and named it after her loving memory."

"If it was not for her bravery and strength the spirits of her kind would not exist in all of us today.'

Firefly walked up the mountain and felt a little shaky as this was much higher than they had flown off before.

Firefly was going to get ready to approach the cliff her father said"your grandmother will always be with you in your heart and mind and she will give you the courage and strength to fly to the highest skies of this Earth."

"Remember my dear child who you are and you then will be able to fly the heavens in time."

"Just believe you can do it as I believe you can."

"Yes, father I understand" as she bowed her head to him to show that she was listening greatly to him knowing that he was not just her father but the great Unicorn King that ever lived.

Now she did not want to let her parents down.

So, she turned around and trotted up to the trees where she took a deep breath and imagined her father when he was young.

There she galloped as fast as she could flapping her wing's up and down until they caused a gust of wind like in the past.

As she approached the end of Moonbeam's Mountain she started to have a soft image of her grandmother in her eyes of a first beautiful elegant black unicorn with a silver horn and second a black mare with a white star where her horn used to be.

This showed Firefly that her grandmother could do these things without magic, in the end, showing true courage and hope which proved to her then that any-thing was possible for her highest good.

She leaped galloping across the sky moving her wings up and down as fast as they could go.

Seequest could not believe his eyes that it was not just a beautiful creature up there but one that he cre-ated himself with great love.

There she was dancing the skies like a natural with her beautiful pink coat shining in the sunlight and her beautiful deep pink and white angel wings moving to the sounds of the winds from further above.

Knight looked up and felt so proud of his big sister flying so high enjoying herself as if that is where she was meant to be.

He then looked at his father as they both smiled at each other and then the great Unicorn King said "It is your turn, my son."

Knight bowed and yet too was very scared as he had bat wings which made them heavier as they were made of bone and skin and will make it more difficult for them to balance properly in the sky, as that is what the feathers do for Firefly.

Poor Knight did not want to upset and fail in front of his father so he put on a brave face and said "yes Father I am ready."

"Very good my son I too am proud of you" and he nuzzled him.

The young colt was opening his bat wings to practice before getting ready to leap off the mountain and join his sister.

When Firefly started to stop flapping her wings and started to fall slowly downwards towards the sea.

Seequest reared on his back legs and neighed loudly that the whole land heard his cry when he shouted 'Firefly wake up and flap your wings now!'

The poor young filly was not used to flying so high for so long in this atmosphere that she had flown to and blacked out because of the different types of oxygen.

She was so excited she forgot to exhale the fumes from the sky and started to fall now very quickly.

Knight saw that his sister was in trouble and straightaway, being Seequest's son forgot about his fears and was more worried about losing his sister.

So, he shouted "I am coming sis!" and flapped his large bat wings as hard as he could and galloped towards the cliff top and jumped into the sky like a pro as well.

His wings were so powerful that they made a storm approach.

He reached his sister in time and called for her to wake up.

She still was out so he decided that he had to bite her to wake her up and he did just that and bit her ear.

She neighed in horrible pain.

But it worked and woke her up, her beautiful rose quartz eyes opened with the light glistened.

She took a deep breath and exhaled afterward and then smiled at her brother saying "thank you, dear brother."

"What would I do without you by my side?"

At the moment she could see that her brother was completely different from her and yet so alike in other ways.

How she loved him so much.

From a distance, their father was neighing and jumping around in relief and thinking how proud he was of his children with Knightmare.

They both noticed that they were starting to flap their wings to the movement and rhythm of their bodies and their legs moved beautifully with the soft breeze of the wind beneath their wings.

Firefly was flying with her brother across the skies of Greece.

She was neighing with laughter and proudness as they flew higher up to the heavens.

Seequest called out and said "do not fly too far yet my children as you're still beginners."

But, after all, they were his children and didn't hear these words and did the opposite and flew even higher.

Both agreed to this wager to see who could fly the highest in the quickest time.

This is part of their mother's traits trying to show who is the better out of the two them, instead of accepting they already were the best fliers just in different ways, they started to climb up towards the clouds higher and higher they flew having fun as they went.

They reached about thirty thousand feet when they looked down and thought wow, we're so high now.

Then through their wings, they produced a great storm that came with heavy winds from the west and knocked both of them out of concentration.

They both started to be thrown around until they both agreed that they had to start diving quickly and get lower again by flipping their wings and galloping quickly as they could go.

But as they did the wind knocked them out of balance and they started to make them fall too fast and once again they lost control.

Knight seemed to pick up and balance himself instantly as he picked up the flow of the gusty wind through his bat wings.

But his sister was blown out of the sky as her feathers made her lighter and easier to be thrown around.

Poor Firefly was flapping her wings as much as she could and yet felt that she still was not strong enough to beat it.

She called Knight to help her.

But he was still diving down to reach her as he is still higher than her.

He saw her falling rapidly and said, "don't worry sis I am coming I will save you!"

At this time Knightmare had woken from her rested sleep and galloped to the edge and neighed out to her children feeling scared as both their parents did not know if they could swim or have any other connections to the sea like Seequest did yet.

So, their parents were waiting to see what would happen next before Knightmare would have to help them herself as Seequest was still weak thanks to Hades draining his magic recently again without him knowing this time!

Firefly gets closer to the sea and her wings are now tucked tightly beside her from above.

Seequest saw his faithful son swooping the sky and flapping his magnificent powerful black bat wings downwards towards his sister hoping to catch her in time before she reached the sea.

But he noticed once again that she had blacked out and no matter what he did biting her gently she would not wake up and was falling to her death.

He had her in his grasp for a few minutes by her mane.

But with her still asleep she was too heavy for him to hold her and so he had to drop her into the sea.

Because she was falling from the sky too fast for him to hold her and control his flight as well.

There she was beautiful to look at once and now quiet with her wings tucked beside her as she fell straight into the sea like a tornado.

She made quite a few waves as she did.

Poor Knight said "no" and then dived straight in to get her not knowing if he would survive himself.

Both their parents panicked when Knightmare kicked Seequest hard saying, "why would you do this to us?"

"Now go and save her before we are done."

Seequest explained that he did not have the powers anymore.

Because of his age and that his magic has been suppressed somehow and he believed this was Hades' plan from the beginning of her not to trust him.

So, she will fall out of love with him which means the great God of Death has them exactly where he wants them to be.

That is making this perfect family become an enemy towards each other now which they are sadly falling apart from their own doing.

Seequest could not blame Hades for this as in their eyes it was his fault!

He bowed his head in shame to Knightmare of feeling that he had let her completely down and said he was so sorry.

She did not accept his apology and carried on walking on in front of him where normally they would walk together as one.

They both turned around to the path and galloped towards the sea to see if they could reach them in time.

As they both weren't strong enough to jump from the cliff top yet and they could take no chances.

So, they galloped as fast as their legs could carry them to the beach where they stood neighing out to their children.

"Firefly, Knight! Please come back to us",

Seequest wanted with all his might to go into the sea and find them.

The unicorn king was so upset that he wished he had the chance for Neptune to meet him so he could also give him back his power to live in the sea as himself again, so he could save his children once more.

But this was not the case and felt that he had let his family down and that it was stupid of him to have taken them there in the first place.

Poor Seequest at this moment in time felt he was going to lose everything again.

What he did not see was that Hades had been watching them for months and felt that they were all getting too close.

Where he find Seequest weakness, was him losing his mare and her children in one go would be heart breaking for the unicorn King that he would give up and hand his horn to be with his family or that's what Hades was hoping for?

Hades planned the heavy winds from his mighty griffon that produced the wind itself by throwing his wings inwards in front of it and by flapping them together to make this ghastly wind appear which made it look like the yearlings had created it themselves as he at the time was invisible.

Afterward, from above he said to the griffon to wait and see if Firefly and Knight would appear safely and could swim in the sea before he planned for the griffon to rescue them on the behalf of his dear mare.

Knight and his sister rose to the surface, awake and alert.

Seequest told them to keep calm and gradually folded their wings into their bodies and started to move their legs as if they were doggie paddling and paddling towards the movement of the ocean herself towards them and the shore.

They listened to their father until a large wave took them under both parents calling out in a frightening panic once more.

Within this time Hades could see they were struggling in the waves and knew it was time to get them out and save them.

He orders his griffon to collect them and the great beast flew straight down into the sea and picked both out with his claws.

He had both of them in each claw as this beast was very strong and large he had a type of lion body on the back and with an eagle head and claws on his front with very powerful large eagle wings to carry them with both.

Knightmare reared on her back legs with delight and said "we are done Seequest"!

"Stay away from me and our children as you nearly killed them both today."

"But thanks to my master he saved our children from death so he is not as bad as you have said as he has shown his love for us today."

She was speaking with anger in her eyes as they were lit up as red as fire at this moment in time and her black coat was streaming with red pulsing veins through her skin once more.

Seequest could see now Knightmare the demon horse he first saw and hated for while had come back and his true love was disappearing right before his very eyes.

Knightmare galloped off back to the cave while Seequest felt defeated and followed slowly knowing that he now deserved whatever feat Hades had set up for him.

The old mysterious white unicorn at this moment could not see a future anymore only his death.

Chapter Twenty

The Hippocampius
are Magnificent

The queen was out with her chariot of dolphins doing her chores when she met up with Neptune's dolphin his mammal daughter Neptuna.

She was beautiful with strawberry lilac hair and lilac and purple shades in her shaped scaled body and pretty fins. These colours also mixed into her bodice that she wore to cover her feminine beauty and she wore a pearl crown gently on her head.

Her eyes were like the ocean itself, such a soft sea green.

She was chosen many years before to be the guardian of the sea creatures like dolphins; crabs; sharks; whales by Neptune.

The only power that she did not have was to change into a Pisces (human type) out of water.

But she can turn herself into a dolphin with special powers of the sea.

As Zeus mated with her powerful mother who is an amazing dolphin to strengthen their intelligence in the sea and she was the result of it, as her siblings were dolphins.

Neptuna did not care that she could not change like her uncle or cousins, as she loved her job all the same.

As she was swimming, she saw the queen and swam towards her and said "your Highness I have not seen Seequest for quite a while."

"He normally swims with my great friends and they have said that he has not been swimming with them and the pods for a long time now.

Because he is so helpful to me in teaching the young ones the ways of the seas and the rules as well, I miss him so."

The queen could see that she was upset and concerned and told Neptuna what had happened to her daughter and how Seequest gave up his life to save his best friend.

Neptuna's heart was broken and she was angry and said, 'do not worry.

"With father's strength and army, I am sure we will be able to get Seequest back, right?" Queen Sera said, "that's our plan my dear but it is not as simple as it seems" with hesitation in her voice.

"Has we would be fighting against the second most powerful god on this earth, Hades himself"

"I loved him like a brother and friend once and I know you did too."

"But sometimes we have to protect our own flesh and blood first and sacrifice the ones we love as well."

The queen replied, "I do not like it either but it is out of my hands as Neptune's away on business at the Great Olympus with Zeus himself and does not know about this update properly yet".

"I am trying to carry on normally and check on how the sea creatures are doing of keeping the waters clean and at peace."

Neptuna ignored the question and shouted out, "I do not care who his with!"

"We will not leave him to rot in the company of Hades."

The queen was very cross with the way that Neptuna had spoken and then said "Neptuna I will ask you again and this time you better answer politely or I will feed you to the sharks."

She shuddered and then said "yes sorry your highness, everything is good."

She then turned and swims away further into the ocean moving her tail side to side as she went thinking that she was done.

The queen was annoyed and flagged her reins to the dolphins whom then swam back to the palace as quickly as they could go.

But on the way, they caught up with Neptuna.

She turned and saw the dolphins nudging her for attention and the queen said "come with me I have something to show you",

Also feeling that Neptuna was right and that if she had the chance she would free Seequest herself but she thought "how could it be possible?"

They reached the palace gates where now Neptuna was riding with the queen and she said to the guards "she is with me it's ok let me pass."

The guards bowed to their queen and opened the grand golden gates to Vissen instantly bowing their heads as she went through.

Neptuna was confused and said "why are we coming here?"

"Wait dear friend be patient and I will show you, come to the stables with me."

They both swam off the chariot and released the dolphins to be free to swim back to their patch where they have extra protection and food waiting for them instead of hunting for it.

They arrived at the stables so great and true and went past quickly to the sea horses, while Queen Sera went and saw Sea Spray and said, "Come girl you're going to see your child."

The hippocampus gets all excited and swayed up and down in her stall.

The queen put on her sea cotton bridle covered in silver and her pretty shell saddle and rode through the grounds where she saw Neptuna waiting for her she said "climb on."

Neptuna did and held tight as they swam further into a dark blue shade of water.

The queen said "put this mask on your face, as where I am taking you has these waters that you have probably never breathed straight away without the help of Neptune himself."

"OK", she said and put on the mask.

The queen replied, "I am going to take you on a journey to a pretty place called Scotland and the most important part is where we're going is the Loch where I have one of Sea-Spray's and Tidal Wave's children living there as she is different from the others."

"Now before we approach there you must promise me that you will not tell another soul or fish about her".

"Otherwise you will put her in danger and us too as she is an incredible beast of her own kind".

"But I can guarantee that she is the family of the original hippocampus before her."

Neptuna forgot about poor Seequest and wanted to meet this new incredible creature that was born in secret until now.

"I promise with all my heart, your highness".

"Good, then that's that".

"Sea Spray, take us to the Loch and let's go and see your child Kessy."

Within that Sea-Spray was also excited again and neighed making bubbles as she did they rushed through the beautiful waters as fast as she could carry them.

They reached the dark porthole, which they swam into and it took them through to another side of the world to Scotland.

Kessy hears her mother's neigh as and starts to swim towards them.

Dolphin child swims up to the surface and looks out at the Loch when the queen mentions "it's beautiful, isn't it??"

Neptuna has only known and seen the ocean, never a large lake bigger enough to be called a loch before, which contains not seawater that she knew and loved but kindly called fresh water instead, where salmon lived.

"Wow", she said, still wearing her delicate refined mask on her face to help her breathe these waters.

But the queen was lucky, as her husband gave her the gift to swim and breathe all the waters of the land for her work and for giving him her heart.

As they swam closer to the land, Sea Spray neighed louder and out from nowhere came to her amazing water horse child Kessy.

She was a different kind of water horse than you could ever imagine, as she looked more like a sea dragon than a water horse or a hippocampus as known in the sea.

But in fresh waters, they are known as water horses instead, as that is what the queen decided to call her type of species so far.

But she is still a hippocampus/sea horse by blood.

The queen and Neptuna knew that Kessy was another new generation of sea horse once again but she was called a water horse, as she lived in fresh water instead of the sea.

"Why is she here, Your Highness?"

"She's here to protect the land and the Loch and because she is too large to live in our seas, as she's ten times bigger than our greatest creature, the blue whale."

Originally, this is also where Seequest and the other unicorns in their time were also created and born.

Wow, there have been more mysteries of mine that have been solved in one day she thought to herself.

"What is her name?"

"My daughter, named her Kessy as she's beautiful and yet strange as well compared to her brothers and sisters.

Yet, we still love her all the same".

"But why did Helena name her Kessy, because of her kind heart and sweet temperament as she is a mixture of hippocampus you know?"

Neptuna looked directly at this grand beast and totally agreed with what her queen had just said about her and replied back.

"She is so pretty and yet messy has a different type of water horse to the others" and yet perfect in her own way as well.

"Kessy was a perfect name as we thought for her at the time as my dear Helena had met her recently."

First she appeared with just her long neck sticking out of the water to say hello.

The first glance of this amazing creature was a slim-shaped face like a hippocampus with an enormous body with four flapper-type feet with a long tail.

She also had a long fin that was from the back of her head to the bottom of her tail which makes her swim in the strong waves.

If need to she also can swim like lightning and can be missed as she becomes invisible.

Her colouring changes because of where she is or where she wants to be as she could camouflage herself which her brothers and sisters cannot do.

They spent a great time with her and they gave her space to spend some time with her mother as well.

They all enjoyed everyone's company in the sunshine jumping in and out of the water.

But the queen could see that the mask of Neptuna's was starting to fade and said "come on its home time now" where they said their goodbyes to Kessy.

She kissed the queen and her mother Sea Spray and then dived deep into the Loch once more.

"Bye sweet girl until next time."

"Be safe, you hear?"

Kessy put her head out of the water miles away from where they were and she turned her head and nodded and neighed loudly like hippocampus does and then swam further away in the distance.

Neptuna said "wow she is great."

"Yes", the queen said 'she is and she's one of Sea Spray and Tidal Wave's children.

"Wow, there is more 'yes".

She said "but you must promise me not to tell as they are my surprise to your father and also the god of the sea."

But Kessy is unique as you had seen for yourself today.

The queen did not know that Neptuna was telepathic until she said "aww, Kessy is talking to me" and felt love and kindness in her soft warm voice.

Neptuna's eyes lit up at this time.

She felt like she had now a sea dragon friend for life. She felt so happy that she jumped out of the water over and over again.

Further in the distance, she could see that Kessy was doing the same but forgot her size and caused the Loch to be affected and water was going everywhere.

They quickly had to stop.

Now, the queen said, "It is time to go home" and they jumped back onto Sea Spray who dive deep back into the portal where they swam through until they reached Greece once more and the ocean.

Even though Neptuna loved being with Kessy, she was glad to be home where she could be her true self again and knocked off the mask as she turned into a pretty lilac-blue dolphin and swam further into the deeper parts of the ocean.

As the queen was approaching back to the stables, she was thinking of Kessy and how she had grown and changed again so quickly.

As of now, she had amazing different shades of green, with still her aqua-blue eyes and light blue fin with a touch of this colour on her feet as well her scaly skin when she is out of the water for long periods of time too.

For a while when the suns on her face and neck her scales start to harden as if it may be possible that she could possibly be able to live on land as well in time?.

So, is she becoming a sea dragon after all the queen thought carefully?

The queen loved her mystical water and sea horses/ hippocampius and yet also loved the research involved.

She could not wait to get back to the library and write this information down and then log it in the Temple of the Crystal Skulls in her Book of Wisdom and Knowledge as this information will be their history maybe their evolution too. She thought.

As the queen was resting later that night in her quarters she wondered what other abilities does Kessy have and what other things could the sea horses possibly do too?

Chapter Twenty-One

Seequest's Planned Rescue?

Back at Hades cave, Seequest was now put into an invisible vortex and Knightmare wanted nothing to do with him anymore, as she believed that he tried to kill her and his offspring, which was not the case.

But through Seequest's eyes it looked like she believes more in her master now as he saved her children from death or that is what he wanted her to see.

Poor Seequest was not only heartbroken weak and defeated.

But what made it worse was that he felt that he had lost his son's trust and faith in him as well.

Because he was told that his father stood there and watched them drowning been close to dying and he did nothing to try and save them both.

So Knight did not believe in the great Unicorn King anymore.

But Firefly still feels a strong connection with her father as she could telepathically talk to him sometimes when everyone else was asleep this took a lot out of them both.

"My daughter, how are you and the others?"

"I am fine, Father but the others believe that you were trying to kill us, that's why you took us to the mountain."

"No, *no*, that's not true I love you; your mother and brother very much."

"I was just trying to teach you the way like my mother did but I guess I was wrong, as I forgot that you may not produce the sea qualities like I do, sorry!"

"I guess I took the chance to see if you did or did not, which was very wrong of me to have done that to you all."

"From what I saw that day I guess you both do not want to know or see me anymore or trust me either, so I am sorry."

"I should have known better than to risk your lives like that" speaking from his heart that he was truly upset.

"I know now that Hades has played me all this time, as yet I fell deeply in love with your mother."

"I have never done that before with any mare and yet I enjoyed it so much that it blurred my judgement on everything."

"I will never let that happen ever again because I put down my guard which I should of not have ever done".

"Now I have lost everything to this cruel man of a god", Seequest holding his head down in shame and disheartenment.

"Father, please do not beat yourself up."

I understand why you did it but I don't understand, if Hades is so nice to us, why is he so nasty to you now?'

Seequest told his daughter everything and she started to understand what was going on, when she replied to him.

"Fear not, Father, I know that Knight and Mother love you very much."

Or she hoped they did?

But she does not get the opportunity to speak to them properly now for a while because of Knight's intense training with Hades now a days.

"But just maybe they are under a spell as I cannot be sure."

"But she said "I will watch; listen and learn when I am with them and let you know what is going on in future, if that helps?"

Until then, please hold on, I love you Father very much."

" I love you to my child".

"Sleep now and thank you."

Firefly answered "Goodnight Father, I hope to see you very soon."

Seequest lay down with his muzzle touching the floor and felt like his powers were fading quicker than before, as when he sleeps that is when Hades takes his power away as he wakes up later drained from his body, which is making him so weak now.

Because Seequest is falling into a deep depression and his beautiful horn will not light up anymore.

He slept feeling weaker than he had ever.

But I guess feeling heartbroken, unloved and defeated would explain the reason for this, he thought to himself.

Winter had come when Seequest was stuck in this invisible vortex that Hades had made up for him to live in again.

Making him feel that he was still lying next to his family as he can see them and yet he could not feel their love and warmth from their loving energies anymore.

Has they cannot see him or touch him.

This was Hades worst thing he had ever done so far to him that pained him deeply.

Every day Seequest was becoming weaker and weaker as the force was being drained out of his body and also through the great grief his experienced recently as well.

The magic was flowing into Knight instead.

But he did not know or feel this yet.

The vortex was made because Hades could not take the horn away from Seequest; otherwise he would die and his magic would also.

So, he needed him to stay alive and thought of his way of getting Seequest's powers instead, Hades was quite pleased with his great idea!

With Hades genius plan to keep Seequest alive and yet still retrieve his powers at the same time, Hades knew for once that he nearly had the power of the great Unicorn king and of Earth in his hands at last.

That day Hades went and visited his mare and her children when he said to her 'look my dear girl, if he loved you he would have never gone away'.

Has Hades told Knightmare that he let Seequest go free back to the sea and agreed to leave them behind to save himself to poison her mind with hate?

So Hades got what he needed from him after all!

But this was not true.

Poor Seequest was right beside her and yet she never knew or saw nothing of this.

Hades would smile right at him when he said this to her, which made Seequest feel like the smallest creature alive and the saddest one too.

Hades looked and knew that he was winning by starting to laugh as he walked away with his faithful companion Cerberus by his side.

Seequest heard his mare say these sad words due to anger and pain of loss that she was feeling at the time.

Knightmare says to Knight "that he only loved himself and used her to get to them".

Which dragged him down even more as his son was speaking badly about him as well.

Knight replied back, "See I told you Mother that Hades was right that Father wanted all the power for himself still and that he did not care about us at all."

This made Knight's blood boil and so his black shinny coat now started to create red veins appearing through his skin due to his anger and pain of hurt and disappointment of the great unicorn king, his father.

Knight had been poisoned and turned by this god of the underworld.

Firefly would try and change their minds but she had to be careful, as the hate started to become nasty at times and she too had to protect herself from them as well.

So, she then decided to play along for a while.

Firefly could also feel the presence of her father near her and yet could not see him properly in a normal form.

But due to their connection of energy and magic, she could see his aura of great colourful light nearby.

Firefly at that time felt lucky that she was blessed more with his genes than her mother's as she had his telepathic powers to talk to him still which also helped him pull through in this time of sorrow.

She keeps to talking to him in his mind while resting and sending him a green and pink energy healing his way to comfort him and also help him to believe that his family loves him very much still.

Even though Hades seemed to have Knight and her mother under his spell of his dark magic!

The great almighty king of unicorns knew that his time was going to end soon.

But he knew that his daughter would carry on his ways of peace throughout the land somehow, he hoped.

He started to remember the memories of being young himself and spending time with his mother, who taught him to never give up until he knew that there was no other way, which made him come to his senses a little at last.

Because he remembered all her battles and adventures she faced and won in her lifetime and now became an icon in their time!

This made him feel that there was still hope and faith there in his heart, before he closed his eyes and thought he would use the last piece of energy he had in trying to contact Neptune telepathically.

By sending him a message asking for his help and maybe others from the heavens too, meaning his parents Legend and Celestial from afar.

As heavenly Celestial used to be his mother before she died and became something even more powerful than before.

Has a thank you from Zeus to her for looking after the world and the animals on it with great love in her heart for every living being, in all forms and protecting them too when needed from the Hades sabre tooth tigers in the past.

She's also called the queen of the heavens for animals and humans one day in the near future too.

Seequest tried and tried with all his might but the force field was to strong than he was for the telepathic waves to break through at a long distance.

But the old unicorn knew not to give up, until he stood pointing his horn above and then collapsed to the ground with a thud of exhaustion through this he falls into a deep sleep for a long time.

Meanwhile in Vissen, Neptune was thinking how he could rescue his dear friend from his nemesis brother.

Because he knew everything about what happened since he had been away and felt terribly guilty.

Deep down Neptune knows that he should have stopped him and his daughter, Helena going back to land, knowing that Hades always wanted Seequest's horn for many years now!

Neptune knew that his brother would never give up that easily on something that he really wanted for himself especially involving great power to rule the world his way.

Neptune was sitting down on his throne thinking hard that he needs his brother Zeus help.

Maybe even others to beat Hades for good and send him back to the underworld forever, where he belongs.

Hades felt more powerful than ever before, as he collects waves of Seequest's energy through his staff has he puts it onto the old king's horn while his asleep.

The underworld king could see that Seequest was starting to drain so much that he was afraid that he was going to die.

Instead of that happening again he would play another trick on him and let him feel that he was getting up and spending time with his family and everything was forgiven, where he makes up an illusion of thi, while Seequest was originally still in deep sleep.

So, in the unicorn's mind he felt that his dreams were now real and that he could see and do anything like before. But really it was his imagination playing tricks on him as his still lying there helpless in the vortex.

Hades said to Cerberus, "this will help him feel that he is loved and will keep him alive in my grasp forever."

Laughing loudly as if he had won the battle at last!

The old unicorn, while lying there, also had an extra special power that was blocking Hades magic.

Like his telepathic energy and memories away from harm's way.

This was annoying, as Hades hated that very much because that was where the most powerful secrets lay.

Seequest was doing his best to keep them locked away.

Due to them been special memories/ powers were only meant to be used for the greater good.

He tried as much as he could to keep them protected at all times.

He did this by using pure white light which was pro-tecting this special bubble in his mind.

Days had passed Seequest could feel that his time was running out.

He felt that though he was terribly exhausted, he would not be beaten.

Yet he felt that he could not hang on much longer and felt for the first time that in his magical life that he could at last be beaten once and for all.

Hades could see the pain that Seequest was in and that in his mind, he was fighting his own battle.

This made Hades smile and salute to him with victory in his eyes.

Seequest was after all the Unicorn King and knew Hades tricks of the trade and was playing him at his own game, as he would never give up the fight, well not yet anyway!

Chapter Twenty-Two

Pegasus Returns to Olympus Again with Sad News from Afar

After being contacted by Luna the goddess of the moon herself, she then looks to the moonstone crystal and speaks through it to Pegasus while he was back in his kingdom of Andromeda in the eighth dimension.

She told him everything referring to what had happened recently and that he must now go and update Zeus and also contact Celestial and Legend.

They are going to need everyone's help to defeat Hades this time.

Pegasus understood and thanked the goddess for the sad and concerning news and was not looking forward to passing this on to Zeus himself.

But he guessed after all, he is the god of winged horses and unicorns as well, so this involves him highly, has it's his duty as the great godfather to them.

Pegasus then understood why she came to him directly and not Zeus himself, for he had great respect for Luna.

He told the other winged horses that he had to leave and fly to Olympus to see Zeus once more on important business, which can affect them all.

He walked to the crystal-clear pebble pathway that took him to other dimensions and told the guardian, who was a large tiger of white fur and golden stripes with crystal eyes whom he saved.

He was unique to Hades' saber-toothed tigers.

As Hades planned to kill the cub; instead Pegasus took him and raised him as his own.

Now he is the great guardian of great powers to the eighth dimension of the winged horses of the Andromeda star.

Pegasus named him Sabre from where he originated from and classed him as his son.

"My son, I must fly to the fifth dimension of Earth and go to Greece to visit our mighty god Zeus."

"Guard with all your life my herd and make sure that no one leaves till I get back."

"I have spoken to the stallions and mares, so expect them to respect my wishes I will be back in a week."

"Yes, Father, oh, mighty one, I shall do as you command me."

"Please be safe", Sabre said and bowed to Pegasus as he galloped towards the pathway.

Pegasus said his goodbyes and started to flap those golden and white huge angel wings as fast as he could until they made a windstorm.

As he galloped across the diamond pathway it began to change into a rose quartz pebbled path that lit up in the most amazing pretty shades of love and wisdom.

He knew that as he was galloping and moving his wings up and down, eventually the path would disappear before him.

He had to fly very fast indeed to make sure that he had enough strength and balance to fly into space.

As he flew closer to the Earth's dimension he saw the sun and then knew to his knowledge that was close to Earth.

He looked like a sparkling, shining star from a distance.

It took Pegasus three days to get there.

So, when he did, he landed in the same place where it all started before in Scotland all those years ago because no one would expect him to be there on earth ever.

Pegasus landed gracefully in the dark of the night quietly to this golden field of corn where the crystal heart was used in the past.

At this time his beautiful crystal eyes lit the night sky in the area of the field where he first needed to rest from his long tiresome flight from his home above to next Greece.

Later he ate the golden corn which to him tasted like the ambrosia rice he had at home thanks to the magic that Zeus gave as a gift for all his hard work in the past.

He decided after that to drink from the stream.

He plucked out one of his small feathers and dropped it into it and it changed colour to sweet pink nectar and he drank it until he felt full.

Luckily, this magic feather only works for thirty minutes so it would not hurt or harm a living creature of any kind.

Once he laid down, he started to remember the memories of how his great creation of unicorns became and neighed as respect now to the dead.

Because their souls to were killed by Hades' saber-toothed tigers trying to find the stallion and his mare of this actual herd.

They had the full power of all the unicorns put together when Hades had come to know this and wanted it all for himself.

By not caring about the way he would get it either.

So many beautiful unicorns died to keep this secret from him until he finds the last of their kind, the night unicorn Jecco and Moonbeam, Seequest's parents.

He would do anything to retrieve this magic!

Thankfully all the unicorn horns magically disappeared after they died and yet live in the atmosphere of earth, which Hades could not retrieve from as it's now in the Air, Water and Lands.

That's why some of us can feel their magic and energy nowadays as it is still around us every day of our lives showing us the beauty of nature; kindness and love for all creatures and earth herself.

Hades wanted the night unicorn mare as she was carrying this special foal, as she was the last of their kind.

As many years before Pegasus told the unicorns that there will be born a powerful one of their kind who will carry all their powers of them all put together.

Not even did he know which type of unicorn mare would carry it.

Hades planned to kill them all and have the power for himself to rein earth the way that he thought it should be in pain and anguish.

So, he instructed his saber tooth tigers to kill all of them as this powerful foal was a fret to his life and domain of terror.

Hades wanted his revenge this time as before Zeus told him to leave them alone.

The sun rose above the British Isles Sea and that is when Pegasus knew it was time to continue his flight to Greece.

He walked around and visited the forest animals and Truth's image in the silver birch tree by paying his respects before leaving England for a while.

That night was another full moon where goddess Luna was watching from afar.

She began talking to him before he said his goodbyes and galloped towards Moonbeams Mountain where he will continue his journey.

As he climbed the highest mountain where Seequest went recently with his family and jumped off into flight towards Olympus in the dark where he would not be seen by Hades' guardians possibly.

It took him nearly another two days to reach Greece as flying only at night.

Eventually, he saw the great mountain up ahead and swirled to the right and landed into what looked like a massive volcano, which is an illusion of protection for them all.

He was beginning to land so elegantly into the flying quarters as he approached the open way of the golden path.

Pegasus was still flapping his wings as he entered the pathway to land, where he was trying to slow down and stop completely having his feet on the ground again.

Once his wings stopped and it was safe, Hermes was waiting to greet him with a great hug and welcome him back home.

In return, he pushed his head into Hermes's shoulders, as if they were like brothers.

He then told Hermes that he must see Zeus urgently.

Hermes said ok and he nodded his head up and down with his beautiful, long white mane flying everywhere as he did.

His eyes had changed to brown so he could also see properly in the everyday light as only daytime shone there due to Apollo controlling the sun.

Pegasus had now folded his wings to his body and walked to Zeus's palace.

The large, great golden doors opened, and there sitting at the back of the room with the sun shining brightly on him was his old friend Zeus, the king of the Greek gods.

Zeus saw Pegasus and stood up with great excitement and said, "My dear friend welcome home. But can I ask why I have the privilege of your presence today?"

Pegasus bowed his head and tucked his right front leg under his chest and pulled down his left leg out towards the front where he then put his head down to his chest, bowing to Zeus.

'My king and old friend I wish I came with some great news but this time it's urgent that I speak with you alone and now please.'

Zeus stood up and could see that Pegasus looked worried and asked everyone to leave the room even his guards and they spoke for hours.

Pegasus said "I feel guilty and feel that I am partly to blame for what has happened to Seequest."

"As I was sending a blessing to Neptune's daughter for her birthday"

"Plus, a blessing of your great brother Neptune himself that she could be a Pisces form to experience what it's like to live on land instead of the sea all the time," he said.

Pisces was close to being a human form and part mermaid as she wanted to feel what it was to live on land for twenty-four hours and yet still be a mermaid as well.

"Ok carry on!" with great interest in his facial expressions as he listened on.

"Well, things got out of hand, as Hades realized this too."

Had his spies everywhere and been watching closely.

"That he decides to shape shift into a large black fox and kidnaps the princess so then Seequest has to go back and rescue her".

"The unicorn king then agreed with Hades that if he sets Helena free he will stay and impregnate his mare through magic!"

"As Seequest decided that he needed to protect her and the earth first as otherwise, he was putting her life and earth as we know it of great love in great danger".

"Because he felt guilty due to how she was kidnapped in the first place as he was asleep instead of guarding her".

"But he also trusted her to not go and stray away from him or the area"

"Where she's not to blame either because of her interest of new things like us all, she would have been fine if Hades did not see her and find out that she was there?

"First his idea was to capture her as bait temporary and yet she was so beautiful, he decided that he wanted to keep her as his queen too.

"So Seequest knew his fate and gave his life to save hers and earth as well!

"That is why Hades did it as he always wanted Seequest's powers to rule Earth which is his powerful horn of destiny".

"As these powers do not only have yours and mine but also holds the powers of the sea too now".

"That means with Hades' power as well which is the energy of fire".

"Hades will have the magic of the four elements of life".

"Hades knew if he got this power he then would be able to rule the world and even possibly beat you!"

"Nonsense", Zeus replied and spoke with great anger in his voice and told Pegasus to carry on.

"Well, Hades has a demon mare called Knightmare where he thought it would be genius that instead of killing Seequest."

He would get him to impregnate her by magic, which she then will have a foal that will have all the powers like him and he will able to control it one day.

"Where then, Seequest will be no more" with a concerned tone in his voice.

"The worst of it is that Seequest fell in love with her which was his mistake has now been trapped forever, as they have two foals which again are unique creatures to this world and very special and powerful indeed!"

Pegasus put his face down to the ground in embarrassment knowing that he was partly to blame for what had happened to them all.

He was hoping that Zeus can forgive him in time.

Zeus stood up boldly and said "what do mean exactly?"

Now the great god has his lightning bolt staff and banged it hard on the gold floor where it started to spark.

Zeus had this power of fire and yet the full magic that his brother Hades needed to control the underworld.

Zeus's powers were mainly focused by the air energy, which he gives the power to make creatures breathe.

Pegasus was now worried that this was his punishment and tried to speak as boldly and clearly as possible for Zeus to hear.

Because Pegasus thought that due to Zeus being angry he would use his lighting staff on him as punishment.

Pegasus carried on begging the great god for forgiveness along the way as he spoke on.

Pegasus replied, 'well the young filly has wings of an angel like me and she also has a horn of her father too so she is a winged unicorn.

"But my king of great power her brother is even worse!

Because he has bat wings and claws like his mother and a horn as well".

"And you know as much as I if they get into the wrong hands they could destroy Earth and possibly our dimensions as well."

Zeus looked concerned and started to think hard about how he could stop Hades from ever having this opportunity.

Pegasus then finishes off this speech before Zeus replies letting him know his feelings towards this disaster now.

"Because we don't know at the moment what-other powers they possess yet Oh mighty one."

Zeus was so angry and disappointed in Pegasus and said "how is it possible that this happened?"

The great mystical horse god looked back up at Zeus in his eyes and said "I do not know".

"But I know now that we must rescue Seequest and see if we can also capture his children before it is too late."

Zeus agreed and yet surprised Pegasus with his answer "no" this is not possible.

'I am sorry, my king, but it is true.'

'Oh, for heaven's sake, so as you said before that it's my brother Hades doing?'

'Yes, it is, Zeus.

"I am so sorry that I have unpleasant news for you."

"These foals first started as normal and now they are one year's old, which in magic years to us is two."

So, their other powers are starting to come in?

The mighty god said "and who told you all of this?"

The winged horse replied gently as he could with his answer.

Pegasus then said "The great goddess Luna herself, sister to Gaia, Mother Earth.

Who was told by her daughter Queen Sera of the sea, Helena's mother your highness".

Zeus replied boldly "OK, then it must be true, as Luna's daughter Queen Sera lives within the oceans of the deep where Seequest become their guardian as a hippocampus."

"My king, what I fear is what if the filly and colt have the power of the sea too?"

"They will be more powerful than Seequest because that means they would have not only the three powers of good but also the fourth which is the power of darkness that Hades processes".

"As you know as much as I do that fire energy is used for good and is a great help to us all".

But if used for bad then that means they have all four powers of the crystal heart, which then could destroy us all!'

Zeus then says "Yes, I see what you are saying then we must put a stop to it quickly.

You must go back to where Seequest was last seen and disguise yourself as a horse and find out from his forest friends if they have seen or heard about them anymore.

When you have received this information come back and tell me what you know and in the meantime, I will start making up a plan for how we can defeat my brother for good."

"Yes, my lord, of course" when he bowed his head and trotted back to the flying quarters and stood on the path, which rose to the top and the volcano.

He leaped off gracefully and flew back towards the forest to the silver birch tree where Truth's the earth unicorn's head his form was now resting in.

Eventually, he landed once again quietly at night and spoke to Truth's image in the tree.

Once more seeking spiritual guidance eventually he received a sign that he felt from the ground that went into his body that may help them all.

He said thank you dear one "I hope that you are at peace with the Earth now".

Within that red ripe apples appeared on the tree and fell in front of him.

He felt they were a gift from Truth himself which made him feel good that he was ok and not alone as he thought.

They also would be a great help to re-energize his strength and power quickly due to true pure sugar in them and juices as well to clinch his thirst.

The horse god put his muzzle on Truth's wooden image of his head and felt a warm loving touch inside.

He knew then that Truth's essence (the presence of the original magic) was living in the tree and the ground around him.

He looked about him carefully before he changed into an Andalusian stallion.

He said this verse and his wings turned invisible which now made him look like a normal horse where he then shrunk into a smaller size as well.

Has Pegasus been enormous to our elephants today?

"Right," he said. "Now to find the horses first and then the forest animals to find out they may know."

He wondered as he walked towards Paradise where the herds were living now.

This mighty powerful elegant pure white god of a stallion galloped up and saw Seequest's granddaughter Honour, who was taken by surprise.

When he ask her if she had seen the unicorn king at all?

Honor could not help it but she grew a liking towards him as he spoke.

Has he had a graceful and powerful essence about him?

But he then told her he was the great Pegasus in disguise, when she heard this she put her head to the floor feeling embarrassed about her feelings towards him earlier.

She then says to Pegasus that she saw him before it all happened and that is all she knew about him.

That Helena went off for a walk with the forest animals when a fox took her Seequest had to rescue her and by doing this he gave himself up to Hades instead.

She then also advises him to speak to his forest friends as they saw him last.

Honor only repeated what he already knew.

She said that she knew that Seequest was going to see the wolves and his forest friends whom he grew up with when his mother passed.

"Thank you, dear one, for your help" and the stunning white stallion galloped away to the forbidden forest where Seequest and Helena were last seen together.

He reached the forest in no time where the wolves were the first to approach him.

They noticed an unusual and powerful scent that he seemed more than just a horse this made the Wolves cautious because of Hade's spies.

They jumped on Pegasus and he was defending himself and bucking them off and kicking them with his back legs neighing with great courage as he did.

This was starting to make him angry when his wings became visible and grew twice his size and said "back off unless you want me to kill you".

"Where is your pack leader?"

The wolves were snarling and feeling scared and yet protecting themselves.

"Who are you first then we will tell you."

"I am the great god-winged horse Pegasus, now, where is your alpha?"

"I must talk with him urgently".

"It's important as it involves the Unicorn King, Seequest".

After that, the wolves became quiet and said "oh" when the large white alpha wolf approached.

"I am here".

"What do you know about our friend, oh, great one?"

"Well, what could you tell me, as we are planning to rescue him from Hades soon?"

"Ok well, you better come with me."

They followed Pegasus and the white wolf and he was told the updated news that Pegasus needed to know.

Pegasus said "thank you 'I will be back but for now, I must go back to Olympus with this updated news" and thanked the wolves again.

He started to flap his large angel white feathered wings and leaped right into the air a thousand miles away from the land back to see Zeus once more.

Pegasus knew now that this would be a great battle.

He was hoping it would never happen and yet now realized it was real!

Pegasus reached again Olympus in an hour and went and spoke with Zeus once more.

This time, Pegasus was flying straight into the gardens as he got closer to the ground.

He put his two front legs forward to support his speed and put his back ones on the ground deep acting like brakes to stop him.

As he did quickly he slowed down his wings, too eventually they stopped as he folded them straight beside his body.

He walks over to where Zeus was in the Garden of Eden.

There Pegasus was with his stunning pure white coat glistening like diamonds in the light and his amazing large angel feathered wings.

He walks towards the Garden of Eden and folds them into his masculine and powerful yet elegant body as he approaches the great Zeus while his feeding his beautiful birds.

He walks into where Zeus was in the Garden of Eden creating more living animals and testing their weaknesses and strengths before he agrees that there ready to live on earth properly.

Now he reached Zeus sitting down peacefully listening to his birds.

"Oh, you're back, dear friend please tell me the news of what you have found out."

"I have come with some good news that Seequest is still alive and yet his trapped in an invisible vortex next to this family."

"Which he cannot see or touch them anymore".

"As this is breaking his heart and also through this vortex Hades is sharing his power from his horn with his son Knight and himself while Seequest is in a deep sleep, now believing that everything is good with his family once more."

"But it's all an illusion to keep Seequest from dying of a broken heart as he fell in love for the first time with Hades' mare".

"Hades plans to destroy him in another way".

"He seems to have planned this by making it look like Seequest was trying to kill his children".

"When all he was originally doing was teaching his children how to fly and how to use their powers properly".

"Now it seems that Hades has the hand of becoming invincible!"

Zeus was thrilled to know that Seequest was alive but annoyed too by what had happened and became so mad that he was planning to kill them all at first!

But then he decided to change his mind after Pegasus pleaded with him not to go ahead with it.

For hours they spoke again about a plan that Zeus came up with that might work.

"OK, you know what we need to do".

Zeus said with his heavenly and yet firm voice of goodness.

Pegasus answered once again and then flew away toward the sixth dimension of heaven.

Where Celestial and Legend are the guardians of the spirits of animals and eventually in time us humans.

He flew for thousands of miles and wondered how he and his parents could rescue his godson and wondered if it was too late to save him.

As the winged god was flying towards the heavens to meet Celestial and Legend.

He flew past so many universes to reach the sixth dimension and flew by the beautiful planet Venus she is shining in all her glory that it lights up the skies in the day.

He then saw the stunning silver planet and its silver gates with the enormous Great Danes of golden colour guarding them of heaven itself.

"Woof, woof, who goes there?" in a heavy tone of bark.

"I am Pegasus, the god of winged horses."

The dogs bowed and replied, "sorry your grace, and opened up the gates to a silver glittery pathway with soft clouds of mystery.

He walked in and at first he could not see anything until he reached again another gate, which this time was, a stunning golden gate.

The gate opened and he saw a beautiful land of different shades of green and pretty colourful birds peacefully flying by him, singing as they did.

There were horses from the past galloping around all together having complete fun.

As he trotted further into the land, he came to another gate of diamond this time, which sparkled so bright and where Celestial and Legend's home is.

As the gate opened their images appeared on them on each side.

The gates closed as he totted in gracefully seeing these heavenly horses standing there together as a perfect companionship like they once were on Earth.

The only difference was they were both winged horses with no horns that had special duties to do here that need to always be completed, as death is a never-ending circle and yet creating lives as well of good souls to possibly go back at later date?

They do decide if the soul goes back as the same image or different one from its previous life.

As the soul image returns it learns from its mistakes and conquerors them or even helps if needed to teach others too.

Because they would send the spirit of a star that will then emerge into the body of the creature which was chosen to come to Earth.

And its mother will teach it all that it needs to know on how to survive and its future duties plus the rules of life as well.

This is how the personality and character of the creature is being born when Zeus chooses its soul from the planets above like Sirius; Venus; Jupiter or Mars.

That is why we humans of today have also planets that we are connected to in our star signs and birthdays too.

They send the star to the body of the creature to earth for its mother and that is how the personality and character of the creature is being born.

Pegasus neighed and jumped a little with his front legs and swung open his wings which started to flap gently showing that he was pleased to see them.

Has he walked into the mystical horse's kingdom and the statues around them?

They did the same thing back to him in respect and yet even though it was lovely to see him, they both wondered why he was there?

But quickly sensed something had happened on earth or to Seequest.

They just hoped it was the earth that needed their help.

Legend was the first to speak.

"Oh, Grandfather what brings you here to heaven?"

"My children it is great to see you".

But it is not a social visit.

It is one of great importance and refers to your past son, Seequest.

I am sorry to say it is business, as I need your help badly.'

Celestial said, "Yes, what can we do?"

They all approached each other and nuzzled together with respect on their necks.

Then the black star mare answered "has it got something to do with our son Seequest?"

"Is he in trouble again? How do you know this, Celestial?" Pegasus asked.

"Well, I once was his mother and I still watch him at times from the Pool of Destiny I feel like he's trying to communicate with me somehow?"

The great Pegasus replied, "Yes, you are right, my dear queen."

"I am sorry I could not help him this time I believe you know it too."

That it will be his end on Earth if we do not rescue him soon?"

Legend then spoke up and said, "It's impossible."

"How is he in danger?"

"I thought that he decided to stay away from land and become a hippocampus and live out his life there in the sea".

"Where he then kindly gave what magic was left in the world to Mother Nature?"

"Who is the daughter of Zeus and Lady Gaia also having the spirit of Truth in her too, due to his ashes?"

Once again, Pegasus said, "Well after you both left, magic started to die off slowly as we know it anyway".

Seequest felt that he did not belong anywhere anymore because he was different from his new progeny of horses.

Seequest was larger than them and had a horn growing from his forehead, which made the other horses frightened of him in case he accidentally hurt them or bred with them even though he knew not to.

The rules of his kind will have magic in them still from us in other ways in time. Celestial answered back to Pegasus and Legend, "You're right!"

"He spoke to Neptune to see if he would agree on a wager that he stayed in the sea for life and help with the Mer prince and princesses' duties and be their guardian".

"And in return, Neptune will be given his horn as a gift to help protect the oceans and create other great things in the future and then became the god of horses himself"

"That Neptune will take over the title of creator of the future horses as his horn helped create the new species of hippocampus's (sea-horses)"

"Which are still even a secret to Neptune himself as we speak!"

Before the heavenly horses could do anything else, Pegasus then shouted out "the real reason why I am here is that we have another great problem"

"Seequest has been captured by Hades by luring him into falling in love with his demon mare Knightmare!"

You would not have thought that this was the great winged horse god speaking as he was very upset and showed his emotions deeply at this time.

After all, they still had feelings especially Love and Kindness for all.

Hades encouraged him to use his magic on her and by doing that they created your grandchildren Knight and Firefly.

But the problem is that they are all living with Hades now!

"Oh, my dear boy", Legend said.

Celestial replies "what have we done?" she said, her eyes weeping.

Pegasus replied and said, "no, your highness you could have not done anything for him or anything different at the time"

"As this must be his destiny now even though he hated saying these words he believed it to true".

"We must collect my winged warrior horses; the gods and goddesses even Zeus himself to see if we can destroy Hades for good!"

"Because now he has the power of the crystal heart of destiny at full power as he has he owns the magic of the flames; land; sky and now the sea too."

Pegasus continues talking and says next "Hades is becoming invincible and could rule Earth in the end if we are not careful!"

"Has for what had done in the past to our unicorns which had improved recently recreating a beautiful and better quality for all living species on this planet".

"After the dinosaurs would become once again destroyed and Zeus's wished to create human creatures in the future will not happen!"

"It is not just Seequest we are worried about but Earth as we know it could be gone as well."

The heavenly horses have never seen their grandfather so concerned like this before.

They then knew this was a serious matter that they had to help solve as quickly as possible for everyone's sake.

"Grandfather where did Knightmare come from originally?"

"Is she one of our horses that were created by our lines?"

"That's why did she die of a broken heart?"

"If this is the case then she could be reborn through Hades' hand once more in his control and then learn more about our ways too."

She expressed great concern for her own family.

Pegasus then explained and said "thankfully Celestial, Knightmare was once Velvet and is one of yours."

"She is from your family tree as she was from one of Truth's late daughters' lines."

Pegasus then carried on the story of Velvet before she became Knightmare to Hades.

They needed to know everything about her so they knew what powers possibly the foals will have in the future.

"They fell in love as she was deserted as one of her own in the past."

"But what she does not know is that Hades took a liking to her and thought that she was too good to be just a horse!"

And through that, he decided to create a devilish beast in return thinking that she was never wanted, poor thing!

"Quietly, he killed the stallion of her herd who was also her mate."

Because of this, she was deserted by her own as they blamed the poor mare for his death because he was protecting her from Hades' saber-toothed tigers which have now disappeared for a while."

"Poor Velvet felt not liked or loved by anyone anymore and eventually accepted that it was her fault that her mate died and so in the end she died of a lonely heart."

"That is when Hades one day saw her there lying still and knew then that she was a true black mare of hate and sadness in her heart already he knew that it would be easy to turn her!"

"Who possibly was created by the ancestors of yourselves when you were Seequest's parents?"

"Hades took her body to his lair before you could reach her and bring her soul back here to rest with her family peacefully again."

"Hades knew she would have a spiritual connection to you and Legend."

"He then realized she will be a powerful mare knowing that you were the night unicorns in the past".

"Hades believed that she too would have a touch of the magic inside her as all the other horses do in some way."

"Has they been once connected to your past selves and others of your kind."

"Hades has been planning this for many years."

"Now as I mentioned earlier Seequest as two beautiful yearlings of his own that he loves very much."

But recently Hades fooled even the great unicorn king and made them all reject him as if he was trying to kill them instead of teaching them to fly.

Both star horses grasp and were shocked by what they heard and looked very sad indeed.

"Hades, quietly, has been draining Seequest's powers for eighteen months."

"Now he's in an invisible vortex in front of them every day with a broken heart and seems to be giving up on life!"

But recently Hades decided that was going to play a trick on him, as he needs him alive to receive his powers.

So, he created this illusion that everything is good again when it is not and Seequest is there lying in a coma.

The great winged god then finishes his story by mentioning this.

"The yearlings seem to be a new species again which I have named winged unicorns as they are of your kind the unicorn and now mine as they have wings too."

They are two completely different types as Firefly seems to be like Seequest and Knight seems to be similar too.

Pegasus's tone of voice becomes very concerned as he carries on to his last sentence.

"But Knight has more of his mother's personality and looks!"

"And that is what we are all afraid of!"

"As Hades is going to give him the powers to destroy earth, he will use him as a weapon of destruction that we have never faced before!"

Pegasus looks relieved that he got the story correct and out in one go, as he walks up two the pair to discuss the plans next on how they can help destroy Hades and save Seequest and his family somehow too.

Legend then looked angrily at Pegasus and said, "That cannot happen!

"What can we do up here?"

"Well, Zeus and I have spoken recently before I was coming to see you both."

"Has we have a plan".

"That might work but we need your help as well to guarantee it too."

"The worst possibility to our plan though is that we may have to kill Knight and also possibly Seequest".

"Because then all the powers will not work anymore and the earth will be saved.

"As you know our powers will not work on earth unless they are alive."

Legend walked boldly up towards Pegasus knowing his grandfather looked upset and he pushed his head up and waved his beautiful black wings up and down.

Legend with great courage and strength in his voice said "we will not give up and we will save our son and our grandchildren too."

"Come, Grandfather, let's have some ambrosia rice and drink some sweet nectar from our beautiful spring water where we can discuss the plans further in great detail."

They all thought hard until they reached the perfect plan that may work, even better than before.

The mystical horses had filled their stomachs which now helped them think hard about how they can achieve this miracle on what exactly they needed to do to make it work in their favour!

They decided to go and gallop around in the Fields of Thought and Peace to see if they could save Knight from becoming this monster and use him in another way in the future.

Because these two creatures were not going to be able to live on earth as their powers in the future will be too strong and dangerous in case they got into the wrong hands which could destroy the planet completely.

Both would have to be monitored always.

Because of their powers, they would have to be taught how to use them for the greater good of all creatures and maybe even humankind centuries later.

But for the present moment, there were more import-ant things to worry about.

Pegasus stayed with them that night discussing these great plans of how they were going to save Seequest the great Unicorn King himself.

Maybe use Knight for another important role if they do not kill him when trying to stop Hades' cruel ways.

Chapter Twenty-Three

Knight Is Trained by Hades Himself

Hades had watched Knight grow beautifully and could see that he had more of his mother's personality than his father's and considered training himself.

Knowing that the young colt began to trust him these days, his father was not in the picture anymore.

Hades had become more and more interested in Knight, as he would ride Knightmare, his mother, with them to gain more trust as they went out more together.

Poor Seequest at this point was still in a deep sleep not knowing what was going on with his family.

While thinking and seeing in his illusion that everything is still ok the way it was before.

But it was the opposite of how things were for real.

One thing that Hades had forgotten is that Firefly had other powers that he did not witness yet, thankfully for her father's sake!

Celestial was aware of what was going on now and knew of her powers, that she could use her telepathic ways within her mind to reach out to the filly to possibly help her father.

Celestial decided to go to the temple of the crystals where she looked through the great Diamond.

It lit up like a ball of pure white and she popped it into the Pool of Destiny to see what her granddaughter would look like seeing if she could trust her because of all Hades' tricks.

She used the diamond crystal that was given to her as a gift to see her son still without him knowing, as a thank you from Zeus for her having to leave him earlier than predicted in her life.

As she was told also that she could not get involved in his life anymore.

But with this it allowed her to just watch him and his family from afar.

But for her, that was enough to go on.

Going back Seequest also used a similar power to hers, which was the crystal heart in the past with Truth to help create their daughters, which is history now.

The Crystal's heart gets its actual main power from the diamond.

This time Celestial prepares it to try and connect to firefly telepathically by using the power crystal again with permission from Pegasus.

Celestial tries calling Firefly to see if she would be able to retrieve a message while she was still sleeping in her stall in Hades' lair

Eventually, she sees her and calls and says "My child, listen to me."

"I am Celestial, queen of the heavens".

"I am also your late grandmother from your father Seequest."

At this moment, Firefly was starting to listen when she opened her eyes quickly and began to panic.

"Be still, my child and listen, as you have been watched by Hades' spies since you were growing up and have been told many lies".

"So just calm down and relax, close your eyes and listen to what I am going to tell you".

"Do not reply or make any strange movements otherwise, the spies would pick up you're telepathic too."

Firefly calmed down as if she had woken from a bad dream and then relaxed once more and closed her eyes again.

Celestial told Firefly that she needed to help her father if she could.

And that help was on its way soon coming from afar.

Firefly opened her eyes again and stood up refreshed and yet shocked and worried for her family.

When everyone was asleep, she believed that her father was near and yet could not see him and yet felt his presence nearby.

She started to move around gently putting her small horn into the air.

Has she did, she then knew if there was any slight light glowing from it, this meant that her father's presence was closer than she thought.

This took days to achieve.

Then one night, she found a spark where it shone for quite a while.

She had to plan how to break the vortex or somehow be able to get through it. But there was no luck.

So, she remembered that when she was little, Seequest used to play a game with their mind knowing that he was teaching her to use her powers properly.

She remembered what he did and hoped now she could do the same to him.

Where she begins to call him from her mind "Father, I know you are near but I cannot see you."

But I can feel your presence around me, I know that you are close and yet I cannot feel your skin near mine.

"I also know that what you are seeing and living is an illusion and that you need to wake up from it now".

"Father we need you and Knight may be in great danger than yourself."

"Please, Father, hear me?"

Days and nights passed when eventually Seequest could feel a strange presence around of a bright light, which helped him have enough strength to answer his daughter back but not possible yet.

There Firefly was all grown up beautifully and becoming a powerful Unisos mare indeed who had a heart of an angel and a mind of a warrior of her time.

His daughter was a winged unicorn and with help of his bright glowing light on his head, she can now connect with him by her thoughts.

Hopefully, in time he should awaken and be freed from this hell he had been living in for so long.

A month later Firefly felt that she got a connection with her father at last.

She felt him answer her back one night.

But she knew that it would be a while before he would wake up properly.

At least now she could tell her grandmother some good news that he was alive and he was strong enough to survive and fight a battle that was coming soon.

Meanwhile, when this was happening, Hades the day had been taking Knight and Knightmare for some training sessions while talking to him and poisoning Knight's mind from good to bad.

Poor Knight did not know what to believe in the end and started to trust only his mother's voice after that.

This one morning Hades rode Knightmare and led Knight to the great cave off the coast where it was rough and rocky where he said to her, squeezing his hands together as he did.

"Knightmare, my dear girl you have produced a remarkable son and he will do amazing wonders for me."

She neighed with a happy reply.

"Now I must take him on his own to do some training alone."

Knightmare knew that Hades loved her and her children or that is what she thought anyway.

Knight nuzzled his mother and seemed scared as he had never trained without her before but his mother said 'he is a good man so trust him like me' and so that was what he did.

Hades then got on Knight's back being careful not to get scratched by Knight's bat wings.

As Knights were much heavier and larger than his dam and they flew for miles, away from his mother and the lair to train.

This place had never been seen or found and yet it was one of the prettiest views of the great ocean herself.

Where there was actual image made of rock roughly of an earth unicorn's head dip into the water with half its body still on land.

Knight seemed to feel very unsure as he felt a strange feeling of uncertainty inside him.

Knowing what his father had said to him and his sister in the past about his god of death.

But he ignored it, believing in his mother as he knew that she loved him and would not let Hades hurt him in any way, or that is what he hoped.

Hades was not the man he had known before because his voice had changed.

"Now, my dear boy let me show you what my training is."

He tied Knight tightly to a strong tree on the rocks and put a leather strap around his body to keep his wings from flapping frantically.

Poor Knight was becoming more and more scared and unsure of what was going to happen to him when his worst nightmare became true.

Hades started to hit him with a large leather whip and said as he did "my boy now you answer only to me, not your mother anymore".

"I own you and you will in time do everything I command and ask you to do."

Knight, said in his mind, no way.

But for days Hades carried on the same way until he would break Knight's spirit to become a bad force to reckon with.

Knight would fight like his father and Hades did not like this.

Knightmare could hear the cries of her son and knew that this was how she became herself once before.

She did not like the training but she felt like she had no choice as otherwise her beloved daughter Firefly would be killed instead.

She knew now that the plan was the entire time to create a beast for Hades to control and destroy earth with.

She felt terrible that she blamed and rejected Seequest's love and devotion to them all.

Now feeling broken because of letting Hades destroy her only dream of living happily ever after with her great Unicorn King.

She wondered if it was possible that Seequest would be able to forgive her in time.

That if Hades does not kill him first she thought and started to wonder again what has happened to him and where he could be.

There she was looking at the ground and saw a beautiful stream where she started to drink from as she felt ill and saw the original mare she was once before and collapsed on the grass.

Knightmare saw velvet and she felt that it was all starting to repeat itself like her life before and panicked.

Chapter Twenty-Four

Helena Is Summoned
Back Home

Back in the beautiful blue ocean, Princess Helena was telling Louis to go as fast as he could, as they needed to see her father quickly because her father had called for her urgently and the messenger would not tell her why.

Straight away she hoped that it was some good news about her old friend Seequest or about the race that she had been training for against her father soon.

The mermaid princess felt excited and yet scared regarding what he was going to tell her.

But either way, she knew that she had to go now.

The princess said a verse out loud, and Louis began to change into a different form that looked like a larger version of our seahorses today.

Wow, she thought, as he was slimmer and faster than before.

Louis had changed into this amazing seahorse form more often and seemed to be becoming quicker at this every day.

They started to go through all the holes of the coral and the rocks around them and were dashed by the great whites.

Because of them not seeing Louis due to his new form which made him look slim and smaller in shape, so he can swim much faster than ever before and miss their powerful jaws.

Helena was so proud and happy that Louis was not just a handsome hippocampus like his father.

No, Helena knew that he was more than that as he had amazing speed too.

This creature again had never lived before in this world.

Helena loved the way that he would change so quickly into either form.

When the verse was mentioned and changed how handsome he looked and how strong he became from them too.

They were going home to Vissen to see the great god of the sea she practiced the verse that would change him into either in a flash.

Because he would give her his all by showing the love and bond he had with her.

In her mind, she thanked Seequest for this wonderful gift of creation, swimming homewards to the palace.

As a hippocampus, he was the build of war lander type, which was a combination of possibly Friesian and Arabian put together with his amazing black-bluish scaled coat that glistened in the light when the sun reflected in the sea.

His mane was long and flowing within the water's movements.

His eyes were aquamarine and his fins were beautifully elegant with a swallowtail shape.

His mane and fins were blue which was of light and dark shades.

When he was a seahorse, his face would narrow right down to a shape of a pole fish and yet keep the horse look.

Whereas the rest of his body would become very slim and curved at the bottom with just one fin.

The hair on his neck would disappear and his tail would lose its swallow look and go into the dragon's tail with the tip at the end of it.

His colour would also change into jet-black to camouflage himself around the rocks and corals of the deeper waters and the bottom of the ocean.

Louis was a great swimmer and diver too and could swim places that dolphins could not.

Helena felt that she was the luckiest mermaid alive.

They were still swimming towards the palace gates, as they were out on their duties that morning.

They passed colourful pink reefs and red crabs walking sideways on the bottom of the seabed happily doing their jobs of cleaning up the mess from other creatures.

But as they were still getting there, she felt a feeling that she had not felt for a while and it was of Seequest needing her help.

Now she was wondering how she was going to do that without her father knowing about it.

Poor Louis had not yet had his breakfast and started to feel a little exhausted and yet knew that he would do anything for his friend.

The Princess asked him to do her a favour even though he knew it would be dangerous.

But because he would give her his all for the love and bond he had with her.

Helena said, "I know that you are tired and I promise that "this will be the last thing I ask of you today, dear boy".

"But when we eventually get back to the stables and your stall I will give you your favourite sea grass and pods as a treat for your extra work this morning".

"Please hurry so I can see my father."

Within that, the black hippocampus neighed and made bubbles in the water.

He rushed in his seahorse form as quickly as he could carry her, by rearing his neck and head upwards and then pushing his head forward to make a great speed.

In a flash, they reached the double doors of many great statues of Neptune and her mother with their well-known Hippocampius; Tidal Wave and Sea Spray plus some of their famous dolphins too.

Back at the palace, her father was visited by his brother Zeus, who had disguised himself as an enormous blue whale to get through the gates.

As he changed into his similar human image again, he reached Neptune face to face.

They had just reached the throne room when Neptune and Zeus could not believe what they just saw swam right by them.

Helena jumped quickly off him and said, "I will call you when I'm done here, dear boy."

The great hippocampus neighed.

Her father and Zeus were thinking that they had never seen anything like him before, as he was more powerful than his great Tidal Wave.

Louis's father swam off galloping with his front fin into the abyss.

Zeus was talking to Neptune alone when she disturbed the meeting.

They stopped talking as they could not let her know anything.

As they were afraid she may do something and cause more problems than there were already, as after all, she is the daughter of Neptune (god of the sea and great warrior to earth).

Neptune did not want to put her in any more danger again against Hades.

Zeus was still astounded by the creature that just swam in front of him earlier.

Zeus said he would see his brother in two days back at Olympus to discuss things in further detail.

Then he smiled at Helena and quickly turned back into a blue whale in front of them and swam right by her, leaving a great wave pushing her to the side as he went.

As he was a little annoyed that she disturbed the great Zeus's meeting.

She recovered quickly and started to swim with her father.

"Father, you called for me?"

"Yes, I did. False alarm, sorry" and looked away from her.

"Father, so it's not about Seequest?"

Neptune seemed to struggle with what to say to her and then changed the subject and said, "Was that a hippocampus?"

"One of the new creations from Seequest's magic horn and my powerful Tidal Wave and your mother's mare Sea Spray?"

Trying his hardest to change her channel of thoughts has he spoken to her face to face?

"I know that your mother is an incredible mer-queen and high priestess but I did not think she would do this behind my back."

Helena was thrown off by what her father had just said and forgot about Seequest once more.

Neptune was relieved that it seemed to work as she started to talk about what her mother had done and told him they were a test and experiment of breeding this unique hippocampus which she mentions if it worked, they would become even greater than their parents before them.

They spoke for hours about them and what the queen had been doing for such a long time in the royal stables for days and sometimes nights too.

Neptune stopped and said, "How did you get this magnificent young hippocampus colt?"

She replied, "Mother gave him to me as a gift, that you told me to go to the stables on my birthday remember?

I believe to forget about Seequest and so I could do my duties without using one of the dolphin chariots anymore, as I cannot swim far to do my duties without one."

"No, that is true, my daughter" He laughed and then said, "How about I put you in the great Atlantic race against me?"

When he then says and surprises her "if you win, you can keep Louis and if I win, I have him for myself?"

Helena was shocked about what her father had said to her knowing what she was going through.

But in true honesty, Neptune was the god of the sea and should own a unique hippocampus like that he thought.

He had upset Helena greatly and she replied, "No father you cannot have him throwing her arms around in an annoyed body language.

She replied "he is mine and you're not going to take him away from me as you did with Seequest!"

Neptune was again shocked that his daughter had the guts to argue with the great sea god and yet still listened as he loved his daughter dearly.

When he replied "then if you believe this my child then you would join me in the race on the fifteenth of October?"

Even though the princess always wanted this to happen for them both, she seemed to change her mind now that she could lose another dear friend.

"Father, No!"

"Nonsense, it is done", he said as he ignored her emotions completely.

"Now my child be away with you as I need to see our people and tell them this news of ours that I must go away to Olympus and see Zeus at his home to continue on the meeting that you accidentally disturbed recently, with some other important business too".

Poor Helena did not understand what had just happened and she knew this was not the father that is loved and worshipped.

She could sense that he was afraid and upset in his heart as he forgot that she was telepathic too.

So, she then calmed down and asked "Oh, Father is it about Seequest?"

Neptune was becoming uncomfortable because of his daughter's feelings and he tried not to lie to her face.

So, ignored her feelings and questioned and said "Daughter I cannot talk to you about it and you cannot come with me either."

"I am sorry, only the gods can go to Olympus, my child."

"Yes, Father I know that I am your daughter and no, I am not a god", she said with an angry tone in her voice once again.

"But it still seems unfair that you will not tell me anything if it is to do about our dear Seequest."

Neptune replied in tempter and said "No, you're right, my child, you are not! You are meant to be the new queen of Vissen in time, not a goddess and that's final!"

Helena felt betrayed and upset now that her father wanted to take her companion away from her.

She felt that he was cruel and that because he was a god he could do what he wanted.

She now could see at this moment in time the similarity of Hades his brother.

And yet she had a secret that she did not tell him about either in the end, after the way he spoke to her earlier.

So, there's a possibility of losing her only friend that she cared for like she does for Seequest because her father and Tidal wave have never lost a race before!

So now she became really upset and concerned knowing that she was just started to enjoy life again without her old friend by her side anymore.

She thought carefully about his offer and then remembered that Louis has a greater advantage than any other creature living in the sea.

She decided not to tell him and maybe that might not be all he has? she thought.

All Helena wanted to do now was to win the race more than ever and wondered of a prize that was greater than anything the great sea god has ever created or done before if someone else beat him, she said holding her hand to her lips.

Maybe her dream that she had a vision for so long could come true after all?

She shook off the feeling of being upset and started to think how she was going to beat the top and fastest sea creature with Louis?

She thought about this for hours and she decided to tell him in time.

But then she changed her mind now.

Because she knew that she had a great advantage of winning the race more than ever and wondered if a prize that was greater than anything the great sea god has ever created or done before if someone else won it instead for a change.

Helena was glad she did not tell her father about Louis's secret.

As otherwise, she could lose him forever but with this extra great skill and magic that he has she believed that she will beat her father.

And in time she will be a queen and a better ruler than him.

Neptune could see that Helena was seriously upset with his wager and yet he knew that he preferred his daughter not liking him.

Doing this gave her the strength to succeed and want to achieve winning the race as she loved challenges especially involving her father.

Plus, it will make her feel like she will want to win to prove a point.

Because he knew that this would make her train harder and make her want to win the race by being willing to train more with her steed to become a better rider for the future.

Neptune thought at least this will keep her out of harm's way.

Helena turned away from her father and quickly twisted her body around and said "you are on Father".

"Louis and I will beat you and Tidal Wave, we will see."

"Now, my child, please go and see your mother as she has a lot to teach you knowing that you will be racing against me and Tidal Wave very soon."

Time had flown so quickly while Seequest had been away from home and yet patience and hope were what kept everyone going, in the sea.

Neptune felt bad about what he said and so he rushed up to Helena and kissed her cheek and said, "Now go my child, I will see you very soon."

The sea god hated that he had to lie to his favourite and wise daughter and yet knew, for now it was the best for both of them.

Once she left and the doors closed.

Her father calls for his guards and told them they were going to the town in the middle of the ocean to tell his people to get ready for a race and a big war.

But he then says quietly to them to their face with get power in his voice "do not let my eldest daughter Helena know anything until it is time".

The mer-guards look at their sea king and bowed to him and say "yes sire" and walk away towards the door of his golden throne room.

The next morning, Neptune had spoken to his wife Sera and told her about the plans regarding the race against their daughter.

Plus, about the war against Hades to try and get Seequest and his children back safely.

Afternoon came and Neptune popped in to see the high priestess who knew about what he had to do and say to Helena earlier.

Because it was both of their plans to keep her out of danger, they hoped, yet hated themselves as they had to do it for her own good!

When great queen could see that he was upset when she cuddled her husband saying in a comforting voice "It is ok Helena will understand one day my love."

"Give her some time to see the actual problem and then this hurt for you will be no more".

Neptune then pulled gently away and looked at his queen with complete devotion in his eyes and said "thank you, my love".

She smiled too as he swam boldly out of her temple and back to his palace again.

That evening the mermaid princess Helena and her siblings were taken out on a visit to see Kessy in Scotland which now Neptune knew about.

He was quite smitten with what his clever queen had done by moving her to Scotland, where she would be safe from Hades.

Otherwise, he would probably try and capture her to do his dirty work too.

Now, all the mer-folk knew the truth about what had happened to Seequest and that they were going to war with Hades.

They were getting themselves prepared for the greatest battle of their lives.

But the royal children knew not of the plan yet.

Everyone was getting ready to go to land when Neptune got on his beautiful white-and-blue steed and swam to the ocean's edge to the beach.

Where Tidal Wave galloped out on the water on his four legs and trotted to the surface.

Neptune changed into a Pisces (human like form) when he jumped off his water horse and told him to go and eat and rest and that he will be back soon to go home together.

Tidal Wave was in his watery form until he reached land and as he stayed longer he became a solid horse of flesh.

But he still stayed in the beautiful colours of the sea.

As he changed again, he bowed and then reared on his back legs showing his sea god respect and strength and landed back on his feet.

He was raising his head and down as he understood what Neptune had just said to him.

When Neptune's steed calmed down, he walked back to him and said, 'Go, my dear champion and be safe.'

He put his head on Tidal Wave's muzzle gently and moved away where again the water horse neighed loudly and turned and galloped away into the distance from the heat.

Neptune waited until it was night and just rested on the beach, looking handsome as he looked at his reflection in the seawater that was coming up the shoreline to the sand.

There a few minutes later stood a fair blond, chiselled face form of a man with a broad torso and slim legs now in a white gown with a golden rope around it wearing his stunning turquoise sea crystal crown with dolphins swimming on it.

Wow, he looked very handsome indeed.

Eventually, night came and there was a noise from the distance.

He could see in the night sky, like a white star getting closer to him, a large white-winged horse flying towards him.

It was his old faithful steed Sea Breeze, which he used to ride all the time when he was younger and when he was just a prince not a king of the sea.

The stunning white diamond steed landed carefully in front of him and stepped dead right at his feet.

"My dear boy how I have missed you"

The winged stallion reared and neighed with delight seeing his old friend again.

The stunning white diamond steed landed carefully in front of him and stepped dead right to his feet.

Once Sea Breeze calmed down Neptune held on to his mane and said a verse and there appeared a stunning blue bridle and saddle of turquoise, which he kindly put on his friend.

They both were ready to gallop off towards Olympus to see Zeus the god of all living things.

As he felt more comfortable he said another verse and there his outfit changed to something more ideal for this meeting.

As quickly as a flash, there appeared on his body his amazing gold-and-blue armour with a helmet for pro-tection with the design of dolphins on it.

Now they were ready to meet up with Zeus.

They jumped up and leaped for the skies where they flew as high as they could without being seen by anyone, where there they were enjoying their flight together towards Olympus once more like the old times.

"Come dear boy, let's fly" and Sea-Breeze went and did some of his old tricks as they did in the past.

Eventually, it was time to stop having fun and con-tinue this important mission to Olympus.

They eventually saw the great mountain in the distance.

Neptune could also see loads of Acropolis buildings all made of white and gold.

Sea Breeze neighed at his old master with excitement that they were together again and Neptune said, "thank you dear friend for a wonderful flight I will call you once I am done here."

"So, you can kindly take me back to Santorini, please?"

Sea Breeze landed beautifully on the pebbled path, still flapping his wings.

Neptune quickly took off his bridle and jumped off him.

Sea Breeze was now ready to fly back off to the other winged horses that were nearby for now.

Neptune then moved out of the way for the mighty steed to fly straight off again with others in the sky.

As Neptune walks away from the pebbled path, Hermes walked up to him smiling and much smaller than him and said "welcome back great Sea King."

Neptune replies "Hello Hermes", with his bold voice.

Then he started to take off his armour carefully and handed it all to Hermes to look after him with his helmet and cloak as well.

They both looked at each other, Hermes said, "It has been a while since your last visit."

Neptune says, "Yes, that is true and I wished this was just a visit."

"But it is one of great importance."

Hermes replied, "Zeus is expecting you."

They walked to Zeus' throne room to talk more about the plan of possibly having to kill everyone or save them.

But being gods, they sometimes had the worst choices to do for the better of others.

Neptune was hoping that they could rescue Seequest and get him home safely.

But Zeus did not seem to care about his children and believed that Seequest's rescue will be because of his fate.

Chapter Twenty-Five

Helena's Plan to Save Seequest

The Princess was attending to her duties with the dolphins and the pod (families).

She could not forget about her old friend anymore and wanted to find her father to discuss a plan for them to rescue him by themselves.

She is clever as well as kind and she now can read her father's thoughts sometimes when he is around her for long periods.

He seemed to have forgotten about that gift she has, as he has so many things on his mind nowadays to worry about more.

She sensed that something seemed very wrong or was affecting his concentration recently but she could not get to the bottom of it.

Has the goddess Athena of wisdom seemed to of picked up on Helen's gift?

So, she blocked the mermaid princess quickly because there was too much private information that she must not know about it yet, as it could put herself and everyone involved in great danger

The only part Athena has left open still was that she can contact him for emergencies only, as Athena and everyone else wanted to make sure she was always safe and away from harm.

Helena became frustrated because no matter how much she tried to get into his mind and dig deeper, she could not read anything anymore.

This caused her to start to worry instead, and she felt like something was seriously wrong.

But she had noticed that her father was going to Olympus more than often on more important business, which did start to concern her.

Olympus by winged horse was very fast.

But here on earth, it is months away.

Helena remembered that Zeus had the power to make time stand still without knowing it.

While everywhere and everything else is moving as clockwork with help from the sun god Apollo and the moon goddess Luna's helping it run still perfectly in the correct time on earth.

The mermaid princess called her father many times by the magic reef horn, which means help quietly.

Hopefully, he will hear it soon and come back home and discuss the plan to rescue their friend from Hades.

Neptune heard the horn in his ears like a soft breeze of the sea and his daughter's voice saying, "Father, please come home, I need you urgently."

Upon hearing this noise, he approached his old friend Sea-Breeze and started to panic and once he saw his amazing friend, he grabbed his armour from Hermes and jumped on him quickly saying, "Sea-Breeze, old friend, take me home, as my daughter needs me.

Take me back to the beach as quickly as you can."

The stunning winged horse of pure white and great stature, when touched by the sea god began to change his colouring, has he turned to a beautiful aqua blue on his wings, mane, and tail, even on his hooves and his bridle was also gold with aqua blue running through it too.

He looked heavenly now that Neptune is going back home to his daughter and his people.

Sea- Breeze the winged horse was noticed as a friend on the beach.

Because Neptune from a distance had his mer-knights watching and waiting in the sea in case Hades or his creatures were around.

Neptune speaks louder due to the wind in his ears and says "Now, my dear friend, my daughter needs me".

Within seconds, the beautiful stallion moved his head up and down and neighed.

But because the sea god is telepathic, he could hear Sea-Breeze reply to him as well.

The majestic beast replied to him through his mind "your Highness I will take you wherever you want me to go, Hang on."

The gorgeous sea-winged horse now began to flap his wings greatly that they made a large wind sound and galloped and jumped into the air once more.

Back at Zeus' home he was horrified to see that he had been ignored and interrupted by Neptune's daughter once again in a meeting and decided now that she must be more powerful than everyone expects of her.

Zeus admired that she did not give up and that she was brave to have done this because if it was anyone else, they surely would have been punished for it.

But he understood her pain and anguish and that she's coming of age to be a great queen one day and accepted Neptune's apology on her behalf.

Luckily, he understood her actions and let him go earlier.

It was daytime, so Neptune's winged horse was luminous and stunning with the sun shining on him.

How it bought back great memories of when he lived at the home in Olympus with his family many years ago after the death of their father.

Zeus decided to bring his brother back from the blue planet to readjust to this new planet before Zeus decided to give him the title of being the sea king here on earth.

Back in Santorini,

Neptune began to smile and can see the beach and the sea as they were approaching to land there.

Sea Breeze started to dive down towards the wet golden sand and landed quietly on the ground making a massive hole as he marked it.

Quickly, they said their goodbyes with Neptune patting his neck and in return, the winged stallion nudged his face and closed his eyes showing their love for each other as old friends.

Sea-Breeze quickly changed back to his pure white form again and left Neptune standing on the beach watching his old friend fly away above the sky again alone.

Neptune then shook his sword back into his trident once more and banged it on the sand and there appeared his hippocampus.

The great Tidal Wave himself swam to the shore towards him as he was over the other side of the island in the shade resting.

The waves in the sea started to become rough as Tidal Waves galloped very fast across the ocean.

He could see his swallow tail going in and out of the water as he jumped the waves that he made along the way.

There appeared a hippocampus of a watery form as the sun was very bright, it shone on him as it was a beautiful sunny day.

Tidal Wave then became more solid to the touch when Neptune said, "hello friend".

"Take me home" and he jumped onto his back.

The aqua blue sea horse turned quickly back into the deeper parts of the sea, as they both started to change back from a water horse to the hippocampus when Neptune also changed from Piscean back to a great mer-king once again.

Tidal Wave jumped head first with his front legs into the water diving deeply back into the ocean back home to Vissen where he expected to see Helena, wondering what may of had happened?

As they were swimming back there the sea god saw Neptuna helping a blue whale who had a wound on its fin where she was fixing it.

As they swam together what a beautiful sight it was to see a pretty mermaid commanding nicely this massive creature by showing her kindness to it.

From that in return the whale listened to every word she said, it knew then she was trying to help it not harm it.

Because that is how it is in the great seas of Neptune, kindness and caring.

Neptune asked if Neptuna had seen Helena and she said.

"Recently she had been practicing her skills with Louis and now had gone back to the royal stables."

They both swam together with her still holding on to the blue whale's fin towards Vissen where Neptuna let go and continued to swim the opposite way of Tidal Wave's fish-type body.

She stopped and said her goodbyes and went to the royal stables where Tidal Wave dropped off the king at his palace doors.

Neptune gave the command to his great hippocampus to go back to the stables, which he did with no hesitation.

Neptune swam quickly home with his large thick tail like a killer whale and did not see anyone and thought that they must be out training or up in the stables still.

But he thought that they may be at home possibly in the library, so he swam there first.

He reached the Library of Knowledge and called for his wife, Queen Sera and to Helena but no one was there in sight.

He felt concerned and yet went and relaxed until they arrived, as his meeting had tired him out recently.

He said to himself "I shall wait for them to come home" and had a nice wash in his oyster bath and ate the best caviar (fish eggs) you would have ever tasted before and drank the freshest water of the seas.

While sitting down and looking through his palace's round window, he thought to himself that he hoped that his daughter Helena was safe and OK.

But being a god, he could sense some worry and yet could not pin it down in his daughter's mind as there was too much that she was thinking of at the same time, which confused the thoughts.

So, he gave up trying and believed everything must be fine and sat there chilling watching the dolphins swimming by doing their duties and being controlled by his people as they pass his window.

They all smiled at him as they did.

Eventually, he seemed to relax more and rested in his throne chair quite happily and yet a little worried about why he was called home so quickly.

Later, the queen and Helena arrived home and woke him up to discuss the plans for the race, where she gave up trying to read her father's mind and he did with hers too.

They had a conversation about why he was brought home urgently where then Helena apologized and they decided to trust each other more.

Yet Helena changed her mind about telling her father the plan to save Seequest herself, as she thought now that she was old enough and wise enough to do it on her own.

As now she was eighteen!

Chapter Twenty-Six

The Plan Is Put in Motion from the Heavens

Pegasus had left heaven and had planned to ask for Zeus's permission for the Celestial and Legend to come back to earth and help destroy and stop Hades once and for all.

Meanwhile, Celestial was letting everyone know that she may be going away for a while and that their king and queen were needed back on earth one last time.

While she was telling all the horses this, her memories of her son, when she was a night unicorn came back.

Later when she was on her own, she started to cry as she was going to see her son once more as powerful as he had become and a warrior as a hippocampus of the seas.

She could not wait to see him but first, they will have to rescue him.

She went and got herself ready for the greatest fight ever.

Legend could see that she was excited and yet frightened for the first time in history.

He put his head on her shoulders and said, "Our son is stronger than anything.

He will pull through this."

But they both knew that was not the case.

Legend said that he would be back soon as he has to fly back to his star where he normally watches everything from afar, they gently nuzzled and he went to the pebbled silver and gold pathway, which lets them fly to other dimensions.

He galloped across the sky with his stunning, powerful angel black wings with touches of sapphire blue in them and his mane and tail with soft blue tones through his coat as well.

They were both beautiful in flight, as they also have diamond sparks reflecting on them as they left sparkles of dust across the night sky.

He was even quicker than he was before because this time he changed himself from a star now he was his Spirit.

He flew and flew until he felt that he was getting tired and landed peacefully on the cloud.

Again, it became night and so he said a verse when his whole image changed into a sparkling star from afar once again.

There he had the chance to get closer as his actually on earth's plane to see in easier detail.

He watching Hades at night, as that's when it was best to train Knight now.

Legend was heartbroken to see his grandson had been seriously ill-treated to make him mad.

But he could see from the distance this black Unisos had a kind heart of an angel.

He could see and feel that he was losing the battle because of being tied up and feeling useless to defend himself from the pain that Hades had been inflicting on him to become a demon horse of hate.

Legend thought he could help him somehow and began to shine very brightly in the night sky, like a beacon.

Legend shone himself as brightly as he could into Hades' vision and caught the eye of Knight, which seemed to have calmed him.

Knowing that Knight then felt as if someone was watching over him like his father said they do in his past when he was a foal.

When he looked up he saw the shining star and when he studied it and looked deeper as if believing in it, he sensed it could be a guardian.

That he saw a black and dark blue winged image similar to him up in the sky and remembered the tale about his grandfather that Seequest told him when he was younger.

Knight started to feel guilty that maybe he was looking at things the wrong way and reared in front of Hades.

For doing this the underworld god punished him badly that he would not take him out anymore at night.

But in the day instead when it was hot too sure that no one could ever disturb him again.

Knight felt that he had betrayed his father and wished that he had listened to him all those years ago.

Yet he was frightened of what else would Hades do to him to break his spirit even more.

But what Knight did not know was that Hades was not finished with him yet, Hades had not even started his full training!

Chapter Twenty-Seven

At Olympus, the Plan Was Coming Together

The battle and rescue took time to plan correctly.

As there was only one time to get it right.

Pegasus had all the details from everyone that could help and told Zeus all the news about what Hades was trying to do to Knight and Seequest.

Pegasus said quite happy and relieved "I believe he's still alive now playing along with the plan that they put in place earlier".

"Hermes has been visiting him in secret where he is now".

"While Firefly was on their side leaking as much information to Celestial as she can before she gets caught!"

Meanwhile, Zeus had summoned all his family to come to the meetings individually and together from time to time to hopefully have the upper hand over Hades.

It was now Neptune's turn again and he said, "Hi, Zeus".

"What is the great plan I am getting upset of keep lying to my daughter like this?"

"Now brother I am sorry that you must."

"But you know it is for her own good right "because we do not know yet if one, Seequest will be rescued and go back to the sea?"

"Two we may have to kill his son to save our earth from Hades' evil idea as well?"

Neptune looked angry and nodded.

He knew that his brother was right.

"Ok, then, brother"

"What is the plan?" he said with great interest.

"Are you going to rescue Seequest or are you just going to kill them all and be done with it?"

Neptune asked with great sorrow in his heart as he did.

"Neptune, I wish it was that easy brother"

"But you know it this is not"

"I shall not kill Seequest", with a soft loveable tone to his voice

Zeus said with heart "I must try and save him knowing that is the godson of our friend Pegasus"

"Seequest is the progeny of the original bloodline of unicorns and Pegasus mystical winged horses"

"That are warriors and friends from the battle who kindly saved us from the Titans thousands of years before"

"Let's call in my daughter Aphrodite and see what she can do to help."

He called for Aphrodite, who came in walking elegantly with love for life written on her face with beauty.

She walked up to her father's throne looking beautiful with a fair complexion and with golden wavy hair and her robes were of white and cerise pink with pink roses in her hair.

She smiled which lifted the light of the room and bowed in front of her father's feet.

"Your Highness, oh, mighty one, why do you summons me today?"

"My wonderful angel of a being, I need you to make up a love and peace potion to try and get Seequest's son back to his natural innocent self before it is too late!"

"If that does not work, then we will have to decide on the worst if it comes to it."

Aphrodite said "father, I will get on with that straight away for you."

He replied, "thank you, daughter"

"I knew that I could count on you to help us in this time of great hurt and sadness to us all."

She smiled; bowed and turned walking away.

Zeus and Neptune agreed with the plan and sat for hours until it was time for Neptune to leave again.

Zeus called Artemis in and asked her to send one of her white doves with a message to the Celestial to be prepared for Hermes' arrival afterward.

She agreed and went and designed the biggest, strongest, and purest white dove they had ever seen.

The pretty white dove carried the message to Celestial across the universe through the dimensions which she will then pass onto Firefly telepathically about their arrival soon.

Days later, Zeus then called back his daughter again Aphrodite, goddess of love when she showed him the potion the muses had kindly made up on her behalf.

Zeus said, "Get ready for the family to become one again", they smiled.

Then he said "go my daughter and bring love and peace back to earth"

Artemis was told by Luna that the white wolf would be able to help them as she approached him one night at the pool where he drinks and tells him the plan too.

He then passed the information to the forest animals.

But he had been told to keep it a secret till the day.

But due his experience of being an alpha for years he thought that the forest animals should know to possibly move from their homes before the battle starts.

Days passed when the great god of war arrived and saw his father.

"Father, you called for me?"

"How can I be of service to you?"

"My great warrior of a son I need you to go with Pegasus and meet your uncle Neptune, the sea god with his army, please."

"Yes Father, of course."

He walked to the golden pathway where Pegasus was waiting with him and his winged horse Challenger.

Who was Pegasus's famous fighter in his herds' and the gods' battles?

He jumped onto him Challenger's changed from pure pearl to reddish on his wings; mane and tail as magic his golden and red bridle and saddle appeared.

Ares said, "Challenger, let's go" and he neighed with great power in his voice rubbing his front leg on the ground ready for anything.

They followed Pegasus into the stunning blue sky as they flew for hours until they reached Santorini's beach.

As they flew, Pegasus was contacting telepathically Celestial and Legend that they have permission to come to earth and help them once more like in the old times.

Celestial and Legend are more powerful than they had ever been before and have mighty powers of their own that no one has ever known of.

They can help in some way because of these powers that they have and know how to use well in battle.

Even though they are different beings now, the night unicorns' courage still lives on in them both.

Zeus appeared in the sky as a lightning bolt and said to Ares, "go my son protect us all."

Hermes had come back to update Zeus with the news of Seequest and his children.

Hermes was the last to be spoken to about the plan to save Seequest and his family.

Hermes is a much smaller god than his family for a reason and yet he can become smaller even still if he wanted to.

"Father, what can I do to help?"

"My dear Hermes, you already are."

"Go back and see if you can help Seequest awaken from this terrible nightmare and help them all escape quietly"

"Also tell Hades that I want to meet him in Scotland at Lochmond and I will take no for an answer!" Zeus said.

Hermes said "I will do my best to get him away from his lair where he is at his strongest."

"With help from our family with the winged horses, we can destroy his creatures in the process and hopefully Seequest can then be rescued"

Holding his hands in a prayer form at the time he said this and carried on saying.

"He then can help me rescue his own family and escape from there for good."

Hermes bowed at Zeus, and the great god leaned over towards him and handed him a roundish crystal bottle of a pink liquid inside it, 'Oh here, take this.

"It's a love and peace potion that Aphrodite has made for Seequest and Knight to help them become their powerful selves again".

"It will then bring their magic back temporarily for a short time just to get them out of there in one piece".

"There we will fight for earth for the last time hope-fully all together again as one that we are." Zeus said with great passion.

Hermes replied "yes my lord, I shall do my best to achieve your wishes."

"Good then go now and do not fail me."

Hermes bowed again and flew off to go and get his magic golden boots from the other side of Olympus and then took off towards the side of the Greek islands.

He reached there in the day.

It was very hot, so he rested until night came again and walked slowly into Hades' lair.

He flew around for ages in the cave and could sense Seequest was near and planned to give him the message.

But he was not quite there yet.

Hermes felt he was becoming closer so he flew fur-ther into the deeper parts of the caves until he finds Seequest.

Back at Olympus, Zeus quickly saw Athena, the god-dess of Wisdom and said 'my daughter please send to us all your great power of kindness and intelligence thank you my dear child"

"Plus, we need your mighty wisdom to help save the day and prevent anyone from getting hurt badly from this please."

"She replied father that I cannot promise but I'll do my best to prevent it as remember I can pass on my wisdom to you all".

"But everyone uses it a different way from us, even our blood."

"Yes, that is true, daughter."

"Let us go and fight once more in the history of the gods."

Artemis came back to see him with her bow and arrows wrapped around her side.

Looking beautiful a protector of her planet and everything that lives on it.

"Artemis, please go and see the winged horses and choose twenty of our best mystical horses for this battle."

"Yes, father I shall go and start the tests now"

She replied "I will have them ready in two days, as requested."

"Please go now and get them ready for another battle with us not protecting our home this time but earth herself."

"I also need you to ask the muses to make the strongest swords; bows and arrows than ever before please."

"Agreed, I will tell them now", when she bowed and walked away with great courage in her footsteps.

Chapter Twenty-Eight

Hermes plans to wake Seequest in Hades' Lair

Hermes arrived on the beach connected to Hades' lair and saw hoof prints of Seequest's family.

Luckily, it had been raining recently it kept the prints still fresh and he knew what to look for.

Hermes followed the tracks into another large dark cave where Hermes saw Cerberus and tried to escape being seen.

But it was too late as Cerberus jumped up and tried to catch him in his mouth and yet kept missing due to Hermes having turned himself into the size of a butterfly.

Minutes later, Hades walked through the pathway of the cave and saw his demon dog playing around.

Then Hades said "Enough playing with Hermes, let him talk!"

Hermes was panting after being chased around.

He caught his breath and says, "I have a message from the almighty god Zeus himself."

This annoyed Hades a lot, as it was rubbing it in his face that he was strong but his brother was more powerful than he will ever be.

But he thought this time he might just have the upper hand at last and agreed to meet with his brother on the other side of the world.

He said, "It must be in a few days."

Hades said, "Agreed, now go back to your leader and pass on that message to him for me, daddy's little helper", he laughed and he said to Cerberus.

"He is all yours get this weasel out of my home now."

Hermes grew smaller quickly into a size of a butterfly again and flew as fast as he could go with Cerberus running behind him.

Eventually, the beast heads were all out of breath and stopped chasing Hermes, who luckily got out this time, as remember Cerberus only has one body.

Hermes was thinking that he needed to go back in and find Seequest without being seen or heard and decided to wait until Cerberus was sleeping.

Later, Hermes was resting on the wall in the corner of the cave.

He was lucky he got away earlier and knew that now he had to find Seequest and give him this potion that Athena had made to cure him.

He was hoping that it would work for all their sakes, as he knew that he needed Seequest more than ever to escape the great beast again.

But first, he would have to find where Seequest was, which could take days as the lair was big indeed.

Back on the beach, Zeus had contacted Apollo with an image of him in the sea he said, "Wait for me before you start this war."

"Yes, Father, I will be patient for your arrival."

Zeus said, "Good I shall see you all in two days", then his image disappeared

After this, he got ready for battle.

He remembered that he had been given a bottle by Zeus of a made-up potion to weaken Hades' army of dead souls, which will hopefully weaken them at a quicker pace.

As he shook it up, he started to rub it gently all over his sword and ready for battle.

He made sure that he covered his golden shield with it too, as he rubbed over his guard wristbands also.

Luckily, it does not smell or come off unless you use another potion that cleans it off.

But he needs to make sure that he also must be very careful not to touch anyone or anything else until needed.

Even though Zeus is powerful, Hades still has the great sword of death, which he killed his father.

Who was the great Titan of all before, so they know his sword is highly dangerous and can kill anything in its way?

Hades calls it the Sword of Doom.

Cerberus, his three-headed dog, could kill a god with one bite as well.

But recently Hades had created another creature like a red lion with a goat's head and a snake too with powerful wings as an advantage.

Who had recently gotten into Pegasus's home in the fifth dimension and had killed some of the yearlings of winged horses, of which the horse god has not heard the news yet.

Apollo must first look for his massive creature and destroy it as Hades had made it through Seequest's powers while asleep.

Apollo was also fond of music, thanks to the muses always playing their harps around him.

That he realized recently that music is also powerful in its way due to it also being loud noise and calms you as well.

He decided to make up a tune to calm the Chimera down so he then would be able to kill it easier as it would be in trance, which would also favour to him.

He thought it was a great plan, so he jumped on Melody his winged horse and galloped to the Mystery Woods.

Where he was listening to the birds tweeting and the sea whooshing, he made a sweet lullaby that would put the beast to sleep temporarily.

A day had already passed when Neptune arrived unexpectedly and barged through the palace doors in Olympus.

Neptune looked tired due to worrying about his dear friend Seequest and protecting his people and seas from Hades.

He shouted out to his brother not caring that he was the great god of all anymore!

"I have not heard from you for a few days and I was starting to get concerned about the next part of our plan?"

"Dear brother please do not doubt me, as I am your beloved brother first!"

"But I am also the King of the gods as well!" with anger in his voice that made the building shake.

"I am sorry, dear brother but I need to know how we are going to beat Hades and rescue Seequest."

Zeus replied in a calmer tone "all in good time dear brother, it is all under control now"

"Neptune, please do not worry as you have us all helping you defeat him with my children Athena; Ares; Aphrodite; Diana; ; Pegasus; Celestial; Legend, and even Apollo and Luna who are all here to help you and me win this battle too!"

"Come and relax and rest with me in the gardens with some sweet nectar?"

Neptune felt like he had his answer and they spoke in detail about the plan to destroy Hades for good.

But they knew that they still needed him alive for his duties on earth as still needed to keep the balance of all things.

Zeus said, "Go back and collect your finest mer-guard and knights to defend you and your kingdom."

"Please make sure that you also use the great creatures of the sea, as you know that Hades has the protection of the seawater as long as he has Seequest in his grip."

Once Seequest is rescued he will not have that power anymore.

"Now go home and see your family and tell Sera the plan too!"

"Remember Hades can kill us, so make sure you spend as much time with them as you could."

"Because it could be the last time together if this goes wrong!"

"Again, remember not to tell your children, especially Helena, in case she messes up the plan before it even starts, even though she only would do it to help us."

"We cannot afford any mistakes!"

Neptune agreed bowed and said "thank you, brother, see you soon" and walked towards the golden pathway to pick up his ride home again.

Neptune was waiting for Sea Breeze to pick him up from the golden-pebbled pathway.

Neptune agreed when Sea Breeze walked in and bowed.

He jumped on him and said to Zeus, "Hopefully I won't have to use the Defender this time, because he not only destroyed the dinosaurs but also damaged Earth last time we let him run wild."

"It would be a great shame to kill something that Pegasus's new progeny (the unicorns) has only recreated more beautiful and peaceful than ever before."

"I agree, my brother", said Zeus.

"The defender will only be used if we all are beaten and earth will have to be destroyed once more and us with it this time."

Zeus replied with great empathy as he spoke about this matter.

Back in Hades' lair, Hermes was still a butterfly image flying around looking for Seequest or Firefly.

Chapter Twenty-Nine

The Plan has begun in Vissen

Back in the Crystal Temple, Queen Sera was getting the crystal skulls ready.

She's preparing for the battle of her life and her family's as well.

While she was doing this, she contacted her mother, Luna, the moon goddess when she told her that they needed her help.

Afterward, she met up with the goddess of wisdom.

The high priestess of the Great White Light of the Divine was content due to Aphrodite giving her some of the potion while in their meeting of love and peace to keep her people calm under this great threat to their lives.

She also called on Athena herself to help her give some great Wisdom in those trying few days.

Once the crystal skulls were fully charged to their full power by the sea, sun, and moon, she closed the doors and said a Greek verse where the skulls grew bigger and seemed to have a life of their own.

As she swam out of the temple, it crystal skulls began to shone brighter than ever before and started to emerge into each other as the doors closed.

She said, "I will be back soon to help you."

The sea queen said this and another voice replied, "I know, my queen."

"I will be waiting for you."

She smiled and rode her chariot of dolphins back home to check on her younger children and Helena.

While her elder sons were knights and were preparing for the fight with their father's army of all the great sea.

The creatures were from the hippocampus to great white sharks and to dolphins where they were preparing for the fight of their lives altogether as one in the sea.

Back in Hades' lair, Knight was becoming very strange than normal and seemed to be becoming worse and a little mad every day.

Poor Knight was losing his mind more to Hades, as his father cannot help him because of being still put in a deep sleep.

Yet he was getting a little more powerful every day because of his daughter getting through to him recently telepathically.

But what Seequest was not aware of was that Hades had been training his son at night again.

Hades had been training him in a cruel poor way to hate as Hades knows that once hate comes into Knight's mind for good.

He then can control him once and for all making him the greatest destructor that he images him to be.

The evil god of the underworld felt like he had every-one in the palm of his hand.

Because he knows that everyone in their willpower will try and stop Knight and not destroy him yet.

Because he knew if they realize that earth is threat-ened they would be prepared to possibly kill him to save it!

Hades started to starve Knight of his normal oats and grass for a while.

Has he forced him to eat more raw meat in his meal to pull him to the darkness?

Eventually, Knight gave in as he was starving and needed to eat something before he becomes useless where Hades will kill himself even though that was his worst fear.

Six months had passed poor Knight was going through this terrible training with Hades, when his cruel master started to see that Knight could not fight him inward anymore and started to listen to his commands.

Knight was becoming a different bat-winged unicorn than he was before.

Now this could be the end of Knight and the beginning of something deadlier than he?

Knight was going on three years old and yet he acted as if he was four and as, remember he is magical.

Knight noticed that when he was flying with his mother for practice he was faster than her.

Recently he would do anything to beat her and he even started to bite her back to cheat.

They both flapped their bat wings strongly as they landed when Knightmare screamed at her son.

"What are you doing biting me? I am your mother!"

"I am sorry" seeing that he drew blood on her back and he said "mother I am sorry but something is going on that I cannot explain and it is eating me up from the inside."

Feeling scared of the unknown of himself due to what else was he turning into?

His mother said, OK, we will get to the bottom of this when we get back and talk to our master to see if he could explain this."

They trotted back into the cave.

Knightmare asked what was happening to her colt when Hades said "my dear, you have had him for a while and now it is my time to have him for what I planned to do from the beginning" laughing with an evil chuckle in his voice as he looked at her.

"But because you have been good to me I did feel for you that you were happy".

"So, I took the advantage of you and Seequest to become close so I could drain his powers when he was here."

Knightmare looked at Hades and saw the real evil god that he is now and knew that Seequest was telling her the truth after all.

From onwards she felt terrible that she was the one that was hurting her children.

As Hades now has them under his control.

Poor Knightmare was beside herself and felt ashamed of what she had done to her children which she wanted for so long.

But also, she had a family which may have been destroyed for trusting her master all this time.

She had great sadness in her eyes.

Hades saw this and told her as he was making sure he was looking deep into her eyes while he did.

"Now, my sweet girl, Knight will soon be gone soon and my Tremor the destructor of earth will be born" and walked away as if he had no care for either of them anymore.

Poor Knightmare felt bad that she did not listen to Seequest from the beginning and that it was a trap from the start.

Knightmare got angry with her master and flapped her wings at his face and scratched him with the claws from her wings.

"You foolish girl, I gave you everything and now I shall take it all away from you for good."

He waved his staff in front of Knightmare and he had taken away her wings so she could not fly anymore and put her in the darkest part of the cave to die.

Meanwhile, Firefly was having a tingly sensation and heard a horse in great pain but it was too faint to know who it was and what happened.

The pain in her back felt like her wings had been taken away from her, eventually, the feeling disappeared.

She felt like something was wrong, as she had not seen her mother or brother for a while.

The voice stopped as it was quiet again, Cerberus was sleeping.

She tried to contact Seequest.

"Father, I hope that you can hear me".

"Help is on the way and it seems that it is needed more than ever."

I feel Mum and Knight are in great danger.

"Please hear, Father Wake up!"

Hours had passed when she felt exhausted from passing on this message to her mind she fell asleep.

Seequest twitched his eyes as if he was starting to feel again and heard his daughter's cry, so he answered back, "My dear Firefly, I am ok".

"I have heard your message, who is coming to rescue us?"

But poor Firefly was so tired to even hear her father's message and missed it.

Chapter Thirty

Will They Ever Escape
Hades Grasp?

Knight felt terrible about what he had done to his mother earlier and was starting to become afraid.

He felt like there was another force growing inside him.

When he reached the stall, he noticed that even his sister was out cold in a deep sleep and could not wait for her to wake up so he could talk about what was happening to him.

Hades carried on now watching him with a close eye and decided to come and get him and split them up.

He called Knight from his stall.

"Knight, come with me, we have some work to do and I feel that your sister is now a distraction to your needs".

"Now, be a good boy and come with me or I will get Cerberus to kill your sister.'

Poor Knight knew he had no choice and trotted quickly with his wings tightly held to his side him as he was approaching Hades.

He quickly trotted over to his sibling first and nuzzled her goodbye and yet she did not move.

He walked out of the stall with his head held low looking towards the floor as he now walked to his master to put these bright red reins on him that will now control his mind.

Poor Knight was disappearing and Tremor was waking up fast instead.

Later that day, Firefly felt a cold feeling in her heart as if her brother was dying in his heart where he was losing control of his mind and body everyday,

Firefly got to her feet and flapped her wings to stretch them, when she did she looked around she was in another part of the cave alone, wondering what had happened to her while she slept.

She felt that something terrible was going to happen soon.

That evening, Knight saw his mother and did not recognize her without her wings.

She called but he did not pay attention to her.

Knightmare kept calling her son but he never looked at her, as he did not recognize her anymore.

He also could not get close enough to smell her scent either and so thought it was another creature that Hades had captured to torment too.

Knightmare felt that she had lost to Hades' evil powers and was frightened of what was going to happen next to her poor son.

The mare was heartbroken once again, as she now lost her son to Hades' ways.

His evil master was feeding him more meat and made him drink a red liquid of the dead souls in his water.

His eyes started to turn into deeper red and the red in his veins that recently appeared now glowed while his teeth started to become pointed too.

The Knight that his family loved was no more.

The birth of Tremor had just begun.

Hades saw this and was delighted in his creation.

The last thing that the god of death had to do is kill Knight once and for all and then Tremor can come alive properly.

One day Knight had his full trust in Hades now and yet inside felt scared and knew that some other force was now inside him taking over his mind and body.

He carried on and obeyed his master's wishes even if it hurt him as Hades threatened to kill his family if he did not do what he asked of him.

Hades tied Knight to the strongest tree that he could find and created a large ball of fire in his hands, poor Knight was neighing in fear standing there knowing that it was him or his family.

Because he loved his family so much that he chose to do anything for them, even if it was his life for theirs.

Hades laughed in a cruel way and said, "Tremor, I call on you to waken in this body that I have given you".

"I call on you to waken now and do my bidding for me,"

He then threw the large ball of fire straight at Knight.

The poor colt was burning and felt like the pain was too much he became mad and angry.

So, he agreed to die inside and allow Tremor to now be born to take away the pain he was feeling.

Tremor then had been awoken.

The creature grew twice the size of Knight's body.

It changed his bat wings into Dragons, where they were even sharper and more dangerous than before.

His power was out of this world, as Tremor had the four powers of the universe.

He had fired from his master and the rest from Seequest.

There was the earth power given to him by Truth when they united together in the past to create the future horse.

Air through the power of his grandfather Pegasus himself and then water is given to him by Neptune, god of the sea, to save his father and grandmother in the past.

Tremor was more powerful than the great Unicorn King that ever lived.

Knight was quickly feeling that he was seriously losing to this great powerful dark force inside of him.

When he saw his mother watching in the cave window in the distance has now he can see closely and yet far as well.

Knightmare was watching from a distance, neighing in anguish to her son.

Then he heard her cry and started to fight Tremor in his mind and defeated him for a while and used Tremor's powers to break free.

He decided to jump into the sea away from Hades' grasp, making a horrible splash that made an earth-quake appear and he began to lose consciousness.

Yet he was prepared to die and then live life as a destructor ruled by Hades, he thought.

Knight was dying inside as he did not have the power of the sea to breathe it like his father and sister.

Tremor had awoken again to save them both as at this time he then realized that he too could not breathe the salt water and wondered if could survive?

Knight wondered if he was a hippocampus like his father of another kind that will never appear as Tremor had changed into something worse than that!!

Back on the land, Knightmare was neighing and crying out for her son to come back.

Hades said while looking through the door to her said 'do not worry, my dear, he will come back soon as my Tremor.

"Your son Knight will be gone and Tremor that you see now will belong to me," as he laughed standing there looking at the weak black mare.

Knightmare put her head down on the floor as she now hated Hades for his cruel ways.

She wept quietly to the ground where no one can hear her but herself knowing that she trusted her master to look after her children better.

She wished that she listened to her beloved in the first place.

As she was hidden away in this dark cave further in the liar.

When she was thinking about Seequest, she wondered what had happened to him.

A thought appeared in her mind that she must find out if Hades lied about most things.

Then she started to think was Seequest still here in the liar somewhere or did he actually leave her and his children behind knowing that she deserted him in the past?

Hades went and collected Knightmare from her slumber and grabbed hold of her mane as she tried to ignore him.

He hits her with his whip which made her give in as he needs her at the moment.

So, he jumps on her as he waves his sword across her body and her beautiful bat wings reappear for one last time before he took them away again and locks her back into a darker cold dungeon below the lair where she was warm and comfortable before and could see the sea.

Hades felt like she was on Seequest's side and that she could not be trusted as his own horse anymore.

So, he punished her more for her distrust towards him and said, "I will teach you, Knightmare, you will not betray me, you just watch me".

When they arrived back he shut her away in a darker place colder than she was before again with no wings or powers anymore.

She did as she was told and did his bidding one last time.

Until he was ready to come and collect her again but for now he kept her hidden from anyone and everything.

Poor Knightmare felt that she might as well die as she had lost everything to her master and sank into her own mind to survive her pain.

Back in the sea, the black creature had become enormous evil looking bigger than a blue whale.

Neptune knew that the battle was starting early and called his knights and his sharks to go and check the damage to the sea's grounds.

So, they could sedate this monster until Apollo and Ares can get the potion into its mouth or body.

First approached the great white sharks and threw them around like toys.

Then the mighty Vissen knights on their dolphins threw golden spears into it and they only seemed to scratch the surface of its body.

It seemed faster than any other creature known before.

Tremor was getting angry and started to kill anyone in its way.

Neptune turned up and said, "Let it go."

Tremor spoke and said, "Knight is not here anymore."

"I shall kill all of you once I get back onto the surface and destroy this earth once and for all as this is my master's bidding."

Neptune could see that Knight was not there as Tremor had mentioned and Hades was winning this fight so far.

He did not like the idea of letting it go but he had orders from Zeus to do so from afar.

Neptune and his Vissen knights pulled back and let the beast escape this time and hoped that there will be next time to defeat it.

Seequest felt terrible pain through his mind and heart knowing that he had to beat this enchanted spell that Hades add put him under.

But he was still not strong enough to awaken properly yet.

Seequest tried to contact Knightmare as he starts to feel her pain as if they were connected in the past through her mind.

If she loved him still he could possibly contact her now this way too to find her again?

Thankfully she did and so when he reached her he felt like she had given up on the world and was completely gone.

"Knightmare", he said 'my darling what is happening?

"Let me see in your eyes if you love me and trust me."

First, Knightmare felt scared and unsure and decided the love of her family meant more to her now than ever before.

She wanted revenge and to destroy Hades or at least hurt him badly.

She started to come back and began to pay attention to what her love Seequest told her to do at last.

"Close your eyes and think of all the good times we have had together and vision me there".

"Now as you do that, put your mind to a place that you love temporarily".

"So, I can come into yours and use your eyes to see what is going on while I am stuck in this lair."

She did as she was told and thought of the times when they fell in love.

Knightmare paid attention and stayed in that moment for Seequest to come into her mind and took over for a few minutes just to see what was around her and possibly where she could be.

Seequest expected her to be still with her children until Firefly told him differently recently.

He opened up her eyes and looked to see destruction and chaos around her and heartache in her heart.

He also read her memories and saw what Hades had done to Knight and their family and knew then that he will do anything to make it right again somehow.

He asked her to come back to her body; mind and said "I am so sorry, Knightmare we have lost Knight the way he was.

"But I may be able to bring him back to you another way but I cannot promise you anything"

"I will try with my life depending on it."

A weak reply came back when Knightmare reached out and replies back "Please, Seequest do anything you can to get our son back."

"OK, listen to what you need to do," and he told her the plan for him to escape in time he said that he would do his best to save her too.

But she said "don't worry about me, my love worry more about our son."

"He needs you more than I will ever do."

Even though she said it Seequest, felt in her heart that she was lying for theirs and the children's safety as that was all that mattered to her now.

She then mentioned this: "thank you for everything you have done".

"You helped me achieve my dreams of being a mother and having a family of my own".

"But if you're alive then I will be happy once more."

Seequest replied back "please do not think this way, I can save you all."

"No, great king, you cannot as I let Hades do this to our children and now I have to live with it all my life".

"It's not your burden to carry It's mine, my love."

Seequest was calling her to listen to him.

But Knightmare would not.

He knew then he lost his love forever when he is back to his great strength Hades will pay big time and will not know what has hit him when he reaches and sees him again, he thought.

Seequest felt devastated that the love of his life that he had was gone.

He knew then that he had to save his children more than before.

They are all that he has left in his life now and yet thought that he would not give up on her yet.

Seequest was getting stronger every hour proving that he is a fighter, not a quitter.

Knowing that no matter what challenge he had put in front of him, somehow, he would always beat it.

As he was in the dark at first and now sees the bright light to reach freedom again.

He felt that Hades had greater control over him and that he too was being taken over.

Because he felt that his willpower, he knew then was disappearing from his mind.

The first time Seequest felt that he was beaten and needed help from his daughter Firefly.

That's if he could reach her again in time before he disappeared completely too, he thought.

He contacted his daughter to find out what had happened to her as he cannot do anything for Knight until he was set free once more.

He closed his eyes tightly and thought hard about his daughter's appearance so that the connection in their minds would be much stronger than before.

He said "Firefly, it's me, your father."

"Listen to me carefully".

"My powers are strengthening gradually and yet not quite right",

"I also feel that Hades is draining them at the same time, so my magic is weakening again".

"I need your help, please, daughter, hear me, I beg you."

Eventually, Firefly started to come to him and stood up feeling light-headed awoken from this deep sleep that she tried to fight recently.

She had been out for a long time and had her first drink of water when she started to feel better and then she could hear her father's call.

She answered him and so he continued his message to her.

Of what he wanted her to do for him, as he was too weak and far away from his son and daughter to help them or that's what he thought.

"I want you to talk to your brother for me."

She heard his voice and replied, "I would love to but I am not with him anymore."

"It looks like we have been spilt up while I was asleep and now I am lying with my wings strapped to me in a dark cave that smells of mice and oats."

"Father, I am trapped and scared, what's happening to us?"

Poor Seequest starts to fear for them all, as he then remembered what his mother told him about fear in the past.

That it is what we make it to be, which meant it will feed on our negativity due to pain and hurt then it can destroy us.

But he then shook his head and said "it's never real unless you let it enter your mind and allow it to grow bigger through the pain you are feeling at the moment".

"Otherwise try to ignore it and put happy positive thoughts back instead, where then the fear will grow smaller and eventually disappear for good!"

And positively will live forever until needed for your protection only.

He said to ease the way she was feeling.

After listening to his wise voice, she started to calm down and began to think of a way how to escape this.

From there, he woke up and felt stronger and knew then that he needed to do something and save his family if he could.

He replied, trying to keep her as calm as possible by saying "look, do not worry, sweet one".

"I will tell you in due time, you said to me in the past that Hermes is on his way to us, yes?"

"Yes, I believe so, has that is what I was told from Celestial last."

"What, "you have spoken to the queen of the heavens?"

"Yes, father, quite a few times now and she knew all about you."

"Wow, my daughter, I don't even have the power to do that, Lucky you."

Then he was thinking how lovely it would be just to talk to his mother figure again one last time.

But he knew this to be impossible.

He kept talking to Firefly until he got everything over to her correctly and clearly, making sure that she did not give up as her mother had recently, by letting her pain get the better of her, poor thing.

He repeated, "OK, is anyone else with you?"

"Yes, Cerberus is here sleeping beside me and has been told by Hades to kill me if I try to escape him."

"OK, just stay calm and be patient until Hermes gets there, to distract him and frees you."

She replied, "OK."

Seequest then said, "I have faith, my daughter."

"They will come for us, I know it."

The last thing that Seequest could read from his daughter's memories quickly while talking was that he heard that Hades was going to start a war.

First Neptune destroys his sea creatures and drains them all somehow by using his winged chimera beasts and doing it with Tremor as well.

While Seequest was becoming angrier and more impatient, he heard a buzzing noise and an angel's voice in the distance.

"It is me, Hermes" the demi-god"

"I sound and look like a bumblebee."

"So don't squash me when you see me, OK?"

"I am coming to free you from your misery and pain."

The great Unicorn King neighed quietly with relief in his mind, knowing that he was not forgotten and his loved ones came back for him from the sea.

Hermes said "we're planning to rescue you and get you home again," or that's what they hoped.

That night, the buzzing become louder in his ears when he felt a bumblebee land on his back and sting him badly.

He jumped up and then felt like his strong self at hundred per cent again for the first time in months.

He had a good shake so his circulation and muscles could work again making him able to walk properly once more.

His horn was glowing so bright that it felt like it was even too bright for him to handle.

So, he thought maybe it needed to be a little less bright as he toned it down for him to bear again.

His horn at the time was bright red of anger in his heart and he began to grow larger and broke the vortex.

This made a great noise that shook the cave.

Seequest was free and said, 'we must go and find Firefly and free her too'.

Hermes agreed and sat on Seequest's back to go deeper into the caves.

Seequest was galloping faster than he ever could before.

He felt that his feet were not touching the floor anymore.

Hermes believed that Seequest was galloping in thin air as he was more powerful now, as this magic power had laid dormant in his body has never been put into this position of hate before.

Seequest was going to use the hate and make it into a positive power to defeat Hades once and for all.

"Wow", he said "hold on Hermes", and he galloped on to find Firefly's cave.

They reached the cave when Hermes quickly flew into her dungeon and stung her too.

It made her jump and neigh and kick hard at the door where Cerberus flew backward.

The three-headed black-red Great Dane said, Why did you do that, you stupid thing!

"Now I am going to have to kill you for that."

Seconds later Seequest appeared and said, "You were going to do what, Cerberus, to my daughter?"

Cerberus could see that Seequest was larger than before and his horn was glowing red, which he was afraid of, as that was the time not to mess with him.

Because that's when the great unicorn king will hurt you, not caring about the damage that he would do to you anymore.

So instead he clawed Firefly as she was getting slowly closer to the doorway and unfolding her wings.

She neighed in pain and then Hermes stung the creature loads of times that he whimpered and ran further to his master's lair to tell him what had just happened to him and that they were escaping.

As he was running for his dear life, he cried out, "I will be back with my master, your spiteful unicorn you" and cried all the way, howling through the caves as he went further into the distance.

"Hurry", Seequest said "we do not have a lot of time left before they come back from Knight's/Tremor's training routine."

Hermes was holding on to Firefly's mane as they were galloping straight out of the cave to find the sunshine shining in their eyes.

They had to lay low for a while to adjust to it and it had been a long time since they both had seen the sun.

They rested in the sunshine for a while and drank from the spring that Seequest purified first.

Afterwards, Hermes told Seequest where his son and his mate were too.

The Unicorn King promised his daughter that he will try and find her mother and rescue her from her hell If possible.

If she would follow him, he thought and hoped.

Seequest had the plan to try to rescue Knight before it was too late for them all.

He told his daughter and Hermes to lie low until he came back hopefully with Knight with him and her mother too.

He prayed that he could save them both as he kept repeating to himself in his mind, "I am the great Unicorn King and I am more powerful than any other creature on this Earth I will not be defeated by anything or any-one anymore!"

Eventually, he noticed that he reached the other side of the cave.

Seequest was bright pinkish red, as he was expressing love and anger at the same time, which was a good combination to have as it prevented hate from ever arising greatly and out of control.

As it protected and saved him many times before, his horn was shining brightly on his beautiful chiselled forehead.

Eventually, Tremor reappeared from the sea and car-ried on his training, while the knight was sleeping inside his mind still.

Hades came to collect him as he felt his presence and said "I knew that you would be back my dear boy!"

Leaving his daughter and Hermes to rest Seequest galloped back into the cave to where Hades was training his son.

Near the rock surface, near the sea where Knight could not escape Tremor becoming him again.

But yet Seequest could see in his eyes that he was still there fighting the fight for his own body and then he felt there was hope that they all could save his son in the end, he thought?

Seequest stood there in shock watching the terrible torture that his son was put through.

Yet felt like Knight could hold on for a little bit longer as Seequest seemed to be more worried about Knightmare, his mate, than his son at this time.

Even though he was terribly upset that he had to choose in the first place.

But he knew that Knight would have a better chance to survive as he is part of him as well as his mother.

Knight was more of him than Hades realized.

He quickly tried to contact him and got quickly through before Tremor appeared that he was free and was coming for him.

He was holding on with all his might and thinking of the good memories of them all together in the woods as the family they once were before.

For some time, Knight seemed to stop Tremor from taking over him.

While Seequest then knew his son was more like him than he thought.

He prayed that he would not give up the fight with Tremor yet.

Hades was getting really mad now that he pushed even a deeper power onto Knight.

Thankfully Knight knew his father loved him and was coming to take him home again.

He used all his willpower to fight this evil force that Hades was trying to awaken inside of him again and he tried his best to ignore the pain as well.

After all, he was the son of the King of Unicorns and they could feel the pain which they then would use in a positive manner to create great strength from it instead!

As it strengthens their own powers to full glory because it pushes them eventually to release their own full potential of strength back to survive the fight.

Seequest asked his son at this time if he could hold on a little while longer as he founds his mother and rescues her first.

Seequest mentions in his mind that he would come back for him and promised him this.

Knight then for once believed in his father again.

Seequest at this time could see the brave; handsome black stallion of good that his son was after all and was planning to try with all his heart to save him somehow.

Knight kept thinking of he was originally not this terrible beast that Hades was trying to awaken inside of him all the time now.

Knight seemed pleased with what his father said and raised his powerful head and neighed while he carried on fighting the fight.

Until he became exhausted and could do no more to prevent what happened next.

Seequest was worried about his son's safety and yet knew that he could look after himself or that is what he hoped anyway?

He galloped onto a dark rough jagged path on another side of the lair near the rocks to rescue Knightmare.

Then Cerberus appeared in front of him.

There standing was a large image of a three-headed type of Great Dane whose teeth were razor sharp and had claws that could rip them apart with one go with a completely large muscular body too.

Seequest suggested going back and getting his daughter, as he knew then that he could not do this after all on his own.

As Firefly's powers are different from his own as she has some of Hades' dark magic in her as well from her mother's side.

He started to turn back and galloped towards the entrance of the woods where she could help him this time round.

Cerberus shouted out so Knightmare could hear him say "that's it Seequest you run away like a good little unicorn you actually are while, your love one now fades away here"

Hopefully, Knightmare did believe the hell hounds lies and hoped that Seequest will come back at least to say goodbye.

He arrived back at the woods empty-handed.

Of course, Firefly thought the worst when luckily Seequest mentioned before reaching her, "do not worry" they are not dead".

"I have just realized that you are possibly stronger than me and I need your help, come on and meet me at the cave where we'll all go back together as one."

Seequest met up with his daughter as she flew there quicker into the cave once more.

Hermes followed back into the caves to where he was earlier.

When they were all together again Seequest said to Firefly, "Go and find your mother and I will catch up with you soon."

"Father, no, I can help you", and within that, Cerberus appeared out of the shadows and jumped onto Firefly and clawed and damaged a part of her wing.

She screamed and neighed in pain but now her horn had grown longer.

Her father said, "Close your eyes and believe in yourself, and the wand will work with you."

The Unisos filly did exactly what her father told her to and closed her eyes

Next, she said "Oh, great wand of the magic of mine let me use you for good I need you more than ever!"

Within a few seconds, her horn started to glow a beautiful pink and then red, like her father's, and charged Cerberus with it and killed one of his heads.

"How do you like that, you stupid dog!"

He whined and ran away scared.

"Hurry, he will be back, so we must so go now and find your mum before it is too late.

Fly, daughter, fly as far as you can go with Hermes."

Firefly tried to flap her wings to take flight, but she noticed that she was injured and temporarily grounded for a while,

"OK, then come with me".

They approached the beginning of the sea from Hades' liar.

The unicorn king went into the sea where it was enough just once for Seequest to turn into a hippocampus and told his daughter not to fear the water.

At this time, he thought he could just swim away and forget everything.

But love and devotion for his mare and now children changed his mind and stayed to try and free them all from Hades' grips! Or that's what he hoped he could do?

He told her to believe it was part of her this time, because of her being a young female winged unicorn that has the power of her horn.

At last, she could turn into a beautiful hippocampus.

Meanwhile, Hermes was buzzing above them in the air.

The unicorn king went into the sea where he turned into a hippocampus and told his daughter not to fear the water.

Seequest seemed pleased that Firefly was similar and that at least she may want to come home with him in the near future or that is what he hoped she wanted to do.

Once she got the hang of balance swimming with her pretty swallowtail like his, they dived into the deep sea to the other side of the dark caves into Hades' lair.

They reached the Pool of Souls and quickly jumped back out of it as they could be pulled under by many that lived there now.

These souls were of gods and goddesses that had gone wrong in the past and never learned from their mistakes.

This was their punishment from Zeus's orders to live out in the Pool of Souls of the Forgotten and not be heard about again.

First, Firefly fell back as a few souls grabbed hold of her.

But Hermes helped and buzzed around them until she could once more come to the surface and breathe and come out of the dark waters.

They both shook and changed back to the original forms again and heard cries in the distance.

They both knew that it was Knightmare in pain, so they attempted to go and rescue her.

When they broke open the cage and saw an old horse in emotional pain standing there they both sadly did not recognize her.

Because Hades had done was put her back to her original form as a normal horse before she died those so many years ago.

Then he breathed his powers of life/death into her again to be a beautiful, strong demon mare and now she was just a dead horse living with great sorrow in her mind.

Knightmare's head was down and sunken.

They tried to bring her back by putting their horns on her forehead but it was no use.

The Knightmare/ her mother they both dearly loved so much, was not there sadly no more.

Her voice spoke and said, "The Knightmare you knew and loved is gone and all that is left is me."

The dead horse said, "Leave me to perish, as I did this to you all."

"I am sorry for all this hurt and suffering that I have caused you and now it's my turn to bear it for eternity."

"I love you all but I trusted my master more to do something good for a change I was seriously wrong to trust an evil god"

"Has to I was tricked by the devilish games he plays."

"But I never thought that he would have played me, his one and only faithful mare until now".

"I don't regret any of it until now as I have hurt you, especially Knight."

"He will never forgive me" as bless him he tried to tell and warn me that Hades was doing wrong to him",

"But of course, I trusted that my master would not do such a thing that I did not listen to him because of my poor ignorance my son is becoming now an abomination to the world."

"So please leave me here in the cave and let Hades do whatever he wishes with me."

Firefly walked up to the old mare and nuzzled her, as she believed and knew that it was her mother.

She said "mother this is not your thought, It's is Hades not yours.

Please "No, my dear child, this is where I belong now".

"I know though you have a greater purpose which you will find out in due time with your father I am sure".

Go now, my child, and do not look back on your life.

"Only forward and go enjoy it by living every day that you have with your family and friends in your future".

"Has that's what your father taught me once as you never know when it shall end, my dear daughter."

"I love you so much, now go and leave me behind as your past".

They nuzzled each other and then she walked away sadly.

"Go with your father and try and save your brother and look only to the present day, which in time will create your future too"

Even though the dark old horse was weak she had a wise deposition about her.

As that is how she survived all these years before on her own and probably why she was chosen to be her stallion's mare for his herd in the first place.

The weak mare then said "go, I love you all forever there is nothing here for you all no more, I am done with this life and there is nothing more for me to give to you"

She then kept talking to her daughter saying "Go now, my child, and do not look back on this life.

Leave me here, I ask of you, please?"

But Seequest and Firefly said, "Never."

Then Seequest said "we will bring you home somehow".

"But for now, stay here and we will be back" but they all really knew that they would not, as the Knightmare they loved and adored was completely gone.

Seequest was neighing and screaming in anger.

"He said in an angry tone enough of your pity, my dear."

"You are brave and courageous and if you will not go with us now, that is how our children will remember you as, my love".

"I will ask you one last time".

"Please come with us as my friends the gods have powers too and can beat Hades' powers."

"No, Seequest, you must leave me, as I will always be connected to Hades, as I am dead and an evil spirit of his making."

"Remember, what you saw before was an image he wanted you all to see of me".

I cannot leave, as if I leave the cave this time, you will not see me.

"As I have nobody to live in as I am just an old horse's fire soul of light."

They would not take no for answer and waited while she slept and Seequest carried her out of the cave.

Within seconds the sunlight had been on her delicate body when Knightmare disappeared and all they then could see was an invisible image of a horse she once was.

The ghost horse woke up and said, "See I told you I cannot leave, even if I wanted to."

"As I always been just a fire spirit and soul of a dead horse?"

As she spoke with a sad voice of disappointment, in her tone.

"I am sorry to have put you through this, Seequest"

"But it was the only way that I could experience having children and a family"

"Because it is all I ever wanted when I was alive", please forgive me and send my love to our son"

Then within seconds, the ghostly horse ran back into the cave when she changed back into her black horse form again when she neighed with a deep cry as she went.

"I did feel that I love for you all, so I must still do' and again galloped away until they could not hear her hooves touching the ground anymore."

Seequest and Firefly had tears in their eyes as they could not believe what they just saw and heard were true, when they said in their minds, we still love you too.

And that you will always live on in our lives like you did when we were together as one back then.

Seequest said to her through their minds "Rest now my beautiful black velvet queen, I shall Love you forever more".

"I promise I will save our children for you my love if it's the last thing that I do"

Thankfully, the black mare felt the love from them as they both shone their horns toward her, both their horn's sparkle a pink bright light into her mind.

So, she could feel it in her heart for one last time as she knew them once before.

But she also knew that she would do her best to keep that spark alive in the middle of her dead heart.

She believed then that she was forgiven and that she could rest in peace once more as a good horse in heart, even if not in her mind.

The Unicorn King said, "Come, we have things to do and friends to see", even though he was heartbroken and knew then, there was no hope of saving his true love anymore.

They galloped back towards the entrance of the cave to freedom once more, or that was what they thought was the case this time?

Once again, they headed back through the top caves and out towards the doorway of the forest.

They all rushed out together and landed on the ground of the Forbidden Woods this time which is closer to the beach.

At last, Seequest felt free, or was he?

Chapter Thirty-One

Tremor the Demon Horse and Knight's no more?

The next day Hades decided that he wanted Tremor to go back into the sea and cause more damage, to take the mer-folk and his brother Neptune take off the scent of rescuing Seequest.

Hades gets Tremor to sleep once he throws him into the sea and let's Knight wake up has he begins to drown to get the attention of Neptune once more.

Where Tremor had time to change in front of Neptune and his knights, into a creature with a horse head with longer slim type of body like Louis when he changes into a seahorse.

But with a difference, as it has one fin from its head to its tail that makes it swim very fast and at the moment it can swim in the sea struggling for breath though as after all, it was knight's body and so will still have his allergies as tapping the other part of his mind!

That's why knights can sometimes take over again.

Tremor is not strong enough yet to take over his complete mind and yet will soon!

The beast manages to survive for a short while for some reason, as it does not like the sea very much as it shows its anger and hatred for being there.

Due to the way, it was treated badly last time.

Now the creature wants its revenge and wanted to destroy anything in its path.

Hades has Tremor under mind control.

So now Hades and Tremor are more powerful as they are working together as one.

This time Neptune thought they had Tremor where they wanted him.

When he looked in eyes of the beast it was not how he expected the creature to react towards him.

But there in the deep waters struggling was a sweet calm natured spirit of Knight, so Neptune orders his mer-knight s to let him go again.

But the sea god did not know that Knight can survive in salt water.

At this time Knight cannot swim and went to the depths of the sea and died at the bottom of the ocean after Neptune let him go.

While he was fighting the creature in his mind and yet in the end he felt like he was defeated by it for now.

Eventually the actual beast as awoken as it is completely free again and swims freely away to cause more damage in the sea where it plans to do worse this time round.

Hades sends it the power for it now to breathe in the sea as well.

It has found another secret of Knight's and will use this to go deeper into the ocean and destroy at a closer range.

The evil beast was getting angry.

Has it begun to light up itself with red flames piercing through its body and it became a creature of fire?

That moves its hot fiery body around the sea heating it up which was killing the fish and sea creatures as it went.

Neptune at the time wishes that he kept hold of the beast.

But also was beating himself up as he was a friend of its father's and also was curious about what this other creature actually was.

The sea god could see this happening quickly and decided to call the blue whales with his mind secretly.

The sea god then guided them to all the parts of the ocean.

Where he tells them to wave their tails up and down as fast as they can go, which eventually cools the water down and washes away the flames away.

Neptune said, 'That was close".

He said to his mer-knights "we must get this creature back onto land as soon as possible where he can be defeated by us all."

While Neptune was wondering how they could get this creature out of the water?

His mer-folk were also around trying to clear away the flames from the lands by using their dolphins to squirt water together over it.

Eventually, as they are an army, they beat the flames this time round.

They appeared to help Queen Sera who came riding Sea Spray in her battle gear of great beauty of silver and aqua blue carrying her staff with the most power-ful crystal skull inside of it.

Was the Lemurian crystal which powered up her staff?

Through all four crystal skulls united into one.

She knew of another but no one ever found it in her time yet.

She said, "Behold great beast, you have not beaten us yet.

"I ask you politely to leave this place or I shall truly kill you myself", hoping in her mind she really did not have to".

But she had to show authority in front of her people and her king.

Luckily, she threw the staff's power at the beast and hit it gently for it to swim back to land.

As they all chased it, they could see it was a very unusual creature that they had never seen before.

The king and queen of the sea said that they would chase the beast out of the waters themselves while riding their beautiful sea horses to the shore.

They both wondered what type of creature this beast was, as again it was something completely different from all the other sea creatures.

They also were confused that was this, first, Knight, Seequest's actual son

Even though it was their enemy, they also feared for its life and their own at the same time, as it was being commanded to kill by Hades himself.

They chased Tremor now hurt to the top of the surface where his dragon wings appeared once more, which knocked them both across the sea.

She galloped into the ball of flames in front of them, which took them into a portal to the land above.

They swam back, quickly to see a tormented creature trying to escape them.

The black water creature turned around quickly and bit Sea Spray's back with its sharp teeth, which knocked the queen off of her.

Sea Spray was tough and quickly recovered and swam forward towards her queen, where she jumped back on her again and continued the chase.

Eventually, the king and the queen stung Tremor with their trident and staff and it shook the sea, as the waves grew great that they took the creature under with it to the bottom of the ocean where it nearly drowned.

This spooked the creature and it wanted to break free.

They did their best to keep the creature from burning up to its true potential again.

They decided that they wanted out and started to recover its wings from its body.

So, they helped it pull itself back to the surface of the land and tried to get away from them for good.

Tremor's front legs were slightly different from the hippocampus as his hooves had turned into fins, which made him a bigger swimmer in calm waters.

The black beast felt like he had time to recover from the pain and reacted again to attack once more.

When he poked his head out of the water and squirted out the salt, there in the background were Neptune and Queen Sera ready to attack again.

But this time, they watched as if Tremor's personality changed for a split second and his eyes went orange instead of red.

Hades had a plan and used his own magic to pretend to be Knight, while really Seequest's son was still sleeping while Tremor was in command of his body.

Tremor then said, 'leave me alone.

"I am Seequest's son and I do not want to harm anyone."

So, they drew closer.

Seconds later, the creature jumped up and splashed right in front of them as they fell off their hippocampius's, which made them sink to the bottom of the ocean with their riders swimming hopelessly with them in the sea.

"Ha-ha, I tricked you, you silly Vissen's," even though it was knight's voice.

The king and queen of the sea realized it was Hades in control due to its sarcasm.

It reappeared and jumped out of the sea onto the land near the cave where he breathed in and blew out again a large gust of wind.

That pushed Neptune and Sera further back into the ocean.

He then reared once again as the evil-winged unicorn he was.

Red-hot flames grew all over his body with his eyes that looked like red rocks.

As he flew and landed on the land, he accidentally burnt everything as he went.

But this was why Hades created him in the first place to destroy earth and rule it as he sees fit.

Tremor was in so much pain and hated that the creature felt like his mind would explode from inside him.

He was in great pain because of the saltwater on his skin and in his body, thinking that he was immune to it and even with his power he wasn't!

This angered him greatly.

Because at this point Hades did not care if the beast felt pain while it was damaging the lands and seas.

Knight had woken and had a great advantage of still occasionally being in control at times.

Tremor just had the strength to get away, so he leaped straight into the sky until he found a nice piece of land.

As he was burning the fields, woods everywhere which all became covered in flames.

Because his whole body was lit up like a ball of red lava, everywhere he went or passed got burnt in the process.

Tremor was exhausted and fell asleep in the burnt woods, where then Knight could wake up and be his self soon.

When Tremor was resting, Knight looked around feeling awful and sorry for the damage that Tremor had done and was doing to the lands that he grew up with and loved.

Seequests' son was upset as the woods that his father used to take them to as foals was on fire.

It broke his heart to see and then said "I may have to die after all to save my family and friends, even though he did not like the idea."

He knew that it may come to it.

Luckily Tremor taught Knight to use his own horn without knowing, it lit up bright blue which flashed as it helped to put out fires around him.

Has it appeared to produce water and blew from his mouth to help reach all the areas, which seemed to drain out the fire everywhere he could see.

He realized that he must find his father asking for help before Hades gets his body; mind back where he will make him into a destructor of earth once more forever.

Knight was terrified of what he became, so he hid for a while in one of the caves on top of Moonbeam's Mountain.

Where he felt was the last place he was liked and loved for who he originally was.

He now wanted to live this day forever and try his best to keep Tremor at bay for a while.

Knight lay there looking at his new body, which was covered in burns and red veins.

His mane was longer as well.

He walked to the birch tree to drink from the spring water when he looked in the pond and he did not rec-ognize himself anymore,

Tremor looks back at him, saying "did you miss me?"

"I am now part of you, like it or not".

So, get used to it, as you know your body and mind belong to me now and I will control you always'.

He put the red horn into the pond which killed all the fish in it by accident as trying to get a drink to cool down.

Straightaway, Knight was upset about what this evil force had done to these harmless fish and started trying to fight Tremor from the inside.

But once again, the evil winged unicorn was in control of Knight's horn and puts it on his chest and burns him.

Doing this bought back the strength of Tremor to awaken again and made him feel terrible pain and caused him to become angry once more.

"See, Knight," Tremor said, "I will win" and laughed.

Knight is very upset and quickly jumps and trots away when thinking what had he become now?

Poor Knight felt that he was getting tired of coping with all this pain that was afflicted onto him and fell into a trance again.

Tremor said "that's it sleeps tight old friend and he opened up his wings and started to flap them viciously, making the tree's bark fall down as he was digging his hooves into the ground."

He feels bored, so he jumped into the air back home to Hades' lair where he was summoned to go.

"I hear our master calling, Knight and now we must go to him."

Poor Knight, now was feeling useless and trapped in his own body again.

He wondered if he ever be free of this force of evil power?

He felt like it was becoming a part of him now and started to wonder if he would ever be the true dear caring and loving knight again and if he could, will they save him from bad self?.

Has he may have to be killed in the end to stop this evil force that was trying to destroy Mother Earth which he loved so much in the past?

He felt terrible that he had no control anymore and just lay dormant in his own body for now.

While Tremor had full control of Knight's mind once more.

Chapter Thirty-Two

Tremor Arrives Back
at Hades Lair

Hades could feel the presence of Tremor coming home, so he mentioned it to Knightmare.

He told her that her son is a demon horse and that this is her true son's destiny not just another black bat-winged horse like her.

He walked over to her and put her red reins and saddle on her back.

As he did this, she changed once again into his demon mare with her wings once more.

Hades said, "As long as you do not betray me, girl, you will always be this mare of power, not the one you were once before."

"Do you agree with my conditions?"

The poor old mare agreed by neighing with delight to think at least she will have the strength and powerful body with an intelligent mind once more that she seemed to like.

As she still felt that she was useful again in death as this demon horse.

Seequest and Firefly were now Knightmare's enemies, as when Hades put on the reins, it wiped her memory of them, apart from her son Tremor and that is all she remembers.

Hades liked her reply and said "Good, then let us go and meet him."

Her eyes start to glisten of fire red and the red veins start to appear once more with revenge in her mind.

He climbed on her back when she rears with smoke coming from her nostrils and her eyes were now like fire with flames running through her body again.

This time, she grew twice her size than before as they were getting ready for battle against the gods.

She galloped into the ball of flames in front of them, which took them into a portal to the land above.

They reached the Forbidden Woods where there was flying above them was Tremor himself.

Hades called him and said "Come here, my champion of hell."

At this time, the god of death did not know that it was Knight who was in charge, as he was not giving up on claiming his body back from this evil force that was now living within him.

Hades could see that Tremor was not paying attention and looked like he was having a battle in the sky with himself.

So, Hades got out his Sword of Doom and pointed it towards Tremor/Knight, where it lit up a red-hot blaze and he threw it at the dragon-winged unicorn, which caught the flame on its neck and burnt him making it angry again.

Only Tremor could take that type of pain being a fire force of darkness.

Knight had to become dormant once more and let Tremor command his body this time.

Seequest's son fought with all his might and tried his best to bear the pain.

But he still cannot win the battle between himself and Tremor in the sky just yet.

Hades said a verse with his sword and says "I command you, Tremor you shall do as I tell you, my boy."

When he pointed the sword again toward the black-winged unicorn and this time, the ball of fire hit his forehead and went straight into his mind.

There, Knight was knocked out and put into a coma in his own body.

Tremor now lives and controls him completely.

The Evil horse neighed, which made the skies terrible and dark, as he started to breathe fire and his wings; mane and tail were lit in orange and red flames all over him.

Hades said, "Excellent, that's my boy."

"Now you are mine,"

Hades called Tremor to come and see him and his mother again on the ground.

Knight was out for count because the underworld god was tormenting him with all his great memories all in one go.

This made him feel overwhelmed that there was too much happiness and pain at the same time for him to handle.

Until hopefully one day he could awaken once more or that is what he hoped in time?

Before the black dragon-winged creature landed Knight decided to see if his mother was the sweet mare he first knew and love still?

Where maybe she can still help him beat Tremor, from within?

Because of his thinking, he thought that he could kill Hades with all the great powers he possesses now.

Knightmare landed right in front of him and Knight was hoping that he could knock the sword out of Hades' hands.

When Knightmare saw what he was going to do, she reared into him and protected her master and bit her son.

Knight was shocked and yet respected her wishes.

So, to play along, he nuzzled her and said quietly in his mind, "mother, it is me, your son, Knight."

"I am trying to beat Tremor but you must help me, please and rescue our family from harm."

"We can do this together."

Knightmare reared with anger and said, "I do not have any family apart from Tremor."

Poor Knight was devastated and looked into her eyes and could only see evil and hatred and then realized that his mother was gone forever which broke his heart to see this.

Because she bit him again and burnt his neck with her pointed teeth scratching him with her claws from her black wings waving them up and down and striking him to the floor.

He collapsed and felt heartbroken and lay still.

Knightmare shook him to see if the beast was still alive and looked into its eyes.

There she saw her son being trapped in his own body forever.

Then as he was lying there, she could see tears falling from his eyes.

But Knight realized then his mother was now gone.

He closed them for the last time, becoming angry.

Then Tremor was back and Knight had disappeared completely.

Has Knight from inside felt that his life had ended?

He shut off from the world, hoping that one day his family will once more be able to wake him to the life that he once knew and loved so much.

Before he did this, he first closed his eyes in front of his mother.

When in his mind for the last time he thought he will call out to his sister, saying, "Firefly, it's me, Knight."

"Sadly, I am no more!"

"Please kill this beast that now lives in my body if you have to save the world I forgive you and understand why this was done".

"And if you do, I will still love you all forever."

There, Knight's body was lying on the ground, which made the land shake terribly.

The large black-winged horse's wings were lying limp beside him when Hades said, "Enough of this nonsense."

"I tried the easy way and this has not worked knowing that you are Knightmare's son."

"But to control you fully, dear boy, I will have to do this,"

So, he jumped off the mare and approached the helpless colt and began to cut half of Knight's horn and in replace he put his sword there instead, so he had complete control from now on.

Luckily none of the beasts felt this happen as they were out for the count.

Hades' sword then emerged with the rest of the horn and became a jagged shape, which looked more like Hades' sword and meant that Hades had full control from there onwards.

The black hell horse arose and stood up boldly and wisely answering Hades' commands instantly.

"My master, what do you want of me?"

"I am Tremor the Destructor."

"Excellent", Hades said with a smile.

There in the background, Knightmare reared with sadness and excitement too.

Knightmare that everyone knew was now, lost because Hades had her under his spell as well.

"Awaken, Tremor.

I command you now and you shall do my bidding."

But inside, even though Knight is gone, he can still feel the pain of his powers now being taken over by Hades.

Has he disappeared into his thoughts as if he died?

Tremor stood tall even more powerful than ever before and obeyed everything that Hades told him to do.

Tremor now bowed in front of Hades and said, "Yes my master, I shall."

"Good", the evil god said.

'Then let us practice more of your skills, as tomorrow you will bring chaos to this world again.

I will make a monster out of you yet and you will help me become the new ruler of earth,' as he laughed with an evil chuckle in his voice.

Something else happened to Tremor as the jagged horn grew back into a sharper, larger-looking horn than before.

He seemed to have no fear of anything, as Knight had died now inside, which meant that Tremor could do anything with his body as he pleased.

Hades said, "Excellent, now I have the true powers of the Unicorn King and more, as you are working beside me."

"I cannot fail, as I now have all the powers of earth working beside me and not against me at last" and roared a voice of victory.'

Hades was right, as he did have the full powers and he also had bad to help him too.

"Rise, Tremor, my fire horse of hell."

Knightmare saw something that she recognized.

It was the silver birch tree that she used to lie down with Seequest and remembered what he told her about will power and strength of mind control.

From that moment, she felt a little part of her memory come back and thought, is it possible she could save her son still from Hades one day?

Knowing that possibly Knight would forgive her for all that she had done to him recently she thought?

Knightmare also thought that would he still love her like before.

She played along with Hades' plans to see what the future brings.

But then she felt Hades touch her side with his sword on her forehead and again the memory of that moment was gone.

In another split second, she was fighting his command as she looked again at the tree.

But this time she could only think of the present day as Hades had her under his mind control.

Before this happened, she knocked some flowers off the tree that would not have fallen themselves because of the time of year.

It was her way of showing Seequest or anyone the way back to Hades' lair to hopefully rescue them both before it was too late.

The black demon mare was praying that someone will rescue Seequest and that he may see them, knowing that she loved him still.

By collecting these flowers from the tree for her as they were her favourites and guessed that she was the Knightmare that he loved and knew still did inside.

So hopefully Seequest could maybe save her too or that is what she was praying for.

Knightmare started to see the true horrible master for what Hades truly was and that everyone wanted to kill him, even her.

But how can you kill a god that lives under the ground who is dead already, she thought?

They all arrived back into the lair when they saw Seequest had escaped from his vortex.

Seequest was catching up with Firefly and Hermes earlier.

Tremor and Knightmare sensed that he was still in the liar and caught up with him unexpectedly.

Seequest looked at them both and gracefully refused to fight them to the death.

But it was Hades' orders and they had to do now what they were told.

Seequest was horrified that he had to fight his mate and also his son at the same time.

So, they kicked him with their hooves to the ground as he was still weak and adjusting to moving again.

They scratched him and they both bit him, so he had to defend himself.

In the end, he did the same to them.

He looked into their eyes and was heartbroken to see the family that he loved was gone.

But he thought that there must be a way to get them back and always believed there was hope?

Eventually, Seequest gave up and said "Hades you win, as I will not fight my family"

"Do what you want with me or tell me what you want me to do and I shall do it for you?"

Hades was shocked and said, "Well, well, well, Seequest, you can still surprise me."

Hades let them all stay together for a while.

As Seequest was lying there being guarded by his ex-family, he still went and nuzzled them both and put his head on their shoulders.

Hopefully trying to put the potion from his horn which Hermes put there earlier to try and get his loved ones back by brushing it against the top of their heads while resting happily.

Sadly it did not work, so it was no use.

They were too far under Hades' spells.

Then Tremor said "Nice try" and fought with him again and this time, Seequest defended his body and drove his horn through Tremor's chest.

He neighed and then reared up and his wound started to heal straight away.

Tremor said, "Yes, Seequest, you forget I have your powers too."

The Unicorn King then realized that these powers were even too much for him to beat this beast on his own.

The Unicorn King tried so hard to get him away from Knightmare.

Seequest lit his horn up with anger which became bright red and burnt this beast on the head.

Now, Tremor ran off and was alone and had escaped, jumping through the fire, and burning himself in the process to escape Seequest.

Seequest created a ball of white light to protect them while sleeping.

Tremor seriously got burnt because of the fire.

This time Seequest used his true power, which Tremor received with great force.

Eventually, the unicorn king was strong enough to gallop away and reach his daughter again.

He stops right in front of her feeling shattered and exhausted, not afraid to show his feelings to her.

Firefly saw her father battered and bruised and badly bitten when he says "Firefly I am sorry I failed you."

He fell to the ground with a large bang, which shook the trees and his horn started to dull out.

She rushed to his aid and said, "Father don't you die on me, I need you.

We need you" and she closed her eyes and lay beside him and said a verse when her horn started to light up a beautiful jade colour of light to dark shades of green.

She closed her eyes and thought of healing him as she puts her glowing horn onto her father's wounds, which begin to heal up slowly.

As she did this, her actual body changed into different shades of jade and when she was done, she also said another verse, which is about love and harmony.

Firefly's horn again began to change into rose pink quartz as she put her horn this time onto Seequest's forehead.

As this, happened, the rose-pink tones flowed all over her body beautifully, expressing the full love energy as it glowed and made a pretty aura all around them.

It took hours to completely heal the king.

Firefly was pleased with her results and rested beside her father with her angel-feathered wing's, one lying beside her and the other over her father's body trying to keep him warm.

Later that day, Seequest had woken to see his beautiful daughter had changed once again to this stunning feathered winged unicorn with a great difference.

Has she woken and got up from her slumber?

Firefly started to feel different from before.

She felt more alive and in control of her powers and felt the great powers that lay in her for so long were now more powerful than ever before has had awaken them at last.

As now her true powers showed her love for life and survival.

She now understood her father's role of protecting everything in his path.

Plus, how it could also be exhausting and heart breaking what he needed to do sometimes and even sacrifice his happiness to save his world as well.

She glowed of rose-quartz glimmering light over her and her wings that were even larger and had more layers of angel feathers in them too.

She also had feathered legs like her father.

So, at this time, Firefly was relieved in one way that she was like him as he was the protector and made his own decisions.

Not like her poor mother being controlled by her evil master.

Seequest thought that she was incredible and asked her what she was, as he could fly but without wings before.

Firefly then looked at him with great grace and pride and said with her new angelic voice.

"I am Father, yours and mother's creation."

"I am a Unisos as I have all the powers of the earth and Divine as well."

"Wow, how did you get to know your powers so quickly without any training or practice?" he said to her, shocked at her beauty.

"Oh, my grandmother taught me while I was comatose and trapped in the cave, she sent me her power of the divine through our minds while I was sleeping".

Seequest asked again, "What?"

You have had actual contact with Celestial, who once was my mother?'

"Yes, Father, I did"

Seequest got up and shook himself and then walked away from his daughter, thinking if he could see Neptune again.

Maybe between them, they will be able to save his family after all, as no unicorn or her kind has had contact with the ninth-dimension heavens and Divine before.

Because the Divine was Mother Nature herself and she was born after Seequest decided to live in the sea for life.

He thought to himself, my daughter could be even more powerful than me.

But she may be the one to save life on earth, as she could destroy it another way as well.

The more Seequest looked at his daughter the more he was becoming proud of her.

Yet he also felt and knew that Firefly could not stay with him either, which also broke his heart.

But for now, he kept this to himself until the battle was over.

He was just pleased to know that she was on his side as they lay there together as Luna the moon was a quarter that night and just glowed around them.

Seequest looked up and said "my dear friend please help us"

As he then looked back and went to sleep to recover properly emotionally this time.

In her dream, Firefly was thinking of the times that she spent with her family on the beach when her mother said, "Come, my angel, let's go to the beach and you can swim with your father properly."

The next morning the sun was shining brightly on them so they had to wake up and move to somewhere cooler.

Firefly received the message from Knight and started to weep.

"What's wrong, my darling?" Seequest asked.

She replied, "It is Knight."

"He sounded that he was dying and told me what Hades has done to him", with her head hanging down in sadness feeling her brother's pain and great sorrow as well.

"Yes, I know, my sweet girl."

Firefly reared at her father showing great strength by being angry with him for not saving her brother, as he promised her in the beginning.

Seequest reared too and said, "Now, calm down".

"I am not your enemy", as Firefly looked like she was prepared to challenge him too!

Hermes flew between them and said "please stop"

Seequest spoke and said "there was nothing I could do for him at this time".

"I am sorry, Firefly".

But the only way that we can bring back Knight is with the help of the gods now.

"If you trust me still in your heart then stop wasting your energy on me and let's fight for the right cause, which is to get our family back in one piece".

"If you believe me then enough of this nonsense and ride with me to the beach to contact my friends for help.'

"OK, I understand but if you betray us then I'll kill you father, as they are still our flesh and blood."

"Yes, I know my angel".

"I will do everything in my power to bring them back to you as if it's the last thing I do."

They both agreed and Hermes said, "Hurry up."

"We need to get to the beach before Hades' Griffins out find us."

They thought they had escaped again.

But what they were not aware of, was Hades planned to let them go this time and lead him to everyone else in one go so that he could kill them all for good.

Chapter Thirty-Three

The Meeting Is Cancelled

Pegasus had met up with Celestial and Legend and they were on their way to earth.

Legend and Celestial were looking forward to seeing their son one last time before they collected him for good but it was a special visit that Zeus who had blessed them with due to their help in trying to save mother earth and Seequest, plus his children from Hades if they can?

While they were flying closer to the planet they saw over the horizon, the beautiful hot bright yellow golden light of an original star now called our sun.

Has it been the hottest and most dangerous star in the galaxy to anything that touched it?

The earth from a distance looked like a beautiful round planet of blue and greens and maps of patterns on her, they also saw Mother Nature smiling at them as they got closer, as she lives inside the earth's core.

As that way she knows everything as she feels, sees, hears and breathes air in it every day.

They swirled downwards through the ozone layer and appeared in Greece.

They were getting closer to Santorini, where Seequest is now living at the time.

Hours had passed when Firefly all of a sudden proudly changedagain and her horn glowed into gold.

This happened as she felt the presence of Celestial becoming closer to them and decides to see if she is right where she gallops as she begins to flap her wings fast and takes flight into the sky quietly.

Seequest was resting below with Hermes by his side.

Firefly looked amazing, a true angel-winged unicorn flying gracefully up their beautiful blue sky high up in the clouds.

As now she felt that her wings were heavier and gave her more weight to produce a correct balance in the atmosphere.

Because it also made her feel that her lungs seemed easier to breathe the air too.

She contacted Celestial while in flight.

"Grandmother, the Unicorn King is alive and well and we are on our way to the beach to meet you all.

I have not told Father that you will be there, he expects just to see Neptune."

Celestial replied, "You have done well, my child and thank you for not telling him."

"We will be with you all soon."

"We shall meet you at the main beach, as we planned."

"Agreed", Firefly said.

"We'll see you all shortly there."

The feathered Unisos changed back to her rose-quartz pink colour, as she was flying back down she closed her eyes for a split second feeling the sea air on her muzzle and her underbelly.

She reopened her eyes to see her reflection from the sea below her as she flew over it, that she had changed again as the love and harmony energy lived inside this precious creature and she now was oozing love everywhere.

The great Pegasus and Celestial and Legend have just landed quietly on the field and galloped towards the beach to see Seequest and Firefly and to protect their kind for the final time.

While Zeus was getting ready at Olympus, Neptune was also organizing his people and his kingdom to be ready for battle against his cruel brother who wants to damage and destroy anything that the unicorns had made beautiful seventy years ago in their tracks.

As Hades was jealous, that he cannot live in it anymore and wanted it all for himself.

As in his mind, if he cannot have it, then no one else will either and his prepared to destroy it again.

Hades has now made Tremor the most powerful creature to ever of been created on earth before.

Has Knight's father is the king of the unicorns and horses and his mother is the queen of death and bad through her owner's will.

This deadly creature can now destroy everything it touches; sees or feels and is the deadliest even to the gods if it gets the opportunity to use its powers to the full potential.

Chapter Thirty-Four

Tremor Will Now Destroy Earth and Everything That Lives on It

Time has passed and this battle has been going on for a long time now.

Has summer seemed to be creeping up and has naturally been becoming warmer at night?

The Unicorn King and his daughter were standing in the waves of the sea to keep themselves cool while they were waiting for Neptune to arrive.

Seequest called him with his mind and said, "Neptune, I hope that you can hear me"? has he dips his horn into the cooling salt water like told to in the past

That caused an invisible sound to the sea that only Neptune or their Eldest Daughter would hear, due to their powers of living things.

"I hope you are all OK," he said with a caring tone in his voice.

"It's me, Seequest, I am free and I am with my daughter on the beach waiting for your arrival".

"Please I need your help once again, old friend".

Neptune, at this time, was sitting on his throne giving commands when he holds his head and goes into a trance, looking straight ahead, when his guards go up to him and called him but he did not hear them at all.

It was as if he was not there at all.

But it looked like he was somewhere completely different from his surroundings.

No one had ever seen the sea king do this before and started to panic thinking that it may be Hades doing.

Helena felt something was wrong and came in from training with Louis and jumped off the hippocampus quickly and swam over to her father and said to the guards, Back off.

"He is fine, Leave him."

"My lady, we cannot do that, as we are his guards."

"Yes, I know that, and thank you".

"But I will take over from here."

"Our lady, you are a princess."

"You do not have the authority to command this wish."

"Then stay and get out of my way replied with a hasty tone as concerned about her Father, can you hear me?"

The King did not answer her call either, as he was concentrating on listening to Seeques and at the same time, he was shocked and yet happy to know he was alive and well.

Seequest repeated "My King of the sea you must get all your people to safety and send them to Scotland, which Hades does not know about yet".

"Has he won't go as it's too cold for him to bear".

"Once you have done this then come to me at the beach to help stop Hades".

"Please, it is me, the Unicorn King."

Minutes later Neptune replied, "Seequest how do I know it is you and not a trick to lead me and my people in a trap?"

"Remember what you did for my mother and me by saving our lives?"

Plus, for many years now you let me stay and live with you and your family all these years in peace?'

Neptune came out of the trance and saw that Helena was there and she said, "Father, are you OK?"

"Of course, my child" he said and changed his way of thinking as Helena was there and he didn't want her to worry about it.

"Guards, I am ok, you may go thank you."

The guards bowed to their king as they turned and made their spears small again as they opened the large golden doors and closed them on their way out.

Neptune looked puzzled on his face.

Where Helena had an idea what it was all about, as she had a twitchy feeling of warmth in her body after hugging him for comfort as if she felt the love energy of her Seequest.

"Father was it a telepathic message from Seequest?"

Neptune tried to hide the truth from Helena and said, "Oh, nothing that concerned you, my child".

"Everything is fine now."

"Was it Seequest, as I felt that he contacted us somehow but slightly different from before?"

The sea king tried his best to keep it to himself, as it was secret this time because of what happened before and said, "I am fine, daughter".

"I must see your mother at the temple now."

"Father, let me come with you."

"No, Helena, please leave it and go and do your errands as before, thank you."

The mermaid princess was annoyed and knew that something was going on and that she will find out one way or another or that is what she was thinking.

The mermaid princess knew that she would get to the bottom of it eventually and swam off to the stables to attend to the hippocampus as her mother seemed to be attending the Crystal Temple more these days.

Due to the attack on Vissen by Tremor recently

Chapter Thirty-Five

Tremor Is Destroying the Lands

Hades got Tremor to go out at night and kill all the animals and then eat their souls, as Hades did not feed him anymore.

He had to eat something and that was what he did and seemed to enjoy it too.

Hades could see that Tremor was alive all the time now and that Knight was dead inside.

Zeus was watching from above his cruel brother's ways and knew that he and his children must stop Hades for good without killing Knight, which will be a great challenge indeed.

Zeus was seriously angry with his younger brother said, "It is time to put a stop to this", with a roaring tone as he spoke to the rest of the gods and goddesses.

"Hades, I am coming for you!"

Has he shouted while he was watching Tremor destroying everything?

He became seriously angry.

So, to stop him in his tracks he then put both of his
hands together and created a large ball of silver lighting he then threw it towards Tremor, as it was sent as
a warning that he is watching from above.

Hades looked up in the sky and replied, "My creature
will beat and kill you dear brother you watch and see"

"Or at least he will destroy your precious earth as you
know and love", and started to laugh loudly again.

Zeus called his guards; his family and said "It is time,
my loved ones and friends, to show Hades what power
freedom and peace is all about!"

Everyone went to collect their spears; swords, and
shields as they began putting on their armour before
they mounted their beautiful, winged white mystical
horses to go to earth for the battle of their wits.

Hades told his creatures that he must go on a trip
before this war with Earth and Zeus, which will
change his life as he knows it.

Because it will eventually change it to his way of thinking like his underworld already is.

This time, he did not take Tremor or Knightmare, as he let them rest for a while, as they were needed greatly for later.

He rode on one of his saber-toothed tigers, which also had been resting until needed again.

Before they killed all the last unicorns apart from two, which were Seequest's parents, who at the time were king and queen of the night unicorns, and their names have now become legends of all the lands as Jecco and Moonbeam at the time.

There was one saber-toothed tiger that got away, and his name is Pain

Hades decided that he was too important to keep him around and so he kept him in another part of the land away from everyone, where Hades created a female for him called Curse because of her red eyes and stripes all over her body.

Now they have been together and have produced ten of them just for this special day.

He called the enormous strong pain and said, "your revenge will be sweet my boy your time is coming,"

As he rode to another place to see the powerful sorceress called Dark Moon, as she was related to Luna.

But she kept hidden until today as she too wants a piece of the action with the battle of the gods.

While Hades is away, the Chimera and Cerberus, now with two heads, were guarding the hell-winged bat horse and hell Unisos while he was gone.

Tremor was weak from being out all day long causing trouble everywhere he went.

Knightmare did her best to comfort the beast that had her son trapped inside his body.

But now she believed that Tremor was her son and Knight never existed because of Hades' spells.

She kept him calm as well, as she still felt love for him only, as that was what Hades wanted her to have for obeying his commands recently.

Knightmare remembered a trick that Seequest taught her in the past and thought that it may come in handy now, as she was fighting her mind as well.

She came to and thought that this wasn't her son anymore, but the demon in her was saying, Knight is dead and Tremor is our son instead.

Poor Knightmare was broken and going mad seeing that her son had become this monster and hoped that he will change back someday.

Knightmare did her best to try and connect with anyone, but it was no use.

The signal was too weak in the caves, as they are farther than they were before.

She thought that she should have seen from the beginning that it was a trap for Seequest.

But she still feels the love with this remarkable unicorn stallion, in the way that he fell for her too.

But she thought how this is possible as they both are fighting opposite sides?

It's because opposites attract.

Even though she was bad and he was good when together they were somehow completely balanced.

Fire warms up the water and water calm down the fire.

Back in the sea, Seequest was still waiting for the arrival of Neptune and his mer- knights to arrive.

While waiting patiently, he began to have flashbacks of all the great times he had with Knightmare and how their love grew from nothing to something amazing.

Has would never be planned in the stars for it to have happened normally.

But sometimes the universe takes over and creates creatures that it thinks will have a great purpose in the future.

That is exactly what had happened to their relationship over time together and due to the way she is now, he could not save her through his magi either.

Only the universe carries all the answers to life itself.

Seequest kept thinking about Knightmare and hoped that Neptune could help her.

But maybe with Zeus's help he can, as he praying this to be true.

But what Seequest and Firefly did not know was that Hades wanted them to feel what freedom was like for a while and put their hopes up that everything will be fine and defeat them.

Hades being a true evil god thought that it will make them feel safe and put their guards down for him to fool them once more.

Hades' plan was working just the way he knew it would.

Seequest and everyone felt relaxed and excited to see their friends again.

While it was another nasty trap of Hades playing tricks with their emotions, hearts and again their minds.

Firefly was getting a little restless, so she jumped up into the sky once more and flew around to see if she could see anyone else coming their way.

Chapter Thirty-Six

Will Seequest and His Daughter Ever Be Free from Hades?

Seequest and Firefly were waiting to be freed at the beach resting in the sea, while Hermes stayed on land watching elsewhere, while they are still waiting for Neptune to appear.

What they did not see was the invisible barrier between them and the deeper part of the ocean where Seequest needed to be to change into a hippocampus to get away to breathe properly and regain his full strength.

Hades knew about this, so he trapped him in his seas.

But for Seequest, he still thought that he and his daughter were now safe and free.

Hades had put another barrier around them.

They started to get thirsty, so they drank some of the seawater into which Hades had got his chimera earlier to drop a potion in it, which will make them weak and tired in the water where they will be.

Even Hermes in the end could not resist drinking it himself, as it looked refreshing as salt water is good for him at times and gives him a quick boost as well.

But they must not drink it often, just occasionally.

All of them felt tired of waiting, so they became sleepy and fell into a deep sleep.

A day had gone by.

Not realizing they had slept, they all woke up to a bright light that came over them, thinking that it was Pegasus.

So, they did not hide from it only to find out that it was one of Hades' creatures that had shape-shifted into Pegasus's image and his power, to gain their trust.

It then waved with its wings of a ball of light at them and all they saw was a massive bright light.

When the light had disappeared from them, they then found themselves back in the underworld once again.

Seequest was just starting to feel more like him when he realized that they were all fooled and back to where they started once more, as Hades was playing tricks on them in the first place.

By letting them feel like that they did escape him, when he made up the image of the woods to make Seequest know that he had control of him and his daughter now forever.

Firefly noticed that she was fooled and was thinking she was back in the stables, where her mother was there with her too only to see when she reached out to her she was an illusion and one of Hades' nasty spells, which made her feel downhearted.

Hades earlier could see that Knightmare's feelings were coming back because of Seequest teaching her some tricks of his own while living with her recently.

So, he decided to lock her away in the dungeon with Cerberus, who has been her guard with only two heads and the guardians of the dead souls, with this time, his dragon image again to prevent from being killed by anyone.

Hermes seemed to have gotten away thankfully being in the form of a butterfly earlier and lay low on the wall once more and rested for a while when he heard Seequest talking to him through his mind.

Hermes smiled and turned into blue tit and then flies around trying to find them all again.

When he got there, Cerberus saw him who jumped up in the air and caught him in his mouth gently.

This time, Hermes thought it was game over and quickly turned himself back into his actual size, which was luckily bigger than Cerberus's tongue and slipped out all covered in the yuk and quickly flew away from him fast, not caring that he was sticky and wet.

"Damn you, Hermes, I will get you".

"Mark my words you!" roaring and howling in anger, with his dragon tail swishing around, breaking the wall as it went, not realizing that he was making it weaker for Hermes's plan to work.

Hermes changed into his actual bigger size than normal wearing his flying boots he could not take his weight anymore, so he had to run as fast as he could down the dark pathways of hell passing the lake of the dead.

He climbed a part of the mountain that is connected to it to reach Hades' actual homeland.

Luckily, he just escaped as a soul jumped out of the dark water and caught his feet thankfully lost its grip and let go as he was shaking it off while still trying to hold on for dear life to the rocks.

He eventually got to the top and thought that he made it and that he must find Seequest and Firefly again quickly.

He ran as fast as his body could carry him and saw a light that he recognises could be Seequest's horn sparking in the distance.

Hermes, now having his strength back, changed into a wasp this time and hoped that he can break the spell that Hades had put on Seequest once more.

"Oh, well, here goes nothing" as he flew to Seequest, who looks like he was slightly fighting the spell but did not have the full power of his strength yet again.

Hermes now stung Seequest quite a few times to make him feel the pain, as before as a bee he could only sting once and save himself as being a god.

But being a wasp, he could sting as many times as needed to wake him.

Hermes was not trying to hurt him but to make him realize that the pain was real and that he was not under any more spells Hades.

Poor Seequest was stung about twenty times until he jumped up and reared on his legs and knocked the wasp unconscious.

"What are you?" Seequest asked,

Has also Hades had wiped their memories clean of ever escaping earlier, so to them, it never happened.

Hermes changed back into his normal form.

He said, "I am Hermes, the messenger of the gods, remember?"

Seequest replied, "No, I don't remember anything."

"What has happened to me?"

Hermes explained that Hades has had Seequest under some great spells and in the meantime been using his power to strengthen his own.

Which was his son who is now a creature called Tremor which has gained all the powers of earth and could destroy her for good and everyone on it without his help?

The Unicorn King was listening but some of the words he did not seem to take in about his son Knight.

But the great warrior stood boldly and felt that he had gained some of his powers back as feeling pain from the wasp stings.

First, he thought of healing himself his horn turned green and remembered luckily how to heal his wounds.

At the time, Hermes said, "I am sorry I did that to you."

"But I had to do something to make you know what was real again."

Seequest understood and said, "It's OK."

"We all have to do things we do not want to do some-times, if it's for our highest good" and neighed at Hermes, who then smiled and nodded his head himself.

Seequest was becoming more himself again, thanks to Hermes, and said "Come on, my friend, we must escape properly this time and rescue my daughter and then my son.

Thinking that Knightmare did not remember him anymore?

Because even though he did not remember earlier, his heart for her had not changed somehow.

He lit up his horn to full power and thought of anger as he kicked with his back legs the door down.

Which broke into pieces and then he galloped toward his daughter's scent.

"Wait, Seequest, wait for me", as Hermes changed back into his little self and hovered behind the great unicorn steed.

"Seequest, please wait for me, as I am much smaller than you."

The Unicorn King stopped in his tracks and started to remember some things at this time.

Hades had tried to wipe all his memory of everything he knew and loved for taking Knightmare away from him before.

But he gradually starts to remember this sweet voice that he thought tried to help him before but failed.

Seequest looked back to see Hermes, flying towards him with his god image with his winged golden boots and hat and muscled body the size of a bird.

Seequest felt that his mind was playing tricks on him and did not believe what he was hearing and seeing anymore and becomes so confused about what to do for the best.

He thought that he was going mad but in the centre of his thoughts, was a family that he may have made up once knowing that it was always a dream before his reign ended on earth.

But he knew it was impossible as he now agreed to be a hippocampus in the sea forever.

Hermes tried many times to tell him that it was not an illusion.

That it was a real memory of his family since living and being trapped in Hades' lair for years.

Eventually, Hermes said to Seequest "do I have to sting you a couple of times for you to start listening to what I am telling you is true?"

Seequest quickly shook his head from side to side as if he was saying no, in shock that Hermes even mentioned it to him.

Seequest said, "No, no, no, I believe you" and started to see that Hermes was there and real in front of him.

Hermes said "Luckily I am a god and a messenger and I can help you remember some things again."

Just feel and believe that they were real once in your life and then your memory will be restored once more.

Remember who you were once, the most powerful creature on this planet.

Seequest you must remember, you are the great warrior of this time.

"You are Seequest, the King of the unicorns and horses of this Earth, please remember that?"

The Unicorn King paid great attention to Hermes's voice and messages as he tried to show him in images from Seequest's mind, thanks to Athena passing on some of her wisdom to him when they last saw each other.

Seequest dropped to the floor as he started to remember when he was a young colt himself what Moonbeam taught him about nature and the rules to keep it great and safe from harm.

How she taught him about realism and his imagination too.

The only thing he had to do was believe in his true self again and everything will become clearer once more.

Then he started to feel and see the difference again.

He shook his head and got up and said, "I can hear my mother's voice as if it is real?" as he turned around and ran towards it.

Now at this time, he felt that the actual presence of his mother was on Earth as his heart felt that he could feel her love like before she left him fifty-four years ago.

He mentioned to the messenger, "She is talking to me in my mind."

He speaks, trying to do a telepathic message between them, thinking that he would not get an answer back and yet trying all the same.

"Mother, is that you?"

And she replied, which shocked him, "Yes, my dear son, it is me, but it is not,

"Because if you remember your mother died a natural death"

She was born again to me, Celestial queen of the heavens as Zeus could not have all the animals back at Olympus so he created Heaven for them, which will be also for the future human race to go, if they were good on earth in time.

They would meet back up with their families and fur babies as their reward, Zeus thought.

Due to Moonbeam's courage and will- power her spirit would be the perfect ruler of it and so yes, her soul is in me.

Once more, he was thinking that his mind was seriously playing tricks on him as he knew that it was impossible.

But for him to hear or see her again, or even the new creation she became was a miracle he thought and hoped that this was true.

He remembered seeing her escorted by Tidal Wave and See spray back into the sea to be with Neptune in the past and died.

Then reappeared as reborn a black Pegasus of Friesian form and said that his mother will always be with her because of her memories, but she was called now Celestial, the queen of the heavens.

As she could not stay on earth as her time was up, she had to go away forever, and they would never meet again in this lifetime anyway, or that was what he was told.

Celestial called his name, "Seequest, my son, where are you?"

The message was repeated a few times when she said "great king of the unicorns, show yourself to me."

And then Hades' magic began to die in Seequest's body.

Knowing that he can hear Celestial, he knew then that his powers were coming back stronger than ever.

So, the black smoke started seeping out of his mouth into nothing, as the spell was completely now broken.

Seequest could feel that his heart and mind were more alive than ever before and he was back for good.

Seequest then said, "Hermes, what has been going on while I have been tucked away in my mind?"

"And is everyone all right?" with a worried voice for his family.

"No, Seequest, they are not, as you need to get to the surface and save us all, as Hades has produced some terrible creatures with you and your son Knight's powers and plans to destroy everything we love in this world."

Seequest was shocked at how his son has been treated and planned to free him from Hades' grasp somehow.

But, first, he said that he must rescue his family and get them out of there for good, so he then ran back to the stables where it all started once up in Hades' lair above the caves.

"Come on, we have no time to lose."

He reached Hades' lair and saw that they were not there and started to get worried about where they can be and what state they were in now.

He kept galloping around the lair and did not seem to find them anywhere.

He was becoming frustrated and dizzy.

Seequest stood still for a minute while trying to get his proper balance back in his head and then proceeded on thinking where his children and Knightmare would be now.

When Hermes said, "Are you looking for a black bat-winged female horse?"

"Yes, that is Knightmare' and he got up to Hermes's face and seemed to be squashing him."

Hermes says, "If you stop squashing me, I will tell you" and he moved back so Hermes could rub his face for comfort.

He then said, "She is down in the dungeon below the caves being guarded by Cerberus, but he is in his dog and dragon form."

"Please make sure that you are strong enough before you see him as he is at his greatest strength as Hades could not bring his third head back from the previous fight with you."

"So, he prepared to kill you on sight!

As Cerberus is seriously angry and will kill without mentioning his plan to you as he did before.

"If you want to free her, then you will have to fight him to the death!"

Seequest listened carefully to what Hermes said to him and thought of the previous fight he had with Cerberus started to remember its weaknesses that the three-headed dog let him know last time without realizing that he did.

But thankfully Seequest is very clever and intelligent and learned from his mistakes and his wins too.

He thought for a few minutes and now knew how to defeat Cerberus once and for all.

They carried on talking for another hour when Hermes could see that Seequest was paying great attention at last.

Hermes now was prepared to tell Seequest exactly what he had seen.

Knowing where Knightmare was and how he can rescue her without getting hurt in the process.

Even though he was not sure anymore if the Knightmare loved him and still wanted to be rescued?

Hermes said "you go that way and I shall go and find your daughter."

In the meantime, Seequest calmed down.

They both agreed and the Unicorn King replied "thank you when they went their different ways to find Seequest's family."

Seequest went back towards the sea of souls where the dungeons are near and Hermes flew back towards the caves to see if Firefly was there.

Seequest reached where she was meant to be.

But the place was empty and Hermes hoped that somehow, she had escaped.

Hades had heard from his creatures that he was looking for her as well.

He seemed to be fed up with all these games and he planned to kill her instead.

Hades appeared like smoke to his creatures and tells them to look for her, while he went back to see Tremor.

"When you find her let me know quickly as then I will let you have the privilege of killing her yourselves as a reward for catching her for me again!"

Within that, Hades vanished once more in a puff of smoke.

Seequest reached the pool of souls and wondered if he could pass them again without getting hurt possibly as he was lucky to last time.

The powerful unicorn stallion did not care anymore about himself but about his family and jumped straight into the sea of souls where he planned to swim to the other side.

But the dead souls had other plans and jumped all over him and tried to drown him and gain his powers for themselves.

He said "I do not want to hurt any of you."

"But I will if, I need to."

Remember even though the water is of the dead it is still water and Seequest is a hippocampus.

So, to escape them he changed into this form to breathe while thinking of strength once more and his horn made the water sapphire blue.

The dead souls, now controlled by Hades do not remember being a creature of good so he then touched his horn to the dead souls, which vaporized them.

Eventually the whole sea of souls lit up with these beautiful blue flames.

Because they had become gods once again as he could see the spirits floating up towards heaven above, where they belonged now free.

He threw his head out of the water and changed back to his unicorn self-swimming quickly to the other side.

As he climbed out slowly, he turned around and saw that the water was now just a blue pool of calm.

Cerberus at the time was walking towards him with now two heads, one of a Great Dane and one of a dragons, as he then remembered earlier he had killed one of them and now Hades could not bring it back to life, so instead, he took it away, which he thought would be easier for his demon dog to get over.

But to Cerberus, it was like losing a brother who was sharing the same body, whom he greatly now missed.

The demon dog was a massive image of a muscled Great Dane with two heads now instead of three where his coat was jet-black and red with his ears erected with large pointed teeth and could breathe fire too.

Because even though Seequest was in an illusion luckily his powers can still destroy a creature or a beast.

As Hades was not aware that is how sometimes he has won his battles in the past by using just that!

Hermes told that he was looking angry and more vicious than before as Cerberus wanted revenge for what had happened to him.

The guardian of death said to Seequest with red fluid pouring out of his mouth.

Because he recently fed and was also showing his teeth from both heads says, "Well, well, look who it is, how did you manage to escape your doom?"

Hades so believed that Dark Moon spells could fool you and keep you all locked up in her magic Hades trap forever!

Roaring as a dragon as he spoke while stretching out his claws ready to jump and fight.

Seequest replied," I escaped and bet you in the past with the power and magic that I have inside me that you or your master can never take unless you kill me first."

Seequest continued talking quickly and said "Cerberus where is Knightmare your stupid dragon dog?"

"She's not here, Seequest, she's is in my stomach now and your mare tasted ever so sweet against my lips."

First Seequest took him seriously while watching him licking his paws with his first head while the second one was still watching Seequest's every move.

As he was doing this Seequest became angry and possibly foolish, as that was one of Cerberus's powers of making you believe his lies and making you feel the pain that they are true.

Seequest replied, "She's not dead".

"You cannot fool me anymore with your voice of lies".

"Get out of my way, beast and let me pass".

Cerberus, looking ready to fight to the death, mentioned, "No, I shall not".

"You will have to fight me, your weird horse with a horn."

There they were just eyeing each other up until it was time to fight to the death.

Chapter Thirty-Seven

Helena and Louis's Adventure

The time was close to competing now with her father.

Helena and Louis her stunning black hippocampus, were nearly ready for the great race in Vissen against her father himself.

The mermaid princess felt confident that her steed could win the race because of his other skills that no other creature yet apart from his own siblings have as they were excited about the new adventure that they trained for every day.

Neptune and her mother, Queen Sera, seemed to be busy elsewhere doing things that she was not allowed to know about.

She was aware and was told that her father was on important business with Zeus and her mother was at the Crystal Temple, not to be disturbed.

The mer-knights protected the grounds and temple too, which Helena thought was unusual.

But she did want to go and see her mother for some advice.

So rode Louis to the grounds where the Crystal Temple was where it was gleaming with a beautiful crystal white light that she had never seen before.

The knight said, "My lady you cannot go near there Otherwise you will be burnt"

"Nonsense my mother is in there so I can."

Then she heard the sound of her mother's voice in her mind.

My darling, you cannot enter here for your protection.

Please stay away, I am fine and well, I just need you to do something for our people.

Tell me, Mother, please, what is going on? Why all the secrecy?

My darling daughter, I am sure you will know in time but for now, please do as you have been asked.

"Fine, I shall go now and find answers somewhere else" Helena said with frustration in her voice.

She decides to go to the library after seeing her mother and went to find the book of knowledge, where she found out something that no one has ever seen or heard of for centuries.

Helena was so intrigued, she rips out the page in the book and puts it into her pouch and seems pleased with herself.

That she quickly swims home to get ready for bed, thinking "if I find this skull maybe then I can save my dear old friend Seequest after all?"

While she falls asleep peacefully knowing that her plan was going to be dangerous.

The next day she did all her cores and her training with Louis, when she decided that she had to go back to the land again to see what was going on as the mer-folk were going there more often and not telling her anything.

She thinks that she's going there today and turn's her hippocampus around and says to him, "Come on Louis we are not wanted here anymore,"

Decides that she would go up to the land to see what was going for herself.

She reaches the surface to see the mer-folk play-ing around in the ocean having fun while they could before another attack.

Later that day, she thought she heard some rumours about Hades through the mer-folk chain.

She started to question her parents regarding what they had told her and yet the answers still stayed the same.

She was becoming angry but went home that day thinking she's going to visit the beach the next morning and see for herself what was going on.

Without being seen this time, she hoped.

The next morning came when she sitting eating with her sisters, as the princes who were on a mission with their father as they were old enough now.

Her mermaid sisters were all there brushing each other's hair and making ordinary conversation about mer-boys.

She had a great morning with them having breakfast of seaweed and shrimp.

Helena then went to the dolphins and swam up to the stables to see her close friend Louis, whom she felt that she could trust.

She attended to all the other hippocampus and set them free for the morning.

There were not many left now because they had all grown up and become mer-knight's horses for battle and protect the Vissen grounds from predators.

There was only now Sea Spray their mother, Louis and his sister Moon Stone, who was pure white colour like the stone itself.

She became Queen Sera's mare for battle whereas Sea Spray was used to controlling the waves.

Moonstone seemed to have the same powers as her brother Louis and Sera thought that she would be great to have for traveling all over the world quickly in the future.

Sera always wondered in time if she could change like Louis as well.

Once Helena fed them their favourite shrimp and tuna fish, she gave them sea grass which gave them an extra kick of strength for the day.

Helena was waiting for Louis to digest his food before taking him out for his ride.

But became a little impatient and felt like she could not wait any longer to read more about this new information she finds and begins to swim towards the quiet part of the ocean to her place to think.

She reaches the surface and swam over to her favourite rock, which she likes sitting on while watching the dolphins play in the sunset.

As she's looking at the lands in the distance daydreaming about her life and dreams coming true.

Helena enjoyed sometimes having her own space to think.

She puts her beautiful green swallow tail curled around the rock and gets out her water pouch where she put the papers that she had ripped out of the Book of Knowledge.

She knew that she was safe to look at them properly without being seen here.

The mermaid Princess had to do this even though it was forbidden because the actual book was too huge to carry from the library.

As she looked at the book earlier at the library in detail where it mentions the crystal skulls and where they came from before them.

It said that many years before, celestial beings from other planets had given them in return for having the privilege of feeling what it was like to be mer-folk, as before this they were only a ball of light called the soul beings.

In the book, it mentioned that the crystal skulls were to be given to Neptune and the moon princess to use for the greater good always and now being married High Priestess Sera could control them all.

They were a thank-you for letting the Celestial beings temporarily experience these feelings that the gods were awarded in return to have these crystal skulls of great enormous power even before their time.

But the promise was that they would only be used for good; otherwise, the crystal skulls will be destroyed.

This was written over again to make sure they took these rules seriously.

It said that there were originally five crystal skulls.

Because Hades in the past tried to get them, where they then had to hide the most important one from everyone and it has never been seen ever since.

The pages that she ripped from the book mentioned that a royal bloodline was the only one that could control it.

It says that a prince or princess had to be telepathic; kind and loving mer-person for the crystal skull to communicate with him or her.

"Wow", Helena said, "I wonder if I could find this crystal skull?"

I then could rescue Seequest myself she thought.

She began to read more, when it said it had the power to change mer-folk into Pisces people permanently unless decided otherwise.

Has it could give them the power to live on land and water at the same time.

This crystal stone was the Amethyst one and it controlled creativity and inspiration.

It also holds the highest power and magic of all for protection and spiritual wisdom.

It could make anyone feel strong and full of courage, as takes away any negativity that Hades may try to poison their minds with.

Even though time has gone by and the princess was going to be eighteen years old soon.

She felt like if she could control this crystal then she would have the powers to be a great queen in the future and also help her parents now.

She read more of where it was possibly hidden and as she was clever and she had a great interest in history and research and loved going on adventures of late with Louis that she thought they could find it?

As it was written that it was hidden in a land of great white sharks' lairs.

Plus saying it was also a dangerous mission that she would ever do, as no one so far has ever survived or escaped from trying.

It even said on the pages that Neptune her father, would not risk it!

That it was best not to ever be used or found and classed it in the pages as destroyed in the last battle of the seas before she was born.

Helena loved a challenge and wanted to show her parents that she should be there to help her old friend

Knowing that they all blamed themselves for his pain and sorrow all these years, even though it was an accident.

She was watching the movement of the sun and knew then that it was time to go back and get Louis ready.

She felt so excited that she quickly rolled up the papers back into her pouch and dived right off the rock into the sea.

Swimming as quickly as she could to tell Louis her plan of finding this Amethyst crystal skull or thought it would be worth trying as she had nothing to lose anymore.

The mer-princess knew then she had an upper hand as her hippocampus can change into a seahorse.

Thinking if any creature can get through the sharks' lair without being caught or touched it would be Louis.

She swam as fast as she could back to the stables as she heard "I am ready, In her mind"

She smiled at him and swam into his stall and brushed him down before she got his bridle and saddle off a hook shaped like a starfish.

She told Louis her plan trusting her enough to know they will be ok.

He let her put his sea bridle and saddle on that her mother had made for them.

But she remembered that her mother said only if she feels that Louis was fully trained and that he will listen to every command that she gave him.

She felt like he was ready to do what she asked him and said, "Louis my sweet boy, we are going to go on an adventure across the other side of the Atlantic Ocean."

"Will you be good for me and listen to what I say and tell you to do?"

The hippocampus looked at his owner in her eyes and said in her mind "my lady, I am your steed and your friend."

"I will obey everything you say to me and I will protect you with my life."

"I am ready to become the greatest hippocampus/ seahorse ever."

"I would like to make you and my parents proud of me, let's do this."

She agreed and smiled at him.

She got hold of these beautiful silver reins with blue topaz on the sides of the bridle and saddle with citirine too.

Before she put them on she noticed that stuck deep into the saddle was a saddle shell cloth.

She undid the cloth and there she found a pretty black onyx stone with a message on it.

The message was from her mother.

It said, "Daughter, I have made these special items for you for your eighteenth birthday, "when you're both ready to wear them with pride, as they will keep you and him safe."

"They will also give happiness and abundance too.

As it will protect you at all times with creativity as well.

It will help you in the future in creating your kingdom one day.

Hopefully by winning this race along with your father soon too.

I have put inside the back of the stall also an armoured dress as you will need it for the race.

As it is a rough course to do.

I hope you like it, as I have also put the stones in there that represent you as a person as they are your true birthstones.

As you were born Helena on 20th November so they are Topaz and Citrine, I hope you like them.

Wow, she thought it was perfect timing as her mother put it away in Louis's stall and hid them before she went to the Crystal Temple days before.

While she was peacefully sleeping, she was dreaming about owning her own palace on land.

But then she remembered that her mother was after all the high priestess and would, of course, know and shrug her shoulders as "Oh, yeah she knows everything."

But this time even Queen Sera was in the dark about the future.

The queen knew that she may not be able to celebrate her daughter's special birthday, thanks to Hades' plan now.

So, planned this knowing how important Helena was to her and her father, even though they were going to war with Hades.

Regarding the armour and weapons for races or errands, they wore with their details.

Most of the mer-folk especially the royals would wear their birthstones on their rides, chariots, and armour plus dress wear as they also represent their personality to help them in their lives too.

Helena was so pleased.

She dropped the stone on the floor in Louis's stall, where he then reared to the noise.

So, she went and comforted him telling him it was her stone that was precious from her mother for her birthday, as Helena is holding his elegant Arabian neck and silky black coat.

"Look, Louis, there is also a gift for me and you too", the hippocampus neighed with delight.

Helena swam over to uncover it from under the sea-weed bag.

The armoured bodice was soft but when it was needed in battle she would say a verse that her mother had written on the stone for her to remember by heart and moments later, it turned into solid steel.

Her breastplate had a logo of the two dolphins swim-ming separate ways on it.

It said also in the note that she had cuffs for her wrists and a beautiful helmet that had on the top of it, was her actual hippocampus, Louis.

She loved it because it had her birthstones on it.

Then as moving the seaweed out of the way a gorgeous famine helmet was shining in the stack.

First of all, Helena looked at the beautiful detail that was on it.

Then she grabbed it and put it on her head after admiring it for a long time.

It fitted her perfectly.

She said a verse and it turned into a delicate jewelled crown showing her that she was Neptune and Sera's beloved eldest daughter.

"Oh, my goddess", she said 'how beautiful is that!'

The mermaid princess was delighted with all the gifts that she put on her and Louis too.

She slipped his loose rein over his face and bought him out of the stall when he started to grow twice his normal size than before.

Now he was the size of a great white shark and she then knew that she had a great chance of surviving this life-threatening task of theirs.

Thanks to this extra power of moon magic that her mother kindly gave them.

They were ready and so they swam to the entrance of the first silver gates where they could go and possibly find this lost crystal.

As they were approaching the second golden gates to go out of Vissen, there appeared to be two extra-powerful knights.

Who were guarding the gates instead of the mer-guards.

They said to Helena, "Stop in the name of the king with firm voices as they spoke to her."

"You cannot leave the land as the king and queen have forbidden it!"

The sea knights had not recognize, the hippocampus has it was bigger and more beautiful than before.

Helena was wearing her battle gear and the mer-knights knew that only princes had this type of armour and believed that it could be one of Hades' tricks to get in and out of the palace whenever he pleased without being noticed.

The mer-knights were wearing different clothing as represented the Neptune this time not Queen Sera too.

The princess only wears a pretty covered skin shell top and wears a little silver seashell crown on her head with her blue pouch bag.

But she kept telling them it was her but they would not believe her.

She was wearing a magnificent piece of clothing that they had never seen before she begins to take off her helmet.

They start pointing their spears at her and Louis which made him rear his front legs as protection and she grabbed the reins to calm him down.

Taking off her helmet slowly, her beautiful black hair appeared wavy around in the water and they saw her beautiful face of blue eyes glimmering at one of the knights closely.

Wow, not realizing that it was the princess who had changed now into a pretty young mer-lady, not a mer-maid anymore as she looked much older.

The princess knew one of the mer-knights as she remembered his build working alongside her father at times.

She said to him looking at his face to face "it is me Taylor Princess.'

Where she felt a strange feeling as she looked him in his stunning blue eyes and said, "My hippocampus Louis"

"I'm going out of the kingdom to do some special training for the race.

That's soon, remember?"

All Taylor could see was her and he did not pay attention to what she said, so she repeated it.

"My knight, do you hear me?"

He replied after coming back from his quick daydream of her and said "yes my lady I do, straightaway," trying not to show that he was looking at her.

Because he will be in trouble with the sea king, as Helena was bestowed to another.

"Sorry, your Highness, I did not know it was you."

"Yes, I guess it has been a while since we saw each other old friend and many things have changed now."

"Yes, my lady they have indeed."

"Then let me pass by putting down your spears at once before I do it for you!"

Helena reached for her helmet and put it back on again as she got ready to ride through the gates shortly after.

There she was holding tightly onto the hippocampus' reins excited for this new adventure that could change her life forever from now on.

The poor knights felt bad and so they let her pass this time around.

But as she rode past Taylor, seemed to smile at her as he felt a connection and she did the same to him too.

She wondered did he just show her that he was attracted to her, the princess carried on thinking would the king and queen approve of them meeting maybe in the future because she felt something towards him too.

Wondering if he would spend some time with her on his own, as she is the age for courting now, she sighed gently.

The princess also had a lot on her mind and this was the last thing that she could think of for a while.

So, she cleared her mind when thinking where about this mysterious cave in the Atlantic Sea.

They both were excited about finding this Amethyst Crystal skull.

They swam for hours and hours until they reached the lighter part of the Atlantic Ocean and saw that they were quite a few great white sharks around.

She had to follow them carefully to their lair without being eaten.

Luckily Louis became smaller and slimmer so they were not seen so easily as swimming by them with great speed which luckily, they missed their massive jaws this time as they quickly swam through them.

Eventually, they came to the lair where the king of the sharks lived and wondered if he was protecting the skull for her parents.

They swam past the guard sharks.

Feeling that she felt a presence pulling her to the back of the king's liar, which was cold and dark covered in bones everywhere.

They felt a little unsure whether to carry on but they were brave warriors, Louis has been a small seahorse swam deeper into the lair of darkness wearing his armour too for protection.

Helena had also a special spear that at this time was a size of a small fishing knife.

She spoke to it as it began to grow to its full size lighting up the cave as they went.

Helena felt pulled to some special rocks.

King of Terror was out hunting for himself so she thought they would have time to find the crystal skull before he gets back.

She jumped off Louis quickly seeing that there was a tiny hole through the rock with a small bright purple light shining inside it.

So, she started to use her hippocampus by using him to help pull away the bigger boulders of rock.

As Louis pulled the rock it broke into pieces which made a massive noise.

She was concerned that they had to hurry up.

But they had no choice but to carry on hoping that Terror would not arrive back yet.

Because sharks cannot see very well or hear great noises but they do feel the vibration mostly of them instead.

The princess kept telling Louis to hurry up moving the rocks for her as her armour changed into something lighter for her to get through the hole when ready.

Now there was enough room for her to swim into the hole quickly.

There she saw a large rock that seemed to have a door and she broke it open with her spear, which made a great deal of vibration she knew then she had to be quicker as Terror will be home soon.

He was just finishing eating his tuna lunch and started to swim back to his lair.

King of Terror knew that the skull was found and began to throw his large powerful tail back and forth for speed.

Has he sensed an intruder there because Neptune had put a sensor on his head to let him know if the crystal was taken?

He approached chopping his jaws as he was going back to find out who was there in his lair.

Helena could hear in her mind that he was angry and ready to fight to the death.

She quickly called Louis to go and disturb him while she tries to escape telling him that she will meet up with him somewhere else soon.

There, Louis was now the same size as the shark that was coming at him.

He saw a vicious creature charging at him when he quickly said to Helena, "quick say the verse to me" and she did.

It worked as he could change his form into a small seahorse and darted across the great white's jaws and sat on the back of him for a while, catching his breath and escaping death full on.

The shark then was puzzled and scared because he thought that it was magic and rushed out of the lair.

Louis then swam quietly off him and changed back to his natural form.

While making the shark follow him away from the shark's liar while letting the princess hopefully escape unharmed.

In the meantime, Helena swam into the room where there was a large purple sparkling crystal skull sitting on a large piece of rock.

She tried to lift it but it felt too heavy for her to pick up.

She then remembered what her mother said which will give her the strength and stamina she needed.

So, she said a Greek verse and her outfit and crown turned into battle armour again where she was pro-tected and had the strength to pick it up.

She could not believe she now was holding the most powerful crystal skull known to her people for centuries.

Helena was smiling and excited that she sent a telepathic message to Louis that she had it and that it was time to go home.

She slammed her spear on the floor and by touching the crystal skull at the same time it broke open the other side of the wall.

She pointed her spear at the Amethyst skull and made it shrink to the size of her hands as swam as quickly as her fins and tail could carry her away from the sharks' lair and the sharks completely.

She saw a different type of dolphin and called it the mind that came and protected her while she was looking for Louis somewhere deep in the ocean waves.

The colourful dolphins told her that he was wounded and had been hiding in their pod at the moment.

They were called White Atlantic dolphins, which she thought was very pretty while swimming back to see her hippocampus.

The dolphins took her to him where she said "Louis I am sorry."

She could see that he got scratched by the teeth of the shark before he made himself smaller earlier.

So, she took out the crystal skull from her bodice and held it in both of her hands and said to it, hoping it would work, "I, Helena of Neptune the sea god." "I ask of you now to please heal my friend so we can go back home thank you, mighty skull"

Within seconds, the skull started to glow brightly its gorgeous purple eyes shining towards the hippocampus and he neighed as it was so bright.

Everyone thought that it was killing him even though it was making him stronger than he was ever before.

When the skull stopped glowing, Louis got up from lying on his side and said "I am now called Source."

Helena thanked the dolphins and put the crystal skull back away and jumped on this magnificent and more powerful seahorse as his armour once again changed too.

The dolphins' eyes also were bright purple and said, 'we are your warriors of the sea our queen as the energy bounced through them as well.

This scared the princess a little as she did not know what was going on.

Did the dolphins know about the skull and its powers?

They answered her question by nodding their heads to both of them as they swam away as fast as Source could travel.

She also noticed now that Source/ Louis was wearing a silver and amethyst body sheild himself and on his head was a shield to cover his face with a purple horn on it for extra protection on his forehead too.

She said "just a gift from the celestial beings from afar."

The mermaid princess was pleased and yet felt scared of what she and her friend now have inside of them.

So, for now they decided to keep it a secret until they felt like it could be a secret no more.

Later that day back in the Atlantic Ocean before going home, she thought that she may try and see if she could use and control the Amethyst crystal skull like her mother did with the others.

She reached her little hideout and jumped off Source and took off all his armor and his reins and saddle and let him become again her beautiful black hippocampus, Louis whom she loved and adored very much.

She let him swim freely in the sea to rest while she checked out the skull on the deeper level.

She thought to herself, where did she put the other parts of the papers about the skull?

She thought she put them in her sea pouch earlier or did she leave them in his stall back at the stables?

Now they are back in her ocean again safe and sound.

Helena returns to her rock and saw that she had left some papers sitting on it.

She then realized that she had not put them into a bag after all.

Oh, how she was so relieved and looked at them closely.

But they were not the important pages she was looking for starting to become worried in case they got into the wrong hands.

Luckily for her that her blue pouch bag got stuck on the rock surface to its right side.

She grabbed it quickly opening it to find she had a small pocket that she had forgotten about and there in that secret pocket.

She found the last two pages and read them carefully where it mentioned a special bloodline, hers!

Saying that a warrior must always believe in themselves by helping others, by this the purple skull will be willing to help them if worthy of its true power.

It also mentions that you should hold the skull tightly in both hands and speak a verse that represents the skull from its planet, which was Neptune.

Even though it's blue, they are connected like the aquamarine crystal skull, which belongs to her father as well.

Because the crystal skulls represented the emotions like water as it does on the planet Neptune.

Cronos had created it for her father to live and look after before Zeus asked him to live on Earth.

Zeus missed his brothers and needed a sea god of the seas and sea creatures for his planet too because emotions can be powerful when they are used perfectly.

Mostly of course the positive kind will help conquer great battles of evil always she wondered if she should try it?

But will she be worthy enough to survive its tremendous power?

She also thought Is Louis ok beginning to think hard and carefully too.

Saying that she wondered if was he part of this magic after all and that is why he has become this magnificent creature.

As when he is Source he is a true warrior of the seas now.

She sat for hours looking at this Amethyst crystal skull, thinking to herself that for centuries, the merfolk and others have been trying to find it.

Here she is holding it in her hands as if just another of her treasures that she had found in the great sea.

She took a deep breath and thought oh well I have nothing to lose but to gain if I achieve this.

She closed her eyes and put the crystal skull tightly in both hands and laid it on her heart when she started to feel warmth in her heart.

As she spoke to it "I am Helena of Neptune"s kingdom, I command you to obey me now"

"Because I will do the right thing for myself, my people, and my friends and will use this power for good only, I promise."

The warm heat went into her body and she grew a little bigger as her hair turned purple and her eyes glowed so brightly when she looked at her reflection, she had lit up the ocean.

All her friends were watching in the distance and were frightened of her and swam away.

But when she touched it again, her eyes stopped glowing and she smiled at the sea creatures.

They could see only the good in her and felt safe around her again.

Her body also glowed of this purple light and she too felt stronger, wiser with full courage than before.

Then she heard from the crystal itself, which said

"The princess, I heard your call and for now, I will obey your wishes."

She replied straight away "you know who I am?"

The skull answered "yes I know all about you and your father Neptune, we know everything!

Because of this, she started to answer questions about Seequest and it said he needs help.

Then it said "these are the rules that you must follow always for my services to you."

"As if you use me in a bad way, then you will be punished by my powers and I will destroy myself forever."

The princess said, "I agree."

The mer-maid replied "never will that happen.

"But if it did then I will kindly give you my life in return."

The purple skull replied, "Because you are only young still and not a proper queen yet, you can only use this power of mine only three times?"

The princess agreed.

In a flash of purple, the Amethyst skull disappeared and reappeared as a cloaked form and said again, "I am now your cloak so use me wisely."

She said "wow" as she touched the Cloak of soft velvet and said "I understand and will only use you when properly needed and not before oh mighty one"

Before approaching home, she swam to a jellyfish nest and prepared to take off the beautiful cloak and took out the papers from her pouch.

Has Helena then decided to hide everything that she had been given by the crystal skull in the jellyfish nest for safekeeping?

Because she knew that no one will ever go there as they will be stung to death by their mother, her friend.

As she saved her and her babies a few times in the past, so now she is friends with them and they will help her when needed.

Louis carries the power within him always now as the voice spoke out from the cloak earlier about him.

It said because Louis is the Unicorn King's grandson of great powers of magic, through his bloodlines of some of the powers from the planet Andromeda already, where Pegasus now lives.

That she was speaking to the souls from planet Venus, which is connected to the planet Neptune too where your father originally came from centuries ago and that is why we represent the sea and the skies on your Earth now.

Gosh, she thought and said, "I am taking you off now and hiding you here for your safety."

She unclipped the seahorse silver clip of the cloak and said a verse to make it a small crystal skull again that she could put into her pouch bag for safe keeping with important papers.

When she said "I will be back for you soon"

She reached the jellyfish nest when she bowed to the guard and then swam through as she took out the purple skull from her pouch.

The skull agreed with her discussion and let her put it neatly away where the jellyfish eggs are for complete protection as no one was foolish enough to try and steal them as otherwise they would be killed themselves by trying to.

She was excited and yet tired as it took a lot out of her as she was remising.

She continues to speak to herself saying I actually swam in a shark's lair today and we could have been killed then thanks to the gods and the crystal skull for their help we were chosen for something greater and lucky to be alive.

She quickly swam back to the chambers to eat, drink and be with her siblings before going to bed to rest, thinking of the handsome mer-knight Taylor while she decides to sleep.

Helena was sleeping and thinking of Taylor a lot.

She knew then also that she and Louis were ready for battle and to save Seequest herself and in her sleep, she was saying to herself as she was yawning, "I am going to find Father tomorrow and tell him that I am ready to fight Hades."

Chapter Thirty-Eight

Seequest and Cerberus's last fight

Back in the cave Seequest listened to Cerberus's challenge and thought hard about what to do next when he had an idea that Hermes mentioned to him earlier when they spoke.

He hoped that it would work but he decided that before he could rescue Knightmare, he would have to kill Cerberus first, as he thought that he could not get into the dungeon otherwise.

So he would then speak to his love from the outside of it in case he loses this battle with Cerberus soon when trying to rescue her, as Seequest was strong

but not his full potential yet, as he needed to energize himself in the sea as the sea salt will strengthen him even though knowing his parents created him.

Once Neptune had helped his mother in the past, he then had the powers given to him of the sea as well.

Seequest said his goodbye in another way that he only knew to Knightmare, "Goodbye, my love. Thank you for everything and for teaching me what love is"

And he then saw in front of his eyes an image of Knightmare, which was the love of his life disappear.

He knew now that even though he was hurting inside, he was the Unicorn King, who must carry on without her in his life and continue the battle against Hades to death.

Cerberus was standing there thinking that he got the better of Seequest, as dragon dog then said "you are silly, aren't you?"

With all your powers, Hades has still tricked you once again, as there you are putting your heart out there for a demon horse that was never yours in the first place, as it was planned all along from the beginning.

"Hades is much stronger than you thought, as your Knightmare is not here anyway and she has forgotten you, as Hades kindly took away her memories that you and your daughter ever existed in her life".

"She only knows about Knight, your son, and he has now become the most vicious beast on Earth called Tremor".

"And here you are standing, listening to me, realizing that you have been fooled and used by Hades and his mare from the start"

Cerberus continued and said, "yes, I will tell you this for the first time, Knightmare seemed to be happy somehow and loved you both very much too.

But now that is all over as she is back to her normal demon horse self, destroying the lands with your son."

Seequest was so upset and angry that he did not care whom he hurt anymore and thought that no matter what this demon dog said it had seen its last days.

So, with great force, he bent his head straight down towards the beast and he charged the two-headed dog/dragon in the chest with his horn, which lit up red and killed Cerberus in one blow.

The demon creature took one deep breath, and his head went limp on his body when he collapsed to the floor.

Breathing out fire from his dragon head one last time and his other head dropped out its tongue before he closed his eyes, when Seequest said, "who is stupid now you damn beast."

"I said if I saw you again, I would not hesitate to kill you and this time you have pushed me not only to do that but also to make sure that you could never be reborn ever again."

As Seequest put his horn deep into Cerberus's heart it lit red and showed his complete anger and so it made Cerberus's body go into a ball of red light of flames and blast into dust.

Hades was planning to collect his pet hellhound for his next battle on the lands above.

Hades with Tremor by his side quietly walked back into the cave to get Cerberus who was guarding Knightmare.

He reached him and yet could not believe his eyes that he saw that there was a shadow of where he stood before becoming now just a lump of ashes.

He realized also that Seequest and Hermes were now free again standing in front of him, not scared at all, and were prepared to fight him to the death.

Hades was seriously angry as his dear pet Cerberus had been greatly beaten and was lost by the Unicorn King killing him.

The tremor was standing there waiting for a command from Hades as at the moment he was just staring at the unicorn not knowing that it was Knight's actual father.

Seequest thought that he was looking at Knight at the time, but what the unicorn king did not know was his real son is dead and Tremor now controls his body completely.

Hades looked to see what had just happened to his best friend and said in shock and horror, "No, no, my boy, no, not Cerberus.

"Now you will pay with your life, Seequest, kill him, Tremor,"

Hades said as he moved out of the way for them to fight.

Hermes was upset as told to go away by the unicorn and then disappeared as he flew off as quickly as he could as a fly.

He hoped that Seequest will not get hurt but he was more worried that Knight could inwardly.

The tremor came galloping towards Seequest and tried his best to bite and rip him apart.

As they were fighting, Seequest looked into the evil Unisos's eyes and still saw his son in there somewhere and refused to fight anymore.

Seequest then called out loudly, "my son, please wake up, it's your father, wake up, I say."

But poor Knight was gone and Tremor, now well under Hades' commands was doing everything he can to kill Seequest at this moment.

Seequest had an idea and hoped it will work.

He thought of love in his heart for his son and the memories they had as a family and touched Tremor's chest gently with his horn, which lit up in a pink glow and then seemed to touch Knight's, actual heart.

As Seequest tried to pass on the magic to stop the hate anymore and hopefully bring back his son again.

But it did not happen straightaway so they were continuing to fight.

Seequest was seriously trying not to hurt his son's body in case later they cannot heal him because of the magic that Hades had on him already.

But it did not even touch the black heart.

The Unicorn King could see that Knight's horn wasn't the way it used to be.

It looked as if Hades had bounded his sword to his horn, which means all the good he had in him will be frozen in time.

But for a split second, Seequest's power worked and Knight woke up and said 'Father, please, I don't want to hurt you anymore but I cannot fight Tremor either.

"So please just stay away from me otherwise Tremor will kill you, he said sadly."

Seequest was saddened to hear this from his son who is now very weak because Tremor was hurting him as he defended himself as much as he could without try-ing to hurt Knight's body.

But because the love of his son was still trapped inside he let Tremor hurt him until Tremor became tired and fled.

He knew now that he must find a way to save his son and yet destroy Tremor at the same time.

Seequest was badly hurt and yet was still standing boldly like the king that he was.

Tremor felt tired and yet really wanted to kill Seequest, so he came back rushing right at him full blast and knocked him over.

Hermes heard Seequest whim and so flew back as quickly as he could turning himself back into a wasp on approach.

Hermes, at this time, was buzzing around the demon horse and stung it a few times to get its attention while the unicorn king got himself to his feet.

Knight, at this time, could see that his father was beaten and quickly let Seequest escape from Tremor.

Seequest then galloped the opposite way through the dark chambers to find his daughter hoping that she still remembered him and was on his side.

Tremor shook his head and said "Silence" to Knight as he used his horn on his head to break the cave wall and caused him pain, as that would hurt Knight which made Knight go back to sleep because of anger waking up the dark force completely.

Tremor had a better chance of catching up with Seequest as he had his bat wings to carry him further distances Hades' caves were larger than normal so his creatures could fly out when they needed to.

Hermes flew off earlier, as when Seequest was fighting Tremor he told Hermes to find his daughter in case he got killed.

He did this through his powers of being telepathic as a gift from the gods themselves, thankfully.

Seequest was following the buzzing noise he can hear ahead of Hermes and kept swirling in and out of the corners of the dark caves to which the Unicorn King slowed down.

Hermes had found Firefly with her wings strapped to her body looking tired and more confused than ever.

He whispered in her ear and within that, her eyes sparkled and her coat gleamed again of beautiful bright pink where her eyes shone also bright once more.

"Where is my father?"

He replied to her, "I believe, my young filly, he is still looking for you."

"Come on, then.

It is time for us to go and find him together."

"No. It's best if you let him find us."

"No", she said "It's fine if you want to stay here, but I am going" and tried to leave when Hermes said that Hades still has her under his spell and that she could not leave the caves as he did with her mother.

But she then mentioned that even though being confused for so long she felt her grandmother with her helping her to somehow stay strong through all this happening.

But Hades had been watching her closely and took her deeper into the darker dungeons, as it was harder for the messages to be heard.

Firefly then got upset and said to Hermes, "I have been locked away so I was not able to telepath messages to Celestial or my father anymore."

But Firefly was like her father, who was stubborn and sometimes listened to her advice.

While they were waiting to move her, she remembered that her grandmother could talk to her and so kept silent.

Hermes flew over to the feathered Unisos and comforted her by saying, "Look, I know your father and he will be here soon.

Sorry for your pain and sadness but you will soon heal and you can all be together again." Or that was what he thought might happen.

While the feathered Unisos was being patient for her father to collect her and Hermes, they walked a little further to the entrance of the dungeon where Seequest would have to come through.

She tried her best to contact Celestial who could breathe some light of good into this problem they were in.

"Celestial, can you hear me?"

"I am trapped with Hermes while Seequest is seriously hurt because of a major fight with Tremor as he would not hurt the demon horse knowing that his son is trapped inside it still."

"That is what Hermes saw from a distance and has told me.

Please great one, I need your help."

Back on the beach where Legend and Pegasus had landed earlier, they had just eaten, when she decided to go for a nice walk getting impatient about what was going on with her son and grandchildren.

Celestial walked closer to Legend and explained to him what was going on in the distance of the underworld below them.

She felt in her mind like someone was trying to connect with her but the message was too faint to pick up on her own and said "Legend, I need your help and support please now to help me receive this message, as I feel it is from them in the underworld."

They stopped in their tracks, as they turned around and put their heads together to see if both of their powers could break through the barrier stopping them from communicating with whoever was trying to get through to her.

First, she felt a presence of a great powerful unicorn and believed it was Seequest and they said together, "We call the great Unicorn King Seequest."

"Can you hear us?"

"It is Celestial and Legend, who also used to be your parents many years ago."

Seequest thought that he was hearing strange voices when he heard the call and answered while still looking for his daughter.

"It cannot be, as you are far away in the universe in the heavens above."

"No, we're not, our child."

"We are here on Earth at the moment, as we have come to help with this battle on Earth and so Zeus has given us this opportunity to also see you once more before, one day, you, too, will become a spirit and become much more than what you are now"

"Now, listen, where are you?'

"I am in the dark chambers."

They then received another message who said she is Firefly.

But to make sure, they asked her a question that she should only know about her father's heart.

Luckily, she passed the test and they then carried on the conversation in their minds.

When Celestial and Legend asked where Firefly was as they knew that Seequest was trying to find her too.

They thought that they may be able to help them both at the same time Firefly mentioned where she and Hermes were and Seequest's guardians told him where he needed to go to find them.

"Seequest, Firefly said that you need to go through two more passages, turn right, and there you will find your daughter."

Firefly and Hermes are waiting for you.

"Go now, hurry" and her voice vanished from his mind.

As he was getting closer to them, he became excited thinking he will get to see his image of his parents once more in the flesh.

But what was more important was to find his daughter and get out of hell once and for all together in one piece.

As he was galloping through the last passage, he started to feel his cold heart becoming warmer again because of the love of his family, which made him strong in his time of need.

Seequest called and neighed in deep frustration and said, "Firefly my daughter, where are you?"

And then she replied, "We are here Father, in this cave in front of you."

He turned and put his horn onto the barrier and closed his eyes and broke it.

He then trotted boldly and yet weakly to her side, where he breaks the straps and freed her wings to breathe again.

He walked up to her face and said, "we need to touch horns to strengthen each other's powers, as you process a magic that even I do not even have."

He puts his horn to hers and says "close your eyes" when she does, she mentions to Seequest to say this to himself.

Seequest began the chant.

"I will regain my strength by taking some of yours and I will in return give you some of mine and we will become one together."

He now had enough energy to get them out of there but he knew that it will make him even weaker than before.

But he did not care anymore.

He just wanted to free his daughter and himself from this horrible experience.

Now they were all strong enough to get to the entrance of the Forbidden Woods.

He hoped that someone will have the power to break the spell and get them out of there safely in time, as there was another invisible barrier stronger than the last one that Hades had put at the entrance of the cave as a backup.

Seequest felt at this time that he will never be able to escape Hades' grasp and thought if he could save his daughter and his son then he did not care about himself anymore as he felt that he was getting too old to keep on fighting.

Knowing that peace on Earth was more important than him.

As Hades would not let him settle here on Earth until he probably dies.

Even though they were away from Hades' cave and creatures at last,

They were still trapped in darkness, hoping that someone will free them soon as both of them have used the last of their powers to communicate with Celestial, as they are magnificent creatures and burnt loads of energy connecting with her.

These are the reasons why no one is allowed to communicate with her as she could drain them completely by mistake and accidentally kill them.

And yet Seequest knew they had no choice but to try this no matter what happens to him.

Has he been more concerned for his daughter's safety than his own, as usual?

This gift remained from his mother, Moonbeam.

"My daughter I am sorry that I could not save your mother and brother but I did try my best."

"Yet I was not enough even for me being the Unicorn King to save them" with sadness in his voice as he spoke.

They were lying there by the entrance trying to breathe the fresh air.

How they missed this oxygen in their lungs, which took their breath away at first as it had been a long time since they had to use it.

As Hades made it so they could only breathe his air in the underground.

And it would take a while to recover from this and readjust back to normal before they could even get up and walk away again.

Seequest did not like the idea of being trapped.

But he thought at least they had time to recover and learn to breathe the natural air again before they were officially free from the caves at last.

And then carry on finding Tremor and defeating him for good as they both thought while sleeping that they were going to give it their all to save Knight if they really could.

While they were all sleeping Hermes was thinking about being back in Olympus sitting in the gardens eating his cherries, smiling in his dreams.

Finally, they all woke up and still felt tired and refreshed at the same time.

Seequest said to Firefly 'all because I fell in love with your mother, I put down my barrier and allowed Hades into my heart and mind so that he could control me and my magic.

"I hope that you can forgive me one day, daughter", while looking at his daughter with shame in his eyes.

She replied with love in hers and nuzzled him as she forgave him and replied "I understand why and I forgive you, Father."

"Now, come on and fight the fight. There must be a way that we can stop all of this,' she said.

"There is", Seequest replied "but it cannot happen as it would mean me giving up my horn to Hades, so he can control Earth for himself which would be a great nightmare on earth."

"I will have to die and I would never exist in anyone's memories ever again."

"My life purpose is to keep Earth safe and will, with the help of Mother Nature now or Gaia to me has meant to be the protector from all evil too?"

"I am sorry, but this cannot happen."

"Again, forgive me my daughter but my duties are far too great to break this promise for your liking or my feelings either, there is more at stake than our lives now!"

"It's ok, Father."

"I understand why with tears running down her eyes as they put both their heads over each other's shoulders for comfort."

"Let us get out of here quickly before Hades comes back with another of his nasty creatures."

Did firefly tell Hermes to turn back into a small god and try and fly out of the cave between the cracks of the walls and get help?

Hermes went to find Celestial and Legend at the beach to help them all escape.

As Seequest and Firefly were stuck at the entrance of the cave, they could see from the distance there over the back the great silver birch tree that they all used to lie together at when they were a family once before.

It bought back so many memories to them both but they had to put them behind them, as they needed to escape this place more so they saved their energy for just that.

Seequest closed his eyes and felt all of a sudden both his late parents sent him some warmth of magic and then put all his willpower into his thoughts to break the barrier down and it did which shocked even him as he felt that he did not have the strength in him to do so.

He thanked them dearly as now they are free and that they will be with them soon, he hoped.

They rushed to the beach.

Seequest knew that he must get back into the water to build his full strength and heal his painful wounds.

They reached the rocks where he and his mother used to rest looking out to the sea, which made him feel safe and he tried to walk further to the beach when he felt an electric shock from another force field.

Hades had put a spell on this place knowing that Seequest could still win the battle.

Seequest tried again like before but this time, he was too weak as it took a lot out of him last time, and said, "OK, we're trapped again."

The Unicorn King was now seriously annoyed and mad that he felt down and out as he the unicorn hippocampus, he felt the sea was calling him and so dipped his horn into it like Neptune told him to do before the call for help, hoping that the sea god would hear him?

Even though he was not completely free from Hades yet he felt better as they were out of the lair for good that he will have that opportunity to swim the seas soon.

As he was now a hippocampus that lived in the sea without the water in his lungs he would die from this.

And so even though did not like what he had to do now Hades knew that he had to give some of his power back to breathe on land again as needed him alive still.

Seequest now was strong enough to reach the water.

But Hades felt that he had the advantage, as now Seequest would have to stay in the water to survive for a while in the hot sun.

Yet could go any further as The Demon god had put an electric field in the sea and even though it would not kill Seequest, it would harm his friends the sea creatures instead, which Seequest would not ever forgive himself for.

Once again it seemed that Hades had the better of him.

Even Seequest at this moment in time was losing hope and yet his daughter never did and told her father to just hang in there.

Has his unicorn form been only temporary from Neptune until he and Helena returned home safely together?

He thought that Hades would still win the battle after all as the underworld god could not wait until Seequest dries out naturally to collect his horn once he is gone.

But he would have to be quick because it would evaporate into dust and become part of the earth and produce magic everywhere.

Firefly could see that her father was dying of exhaustion and lack of seawater around him.

She did her best to contact Celestial and Legend again to tell them that her father was in great danger of dying as he needed to get into the deeper parts of the water to recover from his pains and heal his wounds soon.

Now his time was running out as a Unicorn King because he gave up some of his earth powers to Gaia and so he needed the sea to survive more as that is where his powers come from now.

Poor Firefly wanted to fly away and find help but she did not want to leave his side in case he went into a coma or died.

She hoped this was not the case but she was fretting that it could be true.

She closed her eyes tightly and began to pray to the heavens and Zeus that someone would find them shortly, as she was useless even to her father.

As her powers could not heal him when a hippocampus.

Even though she, too can change into one she had the powers still of the land and sea.

But her father was too weak for her to use her powers on him, as deep in his heart he is preventing her to heal him because he seemed to not care anymore about what happened to him and just wanted to save the Earth again.

Seequest had been a hippocampus for such a long time now that he adjusted to this life only.

Firefly said, "Father, I believe you."

"Please do not give up now as we have come so far from where we have been."

Seequest was there lying in the shallow waters trying to breathe as now the tide was going again and the sand was now exposed.

But stood there looking out to the sea as he knew that he needed deeper waters to heal and also feel completely free as one with the sea like when he is a hippocampus should be.

He turns around and says, 'There, there, my precious daughter."

"I am so proud of you, your brother, and your past mother for giving me this dream that I have always wanted."

"But it looks like it cannot be anymore!"

"I love you with all my heart, you will live and become an important Unisos in time I know this, and I shall be watching from afar."

Believing now that is the real reason why Celestial and Legend had come to earth due to his mistakes and taking him away from the earth forever.

But that was not true.

Poor Seequest was terrible and he felt that no one could save him as he felt in his heart that it did not matter anymore.

After his speech to his daughter, he collapses into the shallow part of the sea and became still as the sun above was too hot for him to cope with, as otherwise, he will die from the heat of the sun which was Hades' plan from the beginning and knew it would certainly work.

Firefly neighed with despair having tears in her eyes and said "Father you will not die on me, I will not allow you to"

And yet Seequest was lying quietly on the sea surface, not moving.

Firefly said "Please someone help us" and then watched her father from the beach as she needed to stay away from it for now.

Because she too was weak and the saltwater could make her ill at the moment as well.

So quickly when the sea went out she had to pull her father out of the water so she could re-energize her powers as well.

She was lying down resting, keeping an eye on her father's body so that it did not move anywhere else.

She decided to pull him to the rocks where he could still be in the seawater and yet would not be able to go out further and get destroyed by the invisible force field that was life. But took him here where she also she could stay with him.

And as she did, she repeated and said, "do not worry Father someone will come and save us but for now, lie here quietly and rest."

The sun was just starting to go down.

At least Seequest could breathe a little better now that he felt cooler as the sun was too hot earlier.

As it was colder now Firefly felt a little stronger and so did Seequest who had been in the salt water for a long while keeping from drying out in the sun earlier.

She pulled him back near the trees for shade and warmth as they lay together while Firefly put her wings wrapped around her father's back for comfort and reassurance, as Seequest was ripped to pieces inside as he knew that he will never be able to feel love like that ever again.

As it made him weak and helpless and remembered that he is the Unicorn King and that his feelings of love did not matter as that is not what he was here to do.

But he was beating himself up over his emotions which to drained him badly as the horse that he became earlier when with Helena before was the only spirit left inside him which seemed to only survive for now.

Seequest knew that Hades had found his true weakness and couldn't believe that he let him get to that part of his heart.

But once he was strong again hopefully.

While resting he knew then his emotions will have to be hidden in his mind and never come out again like this ever again once he got his family safe away from Hades again.

He knew that he would never let his guard down again as he was the unicorn king. Have emotions for others and the earth.

But emotions regarding his life were not allowed as could do too much damage in the future.

He realized that was Hades' plan all along and played right into his hand.

Have Hades noticed that because he cared deeply for his mother for so long he then knew that his emotions and LOVE were his weakness and decided to play with them to weaken the unicorn king completely?

It looked like Hades, at last, had found Seequest's weakness and he seemed to see that it worked and from a distance watching through the fire in his lair and started to laugh saying, "Well, well, Seequest does have a weakness after all and it is his heart" and began to laugh.

That night, the wolves were out on the beach and the white wolf Moon Cloud knew thanks to Luna that Seequest was in great danger and had to rescue him and his daughter soon.

Chapter Thirty-Nine

Helena and the Mer-Knight

Months passed when Helena wanted to find her father and she got told that she missed him again.

So, she went and had breakfast with her siblings as usual and headed up towards the stables where she bumped into Taylor who was just getting his hippocampus, Reef, from his stables, which is slightly further up to the royal ones.

She tried to watch him without being seen as he was not wearing his armor yet and she thought that he was very handsome with blonde hair blue-eyed merman with a nice muscled torso and his tail too.

She felt like he could be the one that she would settle down with one day,

Or that was what she was hoping.

An hour had passed after watching him and feeling a little giddy inside when she collapsed and made it obvious that she had been spying on him all this time.

"Helena", he said and lifted her gently into his arms he looked at her face and could see the true beauty in her eyes with her pale white body and green swallowtail.

Without hurting her fins, he held her gently and put his face to hers to make sure that she was breathing still when she woke up and saw these bold blue eyes mer-man looking right at her.

Quickly she jumped out of his arms and said, "Taylor what are you doing?"

And he said back, "my lady I am sorry but you fainted and I was just seeing how you were as you were floating upside down."

"Oh, I was?"

"You were" he expressed with a choked-up and caring voice for her.

"Of course, as your lady, I like you a lot and I thought you might like to go riding with me this afternoon and practice our skills for the race together?"

The princess smiled and he smiled back when she replied "sure, let's do that."

As they both smiled and swam and got their hippocampius ready and met outside the royal stables and went for a ride in the Vissen- grounds.

Helena was having great fun and yet she realized that the time was getting late and that she had to get back, as she still wanted to try and go to the beach and rescue Seequest herself knowing that she has the power to do so now.

So, she began to make up an excuse that she had some errands to do and said that she enjoyed his company and he told her the same and she hoped they could do it again soon.

Once again, they both smiled and seemed to feel to have a connection or bond with each other.

But Helena thought, I am eighteen soon and he will be twenty.

Maybe he would not be interested in a young princess like me and is it possible that my parents would approve of this either as his just being a knight in Father's army?

She got upset thinking too hard about it and answered her answer No they will never approve of him!

But she thought greatly of this handsome merman.

She then realized that she was becoming a mer-woman and felt that she fancied him and started to daydream about him too often.

But she said to herself that she did not have time for this now as she had to go to the beach to try to rescue her dear old friend Seequest, as she thought that he had been waiting way too long already.

But what Eldest Daughter did not know was that Taylor was not only Neptune's best knight but also a prince from the Mother Realm of the sea.

She quickly thought that she might see him again soon and thought that she will have to go to her hideout where the jellyfish live now as she did not want Taylor to know her secret yet.

She reached the jellyfish nest and bowed to the mother and said "my dear friend may I please go into your breeding quarters to collect my special things?"

The large colourful jellyfish replied moving its tentacles up and down and agreeing, so kindly moved out of the way so she can swim in there quietly and reach for the things that belong to her.

Before she rushed off back to the stables again she reached for the reins and sea saddle, plus grabbed it, as she made the skull back into a cloak which she puts into her pouch for safekeeping for now.

She quickly went back to the stables to make sure everyone else is ok, where she saw Louis's parents, as her father had arrived home now safe and his hippocampus (Tidal Wave) was floating on his bed sleeping, from his long journey.

Later that night she goes to get louis ready when the others neighed when she says "no sorry not this time".

"Louis and I are going out for practice before everyone awakes up in the city"

She told the others, "Father will be with you both later for you to use the chariot of the sea,"

As Sea spray and Tidal Wave are his chariot water horses of the sea and they control the power of the waves too.

Tidal Wave cannot overdo it because he is Neptune's champion of the games too.

But she knew Tidal Wave was fast and knew that she will win the race this time around because Louis his son has other magic powers that his father does not.

Helena looked at Tidal Wave and Louis together and Tidal Wave woke up and swam to her and she said to him "Thank you our great champion of the sea races.

But this time, you can be assured that your son Louis will beat you fair and square", and smiled and patted Tidal Wave on his handsome horse face when he reared his legs up and caught Helena's fin in his tracks, which knocked her to the floor where she grazed her arm.

She gets up and says "well if you're going to be like that about it, then we definitely will win" and rushed out of his stall.

Helena was forgetting that this hippocampus is a wild spirit and that her father and mother are the ones that can control him and thought that she was silly enough to have forgotten this and she should not be gotten close to him in the first place.

She looked at her arm all cut and reached out for octopus' ointment which she put on and then put some thick seaweed over it to stop the bleeding.

Then she collected Louis and jumped on his back quickly once more, as she had all that she needed with them as they swam towards the back of the stables where the dark pool was and started to dream of being a queen herself one day.

Maybe have Pisces people and mer-folk in her kingdom in the future too, she thought.

That she could build the most spectacular building that anyone has ever seen with rounded houses for her people who would like to try a similar human form where they could change into a mer-people when they wanted to go back into the water.

She was daydreaming more than ever now as if she felt that her dreams could come true now that she has control of the Amethyst skull but only time would tell.

How she dreamt of the kingdom all the time.

And by winning the race, she hoped that her parents would honour this dream of hers because she will be as powerful as them.

She could be even being unique to any princess before her and it would make her the happiest mer-woman alive, where her life will change forever.

Helena created a brand-new world like no other had seen or known before.

She was thinking her powers would help to protect nature and all creatures on land and sea too.

This seemed to make her smile as she was getting ready to see Kessy in the British Isles of Scotland for help.

She said to her hippocampus, "before we go, we must put back Mum's dolphins in the sea fields."

They approached the dolphins and there beside them were some small pods of dolphins with their yearlings which seemed to be very playful indeed.

Then a male swam at them with great speed saying "please you must come quickly."

"Hades has got a pod of yearlings trapped in one of his nets."

Once she heard this she said, "Louis we must save them",

They followed the male dolphin to help the yearlings because that was one of her jobs to do every day.

So away they went swimming as quickly as the hippocampus could, trying to keep up with it, as dolphins are very fast indeed.

She did not care that it could be a trap.

But followed been prepared for anything unusual after what happened before and her parents would not forgive her if she got captured again while their swimming to save the yearlings from Hades' nets and sea beasts.

She said, "I would love to help but I cannot in case it is a trap?"

The male grey dolphin squealed and said in her mind, I thought you loved us and wanted to protect us as you said you always would as we have saved you many times from sharks, whales, and other creatures, and this is how you repay us, your dolphin cousins?'

"No, of course, I will help you."

"Come on Louis let's go" Remember that she had the cloak and her armour in the sea pouch all the time knowing that the Amethyst crystal skull will always protect her.

But will she use it now to protect her cousins or try to rescue Seequest with it?

She did not care anymore.

She just wanted to help and free her friends from Hades' evil plans if possible.

The male dolphin reached the others in the middle of the sea and stopped and said "my name is Speed I am the leader of the pod of blue bottle-nosed dolphins."

"Whom your parents own so we are fully protected too so it's our honour that you are helping us now."

Before she went any further she said "wait I must go and ask the knight Taylor to help us", and that was what she did.

She dived back towards Vissen where she saw Taylor out Scuba practicing for the race and called him and tells him about the dolphins trapped in Hades' nets and that Speed expected her to help him, as they could achieve this together as a team.

Taylor seemed to like the idea of them being together in any way but as a team member, for now, was close enough, he thought.

When replied to her "yes, of course, Helena I will help you and the dolphins."

She replied "Great follow me."

They dived deep again when they came back to where the male dolphin was waiting for them to help release the yearlings from these terrible nets.

Swimming towards the dolphins they seemed to be close together with both of their hippocampius swimming at great speeds.

Scuba is stunning like his brother Louis.

But he is a bigger and heavier build than him.

But he cannot change into a seahorse as he was not shown when he was younger.

Helena promised herself and Louis that no one else would know their secret until at least the day after the race in case they get disqualified because of it.

They saw the pod of yearlings looking sad and distressed, floating around squashed together in this large strong black net, and wondered how they were going to free them.

Helena come up with a great idea about changing into a smaller form by swimming into the net not seen, which would break the net in half.

But she could not do this as it was a secret.

So, she asked Taylor "please go and get some help while I keep the yearlings calm while you do." He smiled at her and did exactly that.

He and Squeal turned around dived head first back into the bottom of the ocean towards Vissen.

While Helena and Louis did what she thought of doing in the first place as a last result?

The Hippocampus changed quickly into a seahorse and swam straight into the net, trying not to get squashed by the yearlings at the same time.

Luckily, he was small enough to get in there on his own but he was still bigger than Helena herself so she could still ride him skilfully and comfortably too in this form as well.

Louis now feels that he had weakened the nets he came out and swooped Helena up onto his back when she said to him, "Come on, boy, we must get them free."

They kept working on them until they did their best swimming carefully around the poor stressed young dolphins in the distance at the time.

The females of this pod were watching further out at sea, as lookouts for sharks at the time.

She remembered her spear can go smaller and also that Louis was just going to change into the other form again, then the net split opened and the dolphin year-lings swam out of it quickly moving their thick tails up and down at a quick pace to be completely free once more.

As they did Helena put her lips to her mouth as if tell-ing the yearlings, it was their secret.

All the dolphins squeaked back and promised her as they thanked them both and began to swim towards their mothers again.

They were all together jumping in and out of the water with joy and splashing the water in front of them as a great thank-you.

Then they did somersaults in front of them and began to swim further out to sea for safety in pods.

An hour had passed.

Taylor returned with Speed with some more knights, when Squeal appeared jumping straight out of the water as his female had told him that the yearlings were already had been freed and are safe.

Expressing this body language showed that he was happy and that his pod could see that too.

He swam closely to Helena where she jumped off her hippocampus and approached the large male dolphin when he brushed his nose to her face as he thanked her and squirted water from his blow hole to breathe before he dived back into the ocean to his pod again.

As this was going on Taylor felt like a fool as Helena did not wait and yet also wondered how she got them free at the same time.

She says, "I am sorry".

"I don't have time to explain the details to you now."

Taylor replied "when shall you then?"

Helena said, "One day, thank you" and dived back into the sea and disappeared.

Taylor was sitting on his hippocampus and said "that princess will be mine, one-day Scuba mark my words".

"She's courageous, beautiful, and kind the perfect wife for me" as he carried on his duties that day Scuba agreed by neighing to him happily as they swam back to Vissen for a rest.

Meanwhile, Louis and Helena were back in the dark pool.

They still had to see Kessy which they were looking forward to all day.

"Come on, my dear friend let's go and see your sister and see how she is doing?"

Louis neighed and said, "Oh yes please" and they shot off in the dark pool which they swam through to the other side of the world to the Loch in bonny Scotland.

Chapter Forty

Helena Goes to See Kessy

Back, in Scotland Sheerness to be exact. Luckily for Kessy time was different there.

In Scotland, it was two hours behind because the sun went around Earth twenty-four hours a day even then.

As they were swimming into the waters they saw amazing different colored fish swimming around with them in schools and colourful crabs and crayfish lying on the bottom of the freshwater too, when they swam up for air they saw a pretty dolphin that seemed to swim in the sea and freshwater too.

She was a grey bottle-nosed dolphin that Kessy used to play with in the past and followed Helena through the pool as she was very intelligent and had been searching for her friend for a long time in the different seas not knowing where she had gone to.

They reached Loch Helena and asked the dolphin why she followed them, when she was just going to call Kessy afterward to let the water dragon know that they were there to see her.

First, Helena approached the dolphin carefully not to frighten it when she looked at the princess in the face and listened to see what would happen next when she called the dolphin over and said, "How did you get here and why?"

The dolphin replied in Helena's mind "I am Kessy's old friend Squirm."

I wanted to know if she was OK, as my other friends the blue nose said that she was living here and that I could go and see for myself as I would be able to adapt to the freshwater like her!

Because she mentioned that she was not going back until she sees her friend again and started to wave her flippers up and down, splashing everyone as she did.

And from out of the blue rise a creature with a long neck with great beauty of enormous hippocampus still.

Squirm looked and dived and then rose again seeing that this great creature was exactly her old friend Kessy.

The pretty dolphin seemed scared and sure that she was safe with her friend and yet realized that she could be squashed.

But her plans were to at least stay for a while and say her goodbyes before leaving for good with a sad expression on her face.

Kessy was excited to see her and noticed too her size and that it would be impractical for Squirm to stay with her which too upset her and felt more alone than ever.

"Kessy, don't worry, girl."

"You always have us" and watched her friend dive back towards the main sea again.

As she did quickly kessy saw further in the distance a pod of blue whales doing their duties of cleaning up the waters as they went, as Squirm swam into the deeper part of the Loch where they are a silver gate and dived out of the water and jumped it and joined the blue whales for fun.

The whales squirted the water from their heads as a hello and then dived deep once again.

The princess waved and Kessy splashed the water to say hello too from a distance.

Later Helena told Kessy of her plan to rescue Seequest, her grandfather whom she had not the pleasure of meeting yet because he had been captured by Hades and she agreed to help in this fight too.

Helena was shocked to see that Kessy could walk with her flappers on the land and rest there in the sun without being burnt by the sun itself.

It seemed that when she was out of the water she could change into the colour of a rock or a piece of land as if she was also some kind of chameleon changing to suit her mood or safety.

Helena realized then that Kessy was evolving again into another creature and she wondered if her mother knew.

How she wanted to tell her and then thought that she could not because she was in the Crystal Temple getting ready the crystal skulls to protect their homes again from Hades.

How much she started to hate her uncle dearly.

She then thought that she will try and contact her mother by reading later the Book of Knowledge to see if it will tell her how to communicate with her.

In a situation like this, she cannot be disturbed even by her daughter.

The Sea dragon was with Helena and Louis and they had a great time racing across one side of the Loch to the other as Kessy always won.

It was great fun though they all thought, as they had not seen each other for over a year and had a lot of catching up to do.

What a great reunion it was for them all.

The princess was watching her when she noticed that she had changed again and saw that when Kessy was on land again later in the day that her scales would harden into a rock scale as it protected her from harm.

With a great possibility that she was beginning to develop maybe wings too.

Oh, how desperately Helena wanted to go and tell her mother all about it and how excited she would be for them all.

But she knew for a while her mother was out of bounds for now.

"Oh, how Mother would love her girl' and smile straight into Kessy's green eyes which were astounding that you could get lost in them because of the sweet calm nature that they gave you when you stared long enough into them."

Kessy felt that the sun was too hot for her again so she slid back into the water moving her powerful long neck out of the water as she went.

She began to hunt for fish to eat by putting her head up and down forgetting that her doing this made a massive big splash all over the Loch which knocked her friends away from her.

Louis and Helena then realized that it was time for Kessy to go out to the British sea to check if everything was OK still, as they dived towards the large silver gates which kept Kessy there in the Loch safety.

Helena saw the gates and opened them up for Kessy to stretch her limbs properly and waited for her to come back when she was ready that day.

As they opened up the gates she then dives into the loch to jump and do whatever she pleased without affecting or hurting anyone as she did.

Kessy loved this freedom that she enjoyed it as much as she could.

While Kessy was out exploring the sea for a while with her special mask on, they went back down and locked the silver metal gates of peace while seeing Kessy in all her glory swimming deeper and further out to the British sea.

They closed the gates to prevent Hades from getting in or encouraging one of his creatures too so Helena said, "Let's make sure that these gates are properly locked, so Hades cannot destroy this land or its waters."

They both hoped that Kessy could look after herself out there seeing her from afar.

Because they had to stay on that side to make sure she could get back in as the lock could only be locked from her homeland.

From the outside it cannot be locked, that is why Hades and his beasts will not get through as it's a special metal made from the moon goddess herself.

Time was getting on when Helena wanted to sunbathe but first she knew that she must train more and be ready for anything.

Helena said "Come on boy let's train" and they practiced both forms for the race and for the fight to save Seequest too.

Helena fell off a few times as she was getting used to the new outfit and the powers too, seeing saw her handsome hippocampus appear looking for her.

In a while she was brushing away her hair from her face and saw his beautiful aquamarine-blue eyes looking at her with great affection for his rider and friend.

His gleaming eyes lit up the night sky.

She quickly said "stop it as it will attract Hades' ravens to catch us."

As it was nighttime when they had been training and waiting for Kessy to come back home again.

The sea horse listened to Helena stopping straight away and dived into the freshwater where he could only swim in at the moment because his reins carried a little white shell that he eats and makes him safe to temporarily swim drink and eat in the loch for eight hours.

After that he would have to go back to the sea otherwise he will die of not having enough salt to breathe in.

"Come on Louis we do not have much time left before Kessy will be back for her rainbow mackerel dessert we have for her and then her rest before we tell her what we plan to do."

His galloping and splashing around the waters with excitement and couldn't wait for his sister to be back where she belongs as now they could not see her at all and began to be concerned.

They stayed there doing some extra special training which involved trying out their plan in action on a deeper level.

They rested as Helena loved lying on the large rock looking at the moonlight thinking if she would ever meet her grandmother Luna in person one day.

But this was the only place that she could get away from it all as it was far away from home.

Now it was time for her to come home so Helena blew the conch horn which she hoped Kessy heard and started to swim back to the Loch seeing that some seals were watching her every move and then realized they were not seals.

They were Hades' evil shape shifters pretending to be sealed as they were trying to find her domain for ages.

Kessy noticed them as she was approaching back towards the silver gates when she dived again changing into the shade of the water that she fooled them.

Hopefully, she was fast enough to lose them before she became visible again to reach home safely.

Helena spoke to Louis "It's taking her much longer to get Kessy back than usual?"

Could Kessy just be over in the deeper waters trying to get away from Hades' seals, she thought?

Helena felt a sensation of fear come over her and dived deep swimming quickly to the gates to unlock them and to get out of the way of Kessy coming back in too.

As you see she would have been killed if she hadn't as Kessy was very large and coming at full speed into the Loch which was even too dangerous for Helena to try.

Helena could see that she was coming at great speed towards the gates which were opened now and Kessy whooshed right through.

Luckily Helena had been practicing been quick in shutting and locking the gates to prevent Hades' creatures from getting in, trying to keep amounts of the sea and its rough waves from getting in.

Killing the fish inside the Loch, as some fish can only survive in fresh water like her.

The other reason why it's there is to protect them all from the sea as she has not been trained in it properly yet and may never be.

Her hippocampus rushed to her aid and dived after she and she wiggled herself onto his back where they swam back to the rock for Helena to catch her breath again.

Has she gone into shock thinking that she could have been killed by her friend if she wasn't quick enough to get out of the way?

Kessy was back safe again in the Loch where she belonged and Hades' shape-shifter seals swam away out of sight to fight another day.

Helena mentions that blue whales will have to be ordered to go and kill them before they go back and tell Hades about Kessy and where she lives.

Because it's a secret from him as there is also an invisible force field over the Loch and it's only when Kessy goes out into the sea that she can be seen and it's down for a short while.

Straightaway Helena calls the blue whales with her mind and tells them what happened and that they must destroy the black seals before they get back to Hades' liar.

The blue whale called Sovereign answered Helena back later and said "the task is done, Your Highness."

She thanked him and told the rest of her friends that again they were safe and sound.

What a great relief it was for them all as they had enough to attend to without worrying about Kessy's secret being broken as well they thought, as they carried on talking about their plan to rescue Seequest soon.

Kessy began panicking that she had put her dear friends in danger by going to sea for the day and started to look for them eventually she found them on the rock and Louis swimming happily around it.

Kessy poked her head out of the water which made Helena laugh as she squirted water straight into her face at the time for fun.

Helena says "It's an ok girl."

It is not your fault and she neighed and jumped out of the water up into the air about three feet and landed with a great splash as if the land had moved.

Helena decided to jump back in from her favourite rock and decided to have some fun before getting ready to leave Kessy for the night.

The princess brushed her tail up and down until she reached the sea dragon's face and cuddled her deeply showing her love for this creature of magic.

Kessy was also much stronger and tougher than she last was when the queen was last here and she hunted for herself independently and could survive on her own.

She was a beautiful of different shades of green in the water,Kessy knew that she had a purpose for why Queen Sera put her there years before.

It was to make sure that the water stays clean and healthy for all the freshwater creatures that live in it and possibly for the future as she is still a secret to everyone apart from Zeus himself and a few others that needed to know to look after her at times for them.

Yes, Zeus visited Kessy himself sometimes as he too is astonished by her greatness.

The princess said 'wow Kessy the last time we saw you were the same size as Bracken and, yes he has grown larger too.

"You are enormous and elegant with it."

"You are a remarkable seahorse with a difference and I hope you do not mind me saying this."

"But I think that from the Book of Wisdom, you are becoming a sea dragon my lovely".

So yes, you are related to the hippocampus line and will always be our family and Louis's.

"But again, you are another species with a difference of a greater purpose in the future."

"I believe Kessy you will be another Legend of your kind like Seequest before you and you will be known for these lands to girl!", the unusual sea dragon seemed to like what Helena was saying "ok, I am going to show you something but don't be alarmed OK, as it is still us."

Kessy said in her soft delicate voice "my dear sweet girl you will always be my family and my friend and there is nothing that you can do that will ever frighten me to change my love and respect for you both."

"You have my word."

Helena cuddled her tightly Louis licked her face before Helena saw another large rock that she can sit on while she gets everything out of her bag and tells Kessy all about the purple crystal skull's history.

Kessy was excited and interested to see the results of what Helena had just explained.

So first, she gets everything out of the pouch and reached for Louis's purple outfit which made him grow bigger by using her small fish knife and tapping on it which made it larger for him to wear again than before.

When also gave him his temporary purple horn on his head with now a webbed mane and long tail with a spear shape at the end of it like a weapon form.

Then Helena asked Kessy to come to her and she did exactly that when the princess pulled out the purple cloak and said "I am going to put this on your face and I want to see if anything happens to you, please don't be afraid it won't hurt you I promise!"

Kessy agreed and trusted Helena by shaking her head up and down.

Helena put the purple cloak over Kessy's face there a flash of bright purple light appeared and within seconds it covered her full body.

There she was with special armor like her brother and it also will give her the power to swim back into the waters of Greece and any sea before.

Because of this Helena promised that she could see her parents and siblings again for one last time, once the war was over.

They were all excited and ready to go back to Santorini and try to rescue Seequest from Hades' clutches or they will die gracefully as warriors if we do not achieve this.'

They all still agreed to this challenge of fate as Helena believed they will win for the greater good or that's what her intuition was telling her.

She felt like she was being watched from above and then it dawned on her while they were having fun in the sun and the moonlight now that someone else knew what was going down there and that they had to get to Greece before sundown.

This time all together for the last time they dived into the dark pool and went through it to reach Greece once more.

She felt that she had a better chance now as she had her friends behind her as she had loads of different powers that Hades did not even know existed yet and felt like she was the lucky one to have them on her side at a time of great need and sorrow.

Chapter Forty-One

Luna Calls for Help to Save Seequest from Dying

Back in the sea, the high priestess still locked away in the Crystal Temple did everything she could with her powers and the skulls to protect Vissen.

Queen Sera contacted her mother Luna the moon goddess for some advice as she too can see what was going on in the sea and above as well.

The sun went down beautifully with a gorgeous sunset that looked like it just settled and the sea had disappeared for the night (magic), and the moon rose as beautiful as she was shining silver and white.

Queen Sera spoke to her mother for hours about everything and mostly about her daughter and this was what Luna said to her 'my grandchild Helena is a champion in her right and one day she will shine my darling, just like her mother has before her.'

"I am worried about her as Neptune has told me through our minds that she was grieving thinking that she will never see Seequest again."

"But we both know he's alive and I thought that it would be a great idea if she said her goodbyes properly before their lives change forever."

"Luna dear mother of mine and goddess of the moon, can she return to land to see him yet?"

"My daughter not quite yet, sorry"

"Has she needs to be strong enough and be prepared for the battle of her life!"

"Let me speak to Moon Cloud the white wolf if he has seen him first.

If he says then yes, I will come back to you and give you my answer ok?"

"Yes, Mother I shall wait here for you."

And then the connection of the queen's image and Luna's of hers both disappeared.

Luna remembered that it was her greatest time as she was full on Earth that night and knew that wolves especially the great white wolf would be near her tonight.

So, she waited for his arrival at the cliff top.

The rest of the pack of wolves of his clan will carry on to the beach to stretch their legs as they loved running on the wet sand near the sea as it also heals their wounds.

So, they used to soak their feet or bodies in it for a short time when the tide is out, as it will not pull them back into it.

So, it's completely safe and that is where they will be now she thought.

Later as she was waiting for Moon Cloud to appear like clockwork he approached the cliff top and stood proud and looked at the moon and howled with all his might.

Seconds later Luna's beautiful goddess image appeared on the actual moon while it was shining down brightly on him and said, "Hello, a dear friend let light be on you always.'"

And he answered, "Yes hello my divine one. How can I be of assistance to you on this gorgeous night?"

"My dear friend I wondered if you could do me a favour."

"Have you or your wolves seen Seequest?"

"His appearance is now again his true form of a large white unicorn."

As she was just going to mention Firefly's image to Moon cloud he quickly replied.

"Does the other creature have wings too?"

Luna replied "yes so you have seen them?"

"No, I have not but my pack said that they saw some creatures on the beach looking weak and tired earlier.

But my pack was too scared to approach them as they also looked dangerous with their horns."

"Oh my", Luna said "your pack has seen Seequest and his daughter."

Moon Cloud shouted out that is Seequest, the Unicorn King.

"Please you must hurry."

The moon goddess looked worried which was a first even for her.

Moon Cloud knew then something was seriously wrong and sat there listening to what she had to say to him with full concentration.

The great white wolf sat there listening to every word carefully and sat in the same spot where Luna changed him in the past.

Luna had turned him into something greater than he was before as a gift for helping her granddaughter in the past.

Now it was her turn to ask for a gift from him in return.

She then said "you said that your pack saw them lying on the beach helpless."

He replied "yes, Luna that is correct."

Luna then says "Poor Seequest."

He must get back into the water as even though he is the Unicorn King he gave up his title a long time ago to become a hippocampus.

"As now he is the protector and guardian of the seas."

"So, he needs the seawater to survive now."

"I believe he originally came with for her birthday when she was sixteen and she was captured when later he returned and Hades let her go if you remember?" Luna said.

"Seequest was stuck forever without any help from any of us as then we could not get involved."

The white wolf then said "oh that is Seequest that Helena told me about those many years before when I saved her myself and that's when you changed me into whom I am today?"

"Yes, Moon Cloud that is right."

"Luna, how can I help you and Seequest?"

"First, did you say that you saw Seequest in the sea?"

"Yes, he was with his daughter on the sand resting waiting I guess for help."

"Oh dear, it looks like he could be trapped on land thanks to Hades' vortex."

"I can see what he is doing."

"Oh I see now" she said and continued saying Hades' big plan from the beginning was to let Seequest escape and then die naturally to collect his horn before it vaporizes into dust.

As she began to see the past images play in her head.

Then he cannot be caught or held for killing him as it will look like he died of natural causes.

"Moon Cloud it looks like Hades has not done this once to him."

But twice and wiped their memories too with a horrified tone in her voice being very upset and also now feeling Seequest's pain as all magic is connected in some way.

It looks like they're exhausted and he has tried to get back into the sea to change into a hippocampus to build his strength and heal himself again and yet to be fooled by the imagination that made him feel that Pegasus came to rescue him.

When it was one of Hades' shape-shifting creatures instead, that took them back to Hades' lair to rot once more.

But this time Seequest believed that he escaped for good to then find out that his trapped in the fresh air on the beach in water but not enough to survive as he needs to go deep to gain his strength and powers properly again.

"In front of his daughter he probably feels that he has nothing else to give and has given up trying and is just lying there now ready to die, I guess."

Because he also knows that if they break the vortex it will kill everything in the sea that he loves and now prepared to give up his life than let that happen.

The white wolf looked saddened by the story of what had happened to Seequest recently and in the past and wanted to help in any way he could to save him.

Knowing, that it is Helena's best friend plus he also protected his late family in the past.

"We must rescue him straightaway.

Moon cloud replied and said "my mistress of the light what can we do to help him?"

She then started to mention Helena and he said "what has she got to do with this?"

Luna replies with full confidence in her voice "I understand white wolf but Helena is here to do many great things in the future and again change the world as we know it now."

"How will she do this?" he replied.

Luna mentioned 'Time will tell faithful friend."

"You need to be patient as it will happen just before our eyes one day."

"Now, as I said my granddaughter.

'The mermaid princess, yes I remember as before that I thought she was like you."

"No, she lives in the ocean as she is Neptune's daughter Helena of Vissen a mer-princess of great importance.

Moon Cloud looked at Luna and said 'wow, she is special already as before her I did not know that they existed in real life."

'Yes, I know."

That's because they could not come onto land normally as it is classed as impossible.

But this time Helena was lucky to be given this gift for twenty-four hours which her parents gave her for her sixteenth birthday from Pegasus our horse god blessing

The white wolf said "I now know everything dear one what is your plan?"

"Go back to the beach and I will contact Helena to meet you there in an hour."

"When she arrives she will be riding her hippocampus Louis who also will come on land."

Please do not frighten him as it's his first time on land.

Plus, she needs him too for extra strength has been together they are stronger as one unit with the power of the Amethyst crystal skull, which I believe she would find someday and that day came just recently.

"When they arrive please make sure she has everything she needs.

Let her see Seequest and get him in back straight in the water.

But first, she will have to go back to the cave where it all happened in the past, yes Hades' liar cave entrance, as the vortex field is run from there."

"That's why Seequest cannot get back into the water as there is nothing to break it from as the power lies in the cave still."

Which, she has to break apart with her new power.

But she must believe in herself and her companion to achieve this large task.

"I know that she can."

"So go back and tell your pack to look after Seequest for us while Helena will be on her way to you very soon."

"Thank you, dear friend.

This means a lot to us for your bravery once again."

"I am honoured to be of service, my dear Luna."

"Please do not forget that you must take her to the Forbidden Woods first as that is where she will be able to rescue her friend Seequest", which is what she has always wanted to do since finding the purple skull.

"Seequest is now lying in the shallow sea again as he has to gain the strength at night to get a drink which has made him feel better but not strong enough yet to gain his full magic again."

But she must go to the cave and break the vortex there which in the end will break the vortex in the sea as well.

"I am giving her the full power of the amethyst skull to help her.

As I have spoken to the guides of the universe and we feel that she can control it properly and will always use it for the highest good of all."

"I think it's time she realizes what great power she possesses and what a brilliant queen she will be in the future as well."

"Yes of course."

"Luna, I'll go now."

He bowed to the moon while looking right at her with his piercing emerald-green eyes which make him see in the dark much easier than before.

He then howled loudly that every creature knew about it and then he walked down the cliff top carefully and then safely ran as fast as he could towards the beach to wait for Helena's arrival.

Helena in the palace resting in the library near her quarters when she heard her mother calling her to the knowledge room.

She sat down and opened up the Book of Knowledge to messages appearing there and then being written as she read.

She read out loud saying "yes, I can hear your dear voice of knowledge.

Give your message to me."

"My dear daughter as I am in the Crystal Temple I thought you may be able to hear me here and that you would know if I called

I am writing this down as your grandmother has kindly given you the full power of the amethyst skull.

"So, use it wisely my child."

"Yes, mother of great priestess.

What service can I do for you?"

"I have spoken to your father and we have decided that it's time for you to be part of the family in a different way."

You have great powers inside you and you too have full control of the Amethyst skull as your grandmother

Luna has given it to you as a gift for your eighteenth birthday.

So, use it wisely to rescue Seequest for us and make sure that you bring him back here to us please, thank you

Helena did somersaults all over the library and was excited as one she will be helping Seequest as she had wanted and two she will be seeing him for the first time again very soon.

With delight, her face lit up and she replied to the voice of knowledge, "so he' is still alive?"

"Yes, he is but his mind has been tricked so many times now."

"He may not listen to even the kindest of words at the minute."

"So, remember to use your instincts and protect your-self from him as at the moment, his, a danger to him-self and us too in this state, bless him."

"Yes, your Majesty I shall do what I can, thank you."

"If you are wondering how I know this."

Your grandmother Luna the moon has contacted me and told me this.

So, after your rest when you reach the shore, you will meet a large white wolf called Moon Cloud.

"He is the alpha of the wolves from this forest to the cave to break down the vortex which will then help Seequest get back in the sea once more where he now belongs."

He knows everything and will tell you your next instructions on what you need to do to save Seequest.

"Now rest, dear child as your quest starts in an hour and you have a lot of research to do at this time."

"So, read more on the Amethyst skull, as there are a few pages further in the back of the book you forgot to rip out recently."

Helena at this point thought Oops being caught and then realized that eyes and ears were everywhere in the sea and home.

She said "Please mother I am sorry."

"Please forgive me for doing that to your precious book."

"My darling I know you did it for the right purpose and that's why I allowed you to do it in the first place."

"Remember that you're telepathic too as this will be a great help to you later."

"I must go now dear child, I love you."

"Oh, and Happy eighteenth birthday Helena, I hoped you liked your gifts."

"Thank you, Mother, I love you too and, yes, we love them"

The hour had passed when she swam as quickly as she could to the stables and got Louis ready where this time he grew bigger and she wore hers.

Both of their armour now was pure Amethyst purple all over.

She felt like she was becoming a great being indeed not just a princess but something even more powerful than that.

Even her hippocampus had already become a powerful sea horse called Source.

She contacted Kessy with her mind.

They all swam up towards the shore once more where she changed into a Pisces again.

The great white wolf watched as she approached with beautiful purple light glowing all around her that lit up the ocean as well.

They galloped out of the sea when Source changed into a beautiful Arabian-type horse with a difference as he was made of a watery image of purple flames glowing around him.

She jumped off her beautiful steed and walked towards the white wolf carefully hoping it was him that she had to meet as told by her mother earlier.

The white wolf bowed as he felt like she was important not only to the sea but to the land too.

There she was glowing wearing her purple and silver with her helmet on, which had now her purple wavy hair sticking out of it.

She took it off and the wolf said while looking into her eyes,

"Oh, my princess it is lovely to see you again."

The princess answered saying that she did not recognize him and he explained that he was the one that rescued her two years ago and for his bravery in giving up his life to save hers,

Her grandmother Luna brought him back to life and made him the strongest known wolf on the planet.

"I am now called Moon Cloud of the Peacemaker clan."

The princess bowed back and said "How can I help you the great wolf?"

She can see that he was of great importance to the lands and Luna herself.

"Get on my back."

"First, we must go and see if Seequest is OK, as he is further up the beach away from Hades' creatures."

"As they are everywhere now and we were told to protect him and his daughter while they are still resting.

Then we must go and see Zeus for the next command."

"OK", she said.

So, he bent down his head and neck so that she could jump on his back and off they went.

"We need to take Source with us too."

Helena then called him over when he stopped glowing purple and stood there as a beautiful Arabian stallion water horse when Helena said, "follow my dear one."

He answered her back "yes, of course, Helena."

They looked for a long time for Seequest and there was no sign of him or his daughter anyway yet.

Moon Cloud took the princess back to another side of the beach where she quickly had to go to the Forbidden Woods.

The white wolf told her that she had to believe in herself and that she had to merge her powers with Source and use them to destroy the vortex once and for all.

She jumps back on her horse where they put their minds together which builds a powerful power indeed.

Once Helena knew she was ready she threw her spear into the cave and it made a massive noise and a bright light appeared.

That it frightened all the birds as now tweeting and making noises as they all fly away trying to get by tremors doubled in the sky as they go.

That is exactly what she did.

She felt relief as pain and sorrow disappeared from her heart and hoped that the feeling was from Seequest and that he will be ok?

Luna then contacted Moon Cloud while he was directing them back to the beach.

She told him there was a change of plans and that they had to go and meet Zeus and the other gods now who were still battling the Tremor copies on land and in the sky.

Both of them agreed and ran off toward where Zeus will be very soon.

The great white wolf galloped as fast as his legs could carry them.

What a great mess there was.

As it was Hades plan thinking that more damage could be done if more of him.

The gods and goddesses would have not known who was the real one and so made it harder to capture him and win this battle.

Trees were ripped up and fire everywhere with the animals running for their dear lives.

Earth looked battered and bruised and when the battle was over it will have to be healed again in time.

But they had no time or point to do it just yet as the battle was still going on.

When they arrived, they saw three beautiful winged horses with the gods and goddesses sitting on them discussing their next plan with Zeus.

They flew to different areas continuing to battle the creatures to their deaths.

But remember even though they died they were magical not real flesh and blood so they did not feel any pain either way.

He stopped in his tracks feeling a little scared seeing that these winged horses and gods were even bigger than him until they shrunk down to his size for his comfort.

He stopped and howled.

"Dear Zeus I call upon you now that you know Eldest Daughter and I am the great white wolf friend of Luna the moon."

"I am Moon Cloud but I was born as Storm son of Max the great alpha of the wolves of all time."

We know that Seequest was on the beach earlier but now we cannot find him.'

"OK" said Zeus "enough of his games" and turned himself into a golden phoenix of full shining light.

It made Pegasus jump as he was slightly burnt

Zeus changed his form to bright golden and orange light and he then flapped his wings and flew into the sky above like a ball of flames

"Moon Cloud you follow me to the beach. Wait there and I shall be back soon."

The wolf stopped there.

Helena was riding Source at the time.

They have not been noticed as she just looked like a mer-knight and they all thought that he was summoned by Neptune himself to help while he was in the sea still.

The princess was waiting patiently to see her friend again after all these years of being apart.

The phoenix flew straight into Hades' lair and lit up with great force.

He used the voice and called Seequest and Firefly when he blew a ball of light on both of them which recused their minds and destroyed the invisible barriers as their souls were trapped still in Hades' lair.

That's why they could not heal or do anything when they were at the beach earlier.

As once again it was all Hades' games and illusions.

They hid away in a place no one could find them until they knew it was safe again to appear as they were both becoming hollow and so clear they both looked like ghosts now.

Zeus said with his powerful voice that shook the liar "Seequest you are again pure free souls of our great friends."

"Go to the beach and find your bodies again where you will become strong and free."

"We will meet you there."

Zeus flew away as a bright massive beautiful bird similar to our peacock of today.

The mystical horse's souls find their bodies at last and slightly fall back into their bodies for Seequest and his daughter to gain consciousness again.

Back at the beach, Seequest felt like he was whole and alive and started to wake up at last from his complete life of confusion.

Seequest stood up and shook his head and saw the great phoenix hovering with its beautiful large orange and white flames all around it flying high above him and said 'thank you, the great mighty one of hope and rebirth."

"I never thought that I would ever have the opportunity to meet you in my lifetime","It is an honour to receive your help in this sorrowful time."

The phoenix replied, "Oh great Unicorn King you are needed to put back the world at peace the way it was before and it may cost you your life in return."

Seequest answered and said back "yes, I will do whatever it takes to stop this creature in its tracks but as long as you do one thing for me in return".

"Anything"

"Please save my family from Hades?"

The phoenix made a noise and nodded his head.

"Agreed" and he flew off with orange and gold light shining their path to freedom forever this time.

Seequest nudged his daughter and said, "Wake up dear one."

We are free from this nightmare of a tale and we can be ourselves again for now.'

She looked at her father and smiled and jumped up feeling refreshed and relaxed.

So, she opened up her wings properly and stretched out that Seequest thought wow, they look like angel wings, and thought he saw her destiny before him.

Yet he did not tell her his destiny, as he did not want to spoil the moment of happiness that they have not had for a long time.

It was good news for all of them and yet bad news for him, sadly.

As the firebird also told him what the possibility was if it achieves his request of saving his family.

The Unicorn king ignores his feelings of vaguely knowing his future now and trotted over to his daughter with full courage and strength in his heart and mind.

Because he put his emotions and love aside until the battle was over with Hades and his horrible creatures of doom.

Both mystical horses were ready to continue the fight by galloping towards the beach where everyone was waiting for them still to arrive.

They eventually reach part of the beach and so the first thing he did was run as fast as he could into the sea where he drank and ate the seaweed that was flowing around, as it was daytime again.

His wounds began to heal properly this time and Firefly galloped in as well and then so did hers.

Both were ready for battle and at last, could not wait to see everyone again.

Just as they were galloping both of the magical horses were glowing, Seequest his pure white gleaming coat and beautiful Aqua blue horn and hooves with beautiful sea blue eyes glowing of great power were now fully re-energized again and his daughter of all shades of pink as well as they were running towards their freedom.

Back in Hades' liar Pain and his new troop of saber-toothed tigers followed behind them carefully not to be seen as they watched from a distance until Hades gives them a command to fight.

Have Hades had created their species again but this time stronger than before and much cleverer and skill full too.

Later that day when Seequest and Firefly had just come out of the sea to relax Hades gave the saber-tooth tigers the go-ahead to attack them.

The pain was a massive red and black saber-tooth tiger with bright burning red eyes being the leader of the pack.

He was very good at seeking around without being heard and approached Firefly quickly as he caught her and pulled her to the ground.

Where she neighed in shock and Seequest stopped and turned around to see that he had the opportunity to meet the leader that killed most of his kind when he was a foal.

Pain said, "I still have a bone to pick with you, Seequest, about your mother".

As he started to crawl and scratch Firefly's legs while she was flapping her wings about to keep him away while she was in anguish and tries to get herself to her feet again while Pain goes now after her father instead.

Seequest then said "your fight is with me not her."

"I thought that Zeus and Artemis had killed you and your kind after killing too many animals for your pleasure?"

Pain then says "no Seequest I was saved and hid by Hades as he created another female for me and so we gave birth again to more as you can see to help me kill you and all your kind at last."

Pain after speaking and expressing his thoughts to Seequest, the large black and red striped tiger came towards him with a great roar at him instead.

Saw Firefly getting up and telling the rest of his pride to catch her, she neighed in great pain and yet ignored it like her father and began to flap her wings again to luckily escape them.

He started running towards the unicorn when Seequest stopped and put his head down quickly as he blinded the cat temporally with a bright glow of light into its eyes and missed judged its whereabouts.

As the silly cat ran straight into Seequest's horn by mistake and roared out in horror.

The pain was dying slowly as Seequest then threw him with his entire strength over his body to the ground as the cat slipped off his horn in the air and landed breaking all his bones.

Seequest knew then that this tiger could never harm a living soul ever again.

Seequest reared with victory expressing a great neigh in his voice as at last, he felt his kind could now be laid to rest peacefully.

Just up in the distance Seequest heard a loud noise approaching them and told his daughter to come close, as he was now ready for anything.

Another noise approached them becoming clearer and friendlier when Seequest saw it was Hermes in his god form flying towards him.

Hermes said that he stayed near and also looked for help at the same time, as he heard Seequest neigh and came to help as he thought his in danger again!

Seequest was pleased to see that Hermes was ok and told him to join them.

The rest of the Sabre-tooth tigers ran off and joined in the battle with the gods as another command by Pain earlier if he was possibly killed.

Firefly watched her father's heroism and flew back down gently on her injured legs. Seequest said wait here as she lay on the beach.

He came back with a beautiful large cockle shell like a large shrimp would live in. holding it gently in his mouth.

And put it on the ground dipping his powerful aqua horn into it, as his magic and the salt water became something even more powerful and there was a beautiful sea liquid instead.

As he told his daughter to keep still as this would burn a little.

He tilted the shell and out came this special fluid of magic which she flinched to at first and then calmed down through her breathing.

Because the saber tiger's fangs and claws were pure vermin poison could kill her.

So, he had to be very quick of healing her before it was too late.

Firefly noticed a few minutes later that her feet and legs were completely healed again.

Hours had passed and the saber-tooth tigers were now been beaten by the gods at the other side of the beach.

Artemis herself agreed that no creature of any kind will kill for the sake of killing only to eat when needed.

That was the rules of nature's creatures of all great and small and the balance here on Earth.

Hades' rest of his large pet tigers were a danger to the unicorns and made them extinct, so Artemis decided they should be too, as she loved the unicorns dearly because the god of death and destruction kept, rec-reating them by making them stronger.

Zeus and Goddess Artemis will teach Hades a lesson soon they thought as they were fed up with the killings from each side and so they had another great idea to possibly use the tigers in the future!

Back at the beach Helena wondered what the Amethyst skull powers could do while waiting for Seequest to appear again.

At this time, everyone heard Seequest's voice in the distance neighing and thundering noises coming ahead like heavy hooves digging the ground as they went.

Hermes came flying around them and decided to ride with Firefly again and says, "See, I said that your father will pull through this."

The Unisos filly threw her head up and down agreeing with him.

So here he was still holding on for dear life to her mane.

There were still some saber-toothed tigers around.

The gods thought that they had killed them all, where on the off chance there walked another female of great structure.

Seequest not believing his eyes saw her approaching him with force as she was looking like she was indestructible to kill him.

He was thinking, I just killed your mate Pain and now I have to kill you too?

"Don't you creatures ever give up and leave me alone?"

But he said, "Come on then she still came galloping at him when he used the power of his horn and when she jumped at him in mid-air from the ground, he moved quickly and froze her there."

Eventually, he said "I am giving you a chance to live or die today what it is going to be?"

Chaos answered "revenge dear one is what I want from you" and so Unicorn King said "OK".

He reared up on his back legs and neighed loudly throwing them back to the ground hard that it shook and broke the freeze spell as the Chaos landed badly and died.

The princess in the distance felt something worrying and so jumped off Source and quickly jumped on the white wolf and said "Seequest was in trouble".

He agreed and planned to meet him and his daughter halfway.

Eventually, Moon Cloud caught up with him with Helena still on his back in armor when in the distance Hades appeared on Knightmare and said, "Are you enjoying your torment, Seequest?"

"You did not think that you could get away from me that easy, did you?"

Hades at this time was wondering who this mer-knight was when he noticed a different kind of armour and knew it was powerful and wanted it for himself.

Plus, he thought that the white wolf would come in handy too

That mer-knight was sitting on a large white wolf when Hades thought and said to mare's ear "oh I can use this beast to help me, with an evil laugh and told Knightmare to get a little closer before anyone could do anything else."

Hades had pointed his Sword of Doom right at the white wolf's head and he howled in pain and fell to the ground.

Helena fell off and ran for cover for then the wolf got back up with no memory of anyone apart from what Hades had put in his mind as he poisoned it to hate Seequest.

In the afternoon Helena was still hiding luckily in the trees when Hades commanded the white wolf to kill Seequest.

Poor Moon cloud did not know what he was doing any-more and the princess ran back to the beach without being seen quickly to warn Seequest and the others.

That now Moon cloud was controlled by Hades too.

The white wolf walked towards Seequest and said 'I know you.

"You are the one that killed my parents long ago."

He looked at the powerful white wolf that was bigger than him and he said "Wolf I do not have any problem with you, so let me be."

The white wolf replied, "you do, as these are my friends and my family."

So, Moon Cloud leaped and bit him and scratched him a few times.

Helena had enough and knew that they were all friends originally, but for now, she had to protect Seequest from this beast.

So she said a verse and her spear appeared, and it glowed bright purple like a flame this time and picked him up in her force field of light and said, "Go back where you belong, I banish you to hell forever."

Then a few seconds later there you could see black smoke slip off the wolf's body while he was there recovering from the blast.

Helena said another verse and sealed up the Amethyst crystal skull powers.

Hades was not impressed and then noticed that his mer-knight was someone special.

Helena's powers were even more powerful than his and he could not wait to find out who it was.

Because he felt beaten he roared and rode into the black and red smoke himself and vanished.

She felt happy yet exhausted and fell to the floor to rest.

"Princess", she heard Seequest call her name as he picked her up gently with his horn and laid her over Moon Cloud's back been himself again and said "you carry her as I still have work to do elsewhere."

The great white wolf replied "Yes your Highness, I shall" and they all ran towards the other side of the beach.

Seequest ran towards the beach to find the other super mystical horses on the other side of the beach, Celestial and Legend were waiting at the rocks when they heard hoof prints coming their way on the wet sand.

Legend told her to get out of the way fast.

But she would not move an inch from the spot where she stood her ground, as she felt Seequest's presence stronger than she had ever felt before.

She then said "Seequest will stop in his tracks."

As he came around the corner within a split moment he saw the beautiful image of a black feminine winged Pegasus that he saw after his mother died in the sea in his past.

He stopped right in front of her.

"You are not my mother but I feel her presence inside you."

"That's because my dear she is me and I am her, as we now are one with the universe.

Because my son I am but also I am not."

Poor Seequest was tired and confused from everything as to him Celestial was talking in riddles at this time.

So, she slowly explained it all to him that when his mother died, she was reborn in a different way for her bravery and had been forgiven to make sure that he existed and became the great Unicorn King that he was meant to be.

Thanks to Neptune's help he made that possible for her and also helped Seequest too.

Celestial then explained in greater detail that because of Neptune's gratefulness for everything she had done for him and his creatures.

Plus, her full courage, the gods got to hear about it and passed on the message to the goddess of winged horses, (Artemis) also known as Diana, who then spoke to Zeus himself.

She said, "There he agreed that he would create a beautiful divine place where all the horses; dogs; cats, and one day when humans are eventually created, will go here when their times upon earth".

"If they are good and bring peace to everything while living on earth during their time living there."

"That their spirit does will live on in the heavens above with Celestial and the beautiful stars when they return when their life is complete.

"But their souls will go back to the planets that they came from as well, like Venus or Jupiter, in the future too."

"One day, they may come back as spiritual guides to the living as well."

So, she told him that she is now a sender; messenger and collector of the heavens.

That she is the queen and that Legend was once the great Jecco here on Earth.

Again because of his courage and bravery, he became a true star in the sky in the form of the horse they know today.

Yet he is a winged horse too and still is her mate as their spirits are still his parents from long ago but their souls and spirits are now something much more than that.

After all this talk he reared in front of her and said "Can I call you mother your highness, just this one time?"

Celestial replies "No not normally but I shall allow it this time around."

"Now come with me and meet Legend who was your father Jecco once upon a time!"

Everyone was astounded by this great beautiful winged Arabian-type horse which they followed back to meet the great legend whom Seequest vaguely remembers when he was young, looking at the stars in the sky when he was a colt.

He could not wait to see him as for the first time he will be meeting his father's image at last in the flesh as he died in the great battle by Pain as Jecco killed his first mate Havoc.

When Pain and Jecco should have died together but Pain cheated death.

Because Jecco was still weak and healing from the previous fight with Havoc earlier and so Pain attacked him the same day.

Pain recovered from his injuries as Hades found him and hid him in his liar for years.

"Until recently when you thankfully killed him and gave back Justice to your kind and your father again"

"Thank you, Seequest King, of unicorns and horses of earth, our son!"

They reached where there was a larger type of black-winged horse waiting for them to arrive.

Seequest saw him standing in front of him this huge handsome Friesian-winged horse with enormous angel wings.

His coat was black with silver draping over it from the stardust he produces and lives on and his eyes; mane and tail had stunning dark blue running through it also when the sun or moon shone on it.

He reared in front of Seequest and opened his wings showing his majesties.

He lowered his legs in front of his son and Seequest said to him, 'your majesty it is an honour to meet you.'

With a bold and powerful voice like a horse god, "It's great to meet you too my son' which made Seequest's heart melt for a short while even though he saw not his parents anymore."

But he felt their warmth and presence of love for him.

Inside his mind, he saw them as the image they once were to him.

Seequest felt like it was the best thing that could have happened to him to build his self-esteem back up and to believe in who he was again.

They all came together and nuzzled him dearly showing their love for him and he did the same.

Within thirty minutes their personalities had changed and all became the strong entities that they all were.

Seequest said, "Thank you".

"I shall carry this memory with me always' and they said they will too."

Seequest then mentioned that he must go into the sea to catch his breath properly and also to gain his power and full strength.

But more importantly to heal all his wounds completely as his body; heart; mind; and soul needed it more than ever after having that attack from Moon Cloud when he was possessed by Hades' demon.

He said then "I shall be ready to conquer Hades and Tremor for good this time with no holding back anymore" or that's what he thought.

He bowed to them and they did too when he turned around to face the sea and felt that it was calling him home at last for good!

The mighty old unicorn slowly trotted gracefully into the water splashing the sea all over his legs as he went until he disappeared for a few minutes as he dived deeper into the ocean and changed into the beautiful hippocampus that Helena and everyone else loved him as.

All you could see was his bright aqua-blue light shining all over the sea.

Everyone on the beach said "look!"

As they all turned and saw that there was a massive white and blue high wave coming towards them at a very fast speed and a noise of neighing coming with it as well.

They all looked and yet didn't know where the noise was coming from.

Then they saw and could not believe their eyes until they see Seequest and the seahorses and Kessy following behind him with the dolphins jumping in the background.

Seequest felt himself again and so enjoyed it while he could as he knew it would not last.

The hippocampius became sea horses again and there Seequest was the true leader once more with yet another creation of his mother's magical horn behind him now.

The Unicorn King was now stronger; bolder and more powerful than he has been for a very long time and he looked happy and well once more too.

The seahorses came closer.

They could use their weapons of the sea which was to heal the wounded when it was needed.

Afterward, Source came and trotted up to Moon Cloud as when all this was going on earlier he ran back into the sea for help while Helena and Moon Cloud were doing what they were told.

The source said to him, "please put the princess on my back."

"I shall heal her" and the white wolf nodded and gently turned his neck softly picking up the princess and gently laying her onto Source's back, as she was there still out cold and yet breathing.

Remember she too was a mer-princess who needed the seawater to energize her as well.

So, he took her back into the sea carefully as she began to wake up and started to feel better and more powerful again.

Kessy stayed in the water until called by the dolphins.

She enjoyed their company again even if it was for a short while.

Seequest looked all noble and strong once more with difference again as he has aged gracefully while being out of the water for so long.

Because when he came back out of the sea he had become this lip panzer stallion type of great beauty and elegance.

His coat was now dapple grey with a black mane and tail with aqua-blue stripes running through it from living in the sea for so long in his past and his eyes were like crystals of the sea herself and his horn glowing of the Aqua blue as well.

Celestial and Legend walked up to Pegasus who had just landed behind them and said, "We thank you for letting us do this and seeing Seequest once more face to face.

Now it's time to focus on the true reason why we have been brought here."

Pegasus agreed and when he saw Firefly and felt like he had seen something that was generally not possible as he saw a unicorn with wings.

Seequest then walked up boldly towards his ancestors and told them that by using his magic and his mare that they created two magnificent new creatures on Earth.

That he named their new species after himself and his grandfather Pegasus genes that he had to retrieve his true blessing from him first before announcing the birth of his new species to the world.

"My lord of winged horses, and unicorns may I please use part of your name?"

"As then I can tell you what my actual children are to our family tree?

Pegasus glowing like a golden light replied with a graceful angelic voice 'Seequest I would be honoured".

"Thank you."

"I will now introduce my daughter Firefly the angel Unisos and my son whom I hope you will get the chance to meet in time is a batwing Unisos after his mother".

I have named them this as they are part of me and part of her too "as they are Unicorn and demon blood together as one.

The Unisos was born and now known to all across the lands and skies on the 27th of September B.C and then was registered in Zeus' records of all creations on earth.

Once everyone was strong and healed again all the beasts were gone and beaten.

They all stopped for a moment and the gods heard what was going on and that Seequest was free.

The gods had a good look themselves and liked the idea when Zeus admitted to himself that he would have never thought that his evil brother Hades had such a clever head on his shoulders.

Zeus and Pegasus thought it was a brilliant idea and that he should have thought about it himself and laughed.

Everyone asked why did it happen?

Seequest replied to them all 'Destiny I guess.'

They all laughed together and then discussed how they were going to capture Tremor from Hades.

Zeus thought that they had come far in these couple of months.

Yet not far enough that he told everyone to go and rest and he will go back to Olympus until Hades and this Tremor appeared again.

So for now they got away and yet Zeus and everyone else knew that the battle was just actually starting.

Chapter Forty-Two

The Preparation for the Battle with Hades

Back in the meeting place of now Olympus a few more months had passed.

The great god Zeus had arranged with his brother Neptune; his sons and daughters to conquer Hades for the last time knowing that Hades will be gone and will not be in control ever again.

Zeus heard an amazing sound of neighing coming towards the rainbow path and it was Goddess Dianna leading the winged horses for their last rides as she brought down them to work again against evil.

Yet it was a different type this time.

These winged horses had flown a long way from the star Andromeda.

Artemis was riding her mare called Huntress in leader fashion to her family.

She told Zeus they came to her offering their help and wanted justice for what happened to the yearlings recently too.

Zeus quickly summoned all the gods and goddesses to their steeds as its time to fight the battle once again.

They all turned up and were told to mount their steeds quickly.

That Pegasus still did not know of yet.

Because these winged horses saved their father Pegasus and the gods from the Titans many centuries before.

Hunter and Huntress were gifted to Artemis from Pegasus himself for all the kindness and love she gives to his kind.

Her stallion was refined as his creator Pegasus as he was tall and strong pure white light diamond coat built like an Andalusian type.

His mane and tail were long and angled so they flowed with his beautiful movement as he had a stunning chis-elled neck that he held with grace.

His eyes were like Diamonds and yet when his full power is needed he also has gold run through his coat and wings which makes become a light to be reckoned with.

And there stood beside him was Huntress, who was also a winged horse like a mustang type, a hardy little thing she was.

She looked to have a smaller build than the others but she was very fast as Artemis was the goddess of hunting and nature so used her more on earth.

Huntress's coat was glowing pure white. When the goddess rode her, it changed glistening in the light of green and brown shades on her body and wings and her eyes were Amber like the sun.

The goddess of hunting was gold as well as her helmet with winged horses on it as she loved and respected them very much and her shield had a beautiful deer on it even though she is the Goddess of hunting it also means to prevent as well.

Lastly, she has a large golden bow and powerful arrows that never miss.

It's so that she can blend with the scenery when they are on errands on Earth making sure that there is a perfect balance between everything great and small.

As for Aphrodite's battle wear, she had gold and rose quartz pink on it to represent her as the goddess of love with hearts on her saddle and shield with the winged horses holding on to a heart with the top of their legs on her helmet as well.

Aphrodite's winged horse was called Passion his eyes were like diamonds until Aphrodite rides him and then his eyes changed to rose quartz and certain parts of his angelic wings have pink over them too.

What magnificent sight they were to see and powerful together.

Aphrodite had her sword called Heart of Love and her arrows would spear love into the creature instead of hate and make it change sides or even give up fighting altogether.

Passion was a very elegant winged horse that when he trotted looked like he was doing dressage.

Behind them came the other winged horses of the other god's themselves.

What a beautiful sight to have them all together again as it did not happen often nowadays from having peace in the world.

There was Ares who too was the only god to own two winged horses due to what he does which is to start wars and stop them as well.

Challenger is his winged horse for stopping it while Revenge will kill until it's stopped.

These winged horses were completely different in every way and that's why Ares loved them both as they had something in common their true Bravery.

Ares's steed called Revenge was a solid type of horse with large eagle wings as he needed them to be extra strong in battles in the skies for so long and to capture what his fighting as well.

Revenge was also known to bite when he needs to win a fight.

Yes, he differently takes after his owner the god of war himself.

His colours were black and gold which blended into his mane and tail and wings too with crystal diamond eyes when Ares rides him.

Ares's shield carries a flaming torch and he lives on Mars.

Next behind was Athena's pretty mare called knowledge.

She was the prettiest of the mares in the line-up.

She was Pegasus's true partner.

As she trotted behind it was as if she was a glistening ball of light as her colouring was gold and white as her rider who was the one and only Athena goddess of wisdom.

Athena's shield and helmet were the trees of life.

This beautiful pair could make you stare for hours in a trance because of their beauty and intelligence.

Next, there was Apollo's winged horse called Rhythm as he loved music added to his steed were a black and white stunning coat.

Its wings; mane and tail with silver matched with a beautiful harp and flute he played too.

The black was in connection with his musical notes as he plays his pipe to make everything relax and put them in his control regarding advising as after this they would generally listen to him.

The winged horses were magical so they did not get affected by their god's weapons or tools they used in the process of the battles.

Apollo himself who was also the god of light lived in the sun with Helios and Sundance and the other horses.

Rhythm can also be a palomino as living in the sun at times with Apollo as well.

So, he can hold quite a lot of heat and shield the others if needed too.

That's why he was always cheery and bright.

Apollo's helmet and shield carried the swan and sun on them both as the swan represented beauty like his music and the sun referring to him making things bright and happy again eventually.

While they were getting ready Pegasus flew off to see what was going on and came back an hour later and updated Zeus that everyone was waiting for them back on the beach.

Thankfully at last Seequest and his daughter were free and they were waiting to fight with Celestial and Legend by their sides waiting for the next part of the plan.

Still, in Olympus, they all had now mounted their winged horses and were ready for the last battle.

There in the distance landed Pegasus himself who bowed in front of Zeus and said "my dear friend, it is time."

Zeus walked up to him and said", Yes I know" and mounted his back carefully due to respect for each other.

Pegasus has been a god it only felt right for the king of the gods to ride a god himself and they both changed into pure gold and silver and on his helmet and shield was the lightning bolt.

While Zeus was mounted he said to Pegasus as they were still talking about the plans to themselves before leaving Olympus'

"That is great news but any news on Tremor yet?"

Pegasus replied "yes, he's back destroying everything with Hades."

Zeus said "then I think it is time for us to all get there and get this show on the road, don't you?"

Everyone nodded while Pegasus agreed gracefully too and bent his head down.

He turned around and said to his children 'if you're already, then let's go!'

One by one they walked up to the rainbow path where they approached it quickly.

Their winged horses flapped their enormous wings incredibly and galloped as fast as they could until their wings were producing enough strength and endurance to make them fly across the sky.

What a beautiful sight Athena thought Knowledge and she neighed back.

Pegasus and Zeus were the first to fly down to a lower atmosphere where they should be able to see everyone better.

Then the rest of the winged horses started to do the same as they were carrying their riders elegantly to Greece in Santorini, where the battle started earlier thanks to Hades and his destruction of a demon creature Tremor and his duplicates again.

They were flying around in the dark blue shades of the night sky with all the stars shining in the distance.

There was Luna the moon glowing brighter than ever to see what was going on every way now so she can update Queen Sera.

Pegasus and Zeus flew further in front of the others who are not too far behind and got ready to land somewhere near the woods where they would not be seen that easily until they wanted to be.

So Pegasus landed in Mysterious Woods a little further away from Forbidden Woods just in case Hades or his creatures were hanging around there as Hades knows that Zeus will come and try to defeat him as that's is what he was hoping.

Everyone was getting ready to land their magical winged horses as they could see two other forms flying towards them.

A light bubble appeared in the sky and out of it was Seequest's late parent's now Legend and Celestial herself.

They all neighed loudly approaching the woods altogether.

Celestial and Legend were looking out for Zeus and the others.

Who was trying to keep a clear way for them to land without trouble as the winged horses had just flown quite away and needed rest?

They drank in the spring waters that Pegasus and the unicorns had kindly created for them.

The other animals also drank there when needed with great power of strength and refreshment too for their hearts; bodies; minds and souls to rejuvenate them fully again.

The heaven horses waited until everyone had landed safely and then Legend went next as he flew down.

Legend looked so powerful this gleaming black and sapphire blue Friesian-type winged horse with silver dust flying off his coat and mane and tail as he did.

As he flew he was still similar to a night unicorn many years before with pearl white eyes because of living in the heavens for so long.

Beside him was Celestial the queen of the heavens herself in the flesh flew down after him.

These mystical horses could see in the dark and gave this power to the winged horses too recently on their births.

She was a pretty lightweight Friesian type with a touch of an Arabian elegance to her and her wings were silver and sapphire blue touched like Legends too.

But when she was flying down she created a beautiful rainbow path everywhere she went, as this was normally her magic for others to pass others in time and yet they're both here today to help stop Hades once and for all they all hoped.

The gods themselves were all dressed in white robes and dresses to protect them representing their gifts and powers.

Their winged horses matched them beautifully so altogether they were the most powerful beings on Earth.

Meanwhile, Zeus; Pegasus and everyone were getting ready to gallop towards the beach while their wings were folded neatly to their bodies.

Knowing now they had a good rest and soon will prepare to meet Seequest; his daughter and Moon Cloud once more for the next stage of capturing Tremor at last!

While everyone was resting Goddess Artemis and Huntress went to the forest and woods and spoke to the animals and told them all to go and hide and protect themselves while this battle was going on.

Has she gone to put over an invisible bubble preventing them from getting hurt on the lands?

But she told them they would have to go now otherwise if the force field is up before they escape then they will be trapped there until the battle ended.

Aphrodite also spread love around the lands with beautiful pink clouds in the sky which eventually become rain and fell everywhere thinking that Hades could be beaten this way or she thought so.

Hours had passed when Neptune approached the beach with his hippocampus pulling his amazing seashell chariot through the waves which were pulled back for them to gallop into the shore.

Tidal Wave was the first one they saw as he was the strongest and toughest of them all pulling his weight through the tide.

He looked like an Arabian built of aqua blue and dark blue mane and tail with aquamarine-blue eyes.

Behind him also was Tide who was fast and elegant and yet youngest as he was Tidal Waves' son.

They gave the chariot an elegant look to it.

Tide seemed a little feisty.

But Neptune knew that he had great potential for the future and may even become his new ride in the future.

While approaching the beach the other gods could see that the water horse's fish tails were changing into legs.

The white seahorses with blue manes and tails and the same eyes were astounding from the gentleness of the glow of the sun.

The shell chariot also seemed to turn flat and Neptune was being glided onto the beach this way.

Neptune himself can change into a Pisces man and be wearing his battle armor with white and blue shades and aqua green with his helmet with great white sharks on it and on his shield too and carrying his famous staff that could change into his trident when needed to.

Another mer-knight known as Taylor approached afterward walking through the shore onto the beach and said 'your highness I have come to fight with you and I have also my kingdom of knights from the Ruby Ocean to help you today as well.

Neptune was pleased with the offer and agreed to smile as he did and said "thank you."

Neptune then asked Taylor "here is your hippocampus, boy?"

"Oh, I left him at home sorry."

The sea god replied "that's fine."

"Luckily, I have here a feisty young colt that needs a good rider.

Please take him for now."

Taylor came and took Tide and climbed on his back as Neptune could not ride two water horses at the same time.

He knew that Taylor was an excellent rider because of being in the great race with Neptune in the past.

Tide is a very slim and yet fast colt and was ready to go to battle when he needed to so he stood next to his father all proud waiting patiently for the next command.

Tidal Wave now walked up to Neptune and bowed as he grabbed hold of Waves flowing blue mane and jumped up on his back.

Zeus was sitting on Pegasus looking so bold when Neptune says "Hello is everyone ready?"

Standing in their glory showing he is god topping up his game now looking very handsome and muscled with his blond hair moving in the breeze from the sea.

He knocked his staff on the ground and it glowed and became his known trident of great wonders.

"I am ready to give word to my queen who is at the Crystal Skull Temple in command of the crystal skulls themselves as she has put herself on lockdown in there as she will protect the sea and the creatures from destruction thankfully,"

Neptune knew that as soon as he was out of the water that he would have Hades' creatures and Hades himself tried to destroy his land as he knew it so they will be prepared this time.

Within this time Helena and Source went back to the palace earlier after freeing Seequest as they knew later that they will be back for the big battle.

But even though Luna and her mother knew what happened earlier, no one else knew yet.

She had to appear as if she never left earlier that day and did nothing until she or the others told Neptune later.

There Helena was saying to Louis as they approached the open waters "ok boy this is our time to shine and show Father what we are capable of together".

Knowing that I process the most powerful crystal skull known to Earth maybe Father will respect me more as mer-knight and not just his daughter?

She began to talk to Louis and said "as I believe he wants me to be a queen one day he wants me to stay his little girl."

Louis said "my dear princess, are you sure that you are ready for this as it will change our lives forever?"

Helena answered "yes I am"

So, Source approached the beach once again.

Before being seen they used the Amethyst crystal skull and she changed into Amethyst High Priestess and Louis became Source all glowing in bright purple which caused a glow of purple in the water.

Ares said "are you aware there is a purple glow in your waters at the moment and do you know who it is?" he asked Neptune.

Poor Neptune did not know where to put his face as no he did not recognize the mer-knight or his hippocampus at all and was concerned that it was one of Hades' tricks shape-shifting his knights again.

He said to be on guard "everyone as I don't know them nor have I asked for anyone to come here today with me.

It could be a trick."

Within that, the purple light got brighter and eventually toned down until they could see the mer-knight in silver and purple, which was on the hippocampus had on its forehead a unicorn horn.

Neptune thought this was very unusual and wondered so badly who this person was as it was not his sons as they were coming there soon when called as they were in the ocean protecting it from Hades' creatures at the moment.

The purple light had completely faded away now and a great surprise arose.

There in the distance, Neptune could see another hippocampus more powerful than his appearing with a soft purple glow around it and he wondered who its rider was that seemed to be magnificent.

The large black hippocampus with purple ran through him as he approached the shore it produced two back legs and its rider looked very powerful with great magic with them as now Source decided that he sometimes wanted to be Louis's colour instead of purple all the time.

The rider took off its helmet of silver and purple and their reappeared Princess Helena in the flesh.

How much she had changed and not even her father recognized this little mermaid princess anymore as now she had become a mer high priestess and yet also a powerful Piscean woman on land.

She approached the sea god and said 'Hello, Father I know you did not expect me here but I came to help you'.

When she told her father that she now controlled the Amethyst skull as she was wearing it as her cloak when she rescued her friend Seequest earlier and then went back home afterward when she knew he was safe.

She said in front of everyone "I am your daughter Princess Helena yes.

But when I am bonded with the Amethyst crystal skull I am called Amethyst High Priestess of the Crystal Skulls" and she was not going to take no for an answer.

Her father couldn't believe his eyes.

He was annoyed and yet proud as he knew in the future that Helena would become a great mer-queen.

That Louis had become Source and he was black with Amethyst purple in his coat and had Amethyst eyes too.

Helena also produced purple eyes and had great power with beautiful purple hair like Source.

Her father was surprised to think that all the mer-people and others have searched high and low for his long-lost skull and never found it.

But his daughter an ordinary mermaid princess and her hippocampus had found it and possibly stolen it from the great king of the great white sharks.

Neptune was again shocked and yet overwhelmed to see not his daughter anymore but a high priestess like her mother, Sera.

She told him that he would not need to let out the beast as she had Kessy in the waters waiting for the action to begin in the distance.

The princess whistled to her and there they all saw while sitting on their mystical winged horses another approaching them fast.

All they could see first was her tall and very long neck of a seahorse face out of the water and eventually, she appeared in front of them very large indeed with green shades and scales all over her body with a large pretty fin going from her head to her long tail.

She bounced onto the beach as she had four flippers like a seal with stunning green eyes.

"Father I would like to officially introduce you to Kessy a daughter of your own Tidal Wave and Seaspray."

She neighed and then slightly roared too.

"Well, my child I did not expect to ever see a hippocampus become like this one."

"Father she is different I agree but she is still the same as the hippocampus as she too has mighty powers plus some of her own.

I believe Father that in the beings before us there were other creatures possibly from other dimensions that we did not know about and she is a sea dragon another new species to our mystical water horses of the time."

"My goodness" Neptune said and he knew then he had a great chance against Hades at last in the seas and on the lands.

Kessy bowed to Neptune and he smiled back at her.

"Kessy please go back into the waters and protect the ocean from Hades' sea beasts."

"We believe they will be here soon."

The sea dragon went and did exactly what Helena told her to do and rushed back into the deepest part of the sea ready for battle.

Amethyst jumped off her hippocampus Source and instead of a swallow tail now she had a beautiful pair of legs when she is a mermaid the hippocampus develops and loses a piece of skin where her tail can link into.

But when she is on the sand with new her powers she can create these fish-scaled pair of long boots, which were comfortable for her to walk on land easily.

She approached her father's horse not being scared of it at all and looked up at him while he was still sitting on Tidal Waves' back.

"Father, I want to fight."

Neptune could not believe his eyes or ears that this sea woman standing in front of him and all the gods were his daughter.

"Helena you cannot be here."

"Please go home where it is safe, my child."

"I won't, Father!"

"I am now eighteen and will fight and save my Seequest."

"Where is he?"

"Actually, he should have been here by now' Zeus replied with a powerful tone in his voice."

"Please Helena it is too dangerous even for you dear child" Neptune said.

"I beg you, go home now, and we shall speak of this no more."

"No Father I won't" and she climbed up onto her water horse and rode off towards the caves on the beach where she heard Seequest call from earlier.

Neptune felt embarrassed in front of his family who are the gods who laughed at him when Ares said "how are you going to protect your kingdom when you cannot even keep your daughter in check?"

This made Neptune very angry and he got his trident and dipped it into the sea there appeared a whirlwind of the sea spinning around his weapon and then threw it at Ares, which he then turned into a wind of water that picked him up and carried him to the sea which throws him in and made a loud splash.

Revenge then galloped to the sea to fetch his master but Ares was angry and splashed him with the sea which then makes Revenge rear with rage himself.

"Enough" Zeus said "we're here to fight not to play silly games with each other!"

Eventually, Ares appeared in the sea just wet, and brushed the water off his brown hair.

He spat out the salt water from his mouth feeling sick as he did.

Has Ares hated salt water at the best of times and is now to be thrown into it?

Possibly drunk it too made him feel not only humiliated in front of his family but also angry than ever before with a bruised ego to match.

After he started walking back to the shore on his own as Revenge had run away from him Neptune said to him 'and now who is in charge of whom here?'

Later Revenge was flapping his large wings and landed back on the beach all dry tucking in his wings as he went.

Once again because Zeus was watching him Ares decided to jump on his winged horse and climb the skies to calm down and dry off around the sun.

Zeus said "Leave him.

He will be back soon."

Helena was on her way back to the others when she spoke to Source regarding how her father was treated earlier as could not still find Seequest as the beach was a massive area to look for him properly.

She had run off to see Seequest before everyone else did and yet to was coming back with no joy.

She was upset that even with the powers that she still has her father treated her in front of the gods like a little mermaid only.

She said to Source "I will show my father what we can do with or without his permission as by the laws in Vissen our mer-people when they become eighteen can choose their carer and now I have chosen mine for him."

Source just told her to calm down and to remember that her father the great water god had just spoken to his daughter in front of all his nieces and nephews of Olympus just as a man or a father.

"What you need to remember my dear child is that he is your king and a true god as well."

This is where you need to practice and meditate on the goddess Athena for her wisdom which you will learn in time.

"But please listen to him and obey his commands, Helena."

When Source had spoken to her like this she then real-ized that he was right and that she was stubborn and letting her ego rule her head.

When she should remember that the Amethyst skull will not work for her anymore if she does not respect him as after all it was given to Neptune to use in the first place from his actual planet.

Once she understood she said "Source you are right!

Thank you for your wisdom, dear friend.

I shall apologize to him later when he is alone not as a high priestess but as his daughter."

"Great then" Amethyst source replied.

"We must get back as I believe that Seequest will be there soon."

They ran back to where the others were waiting for Seequest's arrival.

There Helena arrives just in time to see Ares flying down on revenge as Source gallops up to where Neptune and Tidal wave were waiting patiently with Zeus.

Revenge had just landed on the sand as he trotted by her all proud with his head held high with Ares looking with hate and embarrassment in his eyes.

Trying to show his strong personality and pride while he then walked up to her father with courage as he was humiliated in front of everyone.

This made Helena giggle as he passed forgetting that he was God Ares was not impressed.

He turned around and saw these beautiful lilac eyes glaring back at him and her purple hair flowing with the sea breeze with a cheeky smile on her fair face.

Ares thought considering she was a mermaid and now a high priestess that she was quite beautiful as before he saw them as fish people, not human-like beings.

Ares walked up to his sister's horse when his sister said "that will teach you to speak to the great Neptune like that."

"You're so right war God" and she laughed.

As this was happening all the sea gods' soldier's in their full body armour appeared out of the water on their hippocampius too.

Amethyst on Source was calm now and planned to be the woman she wanted to be and not the princess now.

Source still walked closer up to Tidal Wave and neighed where Neptune could also see that on Source's facial piece has a purple horn sitting on it as well.

Neptune believed that that was Seequest's power and the universe's too.

He thought twice about her staying as she took off her helmet again to apologize to him face to face as she respected him after being the king of the sea.

"Right my daughter."

"You can be here, only if you stay out of sight of Hades."

"I don't want to lose you again."

"OK, your Highness yes I promise."

As Helena felt she just had to be Neptune's daughter for now and yet she was just pleased to fight this time!

Moments had already passed.

Squeaks were coming from the sea where you could see another chariot arriving with large beautiful grey dolphins pulling a clam chariot there was Venus herself riding it.

"Hello, cousin".

"I thought you may need some extra help."

She was very beautiful with a pear shape body long curly, golden blonde hair with a soft white silky dress that covers her refining her beautiful curled body.

She had the most piercing aquamarine eyes you had ever seen.

It was like you were looking directly into the sea.

When all the male gods saw her they all fell in love with her beauty and Aphrodite had a little grudge against this.

As Venus seemed to have a softer complexion than her but they were both very beautiful indeed.

She wore a blue clamshell as her crown on her pretty head also.

Venus arose from the other dimension of the planet Venus of the waters far away.

She was given birth by the celestial beings above and from the crystal skulls themselves so she had the power of the planets and the sea too.

"Dear Neptune, I believe you need my help?"

"Yes cousin that would be great".

"Have you brought your amazing large crabs with you?"

"Yes Neptune."

"If you request them then they shall come for you."

"Excellent," the sea god replied.

Amethyst shrugged her shoulders and walked off on her black seahorse steed on the sands.

Apollo a friend of the sun god had flown back to the skies on his winged horse which had now changed to palomino because of the rays of the sun burning him and was making sure that there will be plenty of light when the battle began later.

While they were waiting for Seequest to appear another surprise came instead.

It was Knight in his true form as before a stunning black sport-like Frisian-type horse with bat wings and an elegant red horn.

He slowly walked up to the gods all proud saying as he walked 'do not hurt me.

"I am Seequest's son Knight from Hades mare Knightmare."

"I am unharmed."

But it was a trick as Tremor was using poor Knight's image to get near all the gods and fool them right before their very eyes.

They let him come closer being cautious all the same.

"If you are my friend's son where is your father now?" Neptune said.

The large black bat-wing Unisos replied "he is dead", with a heavier voice and changed his black coat into red and orange tones, flames running through his body.

As he reared and threw fire from his horn which melted the gods' shields they all dropped to the grounds quickly.

Their winged horses reared because fire can damage their wings like the sun.

They would not keep still.

Hermes was not there yet to give them healing as he is the one that carries this potion on him at all times.

Because at that moment the sea horses all quickly ran back into the sea for cover to protect their selves from Tremor.

Neptune tried to get all the mystical winged horses into the sea to use his magic to heal them quickly.

As the gods and goddess jumped off their winged horses ran into the sea to get the flames off their wings.

The gods, for the first time, said "who are you really?"

And he replied, "I am Tremor, the destructor of this world."

With a heavy powerful voice and even Zeus was worried as he could not see Knight in there anymore.

Wondering now if they will have to kill him in the end and break Seequest's heart once again.

But the great God knew there must be a way and then he thought of an idea and hoped that it will work.

But he will have to see if Seequest will have to agree to it first as it was life-threatening to them all if it goes wrong.

Zeus had faith and believed in wanting to help and prevent the death of dear Knight as well.

Zeus was throwing lightning bolts at him.

But all they did was gave him more energy to fight them.

The great god of all things was hoping that Seequest would feel his presence and come now to help them very soon.

Zeus inwardly was starting to worry about what Tremor said about the Seequest being dead.

Zeus was hoping that he was lying.

Where was Seequest??

Chapter Forty-Three

The Battle Begins

Tremor seemed to have better weapons than even the gods.

Athena was sending out to everyone her wisdom.

Artemis was using her powerful bow and arrows, which seemed not to affect him.

Ares even used his sword rays which also did not affect him either.

Tremor laughed and said, "You cannot destroy me as I have all the powers of the earth and the universe while each one of you has some, I have them all."

Zeus said, "Hades" in a blunt angry way.

The underworld god appeared flying above his mare and said "yes, that's right, brother."

"You would not let me help you rule the earth and spend quality time on your beautiful land and so if I cannot do that, then no one will."

Then he looked down at Tremor saying "come my boy, we have work to do"

He pointed his sword at Tremor which made him multiply into more than hundreds before being more powerful than the first ones too.

Hades thought he would just give them a taste of his strength and now he was letting the doubles have it all.

But the difference was that he only knew that each one has a power which is dangerous indeed.

Because he was making sure that each duplicate demon horse knew its enemy's weakness to make sure it wins its battle.

Athena Goddess of love is up against Tremor with the power of hate as an example.

The Dark horse of hate will not be able to kill her or her winged horse.

But it will slow them down and weaken them, as Love is a powerful weapon and yet Hate is its true equal.

As it was mission everywhere!

Will the gods and goddesses have enough time to prevent them all from damaging the earth badly?

The original Tremor has them all in his control and so he could attend to destroying the world in its most sensitive area, which is its core without being touched or disturbed as he did.

All the gods were fighting these beasts and it looked for a while that Hades was winning the fight against them for the first time in history.

The real Tremor jumped up to the sky covering its hot orange and red flames.

The others like him were damaging the lands by just walking on and through them.

Even Neptune felt like the sea water was not strong enough to hurt these beasts and then he told his mer-knights to get them into the seawater properly so they were completely covered and continued the fight there.

His mer-knights and hippocampus plus dolphin riders surrounded it as it got into the sea to escape them.

But realized it couldn't take much salt in its lungs due to the beast struggling for air.

So, they began to aim loads of arrows that splashed it and drowned it until it eventually evaporated into nothing.

One was down.

The gods started to notice the horse demon's doubles weaknesses.

But the true destructor was still up in the sky doing great damage indeed.

Tremor felt the other images of him were dying quickly and wanted revenge.

He flew straight down like a ball of fire, attacking Neptune and his mer-knights in the sea one by one.

Now his eyes and nose were producing hot flames too, looking like a deep red erupting volcano and through his horn and mouth he passed the red fire towards the sea which lit it up.

Luckily back in Vissen Queen Sera had the power of the crystal skulls on their side when a great crystal dome covered the sea and took away the flames before damaging it.

The ocean was safe once more and so were its people.

Neptune could not believe that he had this great power on his side and that he married the great high priestess of all time.

They all were still fighting these creatures and eventually, even Zeus killed one himself with the great Pegasus's help as well.

"Well done, my friend".

"We have destroyed this one together."

Zeus said, "It seems that we're not able to kill the real creature after all, as Knight is in there too still alive somewhere, they thought."

"But we must do something?"

Then Hades appeared in front of the gods and said "I'll give you another chance before I let my Tremor destroy this world."

"What do you want?" Zeus said.

"I want my family to come and visit me so that I can visit you too like before and own half of the planet myself."

Zeus replied, "Now Hades you know the rules that I and the others cannot attend your space as you may try and kill us and we would burn in your world!"

"Oh, great Zeus" he said playing tricks on their minds which he was good at doing as known as the trickster, by his evil friends.

"I would not do that to you?"

"Well, actually you know me too well, brother."

"Yes, I would", with a cunning tone to his voice with evil in his eyes.

He then said "I see you have met my steed Tremor."

"Isn't he magnificent?"

Helena screamed out while she was riding source in the ocean.

And replied "no you cruel thing, he is terrified of himself and fighting his mind."

"As I believe somewhere in there is still Seequest's son Knight"

He would not do such thing as destroy his own family and planet without being pushed or tormented to do so on your behalf, Hades.'

Hades did not like Helena's answer and said, "yes that's right my child it is possible as that steed has gone to sleep forever through me training him to hate," laughing at her.

The mer-princess was horrified with his answer and said, "not if I can help it."

Hades then walked Knightmare into the sea carefully and looked at the Mer knight in purple and silver deeply as he thought that the figure seemed to look more like a woman.

She threw off her helmet when he noticed that it was the actual Princess that he thought he once fell in love with.

But now could not stand the person that she had become.

"Oh, Princess you may have grown into a young woman but you don't have the power to stop me, you silly child."

Neptune then walked over on his powerful water horse Tidal Wave now both turning into seawater itself like a hollow image.

They walked right through him and smothered them both in seawater.

Hades and Knightmare hated sea water and she reared in pain and shouted "Damn you and your horse Neptune."

"Wait and see what my creatures can do to your kingdom while you are gone and then you'll beg for mercy."

Helena then said "Seequest will come back to us and he will save his son and us all."

"Plus, he will stop your Tremor in one blow."

"Oh, my dear I do not think so as Seequest is in my lair underground in a deep sleep forever and his son who is Tremor belongs to me now."

Helena said, "you horrible beast."

Hades replied, "Yes, I am."

This creature that Seequest helped to create will destroy this world and I will rule what is left of it when you are all gone.

If Seequest does come back somehow I will rip out his horn for good and then he shall be gone too.'

"No, I won't allow you" the princess replied to her father, "I am sorry but I must save Seequest."

"No Helena, I forbid it!

But she does not hear him because now Helena is Amethyst and does not listen to know one."

She then put her helmet back on and says a Greek verse as then she and her hippocampus became a ball of Amethyst purple light.

Hades said "how?"

"It's not possible?"

This crystal skull was gone forever or that's what he thought.

The tremor was destroying the lands one by one, Helena threw a flame of purple light onto Hades and it burnt him.

"She said for the light of the good hear my call."

"Destroy this god once and for all,"

The purple light covered Hades and his mare and banished them into dust for now.

Afterward, the high priestess become princess again and believed that what Hades said was true and she took off her helmet with tears running down her eyes.

As she then looked at her father, feeling that she did the right thing at the time.

He said "never again" and jumped off his steed and mentioned to her.

"I told you that you should have gone home as he could have killed you today my daughter as you let your emotions rule your mind."

She looked back at her father and replied "I am sorry."

"I am just worried about Seequest I do not want to think that he is gone."

"I won't!" as she gave him the cloak to look after for now until it was time for her to have it back.

As remember the purple crystal skull did say that she could only use its powers one more time for now as she felt that she had to learn the ways of its magic through time and patience knowing it's the most powerful weapon of the gods.

Helena was very proud that she was chosen and of her achievements as well so far.

Even though she knew that she could use the skull more.

She also realized that day she had a lot to learn before using it again.

They both looked at each other with smiles on their faces, showing love in their eyes.

At this moment in time, she could see that her father forgave her quickly and then mentioned "my girl I believe that Seequest is a great warrior and that he is still alive."

"Have faith."

Next, Neptune said his goodbyes to the gods and Zeus.

"My bit is done here brother and now I must go back into the sea to fight the fight there too."

So, they all agreed.

When he started to walk back into the sea has his water horse begun to change once again into a hippocampus.

When he produced his swallow tail, fish-scaled body with his shell bridle and saddle, and then Louis did the same as Helena followed her father as he turned into a merman once again.

The gods said "Farewell great one."

They turned around on their mounts and waved saying their goodbyes and went back into the sea once more with their mer-knights following behind them.

As the fight was still going on in the sea as well with Hades' sea creatures and now Helena was with Kessy killing the beasts in the sea.

At this time Neptune could see that his daughter was not a princess anymore but something even more powerful than that now.

Back in the sea, Neptune noticed that he may have been wrong about his daughter so before they got home he handed the Amethyst cloak back to her.

Saying "I believe this truly belongs to you now. Use it wisely, my child."

Helena is thrilled and nodded saying "thank you, father", and called out away then Kessy had find the real demon horse and grabbed hold of Tremor, and pulled him into the sea.

Because she thought that would destroy him too or at least weaken him for a while.

Did they work out a way to separate him from Knight's mind?

Somehow Helena passed the power of the Amethyst crystal skull to Kessy like she had done before as a practice run and now this was the real thing.

So now Kessy became a powerful purple sea dragon in the distance and because Helena put the power on Hades and Knightmare he did not have time to worry about his creature but his life instead.

Kessy with excitement is holding Tremor in her mouth gently without piercing him with her huge sharp jaws and pulling him into the deeper part of the sea where he will eventually drown.

The bat-wing Unisos was neighing for his life after being pulled under. Amethyst thought that was the end of him as he did not appear in the sea anymore at that moment.

Everyone was hoping that the plan they had put in place in the past will work.

For now, they had to be patient and wait.

So that's why Kessy followed the king and princess back into Vissen to fight once more afterward as Tremor was not in sight.

Kessy and the seahorses and mer-knights dived back into the ocean and started to fight with Hades and the other sea creatures. Like the hammerhead sharks, tiger sharks are too at their home.

The blue whales were fighting the hammerhead sharks that Hades had created a while ago to protect his monster from hell.

The mer-knights were trying to capture the octopuses and tie them up with their tentacles as they kept on trying to catch the hippocampius as they swam and weaved through them.

Kessy went on to protect the Crystal Temple from the Hades beast.

While Helena was told to go back to the palace until she was called upon.

Because she was very upset about not seeing Seequest yet that she agreed with her father's advice for now.

An hour had passed and Tremor reappeared on the surface of the water catching his breath.

At this time luckily, Hades had now gained some of his power.

And yet not strong enough to fight the gods again, so he gets Knightmare to fly where Tremor was and they jumped into the water.

Hades says "Tremor I shall release you" and puts his sword to his horn which lit up again in red fire and re-energizes the creature to have enough strength to fly out of the sea to safety.

"Come, my boy, we still have worked to do!"

As they flew back to another part of the underworld so they could recover and fight another day when they were both stronger.

Ares was riding his powerful steed Revenge in the battles when he saw Hades getting away with Tremor and said to Zeus, "Please let me follow them?"

Zeus looked at him and nodded his head. Revenge started brushing the floor as he wanted to catch them and Ares says "let's go, Revenge Fly."

Revenge begins to flap his wings and gallops faster until he felt that he was ready to jump into the air.

After a few minutes, he leaps off the ground galloping upwards further into the sky where his wings were large and strong which helped him stay balanced.

Eventually, they caught up as they followed them without being seen or that's what they both hoped?

While flying around on Revenge for hours Ares contacted Zeus by magic through his sword and said, "I am following him now and I shall let you know where he is."

"So soon again we can defeat him, Father."

Zeus replied "Agreed.

But follow him, do not kill him as Hades is mine!" in an angry tone.

Feeling disappointed that he got away this time.

Ares agreed while in flight putting back his sword to the side so that he can concentrate on keeping an eye on where Hades and Tremor were going.

Hades was riding Knightmare as Tremor was flapping his bat wings as fast as he could with just enough strength to fly following his mother's path, feeling as if he was still in great pain from the Amethyst crystal skull's power.

As he received good energy of it in his blood now by Kessy's bite when she grabbed him earlier.

Hades knew that Tremor was weak.

But what he did not realize is that Knight was more powerful than he thought due to the power being sunk into him by Kessy earlier.

As it woke him, the knight inside now could somehow telepath a message to his father and sister now for help.

Without Tremor releasing he was doing it as he wasn't truly wide awake for him to notice and blocked his thoughts from traveling anywhere else.

Ignoring the pain and the hate that he was feeling as fighting it all the time.

He started to feel the Amethyst vibes running through his entire body.

Because it made him remember what his father told him in the past when they were last together that sometimes you have to feel the pain to become stronger.

That was what was happening to him.

So, Knight was just going to do that by being the clever one.

He did his best to keep Tremor asleep as best as he could so they could find them again.

Ares and Revenge are great warriors of their kind and have killed many of Hades' beasts in the past.

Tremor only being a young colt will probably not beat Revenge in flying mode at this moment as he is a great winged horse who has some speed on him.

Hades noticed Ares in the distance and said to him Tremor 'you must fly faster.

Knight mare "I demand you to get us home now as Hades created a bridle for Tremor so he could hold him as his mother gets them home in one piece."

The poor bat-wing Unisos is in great pain and then knows that he must put all his power to his master's command and flapped his wings even faster than before which eventually produced a large grey cloud in which Ares and Revenge lost them for now.

Chapter Forty-Four

Will Ares and Revenge find them?

Hades reappeared riding Knightmare in his full control once more.

She neighed heavily, as she was talking to Knight inside Tremor telepathically.

Luckily, Hades was not aware of this gift they had from Seequest.

She was trying to tell Knight to stay awake, as she could see the difference when he looked at her and she seemed pleased.

Yet was trying her best to not let Hades know, thankfully as she thought this may be her way of still helping her love and children without it being detected.

She was telling Knight that she knew that he was in great pain and yet ignored it as his father taught him, which will stop Tremor from fighting and destroying the beautiful lands that they love so much.

Hades then noticed that Knightmare was getting too close to Tremor, as he started to slow down so he said, "Oh, no, you don't."

He is mine" and touched Knightmare on her forehead with his staff, which at the moment was small for him to hold nicely.

Once he did this, her eyes lit up a deep red, as she then spoke viciously towards Knight, this time saying, "Ignore what I said before.

These are the rules now," she said.

"We must team up together and kill Seequest once and for all and get that horn of his to rule Earth with Hades, our master."

The large black Unisos shook his head confused and then Tremor had awoken again and replied, "Yes, Mother, we will soon."

Hades made both black hell horses rear at his command and they neighed again as he began to laugh with great terror in his voice as if this time, Seequest will lose.

Now all the gods heard the noises from the lands of destruction and fear across all the lands.

At this time Hades' large vultures were flying in the sky to make sure that Tremor will not be hurt anymore as their Hades guardians from a distance.

Meanwhile, the gods and goddesses had done well and destroyed the entire look-a-like with the help of Athena's wisdom because nothing got by the gods that easily.

Diana shot a couple of double demon horses down with her famous bow and arrows.

Ares returns to the battle due to not being able to see Hades and the others in the clouds.

Within the time flying around eventually they gave up on finding them, as they had been flying a long time.

Ares first spoke to Revenge his steed and they both decided that they wanted to still fight the fight back on land, so they came back and helped their comrades hurt the wings of the dark doubles to weaken them to the ground.

This battle went on for one day and one night.

Lightning now lit up the night sky.

The poor forest animals were so confused and thought that the world was ending.

So, they hid anywhere that they could find to be safe from harm from these creatures and the battle itself, as some were not quick enough to escape before goddess Artemis (Diana) put the protective shield around them from the battle.

The creatures decided it was time to go home and the goddess saw the wild animals all frightened down there, so she swooped down and put another protection shield over them all until they were right out of the way again.

They rested that night and it began again at dawn as Hades' beasts would have the advantage as it did not give anyone enough time to rest to strengthen.

So, the crafty beasts thought that they could win the battle as even the gods had to rest at times.

But luckily goddess Athena was wise and had Artemis makeup and potion to keep their energy and strength going until the actual battle was finished.

Back in Vissen Queen Sera woke her daughter through her mind and said that she must go and help on land straight away.

She agrees and gets ready with excitement as she goes to collect Bracken from the royal stables.

Helena says "it's time as they quickly are now ready for battle once again rushing off to the surface where they see Hades' vultures flying in the air."

They swam at the beach when they both changed and heard a noise coming from afar.

Helena changed into Amethyst and her Hippocampus became a source once more.

As when like this they are a force to be reckoned with!

Eventually, Amethyst (Helena) could see a unicorn figure in the distance, there coming towards them all was Seequest not looking his best and yet ready to battle at last!

Zeus saw it too when within seconds everyone reappeared in the skies, like magic, and landed their winged horses on the ground to see if was it Seequest, at last, coming home.

They all stopped.

Helena couldn't believe her eyes that there in front of her was her dear old friend he was starting to look older and weaker than she knew him last.

Yet everyone was pleased to see each other but had no time to say hellos as there was a serious battle that they had to stop first.

Zeus and the others gods and goddess's all discussed the easiest plan to end this last battle once and for all as it had gone on for months now.

Amethyst was sitting on her powerful water horse Source said with a womanly mature voice "so now will we defeat Hades?"

Zeus said "well my child", as the high priestess was still the youngest of the group.

"We are going to do as less damage as we can to this beautiful Earth and her animals also we need to protect our mystical creatures from harm in the process hopefully too" looking right at her with a strong yet hopeful expression on his face.

"Remember that Hades has also made illusions of Tremor has doubled, so we must be careful we don't eliminate the Tremor who has Knight in him by mistake."

Firefly also spoke and asked Zeus, "How do you plan to stop your brother?' have there must be a soft part of his heart that still exists?"

At this point, she was confused and started to throw her head back and forth.

He replied in a heavenly and powerful voice, "No my young wing filly no, there isn't because of his spell.

Yet she may have given him the answer "break Hades' sword off Knight's horn and Tremor will hopefully die without hurting my brother in the purpose?"

Seequest walked up all bold and said "NO let me capture him."

Zeus laughed and said "how are you going to do that may I ask?"

The winged horses of the heavens and Pegasus trotted up together beside Seequest as they created a circle around him and said, "With help of our powers he could!"

Zeus seemed angry but he was still interested to know their plan.

"Pegasus old friend what is your plan then?"

"Well with your permission first oh mighty one, I am going to give him a pair of my powerful wings that are even stronger than my own so you can fly for longer than before so he can keep up with Tremor and Hades in the red hot skies."

Then Celestial and Legend looked directly at Zeus as they too walked and joined the winged horse's circle as well.

They replied to Zeus by saying together "we will give him the power of immortality even though this was not his time yet."

As they looked at Seequest standing in the middle and said but things change all the time.

"We guess this is your time and there isn't a right or wrong to your destiny so be it now as it is needed".

"But if we do this, it will prevent you from dying which is a good thing and yet when the battle is over your body will fall into a deep sleep until you are needed again soon".

But we do not know when that will be.

They were both looking at him with pride and also sadness at the same time saying this directly to his face.

Then it explained to Zeus and the other gods this also meant that Seequest won't be able to feel any pain in the battle.

No matter how rough it gets and he will continue until the battle is won.

But they also explained that they would not have control over when he woke up.

That will be up to the universe to decide when he is needed again.'

Amethyst heard the conversation and was horrified to hear what had just been said, she had just gotten her friend back and now he could be sleeping for years or centuries maybe until her reign of life is over as well.

Seequest could sense Helena inside the high priestess and then turned and looked at her with kind eyes as he felt her pain and sadness.

He turns around and looks at her wearing battle gear while sitting looking bold and beautiful on Source and replies in her thoughts.

As he walks slowly to them breaking the circle.

First Seequest noticed how different and grown up she was and bowed to her as he could see a queen being born with a difference.

When he stops and says "my dear Helena you know I have loved living with you all these wonderful years before and planned to do it again.

But if my destiny is telling us differently now then we must follow it no matter what we want or think about the situation."

"I want to stop Hades and try to get back my son from this dark shadow force that's living in him at the moment and if this is the only way then it shall be so, my friend."

When Helena heard his reply, she thought that he had spoken like the true king that he was and she loved him for it.

The high priestess knew then the true unicorn king was back to strength to strength mentality.

He just now needed the power of magic from the mystical horses to help him capture Tremor and save his son before it was too late!

Helena looked at Seequest right in his eyes and then could see that he was sad about what he had to do.

But being the Unicorn King first, he had rules to obey as well.

Soft tears were running gently down her pretty face when she jumped off Source and threw off her helmet and ran to Seequest with open arms and hugged his neck so tight.

He could hardly breathe as she didn't want to let him go again.

She gradually released her grip as he moved his head down towards her hand, closing their eyes as they did show the powerful bond of love they had for one another.

Because Seequest had bought Helena up in some ways has been her guardian first.

They had such a great bond from the beginning and now it looks like their lives will be changing forever again!

They both were disheartened but now this was the only way they could save his son.

Helena speaks out loud and says to him "I know that you must do this".

"But I don't want you to."

"It's too dangerous, Seequest even for you."

Zeus then noticed that they had been talking through their minds and replied that's enough of the talking about it.

When looked at them both and said "my children it does not matter what you want anymore."

This is what has to happen to save Knight and earth too from Hades.

"So please let us get on with it as we have the battle to finish here!" Expressing with his firm and demanding voice.

From that moment Seequest put his emotions aside and pulled his head up while Helena started to walk away upset and broken inside.

Yet she felt happy and proud that she had this opportunity to see Seequest again before he parted possibly forever.

The Unicorn King agreed with Zeus and apologized when he started to walk also slowly backward away from the high priestess.

As continued walking she turned quickly so he could see Helena's beautiful face properly and replied again in her mind 'my sweet princess please let me go".

"I must save my son!"

If you love me like I know you do then you will let me do this.'

Its broke Helena's heart but she knew he was right and that he had to do this to also save Earth from great destruction.

Because Tremor had already burnt all the grounds and set the seas on fire too, at this point in the background Neptune and his creatures were sorting and healing again.

Helena stopped and turned around looking right at the unicorn king as she held her stare she looked up at Seequest one last moment as he was larger than before.

She bowed to him and said "my king I love you."

"Thank you for all the time I have had with you I just cannot believe that I might lose you forever".

"But I know now that I must give you up in return to save everyone and every living creature here and on our planet too from Hades and his evil forces.'

Seequest appreciated what Helena had just said to him as this warmed his heart again.

He decided to walk closer to her and tipped his horn where it began to shine a bright light of beautiful rose quartz pink as he points it right at her heart.

By doing this, he is placing some fun and happy memories of them together.

The unicorn king's horn is very powerful as it passes over the loving energy of his spiritual presence of love to her.

He mentions in her mind they will always be together by the connection of their hearts and minds always and where ever she goes or does in her future he will be there for her in some way to protect or support her.

She felt a great warmth through this that made her weep as she wiped the tears from her face greatly again.

As she begin to smile and replied in a warriors voice once more putting on her helmet as she does and says "let's do this,"

Has she known then whatever happens Seequest will live on in her from now on?

Because they will always be together in a spiritual way!

Another warm night came and the moon is shining brightly down on him especially when the big ceremony was done.

Seequest was standing in the circle glowing with heavenly divine light.

Everyone said wow as it had never been done before even in their time and thought that he was an impressive and brave mystical horse of his kind.

He gradually stops glowing when the day is approaching morning as the sun is starting to rise.

He then knew that there was no time to waste and rears on his legs showing his great structure.

He told everyone that he had to go back to the temple of the Crystal skulls in Vissen and regain his full complete power of the sea and the skulls themselves to defeat Hades and save his dear children and possibly Knightmare if he still can.

As he carried on looking at everyone like a unicorn king he was neigh with full power in his lungs.

So, Hades could hear it so he knew that he was free and that he was coming for him very soon!

Seequest was ready turned and gallops towards the ocean which glowed brightly of aquamarine as he touched the water with his hooves.

All the special beings saw him changing into this brilliant hippocampus and saw him dive into the shallow part of the waters.

Within seconds later beautiful blue and white shades of his swallow tail were sticking out of the seawater for a while before he dived again and disappeared out of sight.

He swam deeper into the ocean where he stayed for two hours just enjoying his true freedom at last and just becoming himself once more for the final time as him.

He knew that he was never going to be back there ever again, so he wanted to make sure he had the opportunity to say goodbye to all his other dear ocean friends as well.

He took as long as he needed which also gave him more time to heal with the salt water all over his body and inside his lungs.

When he eventually started to feel his strength coming back and was ready to go back to Vissen and see Queen Sera and his progeny one last time before the final battle for the earth!

As he touches the water his gills appear beside his head and he then dives deeper, swimming as fast as he could gallop with great speed of his tail as well towards the darker part of the sea to the portal to Neptune's kingdom.

As he knew that he had an impossible job to do which was to try and save his son Knight still from Hades.

Before he reached the Vissen gates the mer-knights saw this new type of hippocampus as a horn.

Because they did not know it was him?

He had changed a great deal even to them and so they believed it was one of Hades' shape-shifter creatures trying to get through to the palace on their watch!

Has Seequest was even bigger bolder and even more than he ever before.

Because his form had changed once again to heavenly looking unicorn hippocampus with feathered feet like his father and his horn was thicker and gold as his eyes glowed off the pure bright rosy pearl of the flowers as he had his daughter's powers in him too.

He asks the mer-knights to let him in and they said no"!

"You are not the great Seequest we know please go away before we kill you"

Poor Seequest had no choice as he had no time to waste he said "ok and swam away coming back and charging the gate with his horn which broke it wide open.

He continued swimming fast as he could to the Crystal temple where Queen Sera was waiting for him to appear, as she was told by her connections he was coming home for the last time to say goodbye for good and gain his full potential with crystal skulls energy too!

She could see him coming towards the doors when she quickly puts down the shield and opens the massive large doors she said "Seequest welcome home, please enter"

Quickly he swims straight to her.

She waves her hands at the door and the doors slam closed with the shield covering the temple once again.

"Oh, great priestess you know why I have come?"

She answers him "yes I know and I am sorry it has to be this way".

"But it is the only solution to trying to save knight as well"

He replies "I know I just don't like the idea of leaving Helena alone again, knowing that she is just becoming a high priestess herself with an amazing power of her own."

Seequest expressed his emotions about his concern for Helena as he says "I will not be there the way I liked to be regarding protecting and helping her anymore?"

Queen Sera came up to him and held his face carefully and said from the bottom of her heart "my dear sweet Seequest sometimes in our lives things just happen the way they do and we must just accept it as that's the universe's destiny for us in the end".

"But for you, it has changed a little as the plan was not for you to ever mate with a demon horse and so the divine and the universe is trying to compromise the situation as easily as they could.

Has it known that your children have great power and are good inside too?

But because of what Hades has done to dear Knight he now will be challenged when the time comes, to see if he will be killed with Tremor or maybe become something else?"

The Uni hippocampus understood what the queen was saying to him and agreed with her dearly.

She now said to him please keep still as to get the full powers of the crystal skulls she had to gently use her staff to take off his horn for it to be able to gently sit in its original place where it did before charge properly.

The horn; the large crystal skull both charged to their full magic powers for the greater good of them all at the same time.

Then to give them the full power in one go, Sera then divided the crystal skulls to their original state of the four beautiful colours of Aquamarine; Emerald; Sapphire, and Rose quartz so that they could be charged again with Seequest's new powers and also reboot his own with them again as well.

Where now their powers emerged the Crystal skulls will be held to the moon to charge only.

So, while the horn and the crystal skulls magic emerged together they spoke about the old times and the queen promised that somehow that she and her mother Luna will make sure that whatever happens next the power of the Amethyst skull and his powers will be strong enough for him and Helena to be able to connect to him even if he is asleep.

From afar he will be able to answer and still be there for her in some way too.

Yet they both knew that he could not help her if she is in danger in the future as he will not have control of sleep only the universe has the power to do so.

So, it was her way of reassuring him that what he had already said to Helena is true and that no matter where he is or goes in the future, they will be still connected.

Next, they both heard a loud noise of a sea horse coming towards the doors, and then it was Neptune himself appeared.

He came to say his goodbyes to his old loyal friend and sensed he came home for the last time in goodwill.

Again, Sera open the doors when his wife says "my king hurray please" as he jumps off Tidal wave and swims to Seequest saying "wow look at you haven't you changed?"

Seequest replied "yes, I have had to due to all power I have of the sea; land and the crystal skulls your highness."

"I also have the powers of air again and also powers of the heavens as well," Neptune says "yes my dear brother that would explain it completely"

They talk for a while and then they spoke about Helena's future and that he promised the king that he will do his best to be still there for her.

He said she will be a great queen one day too.

The sea god seemed pleased and agreed with his requirements and loved that Seequest believed and thought highly of his daughter this way.

That Neptune promised that they will be twin souls somehow forever no matter how far away they were?

Seequest horn shone brighter than ever before as it was glowing with all the colours individually of the crystal skulls.

Aqua blue; green; dark blue and pink made it now a beautiful and elegant rainbow pastel horn.

While the queen said a universe verse they emerged again to the large great pure white divine crystal skull that it became.

Has it did she made sure that it sent its powers across all the seas, and oceans and protected the sea creatures as well in times of great need.

The great sea god and his high priestess knew it was time for them to put his horn back onto his third eye close to his forehead.

Afterward, they would have to let him quickly go as he wanted to say his other goodbyes to his dear sea friends before leaving the sea forever.

They all could not believe that Hades had beaten this part of the fight if could not have Seequest then no one will.

Neptune hugged the unicorn hippocampus and said "goodbye my warrior when Seequest reared and said "goodbye my king"

Suddenly he was ready to go when queen Sera nodded and opened the doors as Neptune jumped back on the Tidal wave Seequest nuzzled on his way out.

Tidal wave neighed to Seequest with a sad tone in his voice and then the uni- hippocampus shot out of the doors like a flash and not even Tidal wave could catch him that speed.

Telepathically they said to each other be safe

Seequest saw his friends and told them he won't be coming back.

All the sea creatures bowed to him by waving their tails up and down or closing their eyes and tilting their heads and he did the same saying their thank you to him and their goodbyes too.

His two dolphin friends said that they will go back to the surface with him one last time and say their good-byes there.

As they swam through the beautiful blue ocean together passing by a beautiful school of clown fish and saw plaice lying on the bottom of the sand waiting to attack its prey.

They also saw bright yellow and orange crabs walking sideways digging and making holes for Hades' crea-tures to fall into and die.

These crabs were much bigger than normal and saw him swim by waving their right crawl as a goodbye too.

The dolphins were so heartbroken that Seequest will be gone in their seas forever and that he was like a father figure to them as he was the guardian of the sea as well.

They bumped their noses to his neck and he touched them gently with his horn that tickled them a little, so they squeaked.

Swimming back to the shore for the last preparation for the battle of his life, the dolphins were squirting water and talking as he left them they lifted their fins waving them up and down in the water.

Seequest then disappeared towards the shallow parts of the sea.

While his friends were waiting for the Unicorn King to surface near the shoreline, so they could jump in and out of the water for him one last time of showing their love for him and that they will miss him dearly.

But poor Seequest was in great anguish at this moment and appeared not showing it to them as he was now again the Unicorn King of the Earth and kings do not have time to let their feelings get the better of them.

But the dolphins knew by the expression he gave when he nuzzled them before that he was sad and heartbroken too.

Dolphins understood his body language and that was enough for them.

Dolphins accepted their goodbyes and dived back into the sea quietly.

The uni-hippocampus galloped and jumped so fast that he made great waves in the sea that crashed as he came back to the shore.

Eventually, he reaches the actual beach and changes again into a pearl-white unicorn with a glowing light of platinum that has never been seen on earth before.

Zeus was watching in Olympus that it was time to come back for the last battle and told everyone to meet where there was before.

Because this was days later since Seequest had left them on the beach and they had been battling Hades' other creatures in the meantime, while Tremor was resting and becoming stronger too for the battle of his life as well.

The unicorn king arrived back and trotted over to the heavenly winged horses.

When they saw him approaching from above and getting ready to fly back down gracefully and form the circle again to finish the last part of the ritual.

He galloped over to them when Celestial says "it's time my son and king of horses and our unicorns of all kinds" and bowed to him as he bows back to her with great respect.

Seequest is in the circle like before when Pegasus walks up to him with pride and begins flapping his wings as fast as he could and said 'Seequest are you ready for the battle of your life?"

The bold white Unicorn stallion nodded his head and bowed and then Pegasus starts the ceremony once more to its full power when Seequest replies boldly "yes grandfather I am for the greater good of us all".

Pegasus replies "then we will continue the ceremony from where we left off".

Seequest was standing there looking regal and elegant as he carried the pain and troubles of the world on his shoulders from inside.

He then knew that once he had captured or killed Tremor the earth and its creatures will be at peace once more he hoped.

Seequest knew his destiny and had to obey it and yet was hurting because he could not live on earth ever again, as his powers were greater than Zeus' which could even encourage the great god to try and retrieve the powers for his own doing and maybe would become too powerful for earth himself.

Seequest knew that could not happen and so he would have to go away.

The unicorn king would miss his dear family and friends and yet knew they will all be always ok.

He closed his eyes as the unicorn king for the last time.

Pegasus replies with a Greek verse as he did Seequest starts to shine all over with pure diamond white light and within seconds they all see these massive angel wings appear on the sides of his shoulders like his father's.

He opens his eyes looking proudly at his angel wings as he flaps them towards himself to feel the movement of them against him.

These massive stunning angel wings made this powerful now powerful Unisaus very happy indeed as he always wondered what it felt like to have a pair of wings.

Because in his past he remembered that he could fly through the power of his horn before as his parents once were night unicorns and flew and protected the night skies and the stars too.

After flapping a lot, he puts them back beautifully across each side of his body.

The light continued to shine on Seequest's body and within another few seconds there you could see that it worked as he now was more powerful than any winged horse or unicorn of time.

Zeus was angry as now Seequest was even more powerful than any other god temporarily apart from himself and felt like this was too dangerous to give him these powers in case Hades captures him again.

But he believed that Pegasus and the mystical horses knew what was best for everyone.

Another night had passed as it took hours for Seequest to gain his new powers properly and to get acquainted with them in the short time he had to do so.

The day is starting creep up again when it was Celestial and Legend's turn.

They said a divine verse this time and there appeared to be a stunning large rainbow light that shone brightly everywhere and eventually also created a large rainbow in the sky for all to see.

Everyone thought it was out of this world as at this time it was as if it was a double.

After looking into the sky Seequest sparkled so brightly that first, it took everyone a while before they could look at him again.

Because he now stood there with his wings and horn; mane; legs and tail were all the beautiful colors of a rainbow too.

Zeus says "I cannot believe it and asked Seequest are you ok?

Has they felt concerned that even for the Unicorn king's powers may be too strong for him to bear, as this has never been done before in any shape or form."

This power was also too strong for the great Zeus to control and yet he felt a little envious and wanted for himself.

But then he knew there is a really good reason why it does not and carried as the amazing god he was without it.

Because he knew that this power could work both ways and you had to have a strong will plus say it's for the highest good of others.

Its mighty power would end all civilization as they knew it and he could not risk it getting into the wrong hands like his brother.

After thinking carefully in his thoughts while waiting back for an answer from the new improved Seequest.

He thought that it was best that he did not have it as this will destroy the Earth and could kill him too.

A little while later after the bright light calmed down again the rainbow unison replied to him and everyone else.

"I am no longer Seequest."

"My name is Peace Warrior the Great Unisos and mystical horse of the heavens and the Divine herself."

They all backed away and broke the circle when Peace Warrior reared up with great power in his eyes and determination that he will win this fight and save Knight in the process.

"Zeus, oh, mighty one, I am ready to use these powers for the greater good and protect Earth"

"I am ready to win this war for us all even if I have to give up Seequest's life to do it"

"Do I please have your permission to use this power for the greater good oh mighty Zeus?"

"Yes, Peace, you do, and welcome to earth."

Zeus thought to himself wow why did I not think of putting a winged horse together with one of the unicorns in the first place?

But he couldn't even if he tried as that was Pegasus' powers, not his to use.

Zeus now carrying on watching this special ritual being done, like no other before was intrigued as he forgot that Pegasus could read his mind too.

Pegasus walked over to him and said "just in case you are wondering the reason why I did not do this in the past was that the unicorns are healers and creators of great beauty and peace in the world.

While my kind is the warrior winged horse and was born to be fighters and protectors and give inspiration to all with wisdom as well.

But a combination like that unless fully controlled properly or trained to work for the highest good, could be seriously dangerous to us all."

Zeus sighed and thought about it a lot and thought, yes, you're right.

That's why my brother did it as he doesn't care whom he kills or hurts in the process to get what he wants.

The mighty Zeus looked at Peace Warrior who was once Seequest and put his head down closing his eyes to him in respect.

Because now Seequest has the full powers of all the elements of earth and universe put together.

Seequest was relaxing in his body.

As Peace warrior was now in full control instead.

Chapter Forty-Five

The Heavenly Rainbow Winged Horse

Before Peace could approach Tremor in battle he remembered from Seequest memories that he was also a hippocampus.

So, he decides to go into the sea and see what was so special about it for himself.

Has he thought he may be able to use later as another advantage over the fire horse?

So, the next thing he did was run towards the sea.

He galloped straight in as it lit up the whole ocean with wonderful colorful light of the beautiful shades of a rainbow that we know and love today.

From the distance on the beach, Pegasus says "don't go too far as we have one last stage of the ceremony to do under the last full moon before you are ready to face Tremor alone"

All the gods had not seen anything like it before and they were amazed by this great power this Unisos already had and still had more to be given.

They believed that Seequest in the end will be classed as the unicorn god of the stars. Peace was happily experiencing the seawater when he felt Seequest was telling him that one of the greatest powers of all was salt water.

While Peace was swimming in the ocean the dolphins squeaked knowing that they could feel Seequest's presence now with wings.

There was once their Seequest and now there was another greater celestial being inside him who is swimming in their waters with them.

Peace Warrior thought that he would like to experience what the water was like so he dived straight in and explored it for a while.

The sea creatures saw that this great being of light was even another type of hippocampus that could change itself into something of pure uniqueness.

Has it had a unicorn king's horn, wings which it also used in the sea to swim faster than Seequest could ever do before?

This new creature was very beautiful and elegant with a large fin that made him glide in the water elegantly.

Every whale, shark, and dolphin just swam in their stillness when he went by them and made noises.

As they all could the similarity to their dear old friend Seequest in its eyes.

Peace reached the bottom of the sea where the merguards were standing and they noticed in the expression it was still Seequest and yet it was something even greater!

The mer-knights let him swim straight through the large golden gates of Vissen to explore Seequest's home.

Even though Seequest was relaxing in his body Peace warrior could not believe how he felt about this incredible Unicorn before him and started to understand what powers the unicorn King had himself.

The great Warrior thought that he could use them to his advantage as they will possibly help him defeat Tremor and Hades.

Peace swam further into the Kingdom of the sea god where he saw beautifully posed statues of Neptune and his queen with even Moonbeam Seequest's mother due to her horn creating the first hippocampus in the ocean.

He swam also towards the stunning Crystal Temple which was all lit in its glory.

He touched his rainbow horn on the beam of pure white light which was all around it.

The high priestess was still inside the temple and felt his and Seequest's powers energizing.

She knew then they had a good chance to win this battle after all.

Queen Sera were standing in the middle of the temple glowing with a powerful white light herself as she was powering her energy from all the crystal skulls in the temple beforehand.

From this, she also was very powerful indeed.

The winged Hippocampus touches his coloured horn on the doors of the temple, as he spoke to the Queen inside and asked her 'High Priestess of the moon and sea, I need you to give me all the information about Seequest's children and their magic, please?

"Plus, what type of character and personality was Seequest?"

"So, I can use his image to imitate him and try and free his mare as well if I can?"

She gave all the information kindly to the heavenly hippocampus and he then thanked her and continued to swim away towards the beach once more to continue the last part of the ceremony to complete the full powers of the universe to save earth from this evil reign of Hades.

Peace floating with his tail gracefully moving side to side when he heard Sera talking to him in his mind and "said I hope Seequest can forgive me for not telling him his destiny?

He replied and said "I and Seequest understand why and yes of course as we have to go by the rules of the universe too."

He moved his head when an image of her looked right at him.

As he saw a flash of light and there he saw Sera's eyes change to pearl white.

Queen Sera was now the true self of a moon priestess that she originally was before.

He knew then that she too was ready for the battle of their lives.

She said "thank you oh great one."

He neighed and said, "It's the time your highness!"

She then called the power of the crystal skulls to her staff and the diamond shone up onto the top of the roof and pointed to the high part of the dome of the temple.

When she did this he then was completely connected to Seequest's presence, and body and now controlled his horn.

The Winged Hippocampus horn was glowing with white light representing pure wisdom from the crystal skulls.

Which was the power of time itself, he and it was completed as one once more as their powers were part of the celestial beings from other planets.

Before Seequest left forever, Peace felt like he wanted to say something and respected his wishes and so he repeated the words for him.

"Goodbye Sera".

The queen knew it was her dear old friend himself by how he spoke to her through his heart for the last time.

She received the message that moved her to tears and she sadly replied from her heart too "yes, goodbye, Seequest my wonderful friend thank you for everything, you be greatly missed my unicorn king"

Peace warrior swam away afterward.

While the queen began to open up the doors and swam out towards the gates because the temple was now fully protected on its own.

As she needed to help her dolphins and her people get to a safer place before the battle began as she knew that it would be a dangerous time for them all to be in.

At this time, Sera felt in her heart that Helena knew now the truth about Seequest's destiny and felt the hurt of her daughter's pain and for the ocean itself.

But for now, she had to focus on her work by concentrating her energy on the crystal skulls to help her home, as if it never happened.

But inside she was heartbroken like her daughter Helena was.

The queen knew that things would never be the same again and started to fret as she could not see into the future anymore and it worried her as this was one of the powers she always had normally.

But Peace warrior had frozen this power for a while. Because he could not let anyone get between what he might have to do next, even though he did want to possibly do it.

Because the universe gave him messages on how to complete this mission and save the world again from Hades' reign of badness.

Seequest had to become Peace for a while to stop the battle and save his son.

Peace was swimming back towards the shore when he glanced at himself and could see that he too had a pearl-like colored body and shone like he had diamond crystal eyes that were shining like Luna the moon herself.

That's why the last part of the ceremony must be done in her presence too.

He continued to swim as he healed Seequest's heart and pain of sadness.

Then he knew that Seequest was the guardian of the oceans too and so made every creature feel safe in their home in the sea.

With his powers, he cleared all the mess and harm that Tremor had done earlier and he then felt Seequest's heart become warmer toward him.

As if, the old unicorn was saying thank you for his help.

Eventually, his horn was a stunning deep blue, that shone into the water and the sea started to appear calm and clear once more.

But as he went he also changed the shades of blue in the sea to show where it was becoming shallow, so his friends knew it was too dangerous to go up to from now on.

In case they got stuck on the land and died of thirst or became dehydrated by being trapped by Hades' creatures.

He also collected the salt water of the sea into a large see-through ball which he then left until he was ready to come to the shore and bring it with him.

Meanwhile, the queen was concentrating on the sea creatures and her mer-people as she sensed there was one of Hades' creatures coming to try to destroy the temple and gain the crystal skulls power for their master.

But she knew that they can try and yet won't succeed this time.

This creature was the size of a mountain with the strength of a hundred blue whales.

It's called the destroyer of the deep.

It looked like a massive large black snake dragon that could easily make itself self-invisible and poison the oceans with its ink if attacked.

Peace now swimming at the speed of light swam towards the surface as quickly as he could.

He reached the top and started to flap his fish tail as fast as it could go.

He also sensed the beast in the waters earlier and chased it to the shore where the shallow water was and should not go as it would die of dehydration or die from his horn and now it was trapped and could do no more harm to anyone.

Because the peace warrior touched the water with his horn and drained it dry for the beast to get stuck on the sand for a while.

Until one of the mer-knights came and killed it for him as he had other important things to do, like save the world from chaos.

Afterward, the winged hippocampus carried on towards the shore.

The gods could only see a light in the ocean coming closer to the shoreline and could hear massive waves roaring in the sea.

There appeared a bright white massive glowing Unisos galloping onto the sand now having four strong powerful legs to carry him and his hooves were digging up the sand as he went.

His glowing mane of a rainbow lit up the sky again in the evening.

Peace was astonishing and yet his light being was even too bright for anyone to look at him.

Showing how powerful and majestic he was.

Zeus said kindly "Peace welcome back but can you please quieten your aura as it is too bright even for our eyes?"

Straight away Peace neighed as understood that his energies after all were also from the universe.

So, he put his head down and closed his eyes which seemed to calm down his aura so everyone could see this beautiful creature standing in front of them again.

The celestial Unisos was stunning as he looked like a pure white Ferisan type with a large platinum horn again which weaved with all the colours of the rainbow on it.

His mane was long and flowing showing reds; yellows; pinks; greens; oranges and of course Seequest's shades of blues too.

The only color that he did not have yet was black.

But he knew that this was the power that he needed to defeat Hades, as black was also a protective shield from negative and bad energies and highly spiritual too, which carries the power of the heavens in it.

But it can be used as an aura of bad, dead, negative powers too.

Peace warrior knew that is the part he needed most to complete the full cycle of the universe's powers to conquer Hades' magic of his underworld realms.

As he galloped his large angel wings started to unfold and flapping them up and down until they were dry and then he folded them back to lie on his sides nicely.

He eventually slowed down his pace and trotted towards Zeus; the gods and princess Helena, who was standing next to the white wolf as her true self at the moment with no threat going on and wanted to hug this amazing creature as she could still see Seequest in him and yet knew that it wasn't anymore.

Because he was something else using Seequest's body as a vessel to work with at the time.

This extraordinary being had no body of its own as its true form was a pure white light of energy, originally known to us today, as pure white light of all the char-kas of our souls.

Peace warriors with all these other powers will become the supreme horse being of the past; present and future.

He still was gleaming with great power but duller than before so everyone could see him properly for the beauty that he had become.

He stopped and bowed to Zeus who replied 'Welcome Peace Warrior of the full elements we have one more power to help you still.

With his bold voice, he continued saying "Please come and join us again for one last time before we all go our separate ways".

"Hoping that we all will meet up in the future when this is all over to celebrate the earth in its great beauty once again"

All the gods and goddess reared their winged horses to what Zeus had just mentioned and then all said together "Victory will be ours again father"

As he replied by smiling at them all and raising his large gold staff turned into a lightning bolt as he lit up now the night sky like fireworks everywhere.

"Until they calmed down and the full moon was out in her full glory when Celestial said that's nice but there is still work to do here first"

Within that, even Zeus became quiet and was interested to see what would happen next.

The great Unisos agreed that eventually he would be called by Seequest's name for the last part, as this affected the Unicorn King inside.

She called him over and shouts out loud in front of everyone when he was back in the circle for the final time.

"Peace Warrior I know that my son is there with you and will be listening also to what I am going to say next to you both now!"

"As celestial is standing in an elegant posture of her War-lander form (half Arabian / Ferisan) with her pretty mane laying on her neck with her tail held high and neck beautifully arched with her face looking into the eyes of Seequest's body at this moment."

"I am giving you the power of becoming immortal in a unique way as you will not die but you will not live on earth anymore either."

"I am going to give you the Obsidian power that will ground and protect you!"

"It will also give you strength and courage to do what needs to be done for the highest good of us all with-out questioning it at the time".

"This power is connected to Legend and me from the spiritual side and of death too"

Seequest this part is for you my king after this great battle of your life the powers that you process now will put you into a deep sleep and then it will turn you into a star form until called upon soon.

"Your father and grandfather Pegasus and I have spo-ken to Zeus about this."

"And he agrees that you have been a god send to this planet and all its creatures that he kindly said that you could live up in the sky as your father does now!"

"But the difference is that you will not be awakened until you are needed on Earth once again and for now no one knows when that will be, sorry to say".

"Do you agree to the rules of these powers that I am prepared to give to you now?"

"Because this was the only way we could keep you alive in the rules of the universe herself, due to what has happened between good and evil's balance recently."

Peace speaks for Seequest and replies "yes, I do my queen of the heavens and I understand why, thank you for saving me one last time!"

She sighed and within a few moments, she flaps her black swan wings very fast which started to sprinkle bright silver from the sky came a star form which landed on Seequest's body and forehead.

He reared proudly and yet sad inwardly as his body now began to sparkle like thousands of stars at night.

They then disappeared as Seequest knew now that there was no turning back from this.

Celestial mentions that she was done and walked back from Peace once more and thanked Seequest and this heavenly horse for their help to save earth once again from Hades' cruel ways.

Next was Legend shimmering with blue and silver on his gleaming black coat.

He also walked up to Seequest boldly and the proud Pegasus said "my son I am so proud of you so I am going to give you the power of strength; wisdom and courage to help you fight the battle without any fear of any kind."

He too flapped his black glorious swan wings and once again there appeared a dark blue and silver light which then rose into a large dark bubble and went over to Seequest and landed on his horn which now glowed with blue and silver tones and it even sparkled like Legend's wings.

Peace warrior/ Seequest now carries the black aura energy too as Legend had it from being a great warrior and protector himself.

Peace warrior had to have this to destroy anything as Seequest and his hippocampus form was to never hurt or kill anything unless he had permission from Neptune or Zeus himself, which was hardly ever in his lifetime.

But now he had to change his ways of thinking to defeat Hades once and for all.

But he seemed to have the same heart and remembered that he must not truly hurt Tremor in the process, as his son was still the true form and is sleeping there at the moment, thanks to Hades' magic.

Standing there in front of them at this moment was a larger form of himself black as night with a rainbow mane and tail still with his gorgeous diamond crystal eyes which he changed to see everything again.

Seequest was gone and Peace Warrior was back as now had all the powers that not even the gods can ever have in their lifetimes.

And too were astonished by this unique power of the universe herself.

The black rainbow Unisos was prepared to save Seequest's son and defeat Hades and capture him on the return.

Zeus told his children and the other gods and goddesses of Olympus to ride their winged horses and finish the battles above.

As Hades' creatures were ripping up the lands and destroying Zeus's creatures of the forest which he created second.

Peace Warrior was ready and let Seequest say his last farewells in case he dies in the process.

He jumped into the sky and flew towards Hades' hidden lair where Revenge and Ares saw them last go in the end.

Helena is heartbroken about what is to happen to her dear friend and tries to keep thinking of what he said last when he was himself weeks before.

But she was seriously upset as she couldn't in the end save him the way she hoped or liked.

Then she too was happy to put her life in danger for the greater good she decided that she may not be able to save Seequest.

But she can try and save Knight still if they can capture Tremor first?

Firefly sees Helena thinking as forgets she can read minds too and then walks up showing her bravery in front of Zeus and says "I have a good idea."

So, she told them and Zeus agreed to it.

What she mentioned to him was that she had a little power of the heaven horses to he pointed his lightning bolt at her horn when it glowed of cerise pink representing love and anger too.

Firefly then thought that she would give the winged horses some of her power as she believed that it could help them in the battle as well she thought and save many lives in the process.

As she was very upset of now losing her father and she did not want anyone else to lose as well.

And so kindly shared the powers that Pegasus himself did not have like hers, due to her again having some black energy of her own from her mother's bloodline.

As if this power was used for the highest good of all it could be a powerful weapon and shield at the same time, she thought.

As it represents, the shadow of one's self.

Zeus loved this idea and continued to help her achieve this idea of hers properly as remember his a true God of earth and living things too.

Once Zeus's lightning bolt glowed he told Celestial and Legend to bend their heads down looking at the floor.

And so, when they did the other winged horses were told to come back into the circle again.

This time as a command from Zeus as he loved the idea that they all could help in so many ways at his home and anywhere they needed to protect anything from danger in the future as they will be invincible.

Firefly suddenly stood in the middle of the winged horses and told them to close their eyes tight and hold their heads held high no matter what happened next for them not to move an inch.

The winged horses all neighed with the agreement to what she wanted to give them.

As they felt very proud that she wanted to share her gifts with her ancestor's bloodline.

Next, she moved slowly walking around to all of them pointing her horn straight toward their foreheads for five minutes, and then she could see that an image was starting to appear and so moved on to the next one and so on until she had given her power to them all completely and safety.

The winged horses of the mystics' realms started to feel tingly and they all neighed as before them grew each a beautiful horn on their foreheads which gave them great power of once the unicorns of their time.

Zeus seemed pleased with this idea as now his winged horses could have a better advantage.

Has they could use the horn as a weapon and a shield from the rays of evil forever?

They all neighed together in delight as now they are more powerful than ever before in the reign of the great Zeus himself and of Andromeda.

Zeus told Peace Warrior what Firefly did and now they knew that they will be able to defeat anything.

That Hades should watch out as he has never known of these powers like this before.

But thanks to his ideas they now are using it for the good of all creatures' kind.

Zeus said with a proud strong positive tone "now that you all have this extra power use it wisely for good and defend the land and yourselves from harm always no matter where you are or what you are doing in the future."

All the winged horses reared as they galloped back toward their riders.

Once the gods and goddesses were mounted on them again they then bowed and their horns lit up with the colours of their riders.

Who then turned and flew up into the sky to fight the vultures and any other of Hades' creatures with a pure belief that they would always win from now on.

Due to the horn, they can heal themselves to a degree as well.

Through passing on these powers to every other winged horse Firefly collapsed into a deep sleep herself.

Peace Warrior said no!

As it was Seequest's voice who cried out and rushed back to her aid.

Zeus replied and said with a calm and understanding voice "it's all right boys, she's just asleep."

She will awaken soon.

"It's just that that power can drain you as well as give you great energy."

Even though Seequest believed what Zeus had said he still wanted Peace to go and check on her, all the same, to make sure.

He nudged her and licked her face, and an expression came on her face as happy, and then he walked away feeling calm again and relieved to know that she will be ok.

Eventually, it was time for Seequest and Peace Warriors to face their last battle as one!

Once Seequest inwardly knew that firefly was going to be ok they turned around and galloped away from everyone and leaped into the sky once again like a flying white cloud with a rainbow attached to it.

Because now Peace had turned back into his true form which was a pure pearl white coat through the unicorn king's body energy with the rainbow colors everywhere else.

Where has his body consumed all the elements and charka powers fully of the universe?

Once Firefly awakened she said "where is everybody?"

The Princess Helena standing there in her amethyst armour said "It's okay, sweet girl".

"Peace and your father have gone to Hades' second lair to rescue your brother from him."

Firefly said "I must go and help him too" with a demanding tone to her voice.

So Helena said "only if I can go with a hopeful concerned voice as well."

Next, the pink pretty Unisaus agreed and trotted over to Helena, knowing that she was a true friend to her father and that she felt this may give Helena some closure due to the sadness of losing him too soon.

Firefly then bent down her neck and put her front left leg tucked under her chest with her right front leg stretched in front of her and replied to Helena, "yes, you can fly with me".

"Climb on my back my young queen Amethyst and we will help together."

Neptune quickly appeared as Queen Sera had been watching through her staff and the scared moon water.

Letting Neptune know that everyone needed to come back and fight as one to defeat Hades at last.

As he approached the beach he saw Firefly with his daughter on her back beginning to leap to the skies when he shouted in the distance "no, Helena I forbid it!" when Firefly was just starting to flap her wings to fly.

She stopped slowly and the princess shouted back "you have a choice father, you let me fly with Seequest's daughter to help them in this great battle or I shall go away and never come back to you ever again."

Neptune looked hurt but he saw Helena now eighteen was sitting on this pretty pink Unisos as a future queen and replied "ok, as long as you promise to be careful" and threw the Aqua blue crystal stone crown of Helena's to the high priestess and said "use this as it will not only protect you all from harm but also heal you all too".

Like the power of the amethyst crystal skull in her, she did not have to worry about being out of the water as she now had the powers of planet Neptune and Jupiter put together as it represented still a water stone.

That's why it took to the princess earlier and also because of her spiritual connection to the animals of land and sea and her mind, as it opens up your psychic senses and also with the amethyst stone, she is now an invincible knight-ness.

Before Firefly flew off to another part of the land, Helena said, 'let me help you and she put her amethyst staff onto the horn Firefly's mane; tail, and eyes had changed into a shade of light purple and produced this beautiful armor similar to the goddess's.

Firefly then sounded more boldly and said "I am now your friend I am called Magenta"

Helena was now approaching the beginning of her new destiny at the same time as Seequests and his children are too.

Neptune then could see a true queen beginning to blossom with great power on her shoulders as he continued to look up into the sky.

Thinking that he would have never thought he would see his daughter walking on land and now flying in the skies which were beyond even his imagination.

He knew then she will be the future queen to his throne.

Chapter Forty-Six

Peace Warrior

Peace was soaring above the bright blue sky as he lit it up with his powers.

He felt like he was getting closer to the area where the second lair was and stopped himself glowing as he blended himself like a chameleon into the sky itself.

As then Hades or his creatures won't see him coming, or that was what he hoped.

Eventually he came to some mountains, where he saw volcanoes spurting out hot-red flamed lava.

He knew then he had to be careful of this as even though he would not feel it he still did not like the idea of being burnt.

He carefully flew between it without catching his wings as he did and then landed on a dark surface like soil and mud, as there was nothing growing here anymore.

When he landed and Seequest helped him by saying that he was in Wales of the British Isles.

He then noticed that this poor land that was beautiful before was now gone and he said to himself in the future he would do something about it before ever leaving earth for good.

Seequest also mentioned that there was great water dragon living in Scotland and wondered if maybe Kessy could go there and help it bring its greatness back in the future.

As remember she is different from the others and she does have some unicorn magic through Moonbeam's powers and by Helena sharing now her powers with her too.

He walked quietly with his wings still moving and up and down with great speed and gradually started to slow them until he felt that he could fold them neatly back to his sides again.

He began to change into a black horse again to camouflage has been like one of the copy demon horses in the lands at the moment.

He trots slowly towards the cave when the sabre-toothed tiger was standing in his glory, a large black tiger with red flames as his stripes, with piercing red eyes who said "I know who you are, Seequest.

I still need to revenge my poor Havoc that your father killed in the past."

I have been waiting a very long time for you to show yourself back here!

A shock came as Seequest spoke this time and said "I thought I killed you after escaping the Hades liar has you caught my daughters' legs.

When the sabre cat replied back "oh no unicorn king that was some trickery of Hades magic to think that you killed me" and roared with victory in his tone of voice.

"You seriously did not think that you could kill me that easy did you that was a stand in to make you think that you killed me while I was protecting the liar from the gods earlier."

Eventually the old unicorn king spoke to Peace about what happened in the past and how important that the real Pain must die for real this time.

The sabre tiger believed that he could win due to been emerged with Hades blood.

But what the cat did not know that Seequest was not his self now.

That another entity was using his body instead.

The great black bat winged unisos was trying to say I am not Seequest and yet the sabre tooth tiger would not believe him.

Peace and Seequest agreed that they would be ready to kill this evil cat once and for all.

Peace was quite happy to do it on the behalf of his friend that lives on inside him.

So, Peace replies back 'stop making excuses to fight me and just do it, you stupid cat.'

This angered saber-toothed tiger and he charged with all its might towards Peace.

They were fighting to the death as the large cat jumped on his back and scratched him a few times and bite his legs too to get to his level.

But Peace was too strong for him.

Then the cat started panting and said, "how comes you are not getting tired?"

The heavenly horse replied, "I am not Seequest any-more as he now lives on in me."

"I am known as Peace Warrior, the most powerful heavenly creature of the universe."

As they both looked into each other's eyes.

Havoc was beginning to show a deep fear in him and at that moment it was when he was the most vulnerable.

So, Peace went right at him and charged his horn into the cat's chest which pierced the male's heart.

Peace heard another pride of sabre-toothed tigers approaching hearing their king been killed.

He saw them all coming towards him as they did one by one he killed them all.

He knew that Hades would feel their agony and deaths as he made them out of his own blood this time round and hoped it angered him to show himself so he could find Tremor and save Seequest's son Knight.

By Peace doing this, he knew that this unusual creature that he felt was not Seequest and yet felt his presence inside it.

Hades was aware of it being at his lair and ordered Tremor to go and kill that beast as revenge for his sabre tooth tigers and for killing also his pet Pain who he loved as his own child.

Back in the lair Hades screamed 'no my babies!' and said "I do not know who you really are but I know you will pay for what you have done to my cats," looking into the flames of his fire to see not Seequest but another type of creature that he had never seen before.

"My Tremor is stronger than you as he has hatred in him where you only process the black aura for courage and protection."

Hades began to laugh loudly.

Peace now felt that Knight/Tremor was near and used Seequest's power of mind control on Tremor and called Knight instead to wake up when Tremor was resting with Knightmare beside her.

He heard a voice he recognised and it said "my son, please waken?"

"I don't want to hurt you."

Knight was just going to answer him when Hades shouted in his flame of fire and replies "Tremor wake up now and kill this creature for me once and for all."

The black bat-wing Unisos heard his master's call his eyes came open with pure fire in them as he stood shaking his head and body and said to his mother, "I need to go and kill Father now."

He started to become seriously angry as now that Hades had used his sword on his horn in the past he too had full control of his feelings.

As Hades hatred was powerful than ever before when his coat produced red deep veins running through his skin and his eyes were lit up like a volcano and his wings were carrying flames on them now too.

Has he quickly run out of the lair to the volcano where he stood on its soil to feel the volcano's lava which burnt him?

He neighed loudly and started to gallop with flames coming out of his hooves as he did.

When was adjusting to the heat as Tremor could handle it but Knight still inside could not.

He stopped at the edge of the mountain and said back to Peace Warrior rainbow Unisos "I am here now and

Seequest's son is dead" as he reared on his back legs throwing red-hot flames from his body as he went.

He jumped up into the air to get closer to the heavenly horse.

Tremor now flying in the air began making smoke as he came towards Peace Warrior.

Once Tremor was in the skies with him Peace Warrior covered himself with a large diamond white light of good while Tremor was just a hell horse at its best.

There appeared Hades on Knightmare watching from below.

Hades said, "Yes kill him kill him now", still watching through the flames that were around the grounds.

Tremor started to throw fire from his horn at Peace but luckily this time it bounced off.

It was now Peace Warrior's turn and his horn glowed of the white light of platinum and pointed it straight at Tremor's head which made Knight come back for a few seconds.

Knight quickly said, "I have not got a lot of time".

"Where is my father?"

"I am your father, Knight."

"He is here inside me like you are with Tremor at the moment"

"I have the elements of the crystal skulls and of the universe for a short time to defend myself from the other side Tremor and Hades himself."

"Please surrender and I can then save you?"

Minutes later Peace Warrior had his shield down when Tremor awoke once more and pointed another ball of fire into Peace's angel wings.

He flew away from the bat-wing Unisos and the raging flames and felt that he had to get away quickly for now to heal himself again.

Because he could feel that he needed time to heal them as the fire is magic after all and can really do damage.

He remembered the great Loch and flew out of the cave and off to Scotland where he felt that he was safe which originally was Seequest homeland.

Tremor said "fly away you weakling", and all he saw was Peace flying away at the speed of light in the distance.

Hades looked up and said, "Well done."

"You have defeated him."

Tremor landed neighing loudly that he cracked the ground and said "no".

"I have wounded him, he will be back I am sure."

Hades said "then we will be ready for him."

'Tremor says "yes I will!"

Chapter Forty-Seven

Peace Warrior Healing
in Scotland

Peace Warrior eventually arrived in Scotland.

He can see the damage that Hades' creatures had done to it.

He landed quietly at the Loch, as he did not want any of Hades' creatures to know that he was there.

He quickly slides into a hippocampus form and dived deep to heal his wounds, jumping around in the freshwater.

Peace warrior was beginning to recover and thought of the best plan to capture Tremor without killing Seequest's son at the same time.

It was a very hard quest indeed and yet felt in Seequest's heart that he would do anything to save his son so Peace in his mind was talking to Seequest that he would do his best to try and the old unicorn king respected that.

After Peace felt that he was strong enough, he came out of the Loch and rested on the land near some large trees that gave him shelter, as he felt that he will go back again at night and try again!

But this time he won't leave until Tremor will be killed and Knight was saved.

While he was there resting in the freshwater, he could hear the battle still going on elsewhere and hoped that everyone was ok?

But for now, he had his own battle to attend to before helping the others again.

Peace Warrior had been swimming and jumping in and out of the water all day with Seequest's memories.

From thinking of his life with his mother and then in the sea with his Daughter to then living and falling in love with Hades' mare Knightmare believing that he had lived a great life with many challenges too.

But loved his life, all the same, has then Peace started to understand the rules of life on earth that you had to have rough and smooth as that was the balance of knowing when things were great and enjoying them while they were there.

He also understood that he was taught lessons and made Seequest become the amazing King he was to the unicorns and now horses too through it!

He thought that Seequest had felt at one point that he had everything and now felt like Hades had taken everything away from him for the last time feeling heartbroken.

There was Seequest resting inside while Peace Warrior was now controlling him and with Seequest's thoughts to help him win the battle.

Because Seequest Knew about Tremor and Hades' weaknesses he Knew that he was invincible as he was going to use Seequest's pain to make him even stronger than he was today.

He felt that he was ready for another battle with Tremor and hopefully this time he would stop Tremor and save Knight from creating any more destruction across the lands and stop Hades for good.

Peace walked out of the water as he changed to his natural form again and decided that he was going to lie down on a large flat rock peacefully looking around at the damage that Hades had put on the world when he spoke to Seequest and they agreed together that they were going to stop this hell once and for all.

First though he walked towards the loch and put his horn into the water and there appeared a water fountain flowing above his head.

As he moved his head around it blow everywhere and put the fires out on the land and with their beautiful magic emerged together minutes later.

Peace could see that the pretty flowers and fresh green grass were starting to grow again where it was destroyed before into nothing.

He neighed with delight that he helped heal it with Seequest's help too and that it was been reborn again which made them both feel really good again after they both helped heal the lands.

Peace Warrior got up gradually and stretched his back and his whole body with a nice shake to ease his muscles.

Had some fresh grass to eat and drink the fresh water from the loch to gain his energy.

He slowly pulled out his gorgeous angel wings that healed quickly and so he began to flap them up and down and felt that he was ready and leaped into the sky to go back to Hades' lair in Wales once again.

But this time he contacted Tremor with his mind and said look I want to talk first before we fight.

Tremor replied Fine and agreed to meet him back in Greece which took two days for them to get back to as that was where everyone was in case he felt like he needed help.

As sometimes teamwork is better when trying to achieve something big.

Hades at this time was not concentrating on them as he was fighting the battle elsewhere and knew that Tremor did not need a hand and trusted him to kill the heavenly horse for himself.

They met up on the rocks near the sea where Peace warrior had the advantage at the moment when they spoke and Tremor still felt that he had beaten Peace Warrior.

Even with these extra powers, he let his ego rule his head which was the last thing he should have done.

Now Peace Warrior had the upper hand and his plan was starting to work.

The universal horse said to Tremor "we both know that you can bet me"

"I thought that you would not mind if it was now a fair fight where I can stand freely without being burnt by lava, as at the moment it seems unfair".

"As you are using my weaknesses against me we are both true and strong!"

"So, you then can kill me by expressing to everyone afterward back at your liar that it was a good battle and we fought with honor and all our might to the end knowing we are both very powerful horses of good and bad energy?"

Tremor thought carefully again letting his ego answer for him and replied back 'Peace if that is what you want us to do then I know that I can kill you anyway so I will agree to your challenge"

Peace then said "good then follow me back to Santorini to end this once and for all where we will fight to the death and see who is a mighty warrior in the end?"

Tremor's fire aura calmed down and appeared again has just the knight's image as they both flapped their wings and started to fly out of the cave back on a long journey to Santorini, where the others were waiting as Peace had spoken to Zeus and the others before he flew back to get Tremor to follow him.

They landed in Santorini on the island in the middle of the sea as just a lonely little piece living on the sea surface happily.

But Tremor's ego was not now aware that Peace Warrior had another advantage here.

Because Tremor was thinking so much of being the best and strongest that he blind-sighted himself of seeing actually what was going on around him.

Because knowing that Peace was living at the moment in Seequest's actual body that he could survive in the sea while Tremor cannot!

Tremor's ego did not know this as this was Knight's weakness not his own.

The magnificent creatures were there first coming together having a talk peacefully telling each other that they will fight to the death even if they did not want to.

Tremor at the moment had full control of his own mind which also helped Knight awaken and for thirty minutes of their talk as it bored him because Tremor was created as a fighting machine and not for being a warrior of love and peace to the earth.

Thankfully this quickly gave time for Knight to talk to his father as Peace let Seequest talk to his son again.

What a great reunion, when he said to him.

"My son it is me your father Seequest it seems that the god of death has complete control of your mind and your body".

"So, we do not really want to hurt you".

"But I will let Peace do it if I have to stop the evil force from destroying the lands that I love and protected all these years, as my duty of been the unicorn king before and now your father too!."

"I am sorry father but I do not have any control as Tremor is stronger than me."

"I know son but please try to see if you can get into his energy and find out if he has any weaknesses."

"No, he does not".

"Hades has made sure of that".

But father you do know mine!

"We both know it may need to kill me to kill him!"

"But you do need to stop this horrible creature now before it is too late."

"No, I cannot do that, my son."

"I will then and give you no choice," as he started to bite his father until he drew blood.

Then Seequest said "no I will not fight you, son."

"Father you need to fight to kill Tremor".

"I love you."

"And I love you too, son."

"No matter what happens to either of us we are protecting the lands and our friends and family from any more terrible danger."

"If this is the only time we have ever again" knight said.

"Then I shall take it 'and then carried on trying to bite his father."

"Fight me, Peace".

"We all know it's the only way."

Knight said "I am sorry" and he used his horn of flames and pointed at Peace which set him alight.

Luckily, he had the seal of protection on him but it made him angry and he started to use this power too.

"Forgive me Seequest" Peace spoke to him as the large black Unisos was attacking them viciously.

The bat-winged Unisos moved using with all his might his power from its skeleton wings and scratched Peace on the face badly as he was very close at this time.

"He neighed with pain as those claws also carried poison on them."

Peace could see that at the time Knight was in charge as he was just a beautiful black Unisos colt.

So, he started to buck around and shake his head Tremor woke up and said, "Oh it's you" and his coat and body lit up in flames once again showing the red veins in his body and becoming a ball of fire once more.

Peace could not touch him as the ball of fire was also his shield of protection as well.

They began to take flight and fight a tremendous battle in the air away from everyone else around them who were watching them both from afar.

Peace could see that Celestial Legend and Pegasus had been watching from the grounds and now flew up near him as they tried to join in.

Their wings moved at the same time as they approached the heavenly horse and Tremor together.

All three mystical horses flapped their wings in front of them which created a beautiful powerful diamond white light that they pointed towards Tremor and it landed perfectly around him so that it looked like a net of pure goodness.

The evil Unisos was neighing and bucking trying with his horn to rip it apart but it was no use.

Tremor then realized that his ego had caused him now to be caught in a trap and was fighting for his life against these most powerful horses of the time.

When he wondered to himself if he could now be beaten at last and yet would not give up that easily!

Thinking that he would die trying to make sure that he would take Knight with him.

Half an hour into the battle Tremor noticed that they did not want to kill him as such and thought what were they doing?

He started to feel that their powers were stronger than his.

They continued to glide in the sky flapping their wings in front of him it seemed like it was beginning to weaken his shield which started to fade until the demon horse felt like he was defeated.

He flapped his bat wings with his claws trying to break the silver-white light net and he reared up and broke the white energy of good.

This threw the winged horses into the skies away from them for a while.

But they were ok and yet exhausted so Peace thanked them for their help and sent the mystical horses back to the ground where they were told to wait for him there.

They all neighed and said "Peace please be careful, he is very strong."

"Yes", the celestial horse said "But I am stronger."

Peace flew straight up to Tremor and used with all his strength all the powers of the elements but they did not beat him this time round.

So, Peace sadly said to the unicorn king who was resting inside his body at the time "Seequest I have no choice I am sorry" with sad emotion in his voice as he spoke to his soul.

Peace warrior went in for a full attack as he grabbed hold of Tremor's wings and bit them until they ripped which made Tremor start to lose his balance in the sky and land directly to the ground like a crashed fireball.

There now the demon horse was grounded on the land with his body lying on his side and his ripped wings beside him.

The evil Unisos got up and started to throw fireballs toward Peace which grounded him as he burnt his feathers again until there were too many feathers burnt to heal them quickly.

So, he was falling too and he also landed on the ground with a blast.

There Tremor was waiting for Peace Warrior to adjust and recover from the fall and prepared himself to fight once again.

The fight continued on the island where they were fighting, kicking, and biting each other until they became very tired as they felt that they were as powerful as each other.

Until Peace knew he had one last option that could possibly kill Knight and had no choice but to do it.

Peace warrior looked weak and yet strong with his Friesian white body and rainbow mane that still lit up as a rainbow which now blinded Tremor for a few minutes.

And was enough for him with his horn to push Tremor over the edge into the sea.

The tremor was neighing loudly feeling like he was burned alive also felt confused as the salt was going into his skin and making him feel heavy and in great pain that he eventually sank to the bottom of the ocean.

Tremor did not reappear for hours.

This once powerful demon energy now was nothing but fluid in the water and Tremor's body was at the bottom of the sea hopeless and dead.

Peace Warrior reared with delight and dived into it with full speed as he folded his damaged wings into the sea.

Has he quickly turned himself into a large hippocampus looking now for Knight's body to recover it?

Everyone saw the battle and cheered but they were concerned too as Peace Warrior was weak so they all wondered did he die in the sea too.

Peace disappeared for an hour and then he rose back out as the heavenly Unisos he was before.

There he was now carrying Tremor's body on his back.

Everyone on the ground was clapping saying, "Yeah he did it."

"The demon horse dies".

The gods were rearing their winged horses with delight that the battle, at last, was over for them all.

Now it was down to Zeus to finish it with Peace Warrior.

Peace neighed as he was trying to flap his wings upwards from the sea and then landed and gently laid Tremor's limp body on the golden sand.

Straight away Helena saw what had happened and was worried that Seequest's son also died inside.

She and Magenta who were both upset wanted to land where his sister had to say her goodbyes properly to her brother one last time.

The graceful unisos mare landed quickly and yet carefully that she did not knock Helena off by landing swiftly, as they had been watching in the distance from above.

Magenta quickly galloped over to see that Tremor had disappeared completely and there now was Knight's body looking still and dead.

Helena jumped off and said "let me try and save him with the power of the amethyst crystal skull and my Aquamarine crown which also has the power to heal the good only."

Helena jumped off Magenta who then became Firefly again as Helena's powers were not controlling her anymore.

After Helena had said this Firefly replied back to her with your powers and mine of true love maybe we can bring him back again to live together?

So, they agreed to try with both of their beautiful purples; pink and blue rays of love, protection, and healing flowing for ages at Knight's body and could see that there was a shade of pink in him now with his red veins near his heart glowing and they thought there may be a chance yet?

But then it faded again and they walked back feeling completely defeated.

Peace Warrior after the fight shook himself off looking all bloody.

He dives into the salt water healing his wounds from the battle.

After a while, instead of swimming in it, he was actually walking on it for a few minutes as the waves rose and glowed blue all through his veins which they could see happening.

There a bright blue light appeared and it then died down.

Peace Warrior was walking has good as new if nothing had ever happened to him.

He was now galloping towards everyone wanting to see Knight's body like Amethyst and Firefly.

He slowly changed his trot has he then walked over to his Seequest's son's body where he nudged Knight with his muzzle and then lit up a bright green Unisos and put his stunning green horn onto Knight's head, saying, "Wake up my boy its time?"

There seconds later Knight opened up his eyes now bright green and said "father is that you?"

Then within that Peace said 'yes he is here with me and he loves you very much!"

"He is pleased that you have survived thanks to the princess and Firefly's faith in you and the love you all have inside your hearts for each other."

"As the good was still alive in you and no matter what happened to you the good always conquers in the end!"

"As even though there was darkness at times the light is always at the end of the tunnel, so always believe this from now on and you will always be a fine knight"

Knight was not strong enough to move yet as he was still battered and bruised.

The healing that Peace gave him was just enough to wake him from death but not enough to heal him completely yet.

He nuzzled him once more and says "my job is nearly done here now.

It's time for me now to go!" As the rainbow colours fade from his mane & tail.

Helena ran up to this gorgeous pure white Unisos who was bigger than what Seequest ever was, has been now Celestial being.

When she could not help but cuddle his great powerful neck and looked into his eyes

She could see Seequest looking back at her with sadness and yet at peace with himself.

She then knew it was time to say goodbye for good and said, "I love you, Seequest with all my heart and I won't forget you my Unicorn King."

Within that, he reared with an enormous neigh which Helena stepped back from to make sure she didn't get trampled on by accident.

Firefly came over next and said, "Father, is that you inside?"

"Yes, my sweet girl, it is."

"It's time for me to sadly say goodbye, my child."

Firefly replied "but I have just gotten you back."

Seequest replied back to them all "we knew the price that I had to pay to retrieve these powers to save your brother and our planet. Now I must obey them, my child."

Tears drew down Firefly's eyes she put her neck around her father's and hugged him for a few minutes.

He then said "my child I will always be with you and you will be able to contact me in the stars."

"Just call my name and I will be there for you."

"Please keep an eye on your brother and mother for me, I love you, my angel."

"And I love you too, father, thank you."

Peace proudly walked up to Zeus who was standing there boldly ready to avenge his lands and creatures.

Peace knelt down in front of him and said, "Your Highness it is time."

Zeus god of everything jumped off of the great Pegasus and walked over to this stunning creature of love and hope.

Zeus nodded back to Peace Warrior/Seequest this stunning creature.

He pointed his lightning staff at the front of his body where his heart is which lit up with pearl white crystal light to his rainbow horn.

As Zeus was doing this his staff appeared stronger than ever before as he retrieved the power of the universe into it which caused it to glow and flicker like lightning bolts coming from it strongly.

Has the universe believed that he was worthy of this power himself?

When Zeus was surprised and thought maybe in time he now could create another species like his own image too.

Peace bent down and let Zeus get on his back as they flew to capture Hades and the others were getting ready to do the same.

Peace then said "I will be back my children and Hades will pay for what he has done to you all."

Everyone from Ares; to Artemis, to Athena cheered and saw these great gods rise to the sky and disappear like lightning for the last part of the battle of their lives.

Chapter Forty-Eight

Hades Capture

Peace Warrior and Zeus flew back to Hades' second lair looking so mighty and heavenly that Hades did not know what hit him.

When together they destroyed every bad creature there was and then saw Hades scrunched up in a ball feeling defeated, he then saw Peace and said "you have killed my greatest creation."

They landed on the hot grounds where now Peace could not feel it or hurt him no more.

Where Hades saw Peace and Zeus sitting on him said "damn you, heavenly creature."

"I will have my revenge one day."

Zeus said "that's enough of your nonsense for a lifetime."

"Hades I will banish you to the bottom of the Earth where you will live for eternity"

'No, Zeus you cannot do this to me."

"I am your brother after all."

"I know who you are but you have killed and destroyed the earth and my creatures long enough".

"I am now going to take away your powers of killing as you please and now you will have to destroy or collect the creatures' dead souls instead when I give you permission to do so from now on."

"Peace Warrior was neighing while Zeus said, 'Peace are you ready to fight one last time my friend?"

The mighty celestial unisaus let Seequest answer this time that answered in his own voice and said "yes Your Majesty."

"Let's do this for old time's sake."

Zeus said, "Great."

"Then we shall old friend."

Then Seequest went silent again and Peace's voice which was bolder and more powerful now spoke once more.

Hades looked at the heavenly winged horse and said "Seequest is that you?"

Peace answered, "Yes and no as Seequest is inside me thanks to your idea in the first place".

"We played you at your own game which your hate did not see even though it was done right in front of you all this time"

They swooped closer to Hades as Peace was gliding his wings sideways and pointed the white light towards Hades which put him into a force field and grounded him.

Then Zeus's staff pointed at the earth where it started to open up and swallow Hades whole.

As he was falling into this dark hole of despair he screeched "Zeus nooooo!"

Hades vanished into the deeper part of the Earth's core where it was hot and smoky all the time.

With great force between them, they did the same, and all of Hades' lairs that also sank deep into the Earth's core with the rest of all the creatures with it.

They said a verse together.

Hades' time on earth had now been taken away from him for good.

Has will live in darkness in the heart of earth where he cannot harm as the core is protected by the crystal skulls and the universe.

Where he will never get them as he is down there and they'd be hidden from him forever.

Zeus said that's how you get rid of evil once and for all as Zeus laughed.

Peace neighed rearing with joy before they flew back to Santorini.

From that day on Hades had to go by Zeus' rules if he wanted to be not punished anymore for his terrible and cruel ways and pain he caused to others.

He also on his birthday was sent to Olympus once a year otherwise he would be banished forever into full darkness.

They flew back to the beach where Zeus jumped off Peace and said "It's that time sacred one to go back home."

Everyone was saying their goodbyes with tears in their eyes when first they heard Peace say "Before we go Seequest wants to express his final goodbyes to you all."

They all agreed to this.

As moments later Seequest's image appeared again when he said, "thank you for everything for being my friends and for helping me protect the creatures and the earth and the oceans from all evil and danger again".

"Love and light with unicorn blessings dear friends I shall miss you all and wish that I did not have to do this."

But I have no choice as my destiny is calling me like it did my mother in the past and now it's my turn.

"Zeus, please promise me that no harm will come to Knight as it was not his fault for Hades' cruel ways and ideas."

"I promise you Seequest he will be looked after."

"But he will not be able to come to the heavens with the others as he carries too much of the bad energy still inside him."

"But don't fret, my friend he will be ok."

'Thank you", he replied and trusted Zeus greatly.

He says to everyone "I guess this was my destiny after all?"

Everyone bowed to the great Unisos and said 'Goodbye old friend and thank you for being the greatest king of unicorns and horses in history and friend of earth too.

"Thanks to you everyone in the future will live in peace and harmony again."

Within the time he said this it became dark when Luna who was watching from above, appeared from the moon as she made it a night to also say her goodbyes to Seequest.

She shone the moonlight on him and said "my sweet Seequest I am so proud of your achievements and your bravery all these years".

"I shall be watching you forever when you are up here with me but it will be different."

He replies "thank you" and her beautiful image of a beautiful silver-haired goddess was gone again.

She says this before she disappears into the night sky "till next time dear one".

Peace Warrior bowed for the last time rearing up and said in his bold voice, "thank you for making me feel welcome here and helping us defend earth once more.

Farewell gods' children and creatures I shall be watching from afar in space."

Then his image of Peace the white Unisos, was gone, and they were now standing in a bright pure crystal white light was the great Seequest as his original stunning white body with not a silver horn and dappled grey body anymore but instead a platinum horn and hooves.

He walked backward as his wings disappeared too.

He felt himself once again and then seconds later he felt a powerful flow of peace over him as all his thoughts were now silent and erased.

He was relieved that he knew everyone was going to be safe again and that he saved his son after all.

Seequest felt that he was now happy and proud that he smiled with his eyes and then closed them until he collapsed to the floor.

Where he was laying still and started to glow with the bright golden light of the source itself.

His full image of him standing there then turned into pure stardust, where he rears up as he starts to break into many stars as they float towards the night sky appearing now as seven actual stars of his true self.

Zeus mentions as his spirit floats away further into the sky "sleep well my Unicorn King until you are needed again".

"Rest knowing that you died an honourable death like your father years before and that you died the 9th of April B.C which will be celebrated soon as the great Unicorn King that you are, farewell dear friend!"

"I name you to be known in the stars as Monoceros, our Unicorn star of great Virtue"

It appeared beautifully and shone so bright it looked like it was glowing silver and gold at the same time and then sparkled for the last time until it vanished from the night sky.

Everyone was watching Seequest disappear into stardust.

Amethyst the high priestess took off her bright purple cloak where she became Helena again as she took off her helmet where her black hair would shine.

When she began to cry deeply as she was heartbroken about what had just happened to her dear friend she then knew that no one could have saved him in the end.

She was crying she felt light-headed and fell to the floor from great sadness and her father appeared rushing up towards her from the sea on his hippocampus as Tidal Wave neighed in sorrow as well.

There was a black shadow approaching from the sea itself and there appearing was Louis Helena's hippocampus that came running out been ridden at the time by Taylor the mer-knight that Helena fancied.

They galloped towards the beach where Luna then appeared again and lit up the night so everyone could see Seequest one last time as Monoceros star!

Luna made even the sea glisten in her powerful moonlight, she made it look like stars were floating on it and it appeared like diamonds too.

Taylor jumped off the water horse and ran to Helena's side as she got up from the sand and wiped her tears carefully.

There she stood with pride but she could not help her feelings and did not care at the moment that she was a high priestess and this is what her father meant about controlling her emotions in front of everyone before her peers.

Helena was shocked to see Taylor.

And yet she was pleased to see him as she also thanked him for bringing Louis too.

As he is now her best friend and gave Louis a deep cuddle that comforted her dearly and helped take some of the pain away.

But she saw her father get off his hippocampus standing beautifully she cried running to her father like a weepy child.

He opened his arms to her embrace and she said 'father Seequest is gone' and carried on crying a great deal as mer-folk were sweet and sensitive beings as well and loved their creatures as their own family.

Neptune replied 'yes my daughter he is but he is not as he is still here as well in her heart and mind.

Helena felt confused about what her father had just said and then he kindly explained it to her.

"All you need to do my child call his name Seequest and then look up into the night sky to see his seven stars shining above us."

She then moved her head back and looked into his eyes of truth and love of glowing aqua blue and smiled and wiped her eyes when he said "It's time to come home."

"You are needed there, my child."

The princess agreed and says "yes you are right Father."

"He will be always with us in our hearts and that's where he will stay with me forever."

Neptune nodded and said to Zeus and the other gods and goddesses and of course Moon Cloud the wolf too.

"Thank you everyone for your help and for letting my daughter be part of this battle," Zeus my brother and the great gods of all thank you again of beaten Hades once and for all."

Zeus replied "you don't need to thank me, brother, as we beat Hades all together".

"It was a full family quest".

"Now it is nearly time for me to go to, now that Peace and Seequest have healed the lands again for us with help from Celestial and Legend and Pegasus as well

"Thank you, my heavenly horses of the heavens."

When they replied "yes thank you to Zeus for letting us have the privilege of meeting our Seequest again and for letting us become even more powerful than before"

As they all neighed and thanked Firefly for her kind gift to them all.

They again neighed and bowed their heads and ran and leaped into the stars where they vanished.

Next, the Heavenly horses were getting ready to go as well when they thanked Pegasus and Zeus for letting see Seequest one last time as their true son.

They both bowed to Zeus and Pegasus and even Helena before they looked at each other and began to shine black and sapphire blue before they galloped and leaped into the night sky where Legend left trails of stardust behind him and Celestial rainbow dust as well.

What an incredible sight they were thought Zeus and the gods.

There appeared first was Legend who has known the Horse star where only his head shows up.

As when Seequests father died his horn died too because Jecco was the closest to a horse more than Pegasus would ever be today.

So even though Legend is now a mystical winged horse he has his star.

Zeus called it the Horse star as the Pegasus star was already taken in the future.

Legend was not too far away from his Seequest and so they shone brightly together.

It all went silent when Pegasus looked at Seequest's lost children and said "what will happen to Firefly and Knight now?"

Zeus replied "I have two great jobs for them."

Firefly you can become our winged warrior of a new species "I now can achieve this as thanks to Celestial; Legend and Peace I have the power to do this."

There is the spark of his lightning bolt Zeus said, "You are now the warriors of Olympus and I ask of you all to protect us from all evils."

The Unisos all reared with delight that they now have this extra great power as well and that they were now invincible against anything in the future.

Pegasus said "wow Zeus, that's great."

"Don't worry Peg I still need your originals as well for the future too."

"When Zeus looks over at Seequests daughter and says "Firefly I want you to become the queen of my herd of the new Unisos so I ask you kindly will you join us?"

Firefly was delighted and said "I would love to but what will happen to my brother now that our mother is gone and our father too? He needs me!"

Zeus said "If you agree to my offer then I will be happy for you to stay on earth with your brother for another year and then you must come to the ninth dimension and after that, I will grant you four times a year to see him for the rest of your lives."

Firefly said 'that's fair."

"Then yes great one I will be honoured to join your team, thank you for this great opportunity."

Zeus smiled "Oh by the way Pegasus being the god of all mystical horses will be the sire to the new generation of Unisos as well."

So, with a flick of his staff, her wings became large with silvery pink shades through them as the purple has now gone.

Because the purple energy was given for battle only by Helena the high priestess at the time.

Zeus then replies "good and smiled again with great happiness that she was going to join them and he got what he wanted in the end after all."

Once again Zeus said "your name will be known as Starlight of Love, as you will help spread in the future to earth Love as you will help Aphrodite your new owner as she the goddess of love herself."

Aphrodite replies "oh yes father we will be a great team" and bows at Starlight's beauty which overwhelmed her as now she will be her mystical horse when needed as well.

Pegasus reared with great delight to see that he now will mate with the most beautiful powerful Unisos of all time.

Who is a powerful god himself that even her powers from Seequest of the sea will also make his reign and herds of mystical horses even stronger than they were before?

The gods all said their goodbyes as Neptune jumped back onto his hippocampus and started to gallop into the sea.

Helena runs up to Firefly and said, "thank you sweet girl as I and your father know that your real mother will be proud of you and your brother".

"I am pleased that you are going to live in the heavens with the other mystical horses where you differently now belong."

Firefly looked at her and bowed and she gets up as Helena throws her arms around Firefly's neck where in return she nuzzled her face into Helena's body and closed her eyes in the warm embrace between them both.

She then let go as Taylor was riding her Louis trotted over and said "well my Princess are you coming home or not?"

The princess turned around and smiled at the mer-knight differently.

While he was looking so handsome sitting on her steed so boldly as she looked at him thinking is he going to get off Louis or not?

Taylor replied "well I guess you will have to ride with me!"

"As there is no other sea horse for me to ride looking around the beach as he spoke to her?"

Helena smiled thinking that he was been cheeky and yet liked it and so run towards him for a lift home again.

This also helped her pain of losing Seequest that day too.

Taylor put his hand out to pull her up on him when he said "you're be riding and sharing him with me."

Helena had no energy to argue with him so she put out her hand and he caught it.

Where he grabbed her gently and threw her onto the hippocampus which neighed and turned around where she spoke to everyone before she left and said "Great Zeus and my cousin's thank you for helping Seequest conquer his goal of saving his children."

"But sadly, he had to give up his life to do it."

"I know that he will always be with us still in the stars".

"So, thank you from the bottom of my heart for letting him be the hero and warrior that he deserves to be."

She smiled where her hippocampus bowed to Zeus and the others before he galloped off back into the sea, where they all changed back into their proper selves and swam into the deeper part of the ocean where they disappeared.

Chapter Forty-Nine

What happened next to Knight in Santorini, Greece?

Helena and Taylor are riding Louis who caught up with Neptune and Tidal Wave at the Vissen golden gates where the mer-knights were relieved to see them all unharmed.

Neptune; the princess and Taylor arrived back in Vissen they could see that thankfully it was undamaged through the protection of Kessy and the faithful dolphins and of course the power from her mother too.

Who controlled the crystal skulls at the Crystal Temple in the distance of the grounds?

They got off their hippocampius and put them in their stables to be fed and watered and to rest.

Taylor stayed there to attend to the hippocampus while Neptune had just said that he wanted to spend some quality time with his daughter alone for the first time in ages.

Taylor agreed with the king's wishes and Helena saw that the mer-knight was not coming.

She quickly went over to him while he was attending to the water horses and grabbed him and turned him around and as they looked each other in the face she kissed him on the cheek.

And dashed with her tail as fast as she could before he could realize what had just happened.

As she did he smiled and spoke to Louis saying that "he believed that she was the mermaid Princess for him".

He neighed believing that they were well matched.

She caught up with her father as he decided to go to the dolphins and see what damage there were thanks to Hades' creatures.

Helena asked her father when her mother will return home.

Neptune said "when the ocean is cleaned up and everything is as it should be".

He smiled and replied, "soon my daughter we will be all united as one again".

"I know it will never be the same without Seequest but remember he is gone from us in the sea".

"But he is still here in the sky resting and he can still speak to you thanks to your telepathic mind with him which Zeus allowed you to do still so that you two will always be together and never alone again.

"Zeus knows that you put your life on the line to save him and your people so he has granted you this in return".

"But it does not mean that you can talk to him for anything only in time of true need my child".

"Give him at least six months to recover from what he has been through before trying this."

She smiled been pleased that she still could talk to him at times like the old days.

But in a different now he is a spirit not as flesh like before.

Helena agreed as they held the dolphin's fins and swam back through the beautiful sea again as now it was clear and blue like before.

The sea god said "our work is done now please return home to rest my daughter."

She shook her head and agreed as she was feeling exhausted they swam to the large golden gates where they let go of the dolphins who were told to go back to their pods until called once more.

Neptune cuddled his daughter and told her that he was very proud of her bravery and, one day, she will be a great queen in time.

As they swam she looked at her father looking bold and strong and was so proud of him and then they went their ways as she swam to her quarters.

While Neptune swam back to his throne room and continued with his duties until the queen returned.

Back in Wales trapped in the earth's core Hades was not sure if Tremor was destroyed as Zeus had connected his thoughts to his brother's again which was best now after what Hades had done to them all.

Back in on the beach, Zeus called back Legend on his own from his star.

He flew beautifully through space to meet Zeus as requested.

It was now sunrise and they could see this stunning large black-winged horse flying between the suns as it was rising from the ocean.

The sight of him appearing was stunning with the sun behind him of red and gold gently shining on his coat.

As the sun was miles away and it just looked closer from the mind's eye.

All the other gods had gone back to Olympus and carried on with their normal duties from afar.

Aphrodite and Firefly and Zeus with Pegasus had to make sure that Hades will obey his duties soon.

Legend the black heavenly horse flew right in front of Zeus flapping his wings as he gracefully landed.

"Your Grace, what can I do for you now?"

"Well, Legend I know that you look similar to Tremor as you are related to him through your son".

"I wondered if I can kindly use you as a decoy to capture Hades as at the moment all Peace Warrior and I did together was sunk him and his lairs into the hot core of the Earth, where he will reign."

Legend agreed to help capture Hades to make sure he could not harm anymore.

And so, the mighty winged horse listened to Zeus' plan has he then says "I will now change your wings into bat ones and give you a horn-like Knights was temporary of course"

"Then we fly deep into the earth's core together and play him at his own game."

Legend was happy to help for the sake of his progeny and Zeus said "with this blue light it will protect you as we go."

They agreed and Zeus climbed onto Legend's back and used his lightning bolt.

They flew to where Zeus and Peace warrior left Hades before and broke open the ground deep enough for Legend and him to fly into Hades' new home.

It took a few hours for them to reach.

They landed on the hot grounds of the earth's core and thanks to Zeus giving Legend the protection spell he was protected from the fires and the heat.

Hades saw Zeus sitting on Legend as Tremor's image and said 'oh you did not kill my Tremor after all".

"I knew you are too weak, brother."

Zeus smiled and looked at Hades who was right as they were playing along at his tricks as he got off of Tremor's look-alike (Legend) and whispered in his ear 'you know what to do."

He lit up red like Tremor did and then Legend walked up to Hades pretending to be Tremor now and let him get on his back.

Hades said "good now we can carry on from where we left off."

Straightaway Legend used his wings and raised them over his back and squeezed Hades between them.

Then Hades said "Enough Tremor let me go."

Then he glowed the blue shade again and replied "never you evil god."

"You will pay for what you have done to this world and my family here," bucking and trying to bite Hades while he was trying to break loose from Legend's bat wings.

The god of death felt sick and weak as Legend was also draining his powers at the time.

Eventually, Legend loosened his grip and Hades fell to the ground feeling hopeless.

He was down on his knees saying to Zeus "I am your brother".

"You cannot do this to me."

Zeus replied "Hades at the moment I cannot face you as I am too embarrassed to call you even my brother and own flesh and blood".

"So, this is what is going to happen".

As from this Zeus knew that he could never trust Hades again!

"You will now live here in the earth's core where you cannot harm anything or anyone.

But you will have powers to retrieve the dead as normal and if I ask of you to do something for me then you can rise temporarily to the top again and see the light".

"But for now, I have punished you and you will live here."

Zeus pointed his staff at Legend and there a white flash appeared as Legend's wings became feathered again and Hades said "Trust you to trick me, brother."

"Only you could fool me with anger in his breath"

Zeus replied "and that is why I am the god of all creatures and earth".

"Goodbye, brother."

Wait what has happened to Tremor?

"Is he dead?"

"Yes, he is but luckily we saved Knight from death."

"But thanks to you he cannot go with the others".

"He has to stay here and yet on the high grounds being the water guardian to the dead like you".

"Knights name now will be Kelp short for kelpie, which he will become soon when I get back to attend to him."

"He will live between the Scottish and Irish borders to do the duties that I now will request of him".

"Again, thanks to you Hades his veins and body now have tasted flesh and souls so he now has to be this creature."

Hades cried out and said 'no he cannot be I need him still, he is mine!"

"You cannot have him" and Hades was now sulking looking at the hot lava on the ground.

"No Hades you don't".

"You first need to look after Knightmare whom you also tortured through her mind to give her the love and care that she truly needs.

Otherwise, I will get Kelp to collect her and she will go to the heavens where she belongs."

"Understood, brother?'

Hades replied with defeat in his voice, "Agreed oh mighty one."

Zeus said "good!"

As he then climbed back on Legend and they flew back up to the surface.

Zeus then said, "I will be watching you"

"Hades from above no matter where you are."

As he then used his staff to seal the grounds up again and put a beautiful pink rose bush over it to make sure love only protrudes from it.

Zeus thanked Legend for his help before he said it was no problem as he seemed happier to know that his family will be ok for his past son's sake and then jumped back into the sky where he vanished into the clouds.

Zeus was back in Olympus calling Firefly with Aphrodite to where her brother was recovering still from his torment and becoming this nasty creature in disguise.

They all flew down to Knight and wondered if he had recovered properly yet.

Before Zeus could give him this new source of life!

For quite a long while the evil force was now dead when Zeus asked Knight to awaken and he got up being the most handsome bat-wing Unisos he had ever seen.

Zeus said "do you have the ability to swim in the sea?"

Firefly said "I do but Knight does not."

He said "ok" and then Zeus said a verse and now they all appeared standing at the Loch in Scotland where Kessy generally lives.

When they were there for thirty minutes, Zeus requested Firefly to carry her brother until he felt that he could fly again on his own which in minutes he did but he felt like he was not strong enough and landed head down into the Loch.

Firefly screamed out and said "Knight no" with fear in her eyes because she just got him back and now he was dead again as he landed in the freshwater.

Firefly was told to step back when Zeus said a Greek verse and put his staff into the waters of the Loch and a flash of blue light appeared with Knight's head sticking out of the freshwater.

But when he reached back onto the land he was wriggling like a snake as he came up to them slowly as his body had changed into a freshwater horse similar to Kessy but he was now another kind.

His large fin started from his head to his tail and he had sharp teeth with flipped front feet similar to the hippocampus and yet slightly different.

But still, a water horse, all the same, his coat was black with green in it for camouflage in the mucky waters.

Kelp then said "look I can swim and breathe in this water.

I am like you now."

He started to get excited but Zeus looked at him with sadness in his eyes.

He gradually walked back out of the water and appeared as not Unisos anymore but just a black horse that can if he needs to.

Zeus said "Knight I am sorry boy but this is the only way I can keep you alive."

"As I know that Hades had ill-treated you to hate and he also fed you on the dead, so you cannot be like the other mystical horses like your sister will be."

"But I have helped you become another kind to save you from death itself".

"At least this way, you have an occasional visit from your sister still and keep living like I promised your father a while ago."

Knight then walked up to his sister and said, "I have no horn and no wings anymore sister" feeling sad and different.

"I'm not the same as you feeling upset".

"How can you call me your brother when I am just a dead horse now?"

Firefly walked closer to her brother and put her face to his neck because of her horn and said, "no matter what shape or form you are you will always be my true blood brother" and they rubbed their heads to each other's necks.

Zeus then said "I am sorry Knight that I have taken your horn and wings away from you".

"But you did use them for bad without having control I know that it was not you controlling your body and mind at the time".

"But I still have to punish you in some way too".

"You will now work for me and alongside Hades when ask of you".

A kelpie is a water horse whose duties are going into creatures and future human dreams.

"And if they're bad they will come to you and drink from your waters where you then will be waiting for them to see you and follow you into the water where you will grab them from their skin and drag them to the bottom of the depths."

There you will suck out their souls which you will then deliver to Hades' pool.

"Do you understand, Knight?'

When eventually Kelp would appear again his build will change into a Clydesdale yet all black.

And if he had to make a proper presence then he would have the white on his feathered legs and face to show his good as well.

"Yes, your Grace I understand, thank you."

So that's how Knight had become a Kelpie and had the choice to live in the Scottish waters for now and when he was comfortable he could decide to broaden his horizons and could swim to the Irish waters instead.

For a year this carried on and then it was time for Firefly to go back to the ninth dimension as now she was old enough to mate and that's when she became Starlight of love the warrior of the Unisos of her new form.

Unisos warriors will travel all over the world now to help creatures and future humans by giving them the courage and belief to believe in themselves when they lose faith.

Chapter Fifty

Princess Helena Dreams Come True

Months had passed in the seas.

The next day everyone seemed a little dazed from a late night in the sea.

But they had to get up from their shell beds, as they had duties to attend to.

At the palace, Neptune called for his daughter to meet him in the throne room.

An hour later she appeared in front of the great sea god himself and smiled.

The night that they arrived home she nearly slipped up and told her secret about her hippocampus Louis as she told her father if she did win and truly believed in herself she would win the race soon.

That she would like a palace of her own somewhere on land and yet close to the sea too.

As she felt that she was meant to create a new type of kingdom using the power of Amethyst crystal skulls powers to achieve it.

But first of course she would need to have her father's permission as he is the sea god of the oceans and her king!

The following day came when they meet up again quickly for breakfast and spoke some more while eating shrimp and crab milk before they went to the stables to practice for the race soon.

They all practiced as hard as they could.

As Taylor had the experience of the race and its grounds and so taught Helena and Louis everything he knew.

Through doing this they spent a lot of time together and became very close without their parents knowing anything.

As before they bought back their hippocampus to the stables they would go for a beautiful swim on Taylor's great friend his beautiful pure white mantra ray that grew up with him when younger also, his guardian.

Everyone had a great time until that night it was the day before the race and Helena was becoming anxious and excited at the same time.

As she believed that she and Louis would win the race hands down.

And then she started dreaming about your kingdom??

The day of the race had come and everyone over the ocean completed it.

So far Tidal Wave and Neptune had never lost a race until possibly this day.

It was now afternoon when Taylor kindly helped Helena get Louis there rested for later.

They reach an Ocean called the Atlantic where they saw Great white sharks and their riders and large blue whales and even Mantra rays for their great speed in the deep sea too.

It was time to get ready when Helena heard everyone roaring and calling her father him highly and their Tidal Wave lifted his front legs of pride and neigh making bubbles above him.

Eventually, it was time for the race when first she and Louis were behind everyone and also had to watch carefully what another mer-folk did.

Later in the race, it seemed to be her and the king now.

She is rushing around to get ahead of others in the race.

She could see that the King and of course Tidal wave would not give up that quickly.

But of course she had a secret which no one knew about yet as she decided to not say anything, until they won race fair and square.

They reached the large cove which was the last bit of the race when Helena said to Louis "ok boy, it's time then instead of following her father's route they went their way and swam through small holes in the rocks and soon caught up with them."

Her father did not understand what just happened as Louis was back to his natural Hippocampus form again.

There they were head to head, having to dive through a Blue whale mouth's as part of the course wherein a flash they change again, and Neptune did not notice as he was concreting on himself and his sea steed at the time.

As Helena and her famous sea horse swam through all the holes in the hard-old rocks and pretty coloured reefs in his seahorse form when they were catching up with their father's before he changes quickly into his Hippocampus form again as they caught up with them to the end of the race.

But as he did this there in flash quickly reappeared Helena riding Louis to the finish line and her father could not believe his eyes that they had just beaten him like that.

When they reached the finish line everyone was shocked and cheered for Helena and Louis' victory of beating the fastest hippocampus known in the seas.

There she and her hippocampus were floating proudly in shock that they had just won the race and now the champions of the aquatic race until the next one.

Even though Helena was really happy she was thinking more about her dream of owning her own kingdom was about to come true.

She unstrapped herself from her shell saddle and wriggled off of Louis gently were one of the mer-men congratulated them both and gave her a beautiful reef all made of colourful seaweed for the steed of speed.

Where she thanked him by kissing his nose and putting the reef over his beautiful black scaled-arch neck gently, Louis then smiled his way and closed his eyes and said "my queen I could not have done it without you".

Helena smiled as Taylor swam up to her fast has she run into his arms and he returned the kiss from before as he said "Congratulations my Helena I knew that you both would win!"

She looked at him as he looked back at her and there was a deep emotional spark between the two of them.

That they felt deep attraction towards each other and yet thought this was not the time and place to share those feelings now.

So, she swoop out of his arms quickly and said thank you and went back to attend to Louis where she then takes him back to the stables there for the night to rest.

That day they all celebrated and had a great time and then it was time to go home before it became dark.

Her reward for winning the race was to pick the best racers from the heat.

So, she knew that she would not take tidal wave anyway from father.

So, she chose two dolphins to breed with her mothers in the future and for her she will be able to have a kingdom of her one day and she hoped that Taylor will be allowed to rule by her side when asking her parent's permission first in time.

But as she will be the queen of this kingdom it will be her rules so she can love anyone she thought.

Back at Vissen the next morning after a good rest for all Helena got up and could not wait to bump into Taylor again at the stables.

Before that she had to go to breakfast with the rest of her family as usual.

Neptune was sitting in his throne dolphin golden chair and looked at Helena thinking that isn't my daughter anymore and wondered if it was her or she had just grown up to fast for him to even notice as to much was going on, elsewhere he thought.

He smiled at her feeling so proud and she smiled back when he said

"My dear daughter I love you very much but before I can build your kingdom you first need to tell me how you beat me and Tidal Wave in the race?"

"Yes of course father."

"I will not just tell you but I will be happy to show you my secret."

Neptune was surprised of her answer and yet seemed excited like a young merman again and said "what?"

"Come, father do not panic" she said with happiness in her voice.

"I can honestly say we did not cheat".

"Please come to the stables with me as I need to show you something."

The mer-king agreed and swam with his daughter to the royal stables where she swam up to Louis and said "good morning champ".

"Sleep well?"

"I just need to show father how we beat him yesterday."

She opened up the stall and put on his sea bridle and saddle and told her father to saddle up Tidal Wave as well and go on a ride with her.

Neptune at this moment seemed quite confused but he went along with it to keep Helena happy.

They swam outside the gates when Helena told Louis to speed up and then whispered in his ear.

Suddenly he changed from a fabulous black and blue hippocampus to a small slim lined seahorse.

Neptune could not believe what he was seeing but there in front of him was an unusual type of seahorse which to him looked more like a dragon form so he called it a sea dragon instead "Helena said 'no father Louis is not a sea dragon"!

"He is known now as a sea horse in this form and Kessy whom you met at the battle with Tremor is his sister".

Mother has called her a water dragon knowing that she has four flippers/legs and the hippocampius has two legs and the seahorses like him have none in this form.

Neptune put his hand to his face as if he was questioning her answers.

But he began to understand what Helena had just said to him and praised his wife Sera for her achievements of creating these new and incredible creatures for his kingdom.

Either way, Louis was still an original hippocampus of Seequest's bloodlines his was now small and slim with no fins on his tail.

His tail curled up underneath him and his face turned slim too with a slight short snort and once he changed he showed her father that she where Louis could get through the smallest cracks in the reefs and rocks and dart through the sharks and whales safely too.

"Wow I never", he said to his daughter.

"You seem to have gotten another new species of our hippocampius and I believe if we could breed more like him then our people would survive the great battles of the sea much more."

"Father there is only one more like Louis and that is the white one it belongs to Taylor!"

His parents purchased her for his races from Mother a year ago.

"I am sorry they are both one of a kind."

Neptune seemed a little annoyed about that and yet knew that his wife was the one that bred Tidal Wave and Sea spray in the first place and hoped that she would repeat the mating again in a year's time and have a hippocampus/seahorse himself one day.

But he agreed that he was an extraordinary hippocampus and that Helena trained and rode him well and won the race properly to rules of the seas.

Neptune was just happy for her and agreed to sit down and discuss the plans for this kingdom of hers as he agreed that she did not cheat the race as all she did was use her and Louis' talent to their advantage to win fairly.

That afternoon they were putting Louis and Tidal wave back into their stables for a rest for the day.

Helena swam to the palace when she heard her mother was home again.

But first Neptune said I need to talk to your mother first about your reward then you can see her as much as you want"

Helena seemed annoyed and yet agreed as otherwise her father may change his mind about her dream and she did not want that to happen, she agreed to his wishes.

Hours had passed when she was called into the throne room and talked to about this reward of hers.

She was praying that her dream was going to come true and knew she had to be patient.

The high priestess of the Crystal Skulls was talking to her father about their duties when he said to his daughter.

"OK, daughter let's go and sit all together in the Temple of the Unicorn and discuss this matter further regarding your kingdom that you wish to build on land and sea."

After the last battle, the sea god could not thank his dear friend anymore and so they built a temple on his behalf where they also Helena can talk to him in time of need as it had been over six months since he moved on to the stars.

Helena smiled and said "oh yes father let's."

Queen Sera called her chariot of dolphins as they were waiting outside the palace.

They all swam gracefully inside together and rode to the Temple of the Unicorn.

As they approached Seequest's Temple there were two beautiful images of their friend one statue of him as the great hippocampus in gold and the other of him in his unicorn form standing beside the doors before they entered in silver.

They posed true life-like statues of Seequest once again as a hippocampus but the difference was that it had his silver horn embedded on its forehead.

As the agreement was always to give back his horn to Neptune again as he gave it to him so he could live in the sea like before.

So there the only real piece of Seequest left in its true form was his horn and that's why she could still contact him in the universe as it was part of his self and that's where his magic came from.

So now in this statue he is a unicorn hippocampus which he was in the last battle of his life in the sea and this was done one to protect the horn and two to give comfort to mostly Helena's loss of losing him to the stars.

They all kissed it and gave a blessing before they sat around the round table and spoke about Helena's future kingdom that she wanted to create and build.

Eventually, hours passed and they all agreed that the building that she spoke about would work as long there were rules that the mer-people would have to obey.

Helena agreed and promised that if their people did not obey the rules they would be punished by not being able to live there for a few months.

While if they continued to act naughty then they would be turned into sharks of the guardians of the sea as that was what Neptune did to his people and others like them when they were bad.

It took another year before all the preparation was ready and now the mermaid princess had to do was pick a sensible place for this kingdom to be built for the safety of her and her people who will live there.

So, another year and six months passed that Helena had been so patient and yet had not found the piece of land to build on yet.

As she was getting a little annoyed as she felt her life was wasting away as she had been with Mer- knight on the quiet for quite a while now.

On her twenty-first birthday she finds out from Taylor as his gift to her was that he was a true prince to another kingdom.

She was shocked at first and yet was overwhelmed that at last, they could be together the way she wanted them to be.

As he then told her that he truly loved her and wanted to be with her forever.

Prince Taylor surprised her again and took her on Ghost to a secret island that Neptune had named Santorini.

Yes, the battle was there in the past but it was on the other side of it.

Taylor saw this other side of the island and thought that it would be a perfect place for her kingdom to be built as it was not on complete land and it also was very close to the sea which was everywhere.

The island was in the middle of the actual sea it would be away from harm and Taylor knew then that Helena would love it as she could still be very close to her parents' kingdom which is at the bottom of the ocean where her kingdom would be.

He thought that he could not wait to take her there and show her to see her face light up with excitement again since the race.

She and her people can just dive in and become mer-people whenever they wanted to and they could still carry on their duties to the king and the sea.

Plus visit their friends and families who may be the ones who decided that they feel too scared to go there themselves.

As they were riding Ghost through the sea, Helena kept wondering what it was that Taylor wanted her to have or see so badly and could not wait to get wherever he was taking her.

An hour later they swam through the force field into the ocean of Santorini and they came to the surface.

The first thing Helena said was "my love why as you brought me here?"

"This was where I lost Seequest" and started to get upset and annoyed with him.

He said "my darling I have not brought you here."

"We need to swim to the other side of the island" with great confidence and understanding in his voice.

They dived back under with Ghost gracefully with his large flat body holding on for dear life as he was very fast.

Because they went past pods of bottle-nosed dolphins and beautiful fish of all shapes and sizes in their schools.

Eventually, Ghost rose again to the other part of the island when Helena saw just water and then said, "I am confused."

Then Prince Taylor said again "darling stop being impatient".

"You will see soon enough my love" and Ghost dived one last time until he rose again.

But this time appeared a large pretty green island in the middle of the sea.

Helena looked and felt like she had just seen the island from her dream which she did not know existed.

She just felt like it was her imagination only.

Taylor said, "My princess would you like to see more?"

She answered "oh yes please" with a massive smile on her face overwhelmed with excitement at the same time.

Ghost got as close as he could and luckily now Helena was a professional high priestess too.

She had her purple cloak of the power of the Amethyst crystal skull on her and said some words and there they both appeared as Piscean people as she did before.

First Taylor was falling all over the place and then got his grip and then they felt ready to jump off Ghost and step on the green grass.

Prince Taylor looked happy for Helena and yet felt like would really like this type of life with her.

As all his known was in the sea.

So, for him, this was a new adventure and experience too.

The prince felt a little odd at first and then he trusted Helena's instinct as he kept losing his balance and fall-ing over into the sea.

Helena and the ghost were laughing their heads off when Taylor was not amused by it all.

Eventually, he got the hang of it when they all smiled and the ghost carried on closer to the island for them to explore.

As Prince Taylor knew then that Helena would not let harm come to them and so he trusted her to approach with both feet this time.

Eventually, Ghost kindly swam away back into the sea and there they were both standing on this amazing island circle in the middle of no- where.

Taylor was to beginning to become acquainted with his legs and feet now.

So, they began to walk hand in hand Prince Taylor started to feel the grass tickling his feet but he also thought that it was soft and warm.

Then they sat down and looked up at the blue sky above them and then walked a little further and found a small beach on the right side of the island.

Helena said "oh wow Taylor you have made me the happiest princess alive as I do believe you are my knight and shining armour."

They both laughed together and Taylor could see in Helena's blue eyes which lit up and sparkled that she was the happiest she had been since they had lost Seequest in the battle.

They had spent most of the day here and Helena as it was her very special birthday would be expected to be home for the celebration.

So, she quickly jumped back into the sea where she said 'Taylor my love thank you".

"You have found our new home."

She was so delighted that she jumped out of the sea and did a somersault in the air and dived head-first straight back into the ocean in her mermaid form once again.

Within seconds she appeared once more and swam over to Taylor making lots of waves as she came and hugged him tight and looked into his blue eyes and said "Prince Taylor would you do the privilege of living in my new kingdom with me?"

Taylor answered "yes, of course, my queen," which made her feel like the luckiest mermaid princess alive.

Through her excitement, she could not wait to get back and tell Neptune that Taylor had found the perfect place and that her kingdom would work perfectly for their people as well.

That evening she went back and told her parents the news.

They could see she was so happy so they decided that she could show them this amazing place straight away and that is exactly what she did.

Helena; Taylor; Neptune and Queen Sera all rode back to this island in their gorgeous gold and silver dolphin chariots to this actual spot.

The dolphins brought the chariot out of the sea for her parents to see the island as close as they could for now.

King Neptune and her mother said, "Helena it's perfect as it's away from the land completely, and our people can still be mermaids/mermen as they please."

Helena agreed with what her parents had just said as she and Taylor felt the same way.

Helena was now very excited as now she thought that this was where her new dream kingdom will be built soon and her dream which she had been dreaming of for a long time was becoming her reality.

First Neptune looked up above and called for his brother Zeus and asked for his permission as all the lands belonging to the mighty Zeus.

"Zeus, dear brother, I call on you now."

"My daughter Helena has won the Aquatic Race of the Sea and her prize is to build a kingdom on your land and live still in the sea."

"She is now twenty-one and a fully trained high priestess".

"I ask for your permission and blessing that my daughter can have this bit of land here around my land too and she promises to look after it and treat it well".

"Where the creatures that live on it too, what do you think, oh, mighty one?"

Some clouds appeared in Zeus' image who replied "my brother I understand and I congratulate her many accomplishments so I believe that I am happy and give you my blessing that you may have my island of Santorini."

"Use it wisely, my child."

She replied, "Oh, the great god of them all I will with all my heart I promise you that."

'Then Queen Sera you may use your magic and do what you have to do to make this happen."

Neptune said, "thank you Zeus for your blessing as I believe my daughter will do and create great things here and bring peace to the creatures here too."

"Yes, that is why I am allowing this one time only as a trial to something that I wish to create myself in time."

So, watching Helena's kingdom will show me if my idea will work soon for a permanent life.

"But time will tell".

For now, enjoy your new life, Helena, as I will be watching very closely.'

"I would be honoured, your Grace".

"Thank you again," when he vanished.

Next, Neptune and Sera looked at each other and Neptune said, "My darling, it is time to show us what your magic can do."

She nodded and smiled.

Helena then smiled at her mother too while she watched her mother with compassion create this beautiful kingdom of hers from scratch right in front of her.

Queen Sera opened up her beautiful white silk bag.

Inside was Seequest's horn as a surprise to Helena.

Neptune said, "my dear Seequest, I know that you can hear me and I ask of you, please, would you let us use your magical powers to help Queen Sera create and build my dear friend's kingdom?"

An answer came through the wind saying that he was happy for her and gave them his blessing to use his horn with great love and happiness towards them all.

Queen Sera was holding it gently in her hands when Seequest's silver horn sparkled so bright of great light and then toned down quickly again before she passed it onto her daughter to use next.

Queen Sera says "Helena all you need to do is hold the horn and see in your mind's eye the beauty and love that you want to build for the kingdom; yourself and our people."

It was the first time in her life that she felt Seequest's presence through the horn, as before it was placed at the Unicorn Temple since he left Earth.

Helena had ever held Seequest's horn and at first, it broke her heart and then in her mind, she heard his voice saying to her,

"Princess, use my horn to create the kingdom of your dreams, my child".

Then she held the horn tightly as she felt his loving energy gently in her hands which gave her great warmth to her skin as well.

Knowing it bought back a good memory of her great friend who has given her his blessing to let her build her kingdom through the magic he left behind.

She waved the horn around and said a verse as it turned blue and then she heard again Seequest's voice saying "point my horn right at the land where you would like your kingdom to be"

There are seconds it began to create itself right in front of you it will appear.

Neptune was overwhelmed and said "make sure that it is for your highest good."

"Yes, it is father, I understand and it is" she replied.

She was holding the horn in her hands while she was visualizing her dream and seeing it in her mind.

The horn turned a deep sapphire blue and there as she pointed it at the land.

The beautiful mystical kingdom magically started to appear and build gradually through her very hands.

Prince Taylor and her parents were watching with great happiness and sadness as they then knew that Helena will not be living with them anymore as their daughter because she is a fully-grown mermaid Princess with a difference.

Within a few hours, the whole kingdom was built.

It was stunning of gold and silver everywhere with statues of her family around it, a Crystal Temple for the Amethyst Crystal skull to go in, and another one of Seequest's Temple of her own, which is based in her palace itself for its safety.

Her kingdom was smaller than her fathers of course.

The mer- princess kingdom was perfect as then she pointed the horn at herself and there she appeared not as a mermaid princess anymore but a Piscean Queen!

She was still a mermaid on the inside but now on the outside, she looked more humanlike.

She looked beautiful, all dressed in a pretty purple and white dress with a purple cloak wearing an amethyst crystal crown with a uni-hippocampus on it for her to wear as a true queen Seequest saw her be.

There appeared as well a long stunning silver staff that had the amethyst stone sitting on the top of it and inside the actual stone was a unicorn image of Seequest as the Unicorn King he once was.

Helena looked at the staff and said thank you to Seequest and her parents for the perfect twenty-first birthday gift that she could ever love or want.

Through the power of the amethyst skull, she put her staff onto the sea surface and there she could walk on it for a while, seeing her dream kingdom real as she pinches herself.

Helena then pointed her staff at the end of the land to the part where the sea meets and there she created steps inside the salt water so she and the mer-folk can come straight up to the land easily and safely.

When they reach the surface where their heads will come out of the water and their bodies will automatically change into Piscean form.

So, her people then can experience themselves sitting on a beach to adjust to their new bodies and then walk to the kingdom to see Queen Helena and Prince Taylor's new home.

Her parents and Taylor used the stairs that she had just created and walked from the bottom of the sea up them as they built themselves at the same time.

She had created them magically as the steps will disappear so no one else will be able to come to her kingdom without checking with Neptune first, as after all they are truly his people and there were rules to be obeyed.

Last she walked around and could not believe her eyes that the kingdom of her dreams was now built in front of her and Taylor and her to live in happily ever after there.

There her Piscean man was more handsome than before wearing his colors of green and white.

Then there was Neptune wearing a handsome aquamarine blue robe with a darker blue cloak and gold sandals.

Using his trident, he banged it gently on the floor where it sparkled aquamarine blue which then made the kingdom glisten beautifully as if the sea was shining on it too.

Beside him stood his wife and Helena's mother Queen Sera and high sorceress now as the high priestess due to her powers connected to the purple crystal skull.

There she was standing looking quite beautiful with her blonde hair and fair complexion and enlightened blue eyes wearing a silver and white dress showing her legs in her gown as well as a cloak with the emblem of the moon on it.

Sera was wearing her crown holding her staff which had the moon and stars engraved all over it, as a gift from her mother on her twenty-first birthday in the past.

They could not believe how pretty her kingdom was and how proud they were of their daughter that day.

As they then knew that she will be happy and a great queen to this new life of hers and that she will enjoy her new home with their people in a different way.

They all reached the enormous silver and purple gates with hippocampus on them in a circle one going upwards and the other looking downwards and on top of the towers beside them.

Were a tall statue of hippocampus and unicorn as guardians too as gifts from Seequest as a special blessing of protection always to her and her Kingdom!

Her emblem of the two hippocampi was the one facing upwards regarding living on land and the one facing downwards was of living in the sea.

That is why they were facing different ways of representing her as now Queen Piscean being human-like and still a Princess mer-maid too.

It was her mother's turn to give Helena a gift and she also used her moonstone staff it put an invisible force field of moon dust on the whole land and Kingdom protecting it from harm and even if Zeus' creatures come there they will be safe too.

Eventually, Seequest's horn stopped glowing so she gave it back to her mother to put into her special bag for safekeeping, as it must go back to the proper Unicorn Temple in the sea to prevent it from getting into the wrong hands of Hades.

Has remembered he is still around but just living in the deeper part of the Earth's core now.

They all walked further into the city and there on the outside were the round huts with square windows and doors for the Pisceans' homes when they stayed on land.

As they walked through the city she created market-places where mer-folk would trade some of the land goods for the sea goods.

Doing this will create a perfect balance between both worlds on earth.

Reaching her palace there was an image of a mermaid Queen and a Piscean Queen as well.

Helena said "that is how I will be known from now on."

Because she was accepting herself of been two different beings.

Her parents kindly asked her why she picked two sea horses as her emblem instead of the dolphins and she said "because they both represent me first looking up above the sea and by looking at the sky".

"They will represent being on land and the other facing down living still as a mer-princess in the sea" they smiled thinking it was a great idea.

Neptune and Sera were so proud of their daughter.

Neptune said joking with her "well actually the top seahorse could be your feminine side from your mother who comes from the beautiful moon and stars and the one looking down is your masculine side from me the god of the sea."

They all laughed and Helena replied "father I love that idea too."

"I shall call my kingdom Piscean after myself and my parents."

Everyone seemed to love the name.

Her father replied "I have one more thing for you to keep you safe and that is a surprise."

He called with his conch shell that he had in his pocket making a quiet noise.

There appeared in the distance a hundred mer-knights who had already agreed to be her guardians on behalf of their king and queen of the sea.

"Oh Father thank you".

"Well, I know that you can look after yourself greatly".

"That you are still my beloved daughter and I want you to know that when I do not see you often that you are completely safe at all times."

Helena replied "I totally understand and I will treat them well as my knights,"

She pointed her staff at them and their clothes changed to purple and silver instead of aquamarine and white her father's colours with her hippocampus emblem on them too.

Her dream was now real and all she had to do was to live happily with her prince.

Or that is what she hoped to do.

Has thought to herself maybe I will have children soon when she was ready.

But for now, she was very happy because she had her beloved prince; kingdom, and city of dreams.

Once again, they were walking around her palace which had beautiful views of the island all around it.

It was spectacular and very magical indeed.

Through the magic of Seequest's horn as well in a part of the land in the back of the palace was a garden that was growing quickly with silver birch trees and plants that produced lovely fruits and vegetables for her and the Piscean people to eat as well as their fish food too.

Has a memory too of when she was last with her dear Seequest and was alive and having fun together, it was like when the unicorns created and grew them for earth themselves again in the past.

She felt she had their blessing as well as having the magic herself now.

Wow, Helena did not realize how lucky she was until today.

Helena said that she was grateful to every one of her family, Seequest and Zeus with his family above for their help and protection too.

The last thing she asked was have permission for Neptune's people to come and see if they would like to experience their world from a different angle.

She said "now father would you kindly ask our people who would like to share this kingdom with me?"

Neptune said "yes of course daughter we shall tell them all about today after dinner at your birthday celebration."

Helena and Taylor looked at each other and she ran to him and kissed him in front of her parents where her father then said Prince Taylor "I believe you will be living here with my daughter?"

"I expect you to treat her as your queen?"

Taylor looked at Helena and said back to Neptune "your Highness I love your daughter very much and I would like her to be my wife one day" with great happiness in his tone of voice.

"Yes of course I shall always worship and honour her as my queen and I also will protect her with my life."

Neptune and Queen Sera looked at each other and smiled and they nodded and went to hug their daughter as they were happy with his answer.

They all decided it was starting to get dark and saw Luna the moon showing her image inside it as she spoke and said "happy twenty-first, my dear Helena."

She looked up and said, "thank you, Grandmother," and then she wondered if it was safe to leave her new home.

Luna said, "I shall watch it for you while are gone."

Helen thanked her greatly and said their goodbyes for now.

They walked back to the end of the land where they walked down the stairs as they appeared and when they left them they would disappear again straight after as created.

They reached the bottom of the ocean floor where the dolphin chariots were waiting to take them back to Vissen to celebrate Helena's Twenty-first Birthday properly.

Reaching Vissen they all rested and then got ready for Helena's big celebration of her life, as they were not just going to mention her birthday to their people but now about her own home and kingdom too.

Helena thought that everything that had happened that day was a complete dream and that she had to pinch herself again to know it was real.

Even though she wanted to be with her parents and her family and people, she knew then that her Piscean kingdom was her true home and couldn't wait to get back there again.

As she swam to the top of the sea and looked at the stars seeing Seequest and Legends stars in the difference twinkling back at her.

Helena could not believe that she had truly now her kingdom that she designed from her amazing imagination.

Later they all dressed up for dinner.

Neptune called his mer-guards to call on his people and meet them later in the middle of the kingdom called Neptune's Circle where all the celebrations took place.

That evening everyone was having great fun with their families when Neptune announced that she now a fully trained and qualified high priestess who now shall be called Amethyst at the temples when she's working there and that when she was home in Vissen as well.

She will be classed still as his daughter and also known as Amethyst as well.

But instead of stopping there he then said 'my mer-people of Vissen I have asked you to come here today not only to celebrate your Princess of many other titles now.

"But I have something more wonderful and out of this world to ask you all."

The poor mer-people at this time looked worried when Neptune said 'Please it's a great thing I am going to ask you!"

"But you do not have to unless you want to?"

Now the mer-folk was confused and then he said 'look my daughter Helena has created her kingdom through the gift of the great Seequest's' horn and her powers of the Amethyst crystal skull.

"Has now our high priestess as the power of the crystal skull and with it."

"She has created a great kingdom of her own which is safe for you and your families to go and experience for yourselves of a great adventure on land and yet still be with your kind as well."

"Now if anyone wants to go from here or request a visit then you must come and see your princess personally later tonight after the party"

"But not known as Helena anymore but as Queen Helena of the Piscean Kingdom."

Everyone looked at each other puzzled as they all went silent for a while and looked at each other.

Then Neptune knocked on his staff and it got everyone's attention and then they all realized it was not a joke, their king was serious!

The mer-folk then all started to cheer saying "here's to the reign of our new queen on land and sea"

"Here's to Queen Helena, long live our Piscean Queen."

Helena was so delighted she said "thank you to their people."

Helena shouted out "as my father mentioned earlier if you do wish to come to my island and stay for a while you will need to approach my special stairs which will appear and as you do your tails will produce legs and you will then be able to breathe and live on land as well as the sea for as long as you would like."

After the party loads of their people came to them both and put their names down and they mentioned the rules that were in the place that they had to be obeyed at all times.

They then told them about the opportunity of experiencing a once-in-a-lifetime deal of being able to live on land and sea at the same time anytime they wished.

The high priestess then said to their people that this only applied to the ones that always obeyed the rules in Neptune's kingdom before.

Everyone seemed scared at the idea until the sea god used his trident and banged it a few more times and there appeared an image of his Daughter's new kingdom her Piscean Kingdom of Dreams.

Everyone at first could not believe what they had just heard about and then they could not believe either what they saw next.

Others felt like it was betraying Neptune's rules and abandoning their king and his kingdom as well.

But it was not as then Neptune mentioned that he helped her build this and that it was one hundred per cent for his people as well as his daughter to live there on land.

Because there was a special force field so they could breathe out of the water and this island was like a floating island as no other creature could reach it.

Neptune said that he gave it his blessing and now Queen Helena will rule her kingdom.

Also, that evening high priestess was crowned by surprise in the circle with her throne made of pure silver with two rearing unicorns rearing beside her on the tops of the throne.

It was stunning and her father said "Please daughter sit here then her mother came with a smile holding an unusual crown."

The crown was made of all her birthstone crystals and in the middle was the purple stone.

It was an absolute delight to see.

Their Helena was all dressed in her silver and purple dress and silkweed cloak and now she had this beautiful crown too.

She sat on this amazing throne not believing it was real till she touched it.

When Neptune said "I call on my mer-folk of our land of the seas to bless and protect the new Queen of Piscean.

Please always protect her and our people and also may she reign with great happiness and health too"

Next Queen Helena is there thanking her father and mother and then stands gracefully saying "thank you the mer-folk of Vissen and now my kingdom too.

"I will not fail you, I promise!"

Her parents smiled with pride when they both shouted out "Oh reign Queen Helena and her Piscean kingdom of land and sea" with great warmth in their voices as they said it.

Next, the mer-folk repeated to Helena "here's to our new Queen Helena long live our queen of the kingdom Piscean"

After this was mentioned loads of mer-folk wanted to experience it for themselves and months on end it was a hit and everyone was very happy for a while.

Chapter Fifty-One

Piscean, Helena's Kingdom

Queen Helena and Prince Taylor was living in her home for six months now when one afternoon up in her palace the prince approached her and got down on his knee and asked her to marry him and she said yes.

They could not wait to tell their parents so they first danced on the sand and then ran quickly to the stairs of the sea and ran down them as fast they could until they jumped off through excitement and turned into grand mer-folk as before.

They swam off to collect their hippocampius's, even though she loved Louis as he seemed to not settle away from home being away from the stables of his family.

So, they decided instead to keep him there in the sea where he belonged but she did miss him very much and he missed her too at times, as she got used to walking on land, more than swimming in the sea now more than he hoped her to.

Zeus had been watching for quite a while now and thought this may be an idea that he too will possibly use to create us humans in the big future.

They reached the stables and collected the seahorses ready to swim as fast they could first to see Prince Taylors' parents on the other side of the world.

They were delighted and then the next day they went back to Neptune's palace and told her parents the great news.

Neptune and Sera were delighted and yet sad as they know that she will want to live on land more than the sea in her domain.

The mer-people were loving the idea of having feet and experiencing walking; running; dancing and touching the gorgeous golden grain which was called sand and yet realized that in the sunshine it was too hot for them to step on for long.

So, they thought maybe her people should walk on the sands at night so then they can enjoy it more.

Also, they liked the idea of eating fruits and vegetables instead of just eating seaweed and fish all the time knowing that it was very good for them.

The high priestess Helena also asked Pegasus to kindly help her create pools and baths which had salt water to make her people still feel like they were at home which she had collected from the sea itself.

But it was not allowed to use the seawater in the king-dom as it belonged to the sea only.

When a mermaid or merman came and stayed at Piscean Kingdom that is what the form was called Piscean woman due to them being thought of highly in their form and there was Piscean man.

It also worked from the amethyst crystal skull and sea horse's energies.

The crest she chose to represent her kingdom and pal-ace was two water horses looking in opposite direc-tions to each other which were connected to a beau-tiful piece of jade green seaweed silk.

One was sapphire and silver and the other was Aquamarine and silver.

The green Emeralds were for her land, the sapphire and silver for the sky and Aqua blue and silver were for the sea.

The actual crest represented herself and Prince Taylor for their feminine and masculine form as mer-people and Pisceans now too.

It represented: peace; healing; joy; love; helping; spiri-tuality and creativity.

When the mer-folk visited the kingdom, they wore pretty short dresses and shorts that had the emblem on them so they knew they had permission to visit there in the colours of their Queen and King flag.

And if anyone broke the law they would possibly be turned into dolphins if they were intelligent or sharks if not that creative or clever with their hands like trades folk, who then became guardians of her land and seas too.

Because if they disobeyed the rules they then would be turned into sharks and be under control at all times of Neptune himself.

The Piscean Kingdom and the queen were liked and adored for many years now.

Queen Helena had made the land spectacular as it had many gorgeous salt waterfalls, so it was safe for the Pisceans to still bathe and swim in without actually going back into the sea and becoming a mer-people again for a while.

Everyone loved Piscean.

The mer-folk believed it was a land of dreams and in the future for years it did trades across the world also there.

The time was getting closer as Queen Helena was getting excited as she will be marrying the mer-man of her dreams soon and could not wait for that day to come.

It was spring once more when Queen Helena had been waiting a long time to marry her prince charming.

Her wedding day had come and she was so excited.

She wore a beautiful pure white dress that her grand-mother created for her special day from the energy of the moon itself and it shone just as bright as it with of course a perfect crown to match it of silver and her stones.

She decided that she wanted the ceremony to be at sunset when her grandmother can watch and join in too as that is when the moon is getting ready to appear for the night.

Now the sun had set and Apollo had just made his sun horses move it over to the other side of the world.

There her grandmother was watching from afar.

In the sea around them were the dolphins and whales flapping their tales making a wedding tune for her to ride to who were so happy for her as they are all great friends and she was their guardian once.

Then her parents appeared on land with a difference as for the day Neptune had brought up Tidal Wave and Sea spray to help Louis pull Helena's chariot as originally, she stayed at home in Vissen for the night like tradition.

King Taylor did the same who stayed in his quarters like when they first met nearly two years before.

The mer-folk came out of their homes to cheer her on and the sea creatures too.

They approached the Vissen gates where the mer-guards bowed to her and the royal highnesses and opened the gates where they all swam to Santorini which was two hours away from Neptune's kingdom in Athens, Greece.

In Santorini, King Taylor's manta ray Ghost had carried him all the way.

The mer-king swam with his faithful friend and patted him gently on his head and he swam to the other side of the island where he would not be seen until it was time to do so.

Ghost arrived and let his master jump off gently before he swam away and dived elegantly while Taylor started to swim to the stairs where there was a glow of light which was embedded to the stairs of Seequest's horn for the power to change into a Piscean man again.

As he reached the top Taylor saw a form waiting at the back of the entrance.

The hippocampius's now water horses for Helena's special day were there with a complete difference as they seemed to be happy on land with four legs instead of two and tail out of water for a while.

But they were drinking the water from the sea and the stable hands were there keeping them wet with the sea water too which keep them from drying out and their special coats were put over them until the next surprise was ready from her mother later.

As Louis was not a fan of the land and because of this he used to dry out more than the others.

But his parents did not mind the land.

But do remember that Moonbeam was a land creature.

Where Sea spray and Tidal wave his parents live mainly in the water all the time.

Queen Sera had made white roses grow around the land and surrounded Helena's kingdom and the blue moon rose ones did too represent herself.

Now the Piscean Kingdom itself as part of the unicorns' purity and part of Helena's actual home Vissen in the sea.

There the water horses were Tidal Wave and Sea spray as pure white glistening with their blue tones running through watery manes.

There in the front was Louis as his dashing black handsome self as he too had matured into a stunning stallion of the sea like his father.

There they were wearing purple and aqua-blue fluffy feathers in their head collars and the chariot was made of pure white mother of pearl for the day.

Helena first looked at her sweet friend looking so beautiful and she hugged him.

Has he said in her mind "my queen you look so divine" through their minds.

She smiled and kissed him on his nose and then came over and said hello and stroked the others and patted their neck too before they all climbed in and started to trot elegantly towards Helena's home to Seequest's Temple where she was going to be married by her own mother knowing that she's a powerful queen of the seas and sky.

The Piscean gates opened where Helena's guards were standing there proudly bowing as she came through and they said "your Majesties" and they all smiled.

Helena felt that she was on cloud nine and that she was the luckiest Piscean/ mer-queen that had ever lived on this actual day.

Then they reached Seequest's Temple.

It was night now.

The roof was open for him to watch as well from afar.

Helena was so pleased that she decided to get married in her own Kingdom of Dreams.

The water horses of solid colours stopped beautifully and Queen Sera got out first and said "I shall get everything ready."

Has walked into the temple where she had a surprise for Helena later and could not wait for her to see and know about it.

But she knew that she had to marry them first and just kept smiling at her daughter.

While they were still outside waiting to come in when told too.

In the Unicorn Temple Queen Sera opened up the roof so that her mother Luna; Seequest; Legend, Celestial with Pegasus and the mystical horses all could look on from above.

And be part of this wonderful and miraculous night!

The moon appeared as bright as the day when it shone the whole room with bright white light, magical.

Sera also welcomed the forest animals and the white wolf and his pack too as after all he did save her daughter from Hades in the end.

Second it was her father's turn and he turned around to help her get out of the chariot in her stunning dress and smiled and said, "My darling daughter look at you how much you have changed since these last two years."

Queen Helena looked at her father who was preparing to talk to her and said "are you ready my darling?"

When he looked hard for a few seconds and then knew this was for the last time she would be classed as his little mermaid.

"Believe me daughter you are ready for this adventure of yours to truly begin with great joy on his face."

Neptune's eyes started to tear up with happiness as he felt it for her.

Helena smiled and wiped his tears.

When she stopped in her tracks and heard Seequest's voice and he said "oh how I have missed you and hope that you have a destiny like me?"

"I am so proud of what you have achieved so far my dear Helena he said in her mind" as she looked up to his star shining above her that special night.

Helena was shocked to hear Seequest's voice on her special day that tears were falling down her face onto her dress.

Luckily, she had a piece of seaweed silk cloth that she used to dry them with and said back "my dear Seequest I am so pleased that you kindly came here today for me in spirit."

"But it would be great to see you face to face one day but for now this is enough."

"Thank you, my dear sweet friend."

Seequest answered back "you're more than welcome my queen of Piscean."

There at Seequest's Temple, she felt his stars shining straight on top of it.

It shone with pure silver everywhere for her night and the purple was there to being the high priestess of the amethyst crystal skull.

There he was handsome with blonde hair and striking blue eyes still.

The doors opened for Queen Helena to see all her people queuing inside who now live in her kingdom with her and then she walked past them as they bowed and curtsied to her and the sea king.

There was a second door and this time with her beautiful now purple hair because of the powers that she used all the time there she was walking gracefully with her father holding her arm coming towards her prince charming and yet also her king too.

When she quickly waved her hand over her crown and there appeared gorgeous black hair again.

Neptune walked once again in with Helena in his arms calmly walking up to King Taylor looking so handsome and glam.

Helena smiled and kissed her father on the cheek as a thank you and then slowly walked and stood beside Taylor, feeling excited and yet scared as well.

There Queen Helena was standing looking as gorgeous as ever with her beautiful long black hair wrapped elegantly to her head with a new silver crown on.

Her dress was fitted to her divine body with enough room to still move as she wanted it to which made her dress and figure look like she was a mer-queen with legs though instead.

The colour of her dress was white with silk ribbon from the silkworms that the butterflies kindly gave her as a gift for her wedding day and she wore pretty blue shell shoes with a court heel.

Her skin was like porcelain as always with her pretty rosy lips to finish.

Taylor knew that this will be a completely new life that is now beginning and at this time and Queen Helena was part of it which he felt loved and blessed about.

King Taylor looked at his true bride-to-be and had to rub his eyes to make sure that he too was not dreaming.

He felt that he did not just meet a mermaid princess that he was bestowed to before even meeting each other in the past.

But the most beautiful and powerful mer-princess now queen that he had ever laid his eyes on.

They both got glanced at each other before the ceremony began.

Zeus appeared and said his part.

We are here today to celebrate a new life for these two kingdoms to become one on land and sea.

"Will you Prince Taylor of the British Isles take princess Helena of Vissen of Greece to be your true queen and beloved partner forever?"

Taylor replied, "Yes I do."

Great Zeus looked at now queen Helena and said "and you daughter of the great Neptune himself do you take Prince Taylor to be your true king and partner forever?"

"Yes I do."

"Brilliant", Zeus said.

You first must say these with me now together as partners in the soul.

Helena and Taylor did exactly what Zeus asked them to do before Sera could continue on so they said, 'we will hand our rings eventually to each other to always remember that we are loved and bestowed to each other and to never hurt each other in our lives together as one.'

And Taylor now is a true king with you in your kingdom as well.

"God bless you both"

Zeus replied "perfect, and congratulations from me and the others above".

We give blessings of love and light always to you both and your beautiful kingdoms here and under the sea and it is done.

Zeus then said "thank you for your time tonight" and then he was gone once again for Helena to get married to her prince at last by now the sea gods of her people.

But before they did Zeus said "oh I give you also a gift as a wedding present to you both the full land of Santorini, not just the bit that you have but all it as well is now yours"

"So, use the trees nicely by talking to them and they will grow your beautiful flowers and fruits please respect the animals and Gaia herself and they will help you in return.

If you do this for me then it is all yours."

"Yes, your Highness I will."

"Thank you so much" and she blew a kiss up towards him showing her gratitude and love for her beloved uncle Zeus as well as the god of all living things.

Zeus shone his great golden light on Sera and said "your highness it is my honor to have you wed your daughter from my lands to now yours of the ocean."

"Dear Sera it is your turn to wed them in the eyes of your seas."

She closed her eyes and bowed to him with great respect and replied "the honour is ours oh mighty one thank you" when he then smiled and disappeared, while the others were still watching the second part of the ceremony in the distance.

Queen Helena wanted to be married in her own kingdom that first Zeus had to marry them as he owns and rules the lands of earth.

Neptune rules the sea on earth.

Half an hour in them were both speaking their proper vows which they wrote themselves to each other in their mer-folk language?

That sounded like this "we will be faithful and true to each other as long as we both shall live," then she puts on the ring on King Taylor's left wedding finger it was emerald.

This time queen Helena's stones were instead of aquamarine the stone was turquoise which was her actual birthstone as her birthday was the cusp of Sagittarius as well as Scorpio.

He puts on her beautiful ring on her left hand, her wedding finger too.

Once the ceremony was done they were married by Zeus god of the lands and also the goddess of the seas too as she now belonged to both.

After the ceremony had ended everyone came and congratulated the pair and they all went on the way.

Queen Sera then said, ok then I now can pronounce you both as husband and wife you may kiss your bride.

Both Helena and Taylor looked at each other and kissed as she pulled slightly away to look at each other closely in each other's eyes showing the great love that they fell deep from within.

Everyone cheered and celebrated as they looked up in the sky and in the night, she could see Seequests star shone brightly above them and sparkling in and out as he was cheering for them from a far at this time with Legends and the others too.

Helena looked up and said in her mind "thank you" as she loved him and missed Seequest greatly.

Also thanked him for the life that she had now and knew that if it was not for him it would have probably never happened.

Around the kingdom, in the sea, you could hear the Dolphins and Whales making noises and jumping up and down in the sea showing great happiness and celebration for their friend's freedom.

But Queen Helena and King Taylor walked to the back of the temple to see her parents and went into their chariots to the palace for further celebration there.

The king and queen got into their beautiful chariot of gold covered in shells of the sea.

It was pulled by Sea spray and Tidal Waves and in front.

And there the last surprise was that Queen Sera had trained Louis to pull a chariot of silver just for this night and beside him was Moonstone king Taylor's water horse.

They looked amazing in her purple and silver bridles and sea harnesses and for an extra special touch on their head collars, there were copies of Seequest's horn lying on their foreheads through their seaweed bridles.

As a special gift, her father made her a small gift of Seequest's horn into a shell that she could touch and hold when she wanted to feel him still near her.

And through magic, they changed the sea chariot into a carriage with wheels and the seahorses had changed to the proper form.

They looked all perfect

Then as it was the darkest of all nights, Luna made the dolphins and the whales of all kinds squirt water and make water displays which she also added to make them shine and glow higher in the air.

How spectacular it was for everyone to experience and see.

They're all around them were the Vissen people who were watching from the seas as well.

The party went on all night them watching Helena's favorite mermaids who were called Phoebe and Honey they were amazing acrobats in the sea and now on land too, which to us are called today as gymnastics.

Everyone was delighted with the young mermaid's great performance with true skills which also later involved dancing too, where the Queen even joined in having an amazing time with her friends and family as she was happy for all the right reasons at last.

After the great celebration at her palace with every-one it was time to send everyone back home and the palace became over-quiet which she seemed to love at times as she got used to walking on land more than the sea now!

And sometimes she just loved listening to the lovely birds in the sky.

It was time to go and rest in the palace quarters as everyone had gone home now and there in the dis-tance she felt a presence and only for a minute she saw Legend and Seequest galloping in the sky.

As they did the sky sparkled like diamonds shining from above.

Stardust from them landed on her where she felt their love and they both said "this dust that you now possess will always keep you safe from harm".

"No one can hurt you in any way as you are highly protected by us all now too."

They made a heart of stars in the night sky and then they were gone to their stars where they shone brightly for the last time that night.

From that day Helena thought that because of the amazing idea from her parents of having Seequest's horn on her water horses' or hippocampi's head collars, she made it part of her kingdom bridle wear if they came across any horses She thought?

As to her, it was her way of knowing that Seequest will still be with her always.

The mermaid queen was speechless and said, 'Oh thank you, everyone.

"I love you so much."

They all replied with neighs and said telepathically that they loved her too.

Helena was so overwhelmed that she began to cry with great happiness that her life had changed in one way for the better since Seequest left.

But she felt guilty as she also missed him around her and deep in her heart she knew that it was his way of still being with her on this special night and always from now on.

Now they had been married for another six months when it was autumn.

They were happy with their lives together and living on their island too.

But, of course, they were so glad that they could be able to jump and enjoy their original selves, which was a complete delight as well which sometimes they missed with their hippocampus's Louis and Moonstone.

As they agreed that the hippocampi should stay in Vissen.

Queen Helena's parents could ride them and also Neptune could borrow Louis for the next aquatic race in another two years' time.

So, everyone was very happy.

One day she was thinking if she was prepared to have children and she was so excited but she was also scared of one.

What form would they be in or would they try both ways as Pisceans or their traditional way in the sea?

That is a secret that they will only know.

Helena was also thinking that she missed riding her hippocampus Louis and remembered her great adventures of riding Seequest when she was younger on the land and missed that.

Helena also wondered what happened to his daughter then known as Firefly who now is Starlight to the mystical horses of the universe.

She spoke to Seequest the night before with her roof open looking at his stars wondering if she would ever get that chance again to ride on land.

When she thanked him for listening to this time he did not answer his stars just glowed above her in the moonlight.

She then shut the roof and locked the doors and walked back to the beautiful palace which was lit up with purple lights all around it.

There she saw her husband and they sat together for a while and went to their chambers to sleep.

The next morning came.

Queen Helena woke up in her proper bed and from her window she thought she heard horses neighing in the distance.

Helena thought that it was her imagination playing tricks on her as she used to dream a lot of her memories with her horse friends and dreamt and hoped that one day, maybe some of Seequest's progeny will come and visit her.

And possibly want to stay and let her ride around her lands again?

She got up and rushed to her doors and opened them to see her guards and asked what the noise was.

They told her that there was a herd of horses wanting to get to her land and that they were making terrible noises.

She told the guards "well if that is what they are doing put the bridge down," which she created for herself if she wanted to visit her forest friends which she did at the time.

But it took a lot out of her as she had to walk quite a distance to see them.

So, she cut the visits down as it was too much for her to travel all the time and exhausting.

That's when she thought maybe Seequest's horses may return to the land where she originally met them when she was sixteen.

She heard the noises again she quickly rushed back to the quarters washed and got herself properly dressed in her scaled purple and silver trousers and top and boots and ran out of her yard to see.

By this time her guards had out down the bridge and opened up the gates where the horses came running in as fast as they could go!

Helena reached the pathway towards the bridge when all she could see in the distance were loads of different shapes and sizes of these beautiful horses.

She ran to the courtyard where they stopped in front of her.

There were another two surprises.

The main two were a stunning white mare and her stallion black like his father a Friesian type powerful.

The mare was the leader of the herd, and her stallion was the protector of it.

Helena called Taylor to come quickly which he did and there he saw this herd of beautiful horses that were related to the late Seequest the Unicorn King and her friends.

They neighed and bowed at Taylor and Louis believed that he had to climb onto the black one while the pure white mare waited as that one was for Helena to ride.

It felt strange and yet good as the palace was quite a distance from the Pisceans' homes and village.

Everyone cheered as he went.

They're from all the horses appeared a pretty pure white Arabian type mare approached smiling through her eyes at Helena and she neighed and said to her in her mind, "my queen I am a gift to you from the great Seequest.

I will be your companion up here on land and Bracken is for you to ride in the sea."

Please ride with me today and let me carry you with the dignity that you deserve for helping me and others keep away from harm in the past.

"Let me be the one to carry you for a change so you then can visit your forest friends that you also promised to look after for Zeus himself."

Helena replies to the mare "yes this is true".

"Thank you."

Helena smiled again and said "what is your name?"

The mare replied "my name is Magic and my stallion is called Mystery."

"He has already carried your husband to the palace for you."

Wow, she thought.

Magic bowed down for Helena to climb on her back by using her foot on her shoulders to pull herself up holding gently to the mare's mane.

Eventually, she gets herself comfortable and they rode up to the palace too.

Queen Helena loved her new ride on land again, feeling a soft presence of Seequest in this mare in some way.

It was almost like riding one of his actual daughters.

But she knew that was impossible as they had possibly left earth long ago as normal horses only lived till twenty possibly thirty if they were lucky.

But she thought in one way will be a relationship as he was the creator of them in the first place.

Helena loved the fact she had the opportunity of riding on land again and was free as a bird which she adored.

She later galloped through the city where the Piscean people saw her having fun and all cheered on as she went by them.

She eventually came back to the palace, where her husband was looking very handsome on this stunning black horse and there in a field, there was a herd of horses.

Magic trotted over and let Helena get down from her back when Magic said to her "Another gift for you my queen so that you can farm your land and enjoy it more with us helping you do that, and in return, we stay free and that we never are held down and we can go as we please."

"You must promise to always let us go free to roam wherever we please and never hurt us and then we will help you with blessings always on your people and your kingdom."

"You and your people can use our manes to hold on to when you ride us."

Queen Helena thought what a gorgeous gift for her late wedding present that she was not just riding Seequest's late great-great-granddaughter.

But she can use her anytime when she calls them that she has horses to help farm the crops of her kingdom too.

Eventually, they went into the herd of horses and looked at them one by one.

She chose them individually which were chosen for each errand or help they could provide for her people and herself which would be a great help indeed.

They were many different shapes, sizes, and colours of loads of different breeds from Arabian-like Magic to even heavy Clydesdale horses which would be great for the farmers as some of the work is heavy and tiresome.

Then she looked at the others that looked like a thoroughbred and yet a little stockier all bay like Cleveland Bay of today which looked like the colt she met those years before.

She thought they would be nice as carriage horses and of course, she knew that Magic was fast.

She then had an idea she loved to race in the sea but what about on land, she thought?

From that day Queen Helena was the first to create horse racing but with a difference as none of the horses got hurt.

As they ran on their own, no rider just a number that she added to their names for the race only.

The horses agreed as this breed enjoyed running the distance for complete fun.

Helena was delighted and said "yes my girl I promise to obey your rules in return for your help and kindness to me and my people."

"Thank you from the bottom of my heart."

Everyone was happy with the agreement and it was working beautifully.

Helena knew that it would be winter soon and she wanted to go and visit with Taylor this time her forest friends before they hibernate for winter again.

Taylor today was riding Mystery and still felt like it was his first time so he walked slowly and carefully as he has never ridden on land long distance before.

Only in their kingdom on the island and this time, they were exploring going to the Forbidden Forest to be introduced to her friends and Seequest before winter came and they disappeared until spring came again.

Taylor was thinking that riding bareback was different from riding in the sea as he had to use muscles that he was still getting used to himself.

Mystery reared up showing off that he was a stallion and that he should never try him otherwise.

As he would throw the king off his back!

But Taylor was cautious until he gained a bond with him better.

A few days before they're going to the Forbidden Forest Taylor and Mystery were getting better acquainted and practicing around the grounds to please Helena.

Eventually, they started to build a bond together and trust each other thoughts and body language as they started to move nicely together.

After the ride, this time Mystery came to bring back the king to the palace to meet Helena and showed her that they were ready.

She was delighted with both their courage and will-power together and said "Splendid, you two."

Mystery bowed down in front of her and Taylor jumped off him and said "thank you, dear boy."

Helena walked over and fussed him which he loved and then the stallion reared in delight and galloped off to the fields to relax again with the others.

They had a great day on the island and tomorrow Helena and Taylor are going on an adventure across Santorini.

The actual island from home where there is no safety for them apart from Helena using her magic if there was any danger.

But she felt there was none, thankfully.

Even though Taylor wanted to always please Helena he seemed a little unsure of the dangers out there plus riding Mystery on a long journey to the Forbidden Forest to see and meet Queen Helena's forest animal friends thanks to Seequest in the past.

The day had come when they got up and went for a swim as usual before breakfast and an hour later Helena called the horses in her mind and they appeared in front of her after being let in by her guards at the bridge and her beautiful gates.

Magic says "good morning Helena queen of the Piscean Kingdom."

Helena replied "good morning Magic!"

"I hope that your herd is all ok?"

The beautiful graceful pure white Arabian-type mare replied "yes they're good".

"Thank you for asking about them".

"I also was told that my herd said that they are happy here with your people with a joyful neigh afterward" been pleased.

Helena says "yes my people are very grateful for your kind helping us to grow our crops and still collect the seaweed to eat as well"

"Has we been still mer-folk too so we must keep our traditions up as well our new ones "I have also come to ask if you both are ready to ride to see your friends in the woods today?"

"Are you both ready to go?"

"Not quite my friend"

"Soon as Taylor is just talking to his parents about our adventure today and yes then we will be ready to go, thank you"

Magic kindly replied, "ok we will be back in a few hours for you both, please be ready my queen!"

"Because hopefully, he will not be too long as I want to get moving soon as it is a long journey that we are taking today."

"Ok while we are waiting I will go back to the others and enjoy eating the sweet apples and drinking the clear water that you have kindly put out for us all."

Helena replied "thank you again dear one" kissing her muzzle which the mare seemed to like when she neighed up in the air with delight as she trotted with her head and tail held high showing her authority as she went with great speed.

A few hours later eventually Taylor walked out of the palace doors and said to Helena who had been getting some food together for the trip and her friends in the forest "I am sorry my love my parents send their love to you."

"I also just feel unsure it's a good idea to go today as well"

Helena was just using three seaweed pouches to store some salt water for them both to drink and two others of clear water for the horses and red and green apples for them all to share.

The queen turned around and looked at Taylor looking upset and then he said

"OK, my darling let's go."

He smiled at her and wanted to please her knowing that this trip was very important to her and her agreement with Zeus too.

The Piscean queen called back the horses in her mind.

The horses started to run over the bridge through the great gates where within ten minutes Magic and Mystery were galloping towards the palace pathway made of sand and shells sparkling in the sunshine.

First came Magic and behind her the jet-black stallion as they stopped in front of the royals and reared with delight to be of service to their friend Helena.

Both magnificent horses of different sizes and builds then bowed by putting their left leg out straight and their right tucked under them for the queen and king to jump on their backs.

But before they did Helena and Taylor with respect to the horses closed their eyes and bent their heads to them as well.

Eventually, they were on the horse's backs and held on tightly to their beautiful flowing manes.

As she did Helena used her powers and changes her hair and Taylor in case anyone is watching them.

Queen Helena's hair is now a beautiful blonde and so is Taylor's dark.

Helena said to Taylor "hold on tight my love and don't get go no matter what"

Magic first said that they will trot and then canter and then when closer to the forest will then finish off with a great canter of speed to get there on time.

"Helena told Taylor what her mare said and seemed pleased with agreement while riding Mystery today for this long journey they have never done before."

It seemed a lovely ride for them all as Magic said "it is time to canter hold on tight"

They galloped on for hours when they reached the Forbidden Forest late afternoon.

Helena and Taylor jump off the horses as they thanked them both and ran free while Helena calls her friends to come out with a special soft whistle that Seequest taught her.

There appeared first to be the cute brown and black and white rabbits.

Then the prettiest red foxes and the black and white badgers too, who did not stay long as night animals normally.

The squirrels appeared up in the trees.

Lastly the most important of them all had come down to protect them while they were there was the great white wolf, Moon Cloud himself, and his beautiful pack of all different shades of greys; blues; brown to black wolves all connected to his bloodline.

Moon cloud howled with excitement before he and his pack came running towards her and Taylor of course.

Helena enjoyed seeing them all again.

She was also delighted that they seemed to like her husband too.

That Moon cloud mentioned that they had a black and blue wolf cub that had no name yet, as Helena would give it a name due to her part as his clan now.

Helena was delighted by the idea and held her hands with joy and then said "how about Taylor?"

The wolf replied, "why?",

Helena then explained that her husband's name meant full of life; inspiring with great beauty of a charmer as well

Moon cloud and his new mate Wisdom as his other died in a fight year before.

Both smiled at each other and looked at the Piscean king and then thought greatly and then said "yes we like that name and idea as he will be the next leader possibly to my pack when my time comes".

Moon cloud then calls his recent pups to come and see them both and the two nanny wolves then welcome the stunning handsome black cub directly to Helena she holds me dearly with great affection in her eyes and kisses the cub and says "hello my sweet Taylor of the peace clan"

She then carries the wolf cub to her husband who then for the first time held any furry land creature in his life.

And seemed to enjoy the warmth and love this cub was giving him.

He gently held him as he felt his soft yet hard-wearing fur to keep the wolf cub warm, safe, and dry at all times.

Eventually, Taylor puts down the cub gently to the floor where it rans back to its mother arms, nuzzling her with great love showing through its body language.

In return, she licks it with a love too.

Helena smiles at her Taylor and feels proud that she has also named Moon cloud and wisdom's son after him.

Taylor then smiles back at her blowing a kiss as he does to her and is moved by the Wolves' kindness towards him and thanks them dearly

They stayed as long as they could until it started to get dark.

Moon Cloud with his pack offered to escort them back to safety.

She thanked them all for coming to visit her today and they said their goodbyes to her forest friends for the winter and promised that she will see them again in the spring.

She's looking forward to meeting the new generations of their families to come.

She hugged them all and told them "I am still a mer-princess and yet I am not as I am known now as a Piscean queen now in my kingdom which any of you can visit whenever you wish?"

"I am known now as Queen Helena of the Piscean Kingdom of Dreams and as I own my kingdom here on land."

We live just on the other side of the island where you are all living now.

"So, if you need me call me in my mind if there is any danger."

"I will get my guards to pull down the bridge and open the gates for you all to enter if needed."

They all were pleased to hear there was still a protector on land for them in case of danger.

They enjoyed her company and loved her as their own and went back to their dens; burrows before they left them till spring.

Helena ran up to Moon Cloud with a warm embrace and them sharing their love for each other.

As he squeezed his head into her chest expressing this too and they both moved away from each other when he looked at her in her beautiful blue eyes and then kissed her cheek as he did many years before.

She smiled as approached him and kissed his forehead back and then slowly walk away.

She called Magic back.

There she was and Mystery as well.

They were ready for them to jump onto and ride like the wind back home as quickly as they could carry them.

"Come to Magic and Mystery Please take us home to Piscean again."

The mare answered "yes my queen we shall."

The horses both said "hold on tightly to our manes as it will be a bumpy ride."

Helena understood and told Taylor to hold the black stallion's mane as tight as he could for his life.

The king did not like this idea but he wanted to get home safely and trusted Helena's instinct as she trusted the horses to get them there in one piece of safety.

They said their goodbyes when Moon Cloud said "Helena my highness is you both ready to go home?"

"Yes, my kin friend we are, thank you"

They then turned around when Moon Cloud says "Helena I know a quicker way but it is a little bumpy getting there."

This was probably also the way the horses thought was a good idea and so Helena replies.

"I do not care Moon Cloud I just want to get home please."

Poor Taylor was worried that he would fall off along the way.

But he had no choice and he held onto the stallion with all his might even if in the end he had to hold on to the black stallion's solid neck to do so.

Moon Cloud said "great follow me" and the horses started to trot and then canter slowly, which Taylor did not mind until they went to a full gallop like the wind.

The king agreed that he was a great rider in the sea.

But it did not take that long for him to get used to gripping with his thighs and legs towards the stallion's sides and off they went so fast it seemed as if the horse's hooves were not touching the floor and they were flying due to their speeds.

They galloped through the lands quickly trying to get home before it was too dark.

Eventually, they reached the bridge where she thanked the white wolf and his pack for their protection while getting back in one piece.

As everyone knows that's Hades lives underground but that does not stop him from watching everyone.

Hoping that he will never get involved with their lives again?

They jumped off the horses and King Taylor thanked his black and yet quickly bowed at his queen and said "thank you, my love, for an amazing day with you all but please excuse me"

As he walked back into the grounds and let Mystery go free Helena thanked Magic too with a kiss as she galloped off as well.

She then said, "See you soon."

Under Taylor's breath, he said "not for a while love" and walked off to change.

Helena said "hold on I need to change your hair again" and she did then Taylor thanked her and ran through the palace doors as the lighting had stuck.

Because even though he loves riding he prefers riding on his hippocampius in the sea.

But he did enjoy the experience all the same.

Helena and the white wolf came together and gave another a hug where this time he put his paw gently on her back for old time's sake and she too said thank you to him.

He then ran off into the moonlight with his pack howling as he went away.

Helena was now walking into the palace seeing the purple and silver sparkles when the moon is shining brightly on it.

Then she thanked Taylor for his kindness and understanding for coming with her today to meet her woodland friends and making sure that they were ok before they hibernated for winter again.

They were both shattered and so quickly had a nice dip in their saltwater pool changing into their form before they came out again to Piscean's as they both held each other tightly walking back to their room for the night.

When Helena was resting she was thinking that tomorrow she will surprise her husband by taking him back to the sea to visit some of their dear friends that they both missed very much as he always did everything to please her in her kingdom.

They both fell fast asleep instantly due to it being a long day and a great adventure for them all.

While she was sleeping she could hear Moon Cloud howling at the moon and then his pack saying hello to her grandmother for the night and then she fell into a deep sleep.

Knowing everyone in her kingdom and outside of it is safe and well.

Chapter Fifty-Two

Taylor's Surprise

Another sunny day came when they were up in seven hours and Helena promised herself that she will take Taylor back to the sea to see their families and their hippocampius and that's exactly what she did.

They had their breakfast when Taylor said "what is the plan today my love, to see our people or something else we need to do in the kingdom?"

"No, she answered today I have a surprise for you my darling!"

"I am taking you back to see our families and most of all, Ghost and our hippocampus for the day!"

Taylor could believe what she had just said to him and jumped out of his chair with great excitement and hugged her tightly kissing on the lips then moving gently away to look at her and say "I love you!"

After everything was checked and done for the day at the palace.

They walked out of the palace and jumped into the sea as she had the power for them to automatically change back to their mer-folk form.

They swim for hours just enjoying themselves properly again when Helena called Ghost into her mind and in seconds he appeared as the beautiful spiritual omen he was.

There further out to sea was Ghost, King Taylor's faithful friend so they went out to him for a few hours playing around in the sea like they used to.

A ghost appeared making a soft noise and saying hello waving one side of this fin to welcome them back.

Taylor said "Ghost hi buddy it's lovely to see you again"

Ghost was a great mantra ray of pure white which was very rare as they are generally a grey and white tone.

Ghost was chosen to be the leader of his group as he was the biggest of them all with blue eyes and his body was twice the size of the others.

As he stroked gently his head and then they swam towards his back and held tight.

Taylor was overwhelmed by what Helena had done for him.

He knew then that Helena was one of a kind and that he was blessed to have her in his life.

They spent the day with their families and friends and brothers and sisters that they both had not seen for so long.

How much they thoroughly enjoyed it being on their own it's hard now that Helena is a queen as everyone wants to see her when she swims.

For the first time, it was absolute bliss to have Helena to himself in the sea.

There they were as their handsome and beautiful selves looking elegant.

They swam with the dolphins too as Helena was also their guardian like a mother to them.

The whales and dolphins all came to the surface with them and sprayed water from their air holes to breathe again where some of it landed on them.

They laughed with great joy before swimming on with the dolphins towards Vissen.

They finally reached her father's kingdom and visited Neptune and Sera they all enjoyed it.

But mostly they enjoyed spending some good quality time with their hippocampus's Louis and Moonstone who loved having them back for a while too.

They both swam with them as the hippocampus and then raced to change into smaller and slimmer sea horses swimming and darting through the holes of the coral.

Oh, how they missed doing that and what fun they had that day.

The hippocampus was enjoying their company until it was dark again and it was time for the royal couple to go back home to Piscean where they now belong.

Taylor mentions "thank you my darling."

"I needed this with you."

Helena replies "yes, my love I enjoyed it too."

They were swimming together happily on Louis and Moonstone.

The hippocampus was enjoying both of their company.

It was dark and it was time for the royal couple to go back home to Piscean where they now belonged.

Now it was time to say their goodbyes once again for a while as the loving Hippocampus took their riders to the stairs where they eventually will walk up and changed back to Piscean forms again before entering Helena's kingdom.

He and Moonstone were very sweet as the hippocampus gave plenty of time for Helena and Taylor to get their balance so they can just unhook themselves from their saddles and jump off the water horses' backs so they can dive back into the sea to swim off home again to the royal stables.

Taylor mentions "thank you my darling."

"I needed this with you."

Helena replies "yes my love I did too and I thoroughly enjoyed it."

They also saw a Ghost in the distance and waved at him where he jumped

up out of the sea and makes a large splash and then dives deep into the darker part of the ocean again where he lives Taylor shouts to him "so long old friend until next time."

There Louis and Moonstone were gleaming in the night in the sea neighing as they neigh "thank you" when the queen sent them back to the royal stables where they will be looked after now by Neptune and Sera's stable guards.

One minute they were in their large hippocampus forms and then they both changed quickly into their seahorse forms and then they were gone quickly as a flash.

Within the time that Helena and her husband reached the stairs, they were walking up them slowly.

Seequests magic lit up and change them into Piscean forms again when they reached the second stair to last Helena's hair became jet black again and his blonde wearing their stunning outfits of her kingdom as they walked to the last.

The queen's magic quickly dried them off.

The loving couple was slowly adjusting to their legs again as they were walking back to the palace happily together.

For the next two days, they planned to stay at home and chill with each other until their duties were needed.

But they were not aware of is that Hades had never forgotten what happened to him and was involved and became bitter that he wanted his revenge.

He felt bitter especially towards Helena as he wanted her for himself and for what she called him and saw what she finds in the powerful purple crystal skull.

He wanted so badly to make sure that his revenge would be sweet and yet still be ok without breaking the rules of killing anyone.

That he had one of his shape shifters become one of the great white sharks of Neptune's kingdom and had been watching them both having fun for too long!

This time, Hades was watching from afar as a shark swam around the island of her kingdom and noticed that the Piscean woman was not a blonde anymore as for many years she had been a blonde when out of the kingdom as a disguise to protect her from him finding her once more.

Because when back in her kingdom Queen Helena felt safe to be her beautiful fair skinned black haired self with great beauty and in the moonlight as she sat in her pool as a mermaid again enjoying the fresh air at the same time.

Another day just to be sure Hades has one of his spies watching her around the land and watching as she was riding Magic from the sea when Luna from afar could see her green shades seeping through from her original mermaid lines.

Hades shouts out in his new underground core liar "at last I have found you and my revenge will be sweet my girl you'll see,"

Another of Hades' spies was a big black raven who spoke to the shark while flying above it.

It pretends to catch it by opening up its mouth like the guardian shark.

To not break its disguise and then dive back into the sea.

Where it eventually turned back to this dark shadow of smoke and appears back at Hades' lair.

While the underworld god was thinking of a great plan to destroy Helena and the gods too for what they had done to him all these years.

Chapter Fifty-Three

Hades Revenge

Months had passed after their great day with their families and friends in the sea again they were now resting in their new home in the Piscean Kingdom.

But what they did not gather was that Hades had hypnotized one of the guardian sharks that day and used it to watch what was happening and felt that Queen Helena will have her fun now.

But he will have his revenge when he was ready.

But for now, he was just enjoying seeing the beautiful Helena again.

So, he watched and watched until he felt upset that he wanted her for himself and if that would not happen then the life she loves and adores will be gone.

Hades was riding his demon horse one night after being to Olympus that day to see Zeus as agreed once a year.

While he was riding in the dark cloud he thought that he was hurt so much by everyone that he did not care which way he did it now or who was hurt in the process.

As long as he got his revenge somehow and got hold of her power to rule Earth.

He says to Knightmare "the gloves are off" which meant that anything goes.

Not caring who gets hurt in the process.

He also did not care how long it took either but saw a plan to come to the surface and he would strike at the right time to come out of the ground and use an image of any creature that Helena, Taylor, or even her parents loved to use to his advantage to get closer to them.

Where again he can see what their lives are like now and then plan to destroy every single one of them one by one after all he was immortal and would live forever.

He thought that he would pick at them one by one in his own time that they would not even know it was his doing until it was too late to have noticed and he laughed with great victory ahead of time.

From there he decided for the moment that he would spy on the sea first and then come to Helena at another time but he will not forget her that was for sure.

He said to his new creatures of hell "I shall have revenge and it will be pretty as I will wait for Helena and Neptune to be at their happiest and then I shall take everything away from them as they did to me".

"No one gets away with hurting Hades without getting a payback in time."

He now used himself as a great white shark until he reached the Vissen gates and then popped his spirit into one of the guards and stayed like this for a long time.

Once he heard that the queen was married and had a beautiful kingdom of her own on land as well as in the sea he became very jealous and wanted her for himself and knew if he could not have her then no mer-man or king will.

Five years had passed and Helena loved her kingdom as it had beautiful trees and gardens and her people who were still mer-folk who came and went back to the sea when they pleased.

Neptune's people learned a lot about the land and how the water and soil of Earth could produce beautiful and delicious things to eat as well as to drink.

Queen Helena loved riding in the forests with Magic to see her old forest friends especially the white wolf and his pack.

They became great friends and the wolf was named the protector of the lands as he too, decided that he wanted to be near her.

Another gift from her grandmother Luna the goddess of the moon also sprinkled some moon dust at night to keep everyone at peace and happy there too.

The next morning there was Helios the guardian of the sun with his sun horses.

One of them once was a day unicorn her name was Sundance.

They galloped in the sun to protect the progeny of night unicorns in the past and were the main leader of this chariot of palominos.

The sun chariot would be covered in hot yellow and amber flames like the very hot sun it was.

Helios and his horses would bring the sun up in the sky like the day unicorns used to when they reined Earth before and moved it over to the other side of the planet too, so Luna the moon could bring the night time as well.

So, every living creature knew it was time to rest to reenergize for the next day.

Helena would wake up specially to see Helios bring the sun up again when Sundance used to say good morning to her as related to Seequest.

Helena would then go back to her quarters and rest before getting up properly to rule her kingdom once more.

Everything was great for another few years which was complete bliss and Helena could not have asked for a better life all around.

Then she thought it was time to have children as she was getting on now.

One day Helena heard the white wolf howling to Luna and it was his way of saying hello to her when she arose.

She also had control over them at this time.

That's why today we humans now say sometimes when it is a full moon the animal arises in us.

We all have one animal spirit in ourselves as that's what a wolf spirit animal is if you react to the moon and your mood changes for better or the worst temporally of course.

Back in Piscean, the city was amazing to look at as it shone like the sun and stars together with a touch of the mer-folk's presence to it as well.

There were strong walls that were built around the palace and the people's homes so they had their personal space.

And later Zeus decided through the wolves that he would use that form to create one very similar to it which he thought would have a perfect name dog which meant it was a god originally as it would love; care and protect no matter what happened to it as it would never leave their side.

So as a gift Zeus himself created the first form of dog that looked the similar type to our Great Dane which was a stunning hound dog where he got the idea from his creative brother Hades it was of great size and structure and was a great hunter a similar image to Hades Cerberus form with a softer nature and of course no dragon traits on it either.

Everyone thanked and blessed the food and water it would keep them fit and well.

It also meant that they could hunt to keep the balance on the lands for the forest to bloom and grow always too.

And if they chopped a tree down they had to promise to plant a new one from the trunk of the one that they chopped down before so everything constantly is continuing in the circle of life.

One day this Great Dane type of dog turned up out of the blue at Helena's kingdom gates.

The dog told her he was a gift for her protection from her dear uncle Zeus as her reward for her achievements with her people; land; and animals regarding how proud he was of her.

She let him in and she called him Sirius.

He was a fawn dog with a black mask and brown eyes.

He was a true companion when King Taylor at times had to go back to the sea for his duties to his own parents' kingdom.

She had noticed that the mermaids were coming to her city to have their children to be protected from the sea creatures when they go swimming.

Helena had a great idea and put it forward by contacting Zeus through Seequest's Temple if he would be kind enough to create a smaller type of dog for the children as guardians when they were born.

Zeus agreed and that was how the dog was created as a dog is like a god as it watches over you and gives great wisdom and affection and it protects its people too as Zeus did for his families and animals as well.

So, from that day when the mer-folk had children in her Kingdom has a gift and protection from Queen Helena herself when the child was born connected to the months of Sirius, they would receive a puppy.

The dog's form would be a Great Dane or a German shepherd type for the creative ones as they were great companions and guard dogs to the children when they were growing up.

Border collie or English springer types were chosen for the farm worker's children too.

Everyone loved Queen Helena as she said they would be a gift from her for them staying in her kingdom and sticking to her rules which made the place magical to stay at.

The Piscean women would let Helena know when their child was going to be born and she would give a list to Zeus who would then create the perfect dog for every child.

Because Zeus and Helena loved foxes but knew that they could not have these he suggested another similar type created the cat.

So, if they were born on the other months of the saber-tooth reign they then would be given the future a kitten instead.

Month's later queen Helena noticed that some of her people did not suit dogs and yet felt like they needed a companion of some sort.

Instead of a dog, she would give them a cat which was generally an Egyptian/ Bengal type of black cat that seems to know the mysteries of the universe, or a tabby cat as a spiritual type.

Either of these animals came as puppies or kittens and grew up with the child for them to talk to and to confide in when they felt like they needed space from their parents and independence.

But when the children were in their twenties the dog or cat would die and get put into the sea after saying a verse which then becomes a dog-fish or cat-fish to live forever in a different form.

So, the mer-children knew that their sea pets would always be with them in spirit still protecting them and helping them enjoy their own lives without them.

The mer-children in Vissen though had no time to have a pet as they had duties in the sea and land and were away for too long where it needed feeding or looking after to a degree as it was used to being connected to its child only.

So, mermaids would especially come and have their children in Queen Helena's kingdom as she was so kind; helpful; considerate and generous too.

She was loved oh so very much.

The mer-folk loved the city but others felt like it was against their race and forbid them to even adventure there.

Queen Helena on her twenty-ninth birthday, the same age that her mother Queen Sera had accomplished to create the new forms of the hippocampus; water dragons and seahorses.

Helena wondered what she would receive for hers.

As a surprise her parents had made a stunning statue of her and Louis in both forms: as a mermaid princess on a proper hippocampus and the other side was her as a Piscean woman from riding Magic, her horse on the lands.

They arranged for these to be put into palace grounds while she was swimming with the dolphins in the sea one day.

She came home and saw them there on her grounds.

She loved them very much and for King Taylor's thirtieth she also asked her parents to have a statue of her husband as a merman riding his friend Ghost the manta ray and then one of him as a Piscean man on his beloved steed Mystery too.

They both arrived after their swim and did their royal duties.

Here they all were on the grounds of the palace and there standing near their gates to the kingdom were these statues of them both riding their horses on the land.

And on their grounds to the palace near their pool were the statues of them both riding their hippocampus Louis and Moonstone.

They could not believe that her Piscean kingdom was her and Taylor's dream home after all.

Because they were both thrilled with the detail that was put into them and they thank her parents by going into the palace grounds and going to a pool that was personally connected to the sea where her parents came to see them at times now.

Taylor loved Piscean and, in the end, loved it as much as she did and lived quite happily there.

Later they spoke about children and were planning to start very soon they hugged each other and just went with the flow of nature and hoped that it would be soon.

When they went riding they looked at the statues all the time and completely loved them very much and could not be prouder of each other's lives on their own and together as one.

They both loved that they had an image of both of their worlds which they loved very much and yet Helena felt she would like a least one child if any to complete her life and dreams.

Hades heard that they started trying for children and that they were happy indeed and began to build a plan as now this is when Hades wanted his revenge the most.

Poor Helena's and Taylor's lives were going to change drastically.

He had this plan all arranged in his head and thought now was the time to put it into action.

Hades then said while being in shark form once again "now Queen Helena you now will get for better or for worse my lovely as my revenge is quite sweet when you upset the god of the underworld missy payback is sweet" and laughed.

He gradually was strong enough again to make up a potion that he gave to his raven birds to carry on their beaks.

Everyone was asleep the raven birds would arrive in the kingdom and dip their beaks into the freshwater where it forms quickly into a liquid that stayed clear.

The ravens flew away as if no one knew that they had been poisoned it.

The mer-folk drank the water and it began giving them horrible negative emotions that they had never experienced before and made them all sick.

It started them to turn on each other which caused great rivalry at both kingdoms in the sea and land alike.

The liquid started to make her people bad and mad towards each other and cruel.

Poor Helena felt like something must have happened in the sea as mer-folk and Pisceans alike were one of the same.

Until months later Pisceans started fights back in Vissen and rocked the boat with Neptune and his daughter.

Poor Helena felt like her dreams were now becoming her worst nightmare.

Her father threatened her that if she did not get her people positive again they will be banished to dolphins for an entity.

They were not worthy of living in the sea again due to they will kill and destroy for no reason and this was Neptune's way of stopping this from happening.

Because everyone started to believe it was her fault due to them trying to be someone they are not!

But that was not the case at all.

Poor queen Helena had done no wrong and she knew this.

But how could she prove it she thought crying now in her sleep.

Hades had once again messed around and started to destroy everyone's lives by being jealous!

Queen Helena was upset and completely agreed with her father's wishes.

So, she made her people come to the courtyard one day and told them if they did not behave anymore they will be punished.

That day most of her people did not believe in her anymore and tried to get back into Vissen.

But instead of dolphins, he decided that he will make them into sharks.

Because Neptune heard that they betrayed their queen.

The carers became nursing sharks when he made the bad mer-folk become hammerhead sharks too.

The tough ones became great whites.

All the sharks had a purpose still in the sea and this was the only way that Neptune would welcome his people who disobeyed him and his daughter's rules to allow them to still come back and live in the sea.

This started to happen in Piscean as well so Queen Helena had to obey the rules she did not understand what had come over them and started to use this method herself in her kingdom as well to try and prevent it from happening anymore and yet it continued.

Both kingdoms were out of control and had no authority over their people no more.

Neptune thought now it was because the merfolk lived on land too much.

When it was all Hades' fault as usual up to his crafty tricks once again without anyone knowing and loved what he saw happening.

Queen Helena did not understand why it was happening and who was doing it as she believed that Hades could not touch or get near her anymore or that was what she hoped was true.

Poor Helena had to punish her people badly and change them into sharks or dolphins regarding their crimes, as they could not stay in either form that they were before.

They would harm the kingdoms above and below and cause havoc on both kingdoms in the sea and on land.

Vissen and Piscean tried to keep positive and happy thoughts in their people.

By making worship the Zeus and Seequest and yet nothing seemed to work?

One day Queen Helena disappeared from the kingdom which was guarded and still had the force field on it.

Months passed when Helena did not come out of her palace has been pregnant and could let anyone know about it because of Hades.

Luckily the sorceress had the power to keep some things still hidden when Helena became pregnant and decided that it was safer to have her baby boy in the sea in the Unicorn Temple where he and she were until he was strong enough to be handed over to her friend whom she trusted to bring him up for her.

Another year passed when their young son was getting older quickly and both parents visited him a lot.

But in different ways, so Hades would never know about this amazing young mer-boy Ray named after Ghost Taylors loved a great white manta ray that he still rides when he gets the chance.

Ten years had passed and they were in their forties now Helena and Taylor.

Their boy was as handsome as his father King Taylor himself.

He was very much like him in looks but he was like his mother Queen Helena in intelligence and skills.

Everyone was so proud of them all in the sea and they all had a great life together.

Ray eventually became a strong mer-knight in Vissen and thankfully seemed to like it more in the sea than on land.

Helena and Taylor did not see him as often as they liked.

But they also knew that they had to protect him from Hades.

They were happy enough that he was happy doing want he wanted in life and also knew that he was safe at all times with her parents and her friends who treated him as their own.

Queen Helena was sad as she had everything she ever wanted.

But she could not live with her precious son in case Hades ever popped up again and kidnapped him.

Neptune and Sera her parents thought that because they seem to get their people back in control, they believed that only true Vissen mer-folk back home knew about their heir to her kingdom ever.

This was a blessing for Helena in one way knowing that whatever happened in the future that she knew their son would be safe and sound and he will make a great life for himself one day.

Chapter Fifty-Four

Hades Revenge Begins

Everywhere land and sea were at peace once more as the gods had beaten the Titans.

Zeus and his fellow gods and goddesses had beaten Hades and then the unicorns did and then the last battle with all the races beat Hades for a while.

But Hades knew now was the time to strike where it hurt.

He followed one of the mer-folk to Piscean Kingdom one day and got through the gates as a regular visitor and poisoned all waters and ponds himself this time.

Has he noticed that Helena was the one who was in the possession of the Amethyst Crystal skull which controlled all the powers of them all he thought that if he could not have Seequest's horn then he shall have this instead!

Months later he disguised himself as the King one night when he was away from home and she thought that he had come back early as he said that he missed her has going away so much due to his duties in the sea, due to him always working with his parents and their kingdom being away from home a lot now.

Once Hades got his way with her she would have his child.

But Luna was watching from afar and she told her that it was Hades who was with her that night and so tried to pretend to be not interested and just wanted to sleep.

Luckily Luna sent some magic dust to drink and protect her.

Without Prince Taylor knowing she was pregnant again she said that she had duties back in Vissen where her mother used the crystal skulls and Seequest's horn to try and save the baby and thankfully she did.

But it would grow up and be guardian to Kelp Seequest's son Kelpie due to her having some of Hades' traits.

Helena also thought that now at least their daughter and Seequest's son will always have a friend in the same lands as them.

She named her Kindred, short for Kindred spirit as she would always be connected to her by blood and that was all.

Hades was annoyed and unhappy that his daughter would not be born into her world.

So, he planned to make sure that no one would come to her kingdom anymore.

He made the Piscean and mer-folk fight against each other and made them feel that now they were two different races even though they were officially the same.

It became hell and it caused too much stress and attention to her father as well.

Neptune was unhappy as the god of the sea and king to mer-folk he forbids Helena to have anyone there in her kingdom anymore.

She and Taylor were the only ones that lived there ever again and that's when Hades grabbed hold of her and her husband one night and captured them and said, "now my darling I will make you suffer as you did to me."

Hades did something sad first.

He loved her kingdom for a while and controlled it and kept her prisoner until her forty-seventh birthday.

Her kingdom and life that she loved so much at the time knew if she could escape him somehow, she had to go back to Vissen for her safety and leave her dream behind all because Hades would not leave her alone anymore.

But that did not happen poor Helena was trapped in anguish that she could not escape no matter how pow-erful she was.

Hades' powers and magic were stronger than hers.

There was nothing Zeus or her father could do as he did not kill anyone yet.

All he had been doing was poisoning their minds to become negative and that was not a crime to the gods.

But instead, she never returned home for months.

Everyone just knew that she had disappeared and become invisible to the mind's eye and even the powers of everyone.

Hades had conquered so far that Piscean and mer-folk started to kill the animals and fish for fun and ride the horses with reins having full control of them.

Everything that she had created of been perfect was now a complete mess of hurtful mistakes and pain for everyone.

At this time, she wondered when he would take his revenge and that seemed to be this day

The Piscean and mer-folk felt crushed as they did not believe in the crystal skulls or the healing powers of the temples anymore.

Everyone seemed to have lost their spirit for life and wanted to have free will on the lands and sea and Neptune said this cannot happen.

Back at Piscean Kingdom Hades had conjured up a brilliant plan and he knew it would work and hurt everyone involved forever and it too will change the world as they knew it again!

Hades contacted Zeus and Neptune and said he wanted to live on the land in her kingdom knowing that no one was going there anymore and wanted to have people of his own.

Zeus and Neptune said no and what happened next, they would never forget for the rest of their lives.

One day Hades brought Helena and Taylor back to Vissen and met Zeus there.

They could not believe he was back in the first place and then knew of his crafty ways and thought that their powers and magic kept him at bay, which they did.

But in the time, he was in the earth's core, it made him mad with hate and anger so his revenge would be sweetest than ever before.

He told Neptune and Zeus that he wanted Helena for himself and her kingdom as well and they said 'we forbid these Hades.

"You will never live or touch the surface again."

He was not happy with the response and he said "are you sure as I can make both of your lives hell?"

They laughed and said, "You could not hurt a fly", and they both laughed.

Then he got a hold of Prince Taylor and said "Queen Helena," I have given you time to enjoy your life to the fullest and now it's time for me to take this for myself and you will rein this kingdom with me!"

"You will you be my bride to save your husband from pain?"

She said, "Never."

She looked at Prince Taylor in chains and cried with great sadness.

Hades said "Princes, if you will not be mine forever then you will belong to no one."

Helena looked at Hades and replied "what do you mean by that you horrible god of death?

"You cannot kill us as that's against your rules with Zeus himself."

Even though Zeus was there his hands were tied as there were rules that even the greatest god of the gods had to obey as well.

"If I cannot have you for myself my queen, then neither of you will die."

"But you won't live the way you do now or communicate like you do either as I will take it all away from you as quickly as it was given."

Queen Sera was terrified listening and watching from the library in her moon staff as she understood what he meant and yet thought if she could get to the Crystal

Skull Temple in time because she had the other four that could stop him.

She quickly rushed there without being seen.

Hades said "I will give you forty-eight hours which is two days to decide what you want to do."

"I will come back for my bride."

"Otherwise you will pay for your mistakes."

Hades vanished into shark form again and swam away before any of the mer-guards could kill him.

Helena was swimming quickly to her mer-man in mer-maid form as he was chained and could drain unless they get his hands to lose soon to swim again.

It was Forbidden by Zeus, as after all it was their brother, first as it was Zeus' rule to never kill unless been killed yourself.

Neptune said to Zeus that he would never hand over his daughter to Hades for anything and at first they all agreed that together they will destroy Helena's land of Piscean so he could not own it or know the powers that it possessed there.

In one day, Piscean will be no more!

Princess Helena was dissatisfied and yet knew that she and her husband and their mer-folk had to come first so she agreed and it was sadly planned.

The next day Zeus; Neptune; Prince Taylor and all the people of the sea planned to fight Hades and agreed that he would never be able to have the power of the crystal skulls or Helena Amethyst one either.

But they hoped they could trap him with the luck of the beast's protection behind them or that's what they thought.

That day Helena and Taylor went up to the Piscean and had an amazing day with everyone from the forest animals to the wolves and horse's all living in their lands.

Looking out their window the next night they were looking at Luna and spoke to her and Seequest in the stars asking them for help and advice on what to do.

Both were exhausted and inwardly terrified of what was going to happen to them, they tried to not think about it for the night and just enjoyed being together in this beautiful place one last time.

They went to bed holding each other as if they felt it may be the last time together as they knew something terrible may happen soon as they knew that Hades would never let them enjoy life again.

Plus, Helena also knew that he would never forgive Helena for letting their daughter go to the dark lands as well and being allowed to be with him.

Helena at this time said "my dear Taylor thank you for sharing my dream with me all these wonderful years and for our handsome son Ray who is still a secret to all."

"I am sorry now that I have put your life in harm's way and it seems I will do everything I can to save my kingdom."

"But I feel even with these powers of mine they will not be able to stop this from happening."

Taylor looked at her in her eyes and said "my queen Helena and my love I want to thank you for an amazing life too."

"If this is the end let's just enjoy this moment now more than ever, my love."

He kissed her deeply and they fell asleep in each other's arms until morning.

That next morning came when they enjoyed looking out of the window once again at their animal friends and the butterflies flying by with the birds singing heavenly.

They got dressed and walked down the courtyard to tell their friends what happened and how they were going to correct it.

Helena walked through her kingdom the beautiful white and blue butterflies were flying around her with the waterfalls of the sea flowing where she goes to bathe every day.

After talking and saying their goodbyes possibly for good by letting their forest friends and the wolves free from their kingdom.

It came to the most important which was Seequest's progeny of horses that had lived with them all this time happily.

First, they made sure that everything from her Piscean Kingdom was destroyed and she told Magic and Mystery after hugging them tightly that she loved them very much and now she has to go back to the sea as her life depended on it.

The horses were sad and yet understood with tears in their eyes as they and the other horses loved her people very much for the shelter and kindness all those years.

Until Hades had poisoned the waters so now all the animals and the horses cannot go near there again after this day to say goodbye forever.

The herd started to run free back on the lands again as they have to go back to their original home to live because of the horrible Hades plans.

They were upset and yet understood and the white wolf and his pack travelled back to his homeland as well for their safety too.

Neptune and Sera's daughters life of being a queen of her land, was now been destroyed and taken away from her which seriously broke her heart.

She was prepared to fight to the death and kill Hades if she could.

Her life and Taylor's would never be the same again.

That last night Helena was prepared for what she had to do next and she did not like the news that she was given and yet she knew there was no choice in the matter.

She could sense that things were bad and waited to hear from Seequest to hear how bad as now she believed that Hades had got into the kingdoms and now wanted revenge for what they did to him in the past.

They stayed at her kingdom for one the last night of peace where she opened up the Unicorn Temple roof and spoke to Seequest again.

She asked him what she did wrong and asked for his help and he appeared as a ghost image in the sky saying "my dear Helena I am so sorry you did nothing wrong ever it's just Hades wants you for himself and he will do anything to make sure that happens"

"Hades has been coming to your city for months and has managed to have poisoned all your people against you and each other and now they have free will which means they will do more harm to both kingdoms as he had control of them.

"So, it was a good idea of your father to change them into mammals, as now they will still have a memory of being a mer-person."

"It is the only way that your kind could survive this, please Helena you never did anything wrong."

"You did everything right by trying to improve lives for everyone and this planet."

"For doing that you were rewarded with true happiness"

"Always remember that my darling friend, if there were angels yet".

You would differently be one for all the good you've given to your people and this world too"

"You have the powers to do something completely different now but it will be sad for you to do so."

She said with a sad voice and a determined one too "I will do anything to prevent Hades from having my kingdom and my lovely home or my people as he will never deserve it or them!"

She falls onto the stone floor with a great embrace with tears falling down her face.

She paid close attention to what the great Union spirit advised her to do next.

Seequest then said "this would be for the better of everyone involved as you will not be killed or nor will they."

He told her by using the Amethyst crystal skull with the others and his horn will give them a greater power than they have ever known before and she and her father will have to change their people to mammals and sea creatures to survive Hades' wrath with a difference.

Because it will be the only way their good people could still keep their mer-folk memories alive.

She cried some more and said "I cannot do that, we are mer-folk."

"I mean that you will be dolphins still with your true minds."

"At least you all will be together still and be safe away from Hades' grasp."

The unicorn spirit goes on and says, "My dear friend it is the only way to survive and stop Hades from ruling and claiming this power for himself and destroying Earth as we know it and love."

She looked up at Seequest's star and said "There must be another way."

And he said "this is the only one left that will work in your favour."

Then Luna appeared and said "my sweet granddaughter Seequest is right."

"Hades must not get hold of this power."

"But if he possesses these powers then he will reign Earth and can change you all into ordinary dolphins where you won't be yourself anymore."

The differences if you do it yourselves then you can stay in certain pods like royal dolphins do, with your parents and people right?

"But if you decide to go ahead with it, at least you will be together as merfolk and will enjoy each others company for a little longer happily!"

Also, you will have time to hide the crystal skulls away from him.

"Before you do you must tell both kingdoms what is going to happen to them to try and escape and give them a choice."

"Maybe they might want to live on land now as they have this option in the pyramids that you built in the past which with the help of the crystal skulls, as it sends energy to both kingdoms."

"The sea and the lands, for you all, to help the source of magic to stay there and not be used for a while understand?"

"But as long as the crystal skulls remain as they are this kingdom they may build for themselves in the future should survive for centuries to come."

"Goodbye, Seequest old friend."

He replies "it is not goodbye as we will always be able to talk telepathically no matter what form you are".

"But some others won't."

She wondered what he meant by that and yet left it in case it was something she did not want to hear.

In case it upset her too much she thought.

She was heartbroken and yet did not care what happened to her as long her husband's son and people were ok?

She was prepared to sacrifice herself for her family but she hoped that Hades would just take her as his queen and then leave her family to stay as it was forever or that is what she hoped?

She walked out the next morning and enjoyed seeing Helios and his sun horses bring up the sun for the day as normal.

She then waved as Sundance flew over her on purpose who neighed back as she smiled and then jumped on Magic for the last time to the famous steps to the sea.

Before she left her kingdom for good she galloped around the lands before letting all go.

Because Neptune and Helena had already sent everyone back to Vissen, where they had to choose as to what their future lives may be. (A dolphin or Piscean forever in a different way)

Eventually, Helena and her mare enjoyed their last time together when she jumped off her and kissed Magic goodbye and thanked the mare saying "Magic never come here again!"

"You are now free to live your life in peace, please go away from here it is not safe for your kind anymore I am sorry farewell, dear friend."

The mare bowed with closed eyes at this time before she ran back through the city knowing that it was the last time she would ever see Helena again.

Galloping to the other side to freedom neighing loudly as she had lost a great friend, who was more like family to her.

Afterward Helena quickly ran down the stairs and changed into her mermaid form and swam as fast as she could back home to Vissen to tell her father what their destiny was now to be to survive Hades' nightmare.

Chapter Fifty-Five

Now Princess Helena's Destiny

She reached her father's throne room where her mother the sorceress and everyone from the kingdoms spoke.

But there seemed to be no way of defeating Hades without killing their own which they did not think was fair.

They thought there had been enough killings from the previous battle.

Then Helena taught them a way to survive it.

They were all shocked and heartbroken but at least this way they could still protect and live in the sea in harmony for a while they wished.

The last day had come when Neptune said to his daughter that she had to go to Olympus with him and speak to Zeus herself as she will tell the grand plan to survive this terrible mess!

Back in Greece on the beach, there appeared a Piscean form for the last time.

Neptune's winged horse shone a soft bright blue aura around his body as a surprise to cheer on.

In the distance Starlight Seequest's daughter, appeared as a bright pink light in the clear blue sky landed beautifully standing there glowing with a very bright pink aura around her as well.

Telepathically she spoke and said "Hello again dear friend"

The Princess could not believe how she had changed and looked like a pretty elegant young mare now who was delighted to see an old friend.

She said "I shall take you to Olympus where you can tell Zeus the plan of what he can do to help save you and all your mer-folk from Hades."

Helena could not stop crying and yet she had to pull herself together as she was now going to see Zeus himself in person and had to make sure that she could give the correct information as it was critical to get it right as their people's lives depended on it.

Helena agreed running hugging Starlight and said, "thank you have made my day feel much better even though these are drastic times for me and my father."

They both closed their eyes through the pain they felt from each other and Helena jumped on the mystical horse.

Then she flapped her wings and galloped as fast as she could to the mountain, where she started to climb by using her legs as a galloping movement up towards the sky to Olympus.

Even Neptune had a sad expression on his face, as he was a god himself but he could do nothing more than he had already done.

Hoping Zeus can help them find a solution to this massive problem that will change their lives forever in history.

They arrived at Olympus telling Zeus what Seequest said and Zeus said "I am sorry he right!"

"I am the god of gods and of all living things yet I still have rules to obey with the universe too".

"If Hades does not harm your people like killing them or yourselves then my hands again are tied".

"But if he uses his powers to change you instead".

"Then he has won and will rule Earth!"

"Sometimes we have to sacrifice our own to save thousands of others or even a race of our people or ways to survive without hurting them."

"But creating them again, by making them part of the sea in a different way that they would still love and be alive"

Princess Helena understood and said thank you for his time and Zeus also told his brother that he will always protect them in the future.

But he could not change their destinies no matter how much he wanted to.

Neptune knew that being a god one day he may have to sacrifice his home to keep his family and people alive.

They spoke to Luna and Queen Sera as well and told them the plan too.

She was working to get the Amethyst crystal skull to the Crystal Temple and get all their people together as if they were saying a speech and using the power on them.

Helena and Neptune got back on the winged horses and female Unisos flew back to the beach as quickly as they could to spend time with their loved ones for one more night as tomorrow Hades will appear to claim his bride.

If not, he will destroy everything in his path that was in his way to achieve this.

Prince Taylor had gone back to the sea recently because his life had been threatened by Hades already.

Queen Sera had a protection spell on him for now and wondered how long it would protect him from harm as she was powerful.

But Hades was the son of a titan so much stronger than her.

Later that day Neptune and his people decided what they wanted to be and most of them apart from a few wanted to still live out their lives as mer-dolphins and that is what all the powers of the crystal skulls did.

But Neptune said that none of them could live out in their waters anymore as they have slight differences from the other Dolphins.

Their color was lighter than Greek dolphins and they were a smaller build too.

Neptune knew that Hades would find out and so Helena took them all to the British Isles Ocean, where they would be content and happy together until one day the time came to leave earth naturally.

That was the last time the mer-dolphins ever saw their King and their home again.

Helena sneaked back at night to her kingdom one last time, as she had not actually said her goodbyes yet and needed to accept that her life there was no more.

She quickly changed and ran into her palace as she loved looking out into the distance.

She saw a beautiful night sky while sitting in her true mermaid form in her pool where she could still see everything clearly of the beautiful green countryside too.

Yet she was saddened that tomorrow her dream home will be no more as her father and Zeus are planning to destroy it!

She had so many wonderful memories there with her forest friends visiting and living outside her grounds for years happily and the horses helping her people too.

By building a completely different life from what she was born into too.

How she wanted to stay there and yet she knew her destiny was not to be.

But even though she was sad she knew that she was blessed with the best life she could have ever had.

As she did as she pleased and enjoyed her life to the full of having her own home, husband, son, and many great friends around her.

She was also happy and proud of all the achievements she did for herself and her loved ones too.

As Seequest said that she will always be remembered for her beautiful personality and her kind heart to all.

He also told her that she will be a legend and always be thought of dearly forever.

The princess thought that she would miss the great friendship she built up with Moon Cloud and his pack and lastly her close friend Magic.

Dear Helena could not believe that the Hades she met was now this evil God!

She knew how much she wanted to kill him and yet it was forbidden by Zeus.

Poor Helena knew from tomorrow that she would only be known once again has the mermaid Princess of Vissen where she wondered if would Hades turn her and her parents into dolphins.

But when thinking about her and everyone would still be alive and together she thought?

The next day came when the Princess was just going to say goodbye to her dream kingdom.

She was swimming in the sea enjoying her day before things changed for good when a shark came right at her which was unusual.

She thought it could be one of Hades' sharks capturing her instead of collecting her later, as he then could do his worst without her saying goodbye to her family.

Or that he may destroy them and she would not know?

Quickly she swam as fast she could and called for Louis.

Within seconds the loyal black hippocampus was at her side and saw that she was in danger so he changed into a seahorse and made the great white shark chase him while Helena escaped safely back to Vissen.

But what they were not aware of was that it was Hades actually.

Where he got close to Neptune's nursing sharks and changed his image and got into her father's kingdom as the guards let him through with the other sharks that guard and look after the boundaries around the kingdom for Neptune.

Quickly as he could when everyone was asleep he turned back into a shadow and slipped himself into Prince Taylor's body while he was sleeping peacefully next to Helena in their bed happily together in their quarters.

The next day, the mer-woman could sense that Taylor was not himself.

Before breakfast, she swam to see her mother when they both went to the Crystal Temple first and then Seequest's Temple asking some questions about why is Taylor acting so differently and distant from her.

As of now Queen Sera's powers were not as strong as they were before.

Because she used a lot of her powers recently to save their people too

"They both used the large white crystal skull and Seequest star said that it was Hades in disguise and that he wanted Helena for himself and that he will do anything to get her."

Queen Sera was shocked and called for a meeting with King Neptune in his throne room.

Before that, they asked Kessy and the Hippocampus to help them one last time.

They ordered all of them after the Sorceress and High priestess used the last of the full power of the skulls together as they broke them down again into individuals.

Kessy and all the hippocampus had one each and were told to go and bury them where Hades would never ever find them again.

All the water horses went to the ends of the earth and hid the crystal skulls which for centuries were now hidden from Hades' grasp.

Eventually, after speaking with her husband and father the Hippocampus came back and said it was done and that they will never be found again!

As the celestial beings in the universe saw what was going on and also made sure they would never be found again as well.

They began to talk about what had happened to Taylor and difference they see now in him recently.

When Helena said she saw a puff of black smoke near him recently.

As she was telling Neptune that Hades was in the king-dom lingering inside Prince Taylor himself now.

The sea god was horrified and yet told them to relax and they would keep an eye on him.

That afternoon he was sitting in his chair for dinner when the sorceress said a spell quietly and there appeared seaweed around his chair which tied his wrists and his flowing long tail which was now twitching.

"What is going on with you all" he said.

Poor Taylor was not sure what was going on and yet Helena said as she looked closely into his eyes "my love, do you trust me?"

Then Taylor said "yes always my love"

He looked back into her eyes and could see that she also saw something else there with him.

Queen Sera said "Hades we know that you are there?"

"Come out of Taylor and show yourself."

Taylor become quiet and he opened his mouth widely and a large black image of smoke came out and formed Hades.

Neptune stood up boldly and proudly showing his authority when he said "what do you want, brother?"

"Do you not think you have caused enough pain for a lifetime already?"

Hades replied "no, I don't as you and Zeus have taken my home away from me and my demon horse too."

"Why shouldn't I pay you all back for the hurt that you have caused me, brother?"

Neptune replied "we only did what you had to do to survive your battle which you started again Hades"

"We had no choice as you're cruel and evil now."

"You tried many times to steal Seequest's horn and destroy our Earth."

"You failed that time and you will this time too."

"Go back to the underworld in the deep core of the Earth where you belong as no one wants you here anymore."

This annoyed and hurt Hades even more and this time he knew that he would have his revenge.

He also knew that it will be bittersweet.

"Princess I am asking you nicely to come and live with me and be my queen with an eager tone."

The mermaid princess said, "no, never!"

"I belong with my husband Prince Taylor in our kingdom."

Hades again was angry and replied, "Ok missy, if you will not be my queen, then I shall take everything away from you that you love."

Neptune shouted out now and there above was Zeus with his lightning bolts attacking Piscean kingdom, Helena's home.

Neptune banged his trident which enlarged and shone a brightly solid gold light that lit up the sea and then all you could hear were the whales throwing their tails very hardly bashing the sides of the land of the island and the beast climbing onto it breaking and crashing everything in its path.

Because Sera used her staff to show Hades what was going above them, showing him that he would never have the happiness with Helena that she was there with her husband.

The Neptune's Daughter was not there and yet she and the queen put their hands together and said a verse and there appeared in Helena's hands an image of Piscean and what was happening to it which she had few tears as she knew what she had to do.

She said, "I once had a perfect dream life and had it all, so I am grateful and blessed for that."

"But I created it and now I must destroy it!"

She did just that as she held her hands tight as the light of her dreams was starting to dimmer and there in the end were ashes of her kingdom that she once had and loved very much.

Because of Hades, her dreams were now crushed and she now lost her title as Piscean queen and became once again just a mer-woman.

The lightning bolts then created the volcano to erupt which was on the base of the island.

The lava from the volcano came down and destroyed her land completely and there she saw it disappear with her own eyes.

But she knew that it had to be done this way to save everyone as she remembered what Zeus said to them before about sacrificing things you love for others' needs first or priority which in this case was this.

After all the sea creatures and Zeus's handy work, it made a massive large hole in the land that was connected to it.

All you could see now was a tiny piece of an island left.

Everything was gone like it never existed.

"Nooooo", said Hades.

"See, Hades we said that you will never win or get hold of the crystal skulls or Seequest's horn and we will defend them with all our lives.

Hades was really angry and said "then you shall, brother."

"The way that I know can never be undone and in the law of us gods will not interfere as what I am going to do is not kill you no, no, no."

"I am going to do something more upsetting to you all than that."

"You watch and see."

Neptune and Queen Sera were shocked to think what he can do as he had blocked them both from reading his mind.

He then carried on talking and said "now it's my turn and first" he said "Oh Helena if you will not be my queen, then you will be no one's!" Laughing.

She could not believe her eyes when Taylor draw his sword at Hades he pointed his death staff at the prince and there in front of him he started to change into a large rainbow bottle-nosed dolphin.

Moving up and down now, squeaking and only Neptune and Helena at this point could understand him.

Helena put her hands to her mouth in shock as Taylor the dolphin looked sad and tears came out of his eyes.

"No Taylor my love."

"I am so sorry."

"She went over to him and hugged his dolphin body and begged Hades to change him back."

And he replied, "Why should I do that?"

Helena said "because I will go and live with you and do anything."

"Just change Taylor back and leave my family alone."

Hades said "no, Princess."

"You had your chance and now you will pay for not agreeing to my wishes before."

She and her parents thought about what can he do to them which was worse than taking their daughter away from them forever.

The mermaid princess now shouted "please Hades I am sorry, I will go and live with you and be your queen", begging him for forgiveness.

But he carried on.

Her beautiful Great Dane Sirius came and attacked Hades by biting him hard to make him drop his staff and the dog retrieved it.

Hades said "now be a good dog and give back my staff."

The dog was growling with it in his mouth.

Helena shouted "Sirius hand me the staff, good boy."

The Great Dane was wagging his fish tail swimming quickly as he was now a dogfish swimming again quickly towards Helena when Hades said "If you will not give it back to me then I will get it back another way."

Sirius was just a few feet away from handing Helena the staff.

When Hades said a verse and the dog moaned as he dropped the staff and gave a sad look to Helena as he was turning into a sparkling shadow and then appeared as a dog ghost image of a star.

Hades then said, "this will teach you to try to keep my staff away from me you silly dog"!

"After all, I am the god of the underworld", and laughed.

Poor Helena was devastated that she did not only lose her husband but now lost her true companion.

When she used to go swimming she would turn him into a dogfish so he could go everywhere with her on land and sea.

Hades saw that there were similar creatures to this as well around dogs and cats that were changed with the Piscean children, as their guardians and friends while growing up.

Helena made sure before she gives up her full powers that all the dogs and cats in her kingdom went with their children as loyal companions in the sea.

Hades could see that Helena felt that she had nothing else to live for.

So, Helena said "do your worst, you cruel evil god."

"I could never love you or be with you."

"So, do as you please to me screaming at him with great anger and anguish in her voice as well."

Her parents asked her to take back what she just said as they were terrified of what Hades would do next.

But by this time Helena had lost the plot and did not care anymore.

She looked at her parents thinking that she was very sorry for everything and she loved them very much.

He said "now it's your turn."

He said another verse as she turned around and looked at her parents and they all had tears in their eyes.

Neptune felt like he had his hands tied behind his back like Zeus's now as all he could do was watch what happened next.

Knowing that he could not kill his brother no matter how much he wanted to and stop him from hurting his loved ones!

Because if he was dead this would stop his magic from working forever again!

As even though he was bad at times he too had a purpose and if he wasn't around then there would be no more balance in the world to carry it on.

For the first time in his long life, Neptune felt helpless and the queen was not allowed to interfere either.

Neptune's family and kingdom were under the greatest attack of their lives.

Hades now pointed at her and said "Um what can I change you into?"

Helena said, "A dolphin."

He replied "no, no, no, Princess.

That means you will still be together with your husband".

"No, that will not work for me at all!"

Then he rubs his head and says "oh that's a great idea as Zeus has done this recently and now it's my turn to try then says

Oh, Princess, you will never be with your family friends, or Taylor ever again."

"You'll be just a loving memory to them all now."

She looked scared and confused.

She swam quickly to her parents and hugged them for protection.

Hades said "oh look you are trying to keep her out of harm's way".

"Well sorry but this time it will not work" laughing a horrible chuckle.

Taylor now being a dolphin swam over to Hades and whacked him into a corner with his powerful tail and squeaked.

He got up and said "you will regret that and he pointed his staff again at Prince Taylor when it took his mer-man memory away."

Taylor closed his eyes and opened them again waking with no memory of who he was.

As the dolphin became scared so he swam away.

The princess screamed his name while in tears.

But he did not respond and disappeared from sight.

Neptune explained to his daughter what Hades had done.

Helena swam over to him and tried her Amethyst powers on him as she now carries the energy inside her and she lit up the whole kingdom with a beautiful powerful purple flame of light to strike Hades and burnt him.

Her father told her to stop as he had won.

Helena trusted her father and knew then it did not matter if she had powers, they were useless now.

Because she was not allowed to kill him no matter what he had done to her!

Neptune told her two wrongs don't make a right where she and his people were better than that.

So, she decided to give up the fight accepting her destiny of the unknown.

Only knowing in her heart that she had the best life she ever could have imagined.

"We cannot kill him as if we do we will be banished like what Hades is already doing to us."

"So, my darling it looks like our time is up here together."

Neptune believed no matter what happens they somehow will always be together.

Hades had other plans for Helena as this was what he did next.

He shouted out and said "well my child you have seemed to have made a name for yourself with your own kingdom being loved by your husband, family, and friends and now your time has come to say goodbye to it all!"

Helena shouted "don't you think that you have done enough to me already just please leave us alone" bending down in her parent's arms completely feeling weak and defeated.

At this moment Helena was still holding on to her parents dearly saying "Father and Mother I will always love you."

They said back to her, "we love you too, daughter.

"No matter what happens we will always remember each other and that is all that matters now."

The sea god acting bold and brave said "hit us with your best shot".

Hades answered, "very well if you insist" and said, "I know Princess that you loved becoming a Piscean of being form and you love the horses too."

When he pointed his staff at her a large flash of red light hit right into the heart from which her parents got pushed out of the way.

They recovered from the blow and started to swim back to where she was there floating in the water at the moment was now half celestial being and now half horse.

"You Helena are now a female centaur and your kind does not exist yet so you cannot live here anymore!"

"You now princess, are a female Sagittarius Star your full of fire due to your courage and confidence in life which I like very much!"

"I have been watching that you miss your beloved Seequest so much that I have made another dream for you come true with a difference."

She was looking at herself thinking well that cannot be too bad.

"Oh, Princess you misunderstood me."

"Oh no, you are not going to be with Seequest star!"

"You will be there like him and your dog in a star form."

She was crying to her parents "Father, Mother, help me."

They were devastated and knew that they could do nothing about it.

Neptune looked up and saw that Zeus had disappeared at this time as there was nothing again he could do as it was the rules.

Zeus felt upset that he could not watch his evil brother anymore hurt his own family so he vanished.

Hades looked up and said "that's its Zeus you just go away and turn a blind eye to what's happening to your family you coward"

Luckily for Hades Zeus did not hear what he said and that's the reason why he said it to make himself look powerful in front of everyone else now.

Unless Hades killed one of them Zeus cannot help in any way even if he wanted to.

Neptune and his wife then knew that their days in the sea as a god of the sea and king and queen of Vissen and their people were coming to an unpleasant ending.

Her parents sadly watched their beloved Helena being turned into a half-horse and half-celestial being.

She was glowing silver crying loudly and then he was getting ready to banish her into a star form forever.

Dear Helena did not get the chance to celebrate her forty-eighth birthday.

Hades then turned Helena into the ball of light and said "goodbye Princess Centaur" as she shot up into the night sky with the scorpion star sign too.

There she appeared as the image she was as Sagittarius the female centaur of the stars and universe.

Hades chose this for her as she loved life and was full of courage and strength and full of energy until this day.

Hades used his staff to send her to the sky far away from everyone who was already there.

Far, far away from Seequest and Legend's Sirius Star.

Helena was now called the Sagittarian star.

The princess was gone as everyone had known her and that is why the star sign exists today as her memory of a great Queen she was to land and sea in the end.

Hades said to his brother the sea god "now I feel that you are heartbroken already."

So quickly in his mind, Neptune gave a message to the dolphins to do something for him and his daughter and his kingdom.

Hades carried on speaking saying "I shall let you both be together" as he changed King Neptune and Queen Sera into the gorgeous largest dolphins that have ever been created.

Hades says "I know that you are my brother so I will do this for you."

"But your daughter really hurt me and processed those powers inside, that she could probably kill me."

"So, she had to go away and that is why I have done it"

He repeats "I did warn you all but you did not want to listen."

"Thinking that you could beat me the god of the underworld well you are terribly mistaken I have been living on this planet longer than you brother."

"That's why I and Zeus were chosen by father to live here and control the Earth when you were banished to another planet for centuries and laughed."

Neptune at this time thought what he just said was probably true.

Hades carried on talking and said, "but I know that you are destroyed in your heart and mind and so I shall let your wife live with you for the rest of your days like this".

"And then when your dolphin forms eventually die that your spirits will go back to where you came from which is the blue planet for your brother and Sera you will go back to the moon with her mother."

But what Hades did not know was that Zeus could not prevent Hades from doing this and yet helped in some way.

Has he left their intelligent emotional and communication side of them both in the dolphin forms to teach the other dolphins to pass on the information to the future ones on how to protect the planet and the seas without them forever?

Hades had also changed all their people into sharks and seahorses but they not could change like Louis, or could they?

Hades made them small for having to defend themselves for the rest of their lives and the males carry the eggs for females too.

Last, of all, he could not keep the Hippocampius in the sea as they were.

Because having their own magic could possibly banish Hades for good.

Hades then decided to turn all the hippocampus into the waves of the sea for good as that's where their powers would be still useful he thought.

That is possibly how they became known as today the white horses of the sea forever.

Hades then felt that he conquered and won the last final battle and looked for all the crystal skulls from the temples and Seequest's horn!

They were all gone.

He fell to the floor as after what he had put Helena and Neptune through he was still unsatisfied with the outcome because even though he felt that he won that battle.

He did not actually win the war again!

Because earlier Neptune agreed that if something happens to them Seequest's horn will be returned to him.

Queen Sera talked to her mother for the last time as a sorceress before they hid all the crystal skulls earlier too.

So now Seequest was fully complete once more in the stars as the Unicorn star that he is known for today.

Hades was furious and turned back into a shark and disappeared back to the shore where he changed back to his normal self.

Being a god of dark hair and red eyes wearing his black robe and cloak he was going to climb back onto Knightmare his bat-winged black horse.

Above him with the sun just appearing was his elder brother Zeus.

"Brother I am not happy with what you just did to Princess Helena, our brother and his family!"

"It was unfair and was not called for yet I cannot kill you."

"In return, I will take something from you too."

Zeus pointed his lightning bolt into the sea where Vissen was and then destroyed then said "your saber-toothed tigers will be gone from Earth too."

"Your rein is now done."

"All the saber-toothed tigers that were left of Hades vanished into thin air."

But they were not destroyed Goddess Artemis changed them into a kinder type of tiger and for now, took them back to her kingdom until they were needed again.

"No!" Hades said acting furious as he loved his saber-toothed tigers as they were the only beast that could ever kill a unicorn in the past and he liked them for that reason.

Again, he thought that if he could not have their horns or control them then instead he would destroy them and that was what he did, thanks to loyal big cats.

"Zeus", Hades said "why must you be so cruel to me?"

Zeus replied, "Karma my brother"

"If you do something wrong or hurt others, then in time it will come back and fall on you in return"

When Zeus said "be good always to every living creature and earth and in time the good gesture will return to you instead."

When Hades sulked and open up his fire portal to the underworld once more.

For many years Neptune and Queen Sera used to put their heads out of the sea and gaze into the night when the Sagittarian star was around and stayed there for hours thinking of their beautiful daughter Helena now shining brightly as many stars in the sky.

Every night the brightest star the Dog Star Sirius Helena's Great Dane was special because he was made from Zeus' own blood.

So even though he was a star form he also was a god star.

And that is why it shines the brightest all over the world to see at night today, a certain month of the year August it is truly sending love, abundance, and peace to all.

As that was the time he was created into a star through Hades' staff.

Eventually, Neptune and Queen Sera were dying in their now-dolphin form.

Zeus loved his brother and his wife and knew that he could not stop the circle of life.

So, he had an idea that there was a possible way for Helena to be close to them again and that was for them to be the Pisces star sign that Helena herself created for her own personal crest for her kingdom first and then changed to the water horses at a later date.

That is how the star signs possibly became to be in our skies today everyone.

The Unicorn Star; horse Star; Dog Star and Sagittarius and Pisces too.

"Farewell", as he smiled as he knew that he will always see them there in his night sky and he would make sure that their memories and their stories will be carried into the time of us humans today.

But one thing Zeus did do in the future is that Neptune was the first dolphin to die on earth and so Helena's Spirit was now a Sagittarian star.

But her soul eventually went to heaven where her parent's souls came to in the end as well.

Celestial gave them a choice to be souls of mer-folk or human type, Helena chose what she loved the most her humankind.

And that is how Helena was her happiest again to be with her parents for entity once more.

The End of this Fable until next time...

Explanation

This was the story of how the different legends of the Mystical horses could have come about.

Helena lived her highs and lows through her life been a mermaid princess and a queen in her own dream Kingdom Piscean on land which could have existed many centuries before us humans.

Knight was known as Kelpie who became immortal and so in time he was known on land even though he was working for Hades collecting the bad souls he also did some good too and lived in the British Isles as preferred fresh water to live in the form a black and white Clydesdale representing both dark and light energy as a true balance here on earth.

Zeus renamed him in the future Duke as an heir's name like his father.

If you look up at certain times of the year you will see these stars shining brightly.

So once again I shall let you think if this story is possibly true.

I hope you enjoyed it

If you did, then please join me in Kessy's next adventure.

In My personal Fables

Book: 3

The Legend of the Red Dragon and its Kind

Epilogue

You will find that there was an actual place in the sea called Atlantis and the mer-folk were part of it.

Also, this is why dolphins are possibly intelligent because of the presence of the mer-folk and all the mysteries are safe in them.

So that's also possible why they interact with us humans more, as they are our sea mammal cousins.

The dolphin became a protector of all creatures after Neptune's reign as it fends off sharks because Hades' will of sharks became their enemies due to Hades' plan.

Dolphins attack sharks with great force with their noses like a spear like the mer-folk did once centuries before us as it messes up their senses and puts them in a whirlwind in their head and so they swim off to recover from it as it is a hard blow to it.

The dolphins need to come up for air to breathe at times as well as swim in the deep oceans around the world.

A lot of their people did escape on the lands as Hades did and then became gods themselves of Egypt possibly?

That is how the Egyptians came about and reign on earth.

Due to having all the powers and great intelligence of the universe which is why they lived in the pyramids for their safety?

Which were originally built to send energies to the crystal skulls and Seequests energy on land to Helena's Kingdom and the sea as well?

Queen Sera and Helena and Seequest's horn were used one last time together to give some of their special high-up people a complete Piscean body forever.

Who seemed to be able to swim in the sea like before but always as a Piscean never more a mermaid or merman.

The Stars

Minceros (The Unicorn Star)

The actual unicorn star is 700 light years away from earth and yet you can see an beautiful night sky.

If you look for it its brightest star is Sirius (the Dog Star) the brightest star in all of the galaxy and universe put together.

It's been the brightest star for me as it has always been around me.

I am lucky and blessed, thank you all.

So maybe you will see it for yourself and be lucky and blessed too?

It was noticed by a Dutch astronomer in the 17th century.

That's also the reason why we possibly celebrate national unicorn day as it originated from the Greek gods.

Where centuries later it was known that the unicorn was actually from Scotland and that's why anywhere in the world celebrates the ceremony too.

The unicorn was an icon of all time and that's why it is on their crests still today.

Long live the unicorn past, present and future as magic is around us always.

Sirius the Dog Star is always around in the night sky you cannot miss it.

<u>Sagittarius</u>: Is the star of a Centaur half human type and a half-horse that possibly lived on earth before us humans' centuries before.

Where Helena was wearing her cloak now as an archer because it represents that her life was full of action moving through her life and had great energy too. She is also drawing the bow towards the Celestial heavens.

Sagittarius is the star sign from 20th Nov to the end of December.

<u>Pisces</u>: Has been known to be dolphins by the Greek gods first to then became salmon due to another Greek story of escaping a monster Zeus changed Aphrodite and Eros her brother into fish temporally as they were attached to a long piece of silk ribbon.

Also, the Celtics classed it as hippocampus and Kelpie too.

The star dates from the end of Feb 24th to the end of March.

The Horse Star

Is not known in stars that well but if you look at an old star map or even go to Scotland the main castle inside one of the towers holds a beautiful painting of actually that on its ceiling. (sterling castle in the tower section)

It is showing that the horse star today is right beside the Pegasus star. And its head is the only part mentioned and shown in the picture.

I also mentioned Cancer: The large crab as it connected to people born end beginning of July to the beginning of August and protector to queen Sera in the skies and the sea as well.

The Crystal Skulls

Represent today's Charkas which are:

Amethyst was the crown charka's main important one of them all.

Rose quartz was the root Charka

Emerald was the healing and happiness focusing the heart

Sapphire one was throat Charka

Aquamarine was the third eye Charka

Just some of them, as to your body Charka's, there's two more that I have not mentioned here.

But there are thirteen crystal skulls known in history and the Amethyst one is the strongest of them all and is number thirteen.

They are the sacral Chakra and solar plexus too.

I also explained earlier that Gaia Mother nature and Hades control the seasons of today's weather around our world earth and that's the possible reason why they get their names in the season form.

<u>Gaia</u>: Spring Summer and Hades: Autumn, winter.

When things always begin to live again stronger than before in spring and summer they are just enjoying being beautiful and happy and alive to the full.

When autumn comes Mother, Nature tries to prepare the plants; veg and fruits.

Before Hades comes and destroys them again on only a temporally basis.

<u>Pegasus</u>

Decided that his new species of the Unisos should live out its days in the stars of Andromeda near his future place in the stars where they now are these warriors of time of need for them and us here on earth, that's why you are seeing more of them in Art, stories as winged unicorns which they are not.

As they are not one or the other, they are both and process both powers of creativity, healing and strength, and courage too.

The Small Moon around Planet Neptune is Called Hippocamp

It was noticed in July 2013 by an Astrologer called Mark Showalter through the Hubble space telescope, yet he did not name it Hippo-camp (meaning Sea Horse) until later in Feb 2019, funny enough the same year I had finished writing the story to then a manuscript later.

This moon is the smallest of the 14 that are hovering around the beautiful icy blue planet Neptune.

(Poseidon is a Greek name for Neptune as well)

Mark named the pretty little moon this has a love for the creature known today as our sea horses and also, he loved the ocean.

Wow, another amazing fact!

The Falkirk Kelpies

I must add in today's times an amazing 100-foot sculpture of two beautiful and powerful horseheads in Scotland called the Kelpies.

Andy Scott designed them in 2013 as two actual heavy horses as his models and his drawings state they were standing in the water of the canal.

But when he built them, he decided that he would only create two horse heads for us to see and let our imagination do the rest instead.

Funny enough my friend Helena mentioned these to me after she went to Scotland and saw them for herself.

When I said that's funny as I have already written a few chapters of my second book based on the story of a Kelpie has another folklore in Scotland and Ireland that I wanted to add has been dedicated to an old friend too.

They were built and ready for the world to come and see them in real life in 2014 at Helix Park near the Canals in Falkirk.

Mr. Scott chose two beautiful Clydesdales for his inspiration called Duke and Baron to help him create these massive statues of the Scottish horse of today as an honor to them for their hard work of pulling the barges in the past down the canals themselves.

So, this was the perfect way to say thank you like no other before.

Many years later we were going to Scotland which was my wedding Anniversary present from my husband, I had a strong feeling that I had to see them for myself as I felt a strong connection to them even from afar.

That night we were driving to our hotel from sheer-ness when passing by we saw the kelpies lit up in the distance, we stopped and went into the park even though it was closing in 10 minutes.

We walked up to these great horse head statues, which made me feel like quite Erry as it was pure darkness around them at the time, has the Park was closing up for the night.

There was a gentleman taking photos just before and said "sorry you missed them tonight" I said "Oh no, feeling disappointed that I would not get this oppor-tunity again."

At that moment I looked right at the main horse's head, I believe it was Duke where I felt a loving sen-sation come over me as I heard him say to me to stay.

So, I said to my family "wait when I said I would love to see the Kelpies lit up in my favorite color light blue and they all said they are off now we missed it."

But within 10 seconds to my family's amazement, the Kelpies did light back up again.

Please look at my photo on the back of my book where there is proof of this happened!

They lit up in all other wonderful colours too within that 20 seconds magic had appeared right in front of me and others.

I was lucky to experience it, I said thank you to Duke and went home.

As the plan was to see them properly tomorrow has it been a surprise to us at night on their own accord.

I felt like pure magic had just appeared in front of us all, as the kelpies were turned off for the night and yet they relit themselves just for me and my family to see.

I knew then that was a personal gift from Duke and my dear friend Seequest as his true form as a Hippocampus and his son Knight as a Kelpie.

That night and next the day I felt a great Presence of Love and warmth around me all day,

As when I stood in front of Duke, I was overwhelmed by the beautiful energy they both carried and also their greatness too.

To my astonishment on the tour I find out that Duke had sadly died recently, so I was in contact with Duke's actual beautiful spirit that night, Wow!!

Now if that was not magic then I do not know what is.

Now, do you believe in my story even more?

I will let you decide?

<u>There are many statues and pictures of these great legends, which make me believe they once lived here on earth, what do you think?</u>

Kessy will be back in the next book:3 with her own story about her life adventures.

Information

I made this story possible through my thoughts and ideas and yet after I had finished writing my book, I find evidence that it may not be just a story after all.

Because I felt pulled to visit special places and see amazing things for myself by going to Scotland; Greece where I visited beautiful museums to seek the truth and proof that this story could be true.

I planned to go to Santorini (Greece) but it was cancelled due to Con-vid so another place I feel I must visit in time as well.

Through my story, I believe that this is how sea horses possibly came to be as well.

Kessy is my ideal form of the great Scottish folk tale of the Loch Ness monster of how she came about and what could have happened to her in the end.

But her story has not ended yet.

My story is a way of telling how the kelpie was possibly created as another Scottish and Irish folk tale.

The Celtics were very much into the tales of the hippocampus and the kelpies as there is a famous cross in Scotland.

And on it, the cross has an emblem of the hippocampus and a kelpie with a beautiful trinity knot symbol at the bottom in between them which I read was the way of Pisces as these people loved their horses greatly because they worshipped a goddess of horses in their culture too.

I have a copy of this image that I bought in Scotland on my visit there of it now on my wall.

Seahorses also represent pisces orginal animal spirit as well.

<u>The kelpies</u>

I know I have mentioned these already.

Where I had the opportunity to see and feel their magical presence within them these huge statues while I was there.

As mentioned earlier that is where my photo on the back of the book came from, my visit to the Kelpies.

<u>The statues are breathtaking.</u>

<u>Real Possibilities</u>

There is an island in Santorini in Greece that has been proven by documentaries to have possibly been Atlantis.

But others believe it to be somewhere else.

If you go to museums and art galleries and look on the web and even shops, you will find a lot of clothing; books, and even ornaments of these great legends of the time.

You may find that there are so many statues all over the world of these incredible stories and creatures with the Greek gods and goddesses as well.

In certain, museums you will find many types of pottery and pieces of jewelry again from all over the world of this great history of these amazing legends too.

I have mentioned in my book about the star signs and some planets too as it is possible how they came about in the sky.

Regarding Neptune, he was living on a water planet in the far galaxy when his brother thought that when he took over Earth from his father the bad elemental Titan that his brother would be good as a sea god.

Has he lived in the water already on the blue planet which in time Zeus decided to re name Neptune after the great sea god's achievements on Earth?

When he passed on from being a real dolphin thanks to Hades changing him and his wife into dolphins in the past he remembered the emblem of the two dolphins of Helena's dream kingdom and so thought that another way of connecting them again was to create them as Pisces, the star sign as their spirits and their souls were returned.

Neptune went back to the blue planet and Seras to the moon as Hades planned, until Zeus changed it at a later date for their souls to live out in Celestial's heaven.

That's how our heaven today became and why our animals are with us when we die.

Have they been here before our time?

Mermaids possibility of being the closest to our human race today and that may be why they say that Piscean people seemed to have a strong connection to dolphins; the sea the kingdom of Atlantis and the unicorns as they are all connected somehow (like I am myself).

So, it is true that Sirus, the Dog Star, is the brightest star all over the world and the universe that everyone can see it.

The Minceros unicorn star is connected as part of it, I have read.

When looking right at it feels of great warmth and happiness as well.

Also, this may be how dogfish and catfish came about too by the Piscean children having them living with them on land first.

Who knows the truth?

Seahorses were like they are today as Hades thought that he did not want to kill Neptune's mer-knights but made them work for the rest of their lives as they have to carry their babies' full term while the females do all the work of making sure they survive another day.

Hades wanted to take their strength away from the mer-knights for good.

I do love fresh water to drink as it is good for our general health and we're also made of 70 percent water.

So always much sure you drink plenty, as it also stops us from aging as quickly and it always helps by keeping us feeling uplifted or in high spirits in our busy lives.

We Pisceans want to live by the sea because we're still connected to its energies, which help our stress levels and life, in general, to be calm and relaxed once more.

But it does not mean that anyone cannot either.

Also, eat plenty of fish in your diet as it is one of the best brain foods going especially Tuna that's the best.

Why do you think that dolphins are intelligent as their mammals which means they are our water cousins as their mothers produce like us human mothers too?

Tuna is their favourite meal and that's why they are so intelligent.

Now I am not telling just advising as I love seafood as you can see it sparks the brain and your creativity too, enjoy!

I have also mentioned as I did before in my first book *The Legend of the Horse* that the unicorns; hippocampius; and Unisos are similar types to our real horses of today which are why the Arabians; Friesians; Cleveland Bays (Chapman Horse); thoroughbreds; palominos ; Andalusian's and Clydesdales are important in this story.

As their most powerful; elegant; fastest and strongest horses on earth that we use for our business of helping the earth stay beautiful and healthy by attending to the trees, the ground, and its waters.

Mother Nature and these other living beings gave us fresh veg and salad and fruit to eat and we use the trees to help us breathe oxygen to stay healthy always.

Plus, the trees also let us make paper and use the bark to make fires to keep us warm in winter if no central heating or live outside.

So, we should be thankful as without any of these things we would not survive on this planet.

So, I say thank you to Mother Earth and its beings for letting us live here freely and healthily with their help and kindness.

Once again, I hope you enjoyed it

If you did please come and join me in my next adventure in Wales:

In the meantime, look out for

<u>My Personal Fables Book:1 The Legend of the Horse becoming now on Audible</u>

<u>Plus, a new fantasy Series!</u>

<u>Called the Blue Angel Chronicles, Book 1, Aurora</u>

<u>Planning to release 2024 spring time.</u>

Who said dreams cannot come true, all you need to do is believe.

Love & Light to you all x

Authors note

Always be kind; caring; loving and in return, you will receive the same back as karma is a great thing if you stay on her good side.

Also be grateful in life for what you have and there in return you will receive more abundance etc.

Enjoy life to the full as magic is right in front of you every day of your lives just believe, there you will see and experience it for yourselves.

Unicorn blessings

Sa x

www.ingramcontent.com/pod-product-compliance
Lightning Source LLC
Chambersburg PA
CBHW071953190726
48293CB00001B/7